THE
FÜHRER'S
RESERVE

A Novel of the FBI

P A U L   L I N D S A Y

SIMON & SCHUSTER
New York London Toronto Sydney Singapore

SIMON & SCHUSTER
Rockefeller Center
1230 Avenue of the Americas
New York, NY 10020

SIMON & SCHUSTER and colophon are registered trademarks of Simon & Schuster, Inc.

Designed by Kyoko Watanabe

Manufactured in the United States of America

10 9 8 7 6 5 4 3 2 1

Library of Congress Cataloging-in-Publication Data

Lindsay, Paul
 The Führer's reserve : a novel of the FBI / Paul Lindsay.
  p. cm.
  1. United States. Federal Bureau of Investigation—Fiction. 2. Hitler, Adolf,
 1889–1945—Art collections—Fiction. 3. Government investigators—United
 States—Fiction. I. Title.
 PS3562.I511915 F84 2000
 813'.54—dc21   99-086656

ISBN 0-684-85403-1

In memory of Hayes Scott

Historical Note

One of Adolf Hitler's obsessions during his reign as Germany's dicta-
tor was to amass the world's greatest art collection for his Linz
Provincial Museum. It would demonstrate, once and for all, the cultural glory of his thousand-year Reich. Subsequently, more than half
a million works of art were confiscated from conquered countries
and private collections. On July 24, 1939, Martin Bormann, the
Führer's personal assistant, informed governmental art authorities
that all such acquisitions were to be kept intact so that Hitler himself, or his curator, could choose what they wanted. Later the order
was amended to include all works taken from Jews. The huge store-
house of art that resulted came to be known as *der Führervorbehalt*—
the Führer's Reserve.

At the same time, Reichsmarschall Hermann Goering, Hitler's
designated successor, gathered a collection even greater than that of
his Führer.

Today, thousands of priceless objects from those stockpiles remain
missing.

THE
FÜHRER'S
RESERVE

1

"HERR TRAUCHMANN," SAID THE GUARD WHO AC-
companied the visitor, "your new attorney is here to see you. You
have one half hour."

The old Nazi glanced up at the lawyer who had entered his cell at
the Rüdersdorf prison and wondered which was going to be more
difficult, convincing him of the existence of the largest cache of
stolen art in history, or persuading the elegant young man to murder
him. "My right to counsel now has a time limit?"

"If you want to meet with your attorney in the normal visitation
facility, it does not."

"You know my health will not permit that."

With the tinny arrogance that came with minor rank, the guard
said, "Then you should be grateful an exception has been made that
allows him to come to you."

The old man looked at the guard with a false pleasantness that
was intended to heighten the indignity of what he was about to say.
"This job, it really is at the limit of your abilities, isn't it?"

The lawyer was intrigued. If this man's demeanor was any indication, it was not difficult to understand why the men of the Third Reich
had almost conquered the world. Despite history's recriminations,
they believed their power was absolute—what was right then was right
now—and always would be. Even the guard, whose basic tool of survival was control, gave ground to the old man's insolence and left without another word, only able to slam the cell door in response.

The steel lock snapped into place and the lawyer suddenly felt the icy abandon of confinement. Although he had visited men in prison before, this was his first time in a locked cell. The pulse in his neck strained against his starched shirt collar.

Tattered gray light filled the cell like weightless, hovering dust. His eyes adjusted slowly as he felt his way along the wall. Thin bands of gritty mortar separated large, flat stones so cold that they drained the heat from his hand. A sharp, chalky dampness he had not noticed in the corridor caused his nostrils to flare involuntarily. The air was thick with age, unstirred by human movement, or desire.

Confinement was not merely placing a wall between good and evil, but rather an assurance that these men remained untouched by the influences of the outside world, to deny them civilization, to punish them by submersing them in their own lawlessness. The visitor promised himself never to return.

Hans Trauchmann pulled himself upright in his bed and then took a carefully measured breath to recover from the effort. He was one of the last war criminals held in German prisons. An operations officer during WW II, he had been charged with serving in the "Jewish Affairs" office of the *Sicherheitsdienst*, the intelligence service of the dreaded SS. From its inception, the SD had been staffed with only the most loyal of Hitler's men—a necessity because of what they would ultimately be asked to do.

Given the Führer's mandate to eliminate Europe's Jews, Trauchmann devised most of the "legal" procedures used to identify, confine, and seize their property prior to the final solution. In the end, the prosecutors would charge that Trauchmann's efficiency in those efforts was without parallel in the history of human cruelty. He was responsible for the deaths of millions of men, women, and children, eradicating thousands of years of Jewish lineage.

Avoiding capture for nearly two years after the war, he was not brought to trial until 1948. By then the German people had grown to hate any reminder of the war and the Holocaust even more. The proceedings were short and, as much as possible, unspectacular. He was quickly convicted for his "atrocities against humanity," but hanging was feared too sensational for a country waiting to heal its history with the sluggish salve of time, so he was sentenced to life imprisonment. Fifty years later, Hans Trauchmann, the Holocaust's Expeditor, had been all but forgotten.

His visitor today was Rölf Brunner, a member of the German Democratic Alliance party. His name was not well known, but Trauchmann's old contacts had informed him that Brunner was a man who could get the most shadowed tasks accomplished without problem or notice.

The GDA was gaining strength, having won 28 percent of the vote in the last election. But the press had started becoming critical lately. The party was accused of being unduly contemptuous of foreigners, and of trying to censor the media when it attacked the government's methods. Although they were careful not to specifically include Judaism, their platform included the outlawing of "foreign" religions such as Scientology and all forms of Islam. And they advocated a buildup of the military. Such proposals, while appealing to the broad populace of Germany, had also been the cornerstones of the Nazi regime. The media began labeling Brunner's party "the Fourth Reich." As a result, many of the GDA's financial contributors, although still in agreement with its philosophy, started withdrawing their monetary support for fear of being linked with anything remotely connected with the black days of Adolf Hitler.

But Trauchmann believed fascism would always have an audience in Germany. Its roots went back to the Thirty Years War in the first half of the seventeenth century, when the country's population fell from twenty-four million to four million, leaving the strong and ruthless to survive. He believed the GDA, like the Nazi party, represented the thoughts and aspirations of a majority of the population, and with the right help, could come to power.

Tall and thin, Brunner wore a navy blue suit that had been made for him in London. Even in the low cell, he took care to stand erectly. The jacket and trousers draped perfectly. His thick blond hair was cut short, and his suntanned face could have been described as passively Scandinavian if not for the three long, formal scars that crisscrossed his left cheek. Each was wide and pale, inferring that however Brunner had come by them, they had never been treated medically. A history of survival was suggested, and the permanent sneer of superiority left on his face seemed somehow justified.

"Thank you for coming, Herr Brunner." The old man's words came in short, ragged gasps. With some effort, he gestured to a lone chair. "Sorry you had to come to this damned place, but my health . . ."

Trauchmann's general appearance was unkempt—his shirt and trousers were shapeless cuts of dark cloth that covered him dutifully. His hair, now a muted silver, was matted and uncombed. But his face, as evidenced by a scattering of dark red nicks, was freshly shaven. For a man in his condition, Brunner knew it was a task not easily accomplished. "It is my honor, Herr Trauchmann." The stone chamber had a hollow, muted echo and it accented the insincerity of Brunner's words. "How are you feeling?"

Recognizing Brunner's disingenuous tone, Trauchmann said, "I see you are someone who has little use for pretense. Good. For me, this is an indication of an individual's trustworthiness. So I will simply say that, for a dying man, I have few complaints." Besides being eighty-five, sixty years of smoking, in the form of emphysema, were demanding final payment from Trauchmann.

There was no request for pity in the old man's voice, which greatly relieved Brunner. When summoned to the prison, he was aware of the Nazi's failing health and hoped he would not be asked to construct a final will, or worse, be given a list of meaningless requests to perform that would somehow pave the way for the old man's entrance into the next world. Instead, he found himself admiring the callousness with which Trauchmann regarded his own imminent death. "I am honored that you would call me. But I have to confess, I really do not practice law any longer. Out of respect, I have come to see if there is anything I may do for you."

"There are a couple of things." He smiled. "The most immediate of which is a cigarette. The doctors do not allow me to smoke, and I do enjoy them so."

Brunner took two out and lit the old man's before his own. He smiled and said, "I assume the rest of your requests will not be as uncomplicated."

Trauchmann took a shallow drag. After a single cough, he held the cigarette at arm's length and examined it with his still uncorrected eyesight. "American—very nice." He took another drag. "You are correct. What I am about to propose will not be easy, but if you agree, it will allow me to be of service to the Fatherland one last time."

"And how may I do that, *Herr Oberstleutnant?*"

Trauchmann was pleased that this man from another generation offered his respect by using the former lieutenant colonel's SS rank. "I am told you are a man of unusual loyalty who can accomplish the most difficult of tasks."

"I am willing to do what must be done for the good of the party and for Germany."

Contemplatively, the old man drew on the cigarette again. "These are words I have heard many times before, and the closer the Reich grew to defeat, the more emphatically they were sworn. And those were better days. Now deeds rarely outlive their promises. Are your deeds as relentless as your rhetoric?"

Brunner considered the old man's skepticism. "I doubt if you would have sent for me to discuss something that is—I am guessing—out of the ordinary, unless you made inquiries as to what kind of man I am."

"Inquiries are merely another application of words. I am more concerned with what sins you are capable of."

"Since sin is a moral concept, I would imagine my capabilities are without limitation."

"Then you would not mind telling me of one *out of the ordinary* act you have committed for the good of your party."

"You ask a great deal."

"You stand to gain a *great deal*. More than you could possibly imagine."

"What could you offer from a prison cell that would tempt me into such self-incrimination?"

The old man studied the glowing tip on his cigarette before looking up. "If you agree to my terms, when you leave this prison, you will have the means necessary to bring your party to power in the next election. But first, I need to know exactly how committed you are."

Trauchmann's pale blue eyes invited a search for credibility. They reminded Brunner that this man had kept some of history's darkest secrets through half a century of confinement. "There was a certain newspaper which had been investigating my party—until its offices were burned down."

"That was you?"

"I believe they used to call you the Expeditor. It is sometimes an enjoyable position, no?"

That Brunner understood the pleasure of such sabotage told Trauchmann the young man had indeed been responsible for the act. He nodded his head slowly, indicating his approval. "Have you ever killed a man?"

Although Brunner knew what the next question would be, he decided to let the old man unravel his proposition at his own pace. "No."

"Could you?"

As Brunner had feared, whatever Trauchmann was about to suggest, killing was going to be part of it. "Carrying out even the most distasteful tasks is simply a matter of motivation."

"We shall see," Trauchmann said, his voice deliberately unfinished, hinting that Brunner's assurances would be tested. "First you must give me your word—your honor—that this will be kept in strictest confidence."

"If what you are about to tell me can bring my party to power, my word will hardly be necessary."

The old man exhaled cigarette smoke in short, jerky streams through his nostrils. "As I see it, the only thing that can keep your party from succeeding is money to finance its campaigns. I can tell you where to find the necessary funds." Brunner's left eyebrow lowered itself in mild disbelief, to which Trauchmann responded with a short, coughing laugh. "Quite a trick for a dying old man who has been locked away for fifty years, eh? I must be delusional, yes?"

Brunner straightened himself. "I am sorry, Herr, but it is a lot for one man to accomplish with one conversation."

"A successful life is about power. I once had it, but for half a century, I have not. It was what I thought my life would always be about. But—the misfortunes of war. What I am about to propose will allow me to taste it one last time, and take that taste to my grave. Then all these years in a cell will not have defeated my life."

Brunner felt the conviction in Trauchmann's words. "I'm here at your service, *Herr Oberstleutnant.*"

"Good. *Der Führervorbehalt*—does it mean anything to you?"

"The Führer's Reserve? I am not familiar with the term."

"Are you familiar with Reichsmarschall Goering's passion for art?"

"I am an enthusiastic student of the Third Reich. I think every German has seen photographs of Carinhall."

"Do you know how he obtained those objects he stockpiled at his hunting lodge?"

"They were properties confiscated by the Reich."

"That's correct, and those that were actually purchased were done so with, more or less, confiscated funds taken mostly from Jews." Trauchmann paused and then said, "What I am about to tell you must not be shared with anyone other than possibly those at the highest levels of your party. With this revelation will go a terrible power, and a worse responsibility. If you tell anyone else, I guarantee it will spread like a plague and defeat all that you wish to accomplish."

"The weight of discretion is something I have become accustomed to."

"That is your reputation," Trauchmann said. "Have you ever heard the name Josef Rathkolb?"

"I do not think so."

"He is a man who is known in a very small circle of Reich officers as *der Kurator.* He helped gather the majority of Goering's art for him. I never met him until the end of the war, at Berchtesgaden, where the *Reichsmarschall* was under house arrest. I assume you know why."

"For treason?"

"Yes, but he still had visions of some day becoming Führer, and knew to do so he would need a great deal of money. So he gathered us all there and ordered Rathkolb to bring his art collection from Carinhall. By that time it had grown so large, Rathkolb needed to commandeer two trains to transport it."

"I assume that Hitler didn't know that this was being done."

"Goering told us that he did, but I think we all knew otherwise. Then he told us why we had been summoned, to help Rathkolb smuggle one hundred of the paintings out of the country."

"This is what you refer to as the Führer's Reserve?"

"Yes. And remarkably, the entire operation was accomplished within three days."

"Why paintings? Wouldn't gold or jewels have been more practical?"

"Goering was a shrewd collector. Not only did he handpick which hundred paintings should be taken, but he thought that art would grow in value more rapidly than any other asset available to the Reich at that time. And frankly, he did not have access to the amount of gold or jewelry that would have been its equivalent. He was right about the paintings. In the last fifty years, art has unquestionably been the best investment. And with the works he chose, it has been even better."

"Would I recognize any of the artists?"

"Some that I remember are Rubens, Cranach, Rembrandt, Van Dyck, Van Gogh, Renoir, Picasso, Degas, Gauguin, Toulouse-Lautrec. But Goering had an insight into the future of art, he sensed who would become important. A good example of this was his collecting of the 'degenerate artists,' such as Matisse, Chagall, and Mondrian, who, because of their lack of Aryan purity, were largely banned by the Third Reich," Trauchmann said. "Goering was also clever enough not to choose the most famous of their works, as he knew they might be more difficult to sell."

"Where is the Reserve now?"

"Probably in the United States with Rathkolb."

"He trusted one man with it?"

"Goering once told me that Rathkolb was the only man he knew who was more obsessed with the Nazi ideology than he was. Goering saw obsession as a gift and trusted him because of it."

"Exactly what are you proposing?"

"You must recover these paintings and finance your party into power to ensure Germany's future."

"Elections are very expensive. What is the current worth of the collection?"

"The value of the collection is difficult to estimate. I am no expert, but if one Van Gogh can sell in America for over seventy million dollars, and a Cezanne for sixty million, then I would think an extremely conservative guess would be half a billion dollars. I read the newspapers; I know how expensive an election is. That's more than even the United States needs to elect its president and senate combined."

"That's a very impressive figure. I apologize for underestimating your knowledge in such matters."

"There is no time for amenities. Everything must be completed before the guard returns," Trauchmann said. "When you leave here, the first thing you must do is find Rathkolb, and quickly."

"After fifty years, what could be so urgent?"

"I have received word that one of the paintings is being auctioned in New York at a very private sale. It is by Alfred Sisley, one of the lesser-known impressionists, but the auction estimate for the piece is between two and three million dollars. With that kind of money, it will not remain discreet for very long."

"How soon is the auction?"

"In less than a month."

"Would Rathkolb be selling it?"

"I cannot be certain, but that is the most logical assumption."

"Why would he be selling it now?"

"I'm sure you saw the recent discovery at Berchtesgaden."

"The secret bunker of Goering's, with the documents, yes."

"For fifty years the existence of the Reserve was unknown to the world, but now this business has been discovered. Undoubtedly, there are documents detailing the existence of the Reserve. Rathkolb could be worried about any subsequent search for the Reserve which might, in turn, expose his methods in obtaining much of the art. It is logical to assume that he wants to sell them for his own gain before anyone can discover their existence. But he remains cautious—just one fairly unremarkable painting and that at an all-but-secret sale. Most likely, he is using it to see if anyone is watching for the works he has in his possession."

Brunner dropped his half-smoked cigarette and put it out with the toe of his shoe. "Can we trace him through this painting?"

"Possibly, but that course would most likely be futile. I suspect he is going through a maze of intermediaries. And then there's always the possibility that the authorities may be watching the sale."

"Then how do I find him?"

Trauchmann dropped his cigarette on the floor and Brunner reached over and extinguished it for him. He could feel its heat through the thin sole of the loafer. "That is a puzzle within a puzzle. Originally there were only two men who knew the exact location of the Reserve: Goering and Rathkolb. Now there's only Rathkolb—

another reason he probably wouldn't hesitate to profit from its sale. But there was one other man whom Goering ordered to always know Rathkolb's whereabouts—Major Gerhard Braune."

"So I must locate Braune in order to find Rathkolb."

"I can tell you how to find him. The real task will be to get him to tell you where Rathkolb is. The *Reichsmarschall* was paranoid in his caution. He also instructed Braune not to give that information to anyone but me. And since I will be dead soon, it is unlikely he will be telling me."

"Perhaps a letter from you would suffice?"

"Major Braune was one of Goering's most trusted officers. He is absolutely fanatical in his loyalty to the Third Reich. I know him—an order is a sacred oath—a letter will not work. It will be no small task to get Rathkolb's whereabouts from him. He is an extremely determined person."

"He is in the United States also?"

"Unfortunately, no. Goering had him take the paintings by U-boat to Patagonia, in the southern end of Argentina. From there, they were shipped to the United States where he turned them over to *der Kurator.* Then, other than keeping track of Rathkolb, Braune was done with the affair."

"Is Rathkolb living under an assumed name?"

"Yes, but it was known only to Goering and Braune. Braune, however, is using his real name. Besides his loyalty, he was chosen because he was not wanted as a war criminal. If he had been a fugitive and captured like Eichmann, there would have been no way to find Rathkolb. Presently, he is living in a town called San Carlos de Bariloche."

"I must admit I am not comfortable confronting men of such treacherous reputations, especially in foreign countries."

"Your caution is wise. Because of your position with the party, you cannot afford to be directly involved in this kind of business unless it becomes absolutely necessary. You will need some help, especially in the United States."

"Some of your old comrades who have settled there?"

"I am afraid they are *too* old. I suspect this will require a younger man's endurance."

"Then some of our friends in America."

"The so-called neo-Nazis? You know as well as I that they are nothing but beer-guzzling brawlers whose leaders are watched too closely by the authorities. Besides, they have the misconception that the world's problems are due to the black man, and do not realize that blacks are merely a symptom of Jewish socialism. No, we need someone of our own blood, someone bred to understand loyalty and honor."

"I don't understand, you said they were too old."

"Their sons are not. Do you know who Major Erich Lukas was?"

"Hitler's commando?"

"Yes."

"A great hero of the Reich, killed in the final days of fighting around Berlin."

Trauchmann gave the content smile of a man who had achieved a successful deception. "Actually, he was severely wounded. He, too, was smuggled out of the country and eventually settled in the United States. Once there, he became Karl Decker, and married an American woman. They had a son named Kurt who would now be almost forty."

"How do you know these things?"

"At first, we kept account of everyone in the upper levels of the SS because we hoped it was just a matter of time until the Reich would return to power. Eventually we became too old, but since the lines of communication were already open, we kept track, in limited fashion, of everyone. Probably out of a sense of history more than anything. Old men have a tendency to do that."

"So you think this Kurt Decker will help us."

"I think he is our best hope."

"But he is an American. How do we know we can trust him?"

"He has spent some time in prison, and he is about to be sent back. If you can prevent that from happening, I think his assistance can be gained."

"A criminal? What if he does recover the Reserve and decides to keep it for himself?"

"I doubt if he has the sophistication or contacts to sell master-pieces without being caught. Offer him a million dollars cash. I suspect that would encourage even an American's loyalty."

"And if it does not?"

"Herr Brunner, of all the men in Germany I could have entrusted with this mission, I chose you. Of course things can go wrong, and undoubtedly there will be problems, but the rewards are worth the risks. I am confident that you can find a way not only to motivate, but also to control Herr Decker. Anyway, I am told he is like his late father, tough and strong-willed. Hopefully you will be able to appeal to his sense of family history."

"Where is he now?"

"In Cleveland, Ohio. A number of our people have settled there and have done well."

"And he is waiting to go to prison?"

"Actually he is about to go on trial. Something about robbing a cash shipment. These Americans."

"And we have friends there that can help with this?"

Slowly, Trauchmann unbuttoned his shirt, reached down inside the waistband of his trousers, and pulled out a tiny piece of paper not much larger than a postage stamp. He handed it to Brunner. "One needs only to know the names of certain lawyers. Like everything else in the United States, a comparatively small amount of money will take care of the rest."

Brunner held the scrap of paper up to the available light. "Arnulf Mueller? This is a Berlin phone number."

"Yes. He is a man who has many of the secrets of the Reich at his disposal. I suppose in the old days he would have been your equivalent. I have sent him word to expect you. Although he does not know about the Reserve, he will not question any of your inquiries." Trauchmann was silent for a moment and then his voice became more intense. "Outside of yourself and those in your party you may deem necessary, there are only four men in the world that have knowledge of the Reserve . . ."

Brunner looked up at him. "Yes?"

"And they must be eliminated as soon as possible. With this painting surfacing in New York, there could be other attempts to locate the Reserve."

"I understand. Hopefully for a million dollars, Decker will not have a problem with that request. Who are the four?"

"Rathkolb, whose location you'll have to obtain from Braune. Braune himself. And Jonathan Geist, the man who notified me of this auction."

"Why him?"

"The reason he knows about the Sisley is because he was there when Goering selected the paintings for the Reserve. He helped crate up the collection so it could be smuggled out of Germany. Besides Rathkolb, he knows more about the individual paintings than anyone else alive."

"How will I find him?"

"Like Braune, he is not hiding from the authorities and is a known art broker in New York City. Neither he nor Braune should be difficult to find."

Brunner carefully pushed the piece of paper into the bottom of his shirt pocket. "And the fourth?"

The old Nazi's face relaxed. "Did you think I was being hypothetical when I asked you if you could kill a man?"

Suddenly Brunner realized the old man was asking to be murdered. "Herr Trauchmann, I cannot."

The old Nazi looked at the scars on the lawyer's face. "You are Austrian, aren't you?"

"Yes."

"I recognize the dueling scars. They are peculiar to Austrians. I have always appreciated that men could face one another with swords and fight until marked across the face. You wear your scars like medals. Draw from them the courage you swore to when your ideals were pure."

"You are a dying man, what honor would there be in killing you?"

"It is not your honor that will be decided today—it's mine. Let me die with dignity rather than rot away at the pleasure of the Jews." Trauchmann could see the lawyer was afraid. "After you leave here, it may become necessary to kill someone to accomplish this task. Can you do it?"

"If I must."

"This undertaking is not for the tentative," Trauchmann said, his strained voice rising. He took a moment to compose himself. "Let me help you. If you can do this, then I will know you are capable of dis-

posing of anyone who poses a threat to the recovery of the Reserve."
He stopped and took a couple of shallow breaths. "If you cannot, how
can I be sure you will do whatever becomes necessary? Besides, the
most difficult murder for a man is his first."

"What is to prevent me from walking out of this cell and going
after the Reserve without killing you?"

"If you leave me alive, I will instruct Arnulf Mueller, whom I suspect you will find invaluable in your search, to obstruct you, and then
I will find someone else to set on this path, someone more committed
than yourself."

Brunner's eyes narrowed. "Are you sure?"

"I have spent over a half century in this cell, my only wish at this
moment is to not spend another night."

Realizing the old man had taken away all other options, Brunner
asked, "How do you want to do this?"

"It has to look natural, but please be a little more creative than
smothering me with a pillow. I would like to be able to see as it is
happening."

"I understand."

"But first, another one of your cigarettes, please."

Brunner took off his suit jacket and pulled out his pack, handing
one to the old man and put another in his own mouth. With his hand
trembling slightly, he lit both. He looked at his watch. In less than five
minutes, the guard was due back. Trauchmann sat up and moved to
the foot of his bed slowly. Brunner stood and walked around behind
him to the door and peered out the small grate. No one was in the
hallway. He looked at the old man's shallow, desperate breathing and
decided how he would kill him.

"Could you stand up for a moment, I'm going to need some of
your bedding." He helped the old man to his feet and then stripped
one of the sheets from the bed. Carefully, he lowered Trauchmann
back down and turned him so his back was at the end. From the corner of the cell, he retrieved a small, two-foot-long broom. Then he
folded the sheet lengthwise so it was four inches wide. After placing
it around Trauchmann's chest, he tied the ends in a knot behind the
old man's back. Understanding Brunner's method, Trauchmann took
a last drag on his cigarette, dropped it on the floor, and pulled the

sheet snugly up under his arms. Brunner placed the broom handle inside the knot and started turning it. When the sheet became tight against Trauchmann's chest, he asked, "Is that comfortable?"

"Perfectly."

He slowly turned the lever until Trauchmann's chest could no longer expand, then he struggled to tighten it one more turn. He held it firmly until the old Nazi's chin finally fell limp against his chest. He waited for almost another two minutes before unwinding and untying the sheet. Trauchmann slumped forward on the bed.

Brunner decided that the old Nazi had been wrong, the first murder was not difficult at all.

He lifted the body onto the floor and, in a rumpled fashion, remade the bed with the deadly sheet, then gently placed the body back on top of it. The old man's eyes were still wide open.

There were footsteps in the hall.

In the vague, muted light, Trauchmann's glowing blue eyes still seemed to be plotting. For Brunner, the message was unmistakable: In a world gray with restriction and misdirection, the Nazi vision would be eternally clear.

Hurrying to the cell door, Brunner started pounding on it and yelled in a panicked voice, "Guard! Guard! Come quickly, something is wrong with Herr Trauchmann!"

2

IF DANIEL CITRON WASN'T ALREADY DEAD, TAZ FAL-
lon figured the seven year old had less than two hours left to live—if
the kidnappers were telling the truth.

Fallon took out the cassette that had been played at the FBI briefing an hour earlier and pushed it into the car's tape player. While
everyone had been busy getting their assignments, he palmed the
only extra copy of the kidnapper's phone calls. Admittedly it was a
fairly serious breach of Bureau procedure, but one that might prove
useful. At least that's what he kept telling himself.

Nevertheless, an unwelcomed question forced its way into his
thoughts: If he took it for later use, why was he playing it now? An
emptiness came over him, the same one he always felt when he broke
the rules to gain an advantage. An advantage, not for the sake of the
investigation, but, as the discomfort reminded him, for himself. He
wondered why he always felt so compelled to find the solution to
every case. Then, as he always did, he told himself it didn't matter because it gave him an edge. And if Danny Citron needed anything
right now, it was someone with an edge.

But Fallon's mind disobediently closed itself to his arguments and
started falling back through the grainy black-and-white photographs
of time to a tiny basement apartment just outside of Pittsburgh. A
door opened slowly and the thick, coarse rope in his stomach started
tying itself into an unsolvable knot. Then, mercifully, with a brief
scramble of static, the tape started.

Shortly after the abduction, before the family was aware that their son was missing, the kidnappers telephoned the boy's father at work. The caller spoke in a low, hissing whisper, not only in a half-hearted attempt to disguise his voice, but to further intimidate the man from whom he was about to demand a quarter of a million dollars.

When the call came in, the boy's father said he had identified himself as he normally did, "David Citron, may I help you?"

The next thing he heard was his son cry, "Daddy—"

And then, "Citron, we've got your kid. Get a pencil and paper." The father's phone was part of an answering machine that allowed the taping of calls. He hit the button.

Fallon listened as the recording picked up where the father's recollection left off: "It is going to cost you two hundred and fifty thousand dollars to get him back. You understand?"

"Yes." He could hear his son grunting in the background as if resisting. "Don't hurt him, please, he's only seven."

"We want the money tonight."

Not sure why, Citron thought it would be best to stall. "I don't have that kind of cash; I'll have to sell some things to get it."

"Listen carefully." There was a moment of silence and then the sound of a heavy rush of water. "Do you know how tall your son is?"

"What?"

The caller's tone became sadistically amused. "Do you know how tall your son is?"

"No! I mean, I'm not sure."

"Well, you'd better find out, *Daddy*, because we've got his foot handcuffed to the center of this stainless-steel tank, and . . ." As the kidnapper stopped, Citron could hear the sound of water splashing into a deep hollowness. ". . . the way we got it calibrated, it's going to fill at four inches an hour—"

"Oh, God!"

"If you're going to rely on God, or the police, or anyone else but me, you'd better get ready to rely on your undertaker. It's only you doing what I say that's going to keep your kid alive. Put the money in a briefcase and wait by the phone. Make sure the briefcase is black and unlocked. I will call at ten o'clock tonight and tell you where to leave it. When I do, all you say is, 'I understand.' If you try to keep me on the line, or jerk me around, I'll hang up and walk away from the whole thing. Do you understand?"

Rather than listening to the instructions carefully, Citron was concentrating on the rushing water, trying to hear his son. "But what about—"

"You know," the kidnapper interrupted, "he sure looks small way down there, chained fifteen feet from the walls. Real little."

"I understand." Citron finally surrendered.

"That's better. We're leaving here now, but your son is staying. And we're not coming back. The only way he can be saved is if you come here and get him yourself. You get me the money, and I'll tell you where he is. If I see one cop even driving through the neighborhood—or I don't get the money, for *any* reason—I'm riding off into the sunset, and you'll never see your kid alive again. And don't forget about the briefcase, black and unlocked."

"I understand."

"Oh, when you find out how tall he is, don't forget to subtract the distance down to his nostrils. Unless you think he can breath through the top of his head."

There were a few more seconds of static, and then the recording of the ten o'clock call started. "Hello," Citron answered.

"At exactly one A.M. go to the alley behind the old Landsdown theater in Cicero and place the money in the Dumpster at the back of the building."

"I understand."

That was the end of the recording. Fallon looked at his watch again. It was almost one. He picked up the night vision scope from the seat next to him and scanned the area, finally coming to rest on the Dumpster where the drop was to be made. In the area were eight other FBI vehicles. Only three of them had a direct view of the trash container, one of which was Fallon's.

He swung the scope over to the only other car he could see from his position. Inside, his supervisor, Peter Blaney, used his night scope to keep watch over the Dumpster even though the ransom had not been delivered yet. Blaney checked his watch and then picked up the mike. "Does anyone have movement?" When no one answered, he said, "Someone give me a time check. I think my watch is running fast." Surveillance time had never gone by so quickly. Usually the hours dragged on endlessly while the agents waited for the always late kidnapper. A voice reported that it was seven minutes to one. With each minute, someone had calculated, the water rose another fifteenth of an inch up Danny Citron's body.

Fallon put down the night scope and took off his wristwatch. He opened the glove compartment, took out a small first aid kit, and placed his watch inside before closing it. Out of the kit he took a Band-Aid. After peeling away its paper wrapper and protective strips, he stuck it across the small rectangular window in the dashboard containing the car's clock. For everyone there, time was becoming a quantified emotion. As it dwindled, fear, like the water inside the tank, rose. To think clearly, Fallon had to put the time out of his mind. He rewound the tape and played it again.

When the case agent had asked Mrs. Citron how tall her son was, she said, "I don't know," and then added, "but he's tall for his age," as though that might somehow save his life. Calmly, the agent explained how it might be important later on. She took a moment longer, then stood up, using the flat of her hand to cut back and forth across her torso. "The last time I held him against me, this is where I remember his head touching me."

From this, Danny's Citron's height was estimated to be about fifty inches, which meant that, if the kidnappers had been truthful—and accurate—he had about twelve and a half hours to live after the tank started filling, give or take a half hour depending on how long he could stand on his toes and how high he could crane his head back. After the parents had left the briefing, Blaney had announced that at 1 A.M., the time of the drop, the water would have reached the boy's collarbones.

Now the only thing the FBI could do was wait in its time-tested ambush. Their immediate objective was to make the money seem so accessible that the kidnappers would walk up and pluck it from the Dumpster as freely as if it were someone's abandoned garbage. As always, it was their responsibility to create the illusion that the law was nowhere around.

Agents hated staking out a kidnapping drop site. No matter what vehicle or concealment was used, or how inconspicuous they were, they felt obvious. Cars would pass by, people looked out their windows; they never knew who was who. If the surveillance was detected, the criminals simply had to drive away or pull down their shades and go to bed. The agents would never know. All they could do now was wait and hope that they were invisible.

Just before Danny disappeared, two men had been seen driving through the Citron's wealthy Highland Park neighborhood. The witnesses said the men seemed to be cruising at an unusually slow speed and gave the impression they had no particular destination in mind. The only description available was that both men were white, and their car was dark blue with both body damage and numerous patches of rust.

After calling his wife to determine that Danny had not returned from school, Citron did not hesitate to contact the town's police. The chief, knowing Citron's background, immediately called the FBI.

During the late sixties and seventies, David Citron was watched, with at least half an eye, by the FBI. In those days he called himself a Jewish activist; however, some FBI informants labeled him a militant, reporting rumors that he was a member of the Jewish Defense League, a group thought to have committed some bombings in retaliation for anti-Semitic incidences. During the ensuing twenty-five years, he had become a successful investment banker, but remained active in Jewish causes. He was a prolific fund-raiser for Israel and an outspoken critic of the Arabs and their hatred of the Jews. He was also well-known for his association with the Kach movement, which called for the removal of the hostile Arab population from Israel. Highland Park's police chief, fearing the kidnapping might be retribution by some terrorist group, was only too glad to turn the case over to the organization which over the years had contacted him for information about Citron—the FBI.

Because of the haphazard fashion in which the victim was selected and taken, the prevailing theory was that the crime was a "random snatch" committed by men who were without a real plan and therefore not the professionals they had tried to appear to be during the two phone calls. There had been no terrorist rhetoric, so in all likelihood it was a kidnapping strictly for money.

Fallon's car sat a hundred yards from the dark green metal Dumpster waiting for the boy's father to deliver the ransom. The Bureau had offered an undercover agent to make the drop, but Citron insisted upon doing it himself, and as mandated, alone. He thought it would be a further gesture of compliance to the kidnapper's demands. And he had insisted on making the payment in full, not wishing to bet his son's life strictly on assurances based upon the FBI's past successes.

The Bureau had accepted the father's decision, but insisted that he use a special briefcase with a secreted electronic tracker to carry the money. But Citron had read how the FBI's use of a similar device in an extortion case a year and a half earlier had played a major role in solving the crime and was reluctant to go along with any deviation of the instructions that might prevent the safe return of his child, especially one that had been reported in the newspaper. Again he was told that these men appeared to be amateurs, and as such, were unpracticed in breaking the law, and therefore probably unaware of FBI procedures and technical capabilities. Citron was reminded that the Bureau had an almost-perfect success rate in such cases. Besides, the best bargaining chip for his son's safe return was to have the kidnappers in custody. Citron used the apparent logic of the argument to fight off the emotional need to do everything his son's abductors had demanded and, being unable to detect the beeper after a thorough inspection of the briefcase himself, agreed to use it.

A surveillance squad radio broke the silence on the scrambled frequency. "All units, we've got the drop vehicle inbound."

A half minute later another unit closer to the Dumpster reported, "I got him out of the car . . . he's at the box . . . he's throwing the briefcase into it . . . he's back in his chopper . . . and he's away."

Pete Blaney's voice took command. "One-three, do you have a good signal?"

"That's affirm. We shouldn't have any trouble staying with the package. The output is strong enough to give it at least a half-mile lead."

Fallon looked around and couldn't see the head technical agent's van which would track the briefcase. It was a good sign; the vehicle was distant enough to not be seen and was still receiving the beeper's transmission clearly.

After a few minutes, everyone's adrenaline subsided and the radios fell silent. The agents waited anxiously for the next transmission, hopefully that someone was approaching the container. With increasing frequency, everyone checked their watches and made vague calculations as to how deep the water around Danny Citron was.

Taz Fallon was again using the night scope, not to watch the Dumpster, but to count the number of garbage bags that lay on the ground next to it.

He no longer shivered in the darkness; he was too numb. His father had once told him the best way to endure a bad situation was to look for the adventure in it. At first, Danny Citron did just that, occasionally tugging at the handcuffs or examining their locks for any previously undiscovered secrets—anything to deny the water its growing authority—until his dad got there.

But he could no longer ignore the terror of the rising liquid. For ten hours he had felt its steady climb. Suddenly, the water's chill touched the base of his neck with the deadliness of a razor-thin garrote. For a moment, it was difficult to breathe. The length of his throat was all that separated him from the relentless black surface. For the first time he could smell the water's chemically sweet odor. Panic shot him to his toes. "Help!" he yelled, then stilled himself, listening for any evidence of someone within range of his voice. Hearing nothing, he exhaled carefully and let his feet go flat to save his calf muscles to use when they would become his last line of survival. Then, hoping that the hollow metallic echo of his voice might validate his words, he said out loud, "The higher the water gets, the closer my dad is to getting here."

The Landsdown was one of those neighborhood theaters that had all but disappeared from the American landscape. Modern cineplexes, with their wide selections and wider seats, had replaced the single-marquee movie houses that had been built throughout greater Chicago's residential neighborhoods in the first half of the century. The Landsdown had been briefly given a second life, showing adult films, but once they became available at the local video stores, the doors were padlocked for good.

Its closing sent a ripple effect through some of the surrounding small businesses: a coffee shop where people tried to catch a quick meal before or after a movie, a bookstore, and a hobby and magic shop whose spellcasting windows ambushed young weekend movie-goers who had just had their fantasies launched inside the darkened theater. Unlike the Landsdown, those buildings had not survived the wrecking ball, which left only the theater standing. The lack of available concealment in the leveled landscape made it difficult for the FBI agents to set up on the drop site. It was another thing, Fallon decided, that the "inexperienced" kidnappers had apparently gotten right.

As each minute cruelly vanished, the agents continued to watch the container that the quarter of a million dollars had been tossed into. Although technology had made it easier, there were no secret techniques to solve cases in which criminals traded people for money. The FBI's rule was to never let itself get separated from the cash. It was the one, indestructible tether between the kidnapper and the law. Lose the money—lose the criminal, or in this case, the victim. During the Bureau's history, the only variable had been the creative methods the criminal used to prevent the agents from staying with the cash.

The probable sequence of events would start when someone arrived and, with forced casualness, strolled up to the container, looked around, and then took the briefcase out. He or she would be followed to their destination, and then the agents would break in and rescue the victim. At least that was the way everyone was hoping it would go.

But Fallon wasn't sure this time. Not only had the kidnappers picked an ideal location for the ransom drop, but chaining the victim to a tank filling with water was not only original but too violent and calculating to be the scheme of an amateur. Letting the father listen to the rushing water on the phone had all but guaranteed his compliance. If these two men were as inept as the Bureau's plan had considered them, so far they had been extremely lucky in their choice of method.

Fallon was parked on the far side of two houses. A narrow gangway between them provided him with an unobstructed view of the

Dumpster, and it was impossible to see his car from the drop because of the darkness between and around the houses. He was slouched down in the front seat and adjusted all the car's mirrors to watch the street around him. The neighborhood was sparsely occupied and, at one in the morning, its streets were deserted.

A car pulled up behind him with its lights off. Fallon hit the thumb release on his holster. He sat up just far enough to ensure adequate space to draw his weapon. A young man in his late twenties with heavy shoulders and flickering eyes got out and walked toward the passenger side of the Bureau car. Recognizing him, Fallon leaned over and unlocked the door. He was a Cicero Police Department detective. Because the kidnappers threatened that the boy would die if a cop was seen in the vicinity of the drop, the Cicero PD had provided someone with radio capabilities to ensure that no one from their department wandered into the critical area while on routine patrol. The detective got in and extended his hand to Fallon. "I'm Walt Danson."

"Taz Fallon."

"I'm kind of afraid to drive around. Since we don't have any idea which way these guys will come, I don't want to wander into them and cause a problem. It seems like this spot is as out of the way as you can get."

"It does have good cover." He handed the night scope to Danson. "And a decent vantage point."

Danson let his eyes adjust to the green glow and briefly studied the back of the theater. He handed the scope back to Fallon. "Thanks. That thing's great."

Fallon returned his attention to the Dumpster. During the briefing, Danson had noticed Fallon but wasn't sure he was with the FBI. While the other agents varied greatly in appearance, there was an off-the-rack monotony about them. And they all acted with that nonchalance cops love to display during a crisis.

But Fallon seemed different. His wavy brown hair was too long to be an agent's, and he wore it swept straight back. His shirt was a heavy pale cloth that seemed too coarse to be worn with a tie, but it had a rugged formality about it, as did his tie and tweed jacket. His face was lean, almost hard, the product, Danson guessed, of a life with few excesses. He had noticed Fallon earlier in the briefing and began watching him more closely when he saw him steal the tape of the telephone calls. While everyone broke into smaller groups to be assigned their positions, Fallon headed to his car. When Danson got out to the area of the theater, he searched the surrounding streets until he found Fallon. And now he could see that the agent had chosen the best vantage point from which to watch the Dumpster.

Fallon lowered the scope and looked at Danson for a moment longer than was comfortable. "First kidnapping?"

"Yeah, I just made detective. How'd you know?"

"You look like you're having too good a time."

Danson smiled. "Well, for a cop, I figure working a legitimate kidnapping is as good as it gets. Kind of what I signed up for."

"I hope you still feel that way after the Bureau takes all the credit."

Danson laughed. There was something in Fallon's tone that made him feel that, despite his inexperience, he was being accepted as an equal. "I guess these kinds of cases eventually become routine."

"That's always a temptation. You want them to be routine so nothing will go wrong, so you can see all the way to the happy ending. But if these things don't scare you to death, you probably shouldn't be out here."

"Think the boy's still alive?"

"I hope so."

During the briefing, the FBI's confidence had left Danson with the impression that they thought the chances for Danny Citron's safe return were extremely good. But suddenly this agent's caution seemed far more realistic. "How do you think they'll pick up the ransom?"

"I'm hoping they're dumb enough to just go to the box."

"Maybe they don't know we're out here."

"That's always a bad bet."

As Fallon went back to watching the drop site, headquarters came on the radio. "The victim's father is here. He'd like to know if there is anything new."

Fallon and Danson heard Blaney say, "Ask him if he saw anything when he made the drop."

After a few seconds, the radio operator said. "He said he didn't see anyone around, and there were three bags of trash in the container when he put the briefcase inside."

"Did he see any of our cars?"

"He says no."

"Good. Tell him to try and relax. This thing is in good shape. He'll be the first to know as soon as anything happens."

Danson looked at Fallon anxiously. "I'd better get back to my car. I just wanted to introduce myself."

Suspecting the detective had come to him for reasons other than conversation, Fallon said, "Walt, I know we're on your turf here, but that's only because we've got the manpower and the electronic toys. When this is over, the bosses will either have all of us taking bows together, or they'll be looking for someone to blame, so why don't you just hang loose and let us make all the mistakes."

"I appreciate that."

Abruptly another agent's voice came on the radio. "Pete, we've got a problem! The truck that empties these Dumpsters is coming down the alley." Danson jumped out and walked quickly to his car.

After a moment Blaney said, "At this time of night? He's got to be involved. But he might be just a pickup man. They may be using him to see if we're around. Everybody stand by. If the briefcase goes with the truck, so do we."

Fallon watched the truck driver line up the receptacle with the overhead lift and then clamp onto it. Slowly the bin rotated up past and over the cab of the vehicle until its lid surrendered to gravity and the contents began to slide out into the back of the truck. The first thing to fall was the briefcase. It was followed by two garbage bags, and then the arms holding the bin shook mechanically, attempting to dislodge any reluctant items. As the receptacle started down, Fallon could see that the third bag was snagged on something and fell back inside. Gently, the bin was placed on the ground and the driver retracted his lift. As the vehicle backed up, Fallon could hear its beeping in the distance. Once it had enough room to turn around, the driver pulled out onto the street and headed south toward the interstate.

Blaney immediately called the technical van. "One-three, do you have the signal moving?"

"That's affirmative. It looks like it's in the truck."

"Did any of the units with the eye see the briefcase come out?"

Fallon was about to answer when another agent said, "I saw it fall into the truck."

Blaney then gave the order, "All units, let's go." As the FBI cars hurried into the wake of the lumbering truck, the supervisor's tone turned cautionary. "Easy, people, let's give him the full half mile. The only thing we can do wrong now is to get burned."

In less than a minute, a long string of Bureau cars left the drop site and fell into a cautious formation a half mile behind the truck.

Five minutes after the last Bureau car had driven past a parking lot two blocks from the drop site, an old dark blue Chrysler New Yorker with rust spots pulled out and drove toward the abandoned theater. When the vehicle reached the alley, it turned in and slowed to a crawl as the driver, Randy Lee, searched for signs of the police. Lee had been paroled six months earlier after serving four years of a ten-year forgery conviction. He put the car in park and got out. Satisfied no one was in the vicinity, he walked over to the Dumpster and tapped lightly on its side four times.

Inside the Dumpster, under a false metal bottom, lay Pete Evans, the second kidnapper. Evans was also a parolee who had recently completed twelve years of his fifteen-year armed robbery sentence. The two men had met at a welding shop that, in theory, was to help recent prison releasees acclimatize themselves back into the ranks of the law-abiding. But instead, the routine of a nine-to-five job forced them to realize that they could never be part of any civilized society. In their off hours, they had devised the kidnapping plot and, using the shop's equipment, altered the Dumpster in which the former armed robber now lay hidden.

Hearing the signal, Evans fit his right foot into the large metal loop handle of a sliding bolt lock and pulled it open. He then used his right hand to do the same with a second lock next to his shoulder.

As he started to push up the hinged false bottom, he felt the resistance of the one bag of garbage that had snagged on the corner of the door when he had closed it after taking the money from the briefcase. He now used both hands and his knees to force the lid up. When he did, the bag compressed enough for him to be able to climb out of the compartment.

Lee watched as the top of the Dumpster opened and Evans

climbed out carrying a small black trash bag. Both men got into the car and Evans took the wheel. He sped down the alley and turned out onto the same street the FBI surveillance had taken but in the opposite direction.

"It go alright?" Lee asked, his speech quick with adrenaline.

"Yeah, except the idiot locked the briefcase. I had to jimmy it open, but the black tape held it shut just fine."

"Let me see it," Lee said.

Evans handed him the bag. "I checked the bundles. It's all here, and there's none of them dummy packs."

Lee let out a shrill whoop. "You were right about the old man calling the FBI. You should have seen them flying out of here after that truck."

"Morons. They ain't got a clue they're chasing a empty briefcase."

"Wait until they grab that driver and he explains he was given a hundred dollars to make that one pickup by a guy he's never seen before. And while they're interrogating him all night, we'll be getting farther and farther away."

The two men became silent, each withdrawing into thoughts of the immediate future. Lee had decided he would go to Florida to enjoy its climate and, of course, its vices. It was hot there this time of year, but he welcomed the thought of warm weather and even the humidity. His last winter had been spent at a prison camp in northern Illinois, where it never seemed to get warm. And there would be the ocean; he promised himself that each day he would spend some time along its shores, especially at night when the sound of the waves would remind him of a woman's breathy sleep. In prison, every night had been the same; the screams of madmen, the constant threats of the predators, the aching cries for help from those who had, on the outside, preyed on the helpless. But Lee had found his escape; every night his mind went to the ocean, where he would swim in its salty glare, and was buoyed by its swelling warmth.

"I think we better change plans," Evans said.

Lee felt a flash of panic. He had witnessed Evans's volatility in prison and knew his sanity was fragile at best. While working out the details of the kidnapping, Evans, once he decided upon a course of action, was obsessed with not changing "his plan." Warily, Lee asked, "What kind of change?"

"I was thinking about it when I was locked in the Dumpster, we got to make sure that kid don't die. Too much can go wrong if we don't. I want to go back and turn off the water. Don't need a murder charge."

Somewhat relieved, Lee said, "That sounds like a good idea to me."

"Yeah. We got the money, and I got to be out there to spend it. The FBI works a lot harder looking for somebody who killed a kid than for a couple of nobodies who beat a rich guy out of what he makes in a month."

Evans made a U-turn and headed back toward the abandoned factory where the boy was imprisoned.

Danny Citron thought he heard something. The intake valve that was filling the tank was now under three feet of water and its noise had been reduced to a barely noticeable hum. He listened more intently, trying to filter out its distraction. There it was again, footsteps, or was it someone talking? Was it his father's voice? "Dad!" he screamed, and then carefully listened. Suddenly the water touched his chin for the first time. He jerked his head back and vaulted to his toes. "Daddy!" Holding his breath, he strained again to hear beyond the tank's hollow thrumming. But there were no footsteps, no voices, just the phantoms that come within breathing distance in the night. Again he calmed himself and sank down flatfooted. Carefully, so as not to get any water in his mouth, he lifted one foot to test, for the thousandth time, the handcuffs which it to the bottom of the tank. There was no more give than the last time. The hum, though more distant, was becoming harder to ignore. "Come on, Dad," he whispered to himself. "Come on."

Four miles later, the Chrysler turned onto a dirt road. Lee asked, "Where are you going? This isn't the way back to the kid."

Ignoring the question, Evans said, "You know what else I was thinking about in the bottom of that garbage bin closed in with all that stink? I was back in the joint—in the hole. Back then, I made two promises if I ever got out: first, I was going to die before I ever went back, and second, I was going to enjoy myself no matter what." Evans stopped the car. He turned and looked at Lee for a few seconds. "That's what this is all about—me having enough money to enjoy myself for as long as I can. That kid may be able to identify me, and that sure would cut into my enjoying myself."

"Pete, I never thought the kid was really going to get hurt. I always figured his old man would come through—and he did. If we let the kid die, how much fun we going to have running from a murder?"

Evans thought about it for a moment. "Yeah, you're probably right. The kid'll never be able to pick us out of a lineup. That's why we wanted one so young, right?" He picked up the bag containing the money. "We'd better hide this in case we get stopped." He handed it to Lee. "Let's put it in the trunk." Then he reached under his seat and took out a revolver. "I better put this back there, too. That'd be just my luck, for once in my life I've got enough money to enjoy myself and I get cracked for a gun." Both men got out and Evans opened the Chrysler's huge trunk. "Put it as far forward as you can. Maybe you can jam it up under the rear speakers. If cops search, they don't like to have to crawl in." Lee stepped up into the trunk with the bag and let his hand probe the area above the rear seat. Evans said, "And see, there's the other part of my problem. You not wanting to get involved in a murder. To me, that means you'd give me up just to cut an hour off your time."

"Pete, you know better than that." Lee realized his precarious position and started to get out of the trunk.

Evans aimed the gun at him. "The way I see it, I can enjoy myself twice as long with your half."

Lee started to raise his hand in protest just as Evans fired two rounds into his partner's head. He slammed the trunk shut and got back in the car. Once he was safely out of state, he could dispose of the body in a hidden grave that, if found, could never be connected to him.

Evans headed toward the Stevenson Expressway. Half a mile later, he was following the large green-and-white interstate signs that pointed south toward St. Louis. A quarter mile behind him, a slate gray Mustang carefully matched his speed.

Fallon had not gone with the rest of the Bureau cars. That the garbage bags had been taken out of the bin to make room for the briefcase was understandable, but when one of the three bags inside got hung up, it didn't make any sense. During his ten years with the Bureau, he had crawled around inside more of those bins than he cared to remember. They were smooth inside to prevent bags from tearing or getting snagged during dumping. What had held the bag inside? And why use a slow-moving target like the truck to pick up the money? Then he remembered the kidnappers' repeated requests for an unlocked, black briefcase. Unlocked for a quick count once they got it in their possession he could understand, but one particular color didn't make any sense at all.

Every case had inconsistencies, those little irreconcilable details that, no matter how deeply explored, could never be explained. Even after everyone has confessed, some facts stubbornly remain a mystery. When Fallon was a new agent, he would drive himself crazy by trying to resolve each and every one of them, but he learned not to dwell on them unless, in the final count, they generated what he referred to as *the trifecta*. When three things, all at once, didn't make sense, the odds of them being mere coincidences were as astronomically low as picking the right combination of three winning horses at the track. The snagged garbage bag, the slow truck, and the designation of the briefcase color had created one of those anomalies. In all likelihood, he concluded, something else was going on, something the FBI was not supposed to see.

So he decided to stay and watch the Dumpster. There were more than enough agents to follow the truck. Minutes later, when he saw the dark blue Chrysler pull cautiously up to the bin, Fallon knew he was looking at one of the kidnappers. He was surprised when the second man crawled out and immediately radioed the other agents. They stopped the truck to check the briefcase. Once they realized it was empty, they reversed course and started back to the Landsdown.

When the kidnappers drove away, Fallon followed them, broadcasting their movement on the radio. With his lights off, he followed the New Yorker down the dirt road and witnessed the murder of the second kidnapper. As fast as it had happened, there was nothing he could have done to stop it. And more importantly, if he had interfered, he would probably not have been led to the boy's location. It would have been a tough decision to make; he was almost glad that it had been taken out of his hands by the abruptness of the murder. But with the apparent flight west on the interstate, Fallon knew the remaining kidnapper was not going to the boy or to a phone to call his father. It was time to bring up the troops and stop the only man who knew where Danny Citron was.

"Taz, we're up here on your six." It was Blaney. "How do you want to do this?"

Fallon looked at the highway ahead of the Chrysler and held his radio mike low so the kidnapper could not see him transmitting. "There isn't much traffic, so let me get ahead of him, just in case he decides to run, then you can use four of your cars to box him."

The supervisor designated the trailing Bureau cars to the four positions they would take around the subject's car. They all moved closer to Fallon. "Okay, Taz, we're ready—let us know when you are."

Fallon felt his heart pump three thick strokes. Stopping a car, especially on a highway, was always risky; too many things could go wrong. But this had to be done right now and they could not make any mistakes. He ripped the Band-Aid off the car's clock and saw Danny Citron did not have much longer. He pressed down on the Mustang's accelerator and passed the Chrysler as normally as possible.

By the time he eased up, Fallon was a hundred yards ahead of the kidnapper. "He's all yours," he called into the mike. In his rearview mirror, he saw the four Bureau cars break formation and race at the Chrysler. One agent streaked by the New Yorker on its left side and pulled in a little too close to Evans's front end, causing the kidnapper to swerve to the right before the right-side blocker was completely in position. The Bureau car coming up was caught by the rear end of the heavy Chrysler and went spinning into a 180-degree arc up the expressway embankment.

Evans saw the other cars trying to surround him. He swerved again to the right, onto the shoulder, then accelerated. The car to his left stayed with him as did the car in front. He fired at the one on his left. All the agents knew that he had to be taken alive if they were going to save the boy. The agent to the left backed off. Next, Evans shot at the car in front of him, leaving that agent no choice but to pull to the side and decelerate. Evans swerved back into the middle of the expressway and floored it.

Seeing this, Fallon accelerated to 120 miles per hour. "Pete, hang onto him just a little longer. Try to keep him in the center lane. I'm going to get up ahead and try to put a rifle slug into his engine block."

Once he got a mile ahead, Fallon slammed on the breaks and hit the trunk release. Pulling a shotgun out of the trunk, he quickly loaded three rifle slugs into the magazine. The Chrysler was less than two hundred yards away now and doing more than ninety miles an hour. He raised the shotgun to his shoulder and attempted to take aim at the grille.

Fallon's shotgun did not have rifle sights but only a bead on the front of the barrel. He fired. One of the four headlights exploded; he had missed the grille. The huge car was now within a hundred yards and the other two agents had pulled on either side, forcing it directly into Fallon's Mustang. Evans fired a shot at the car on his right but the agent refused to pull off.

Fallon chambered another round, sat down, and leaned back against the rear of the Mustang to steady the shotgun on his knees. He took an extra second to aim and fired. This time he hit the grille dead center. There were a couple of small explosions as the Chrysler's engine shut down, but it was too late; the car was doing over seventy and there was only thirty yards between it and Fallon. He could see the insanity on Evans's face now—he was going to take an FBI agent with him.

Fallon flattened out and pulled himself under the Mustang's rear end just as the Chrysler crashed into it. Tires screeched to a halt as the other agents got out and drew their weapons.

Fallon had held onto the undercarriage knowing the impact would ram the Mustang forward and he did not want to be run over by the Chrysler. He was dragged forty feet before both vehicles finally came to a halt. Still on his back, he wriggled from under his car and crawled beneath the Chrysler. Fluids splashed down on him, some scalding hot. Still unseen by Evans, he carefully came out from under the driver's door.

Evans tried to open the door but his left arm was broken and badly lacerated. The agents, from behind the protection of their own cars, yelled at him to raise his hands. They were on both sides and behind him; he was in a three-way crossfire.

Evans now knew he was going back to prison—for the rest of his life. All his freedom, all his choices would be gone forever. All but one. He picked up his revolver off the floor, thumbed back the hammer, and put it to his temple. To the agents pointing their guns at him, he said, "I'll say hello to Danny for you."

Fallon dove through the window, grabbing at the revolver. But he wasn't as quick as Evans. The .38 exploded.

3

DANNY CITRON HAD NO WAY OF KNOWING THAT THE only two men in the world who knew his whereabouts were now dead. If he had, he might have panicked as the water finally reached his lower lip. Instead, he calmly tilted his head back and stretched his neck.

Blaney ran up to Fallon. "Taz, you alright?" He took the agent's arm and turned him slowly. His clothes were torn in several places where he had been dragged across the pavement and his back was scrapped and bleeding.

"I thought I could stop him."

"He was going to do it anyhow." The supervisor looked at his watch, "Time is getting critical." Fallon, who was staring at Evans, didn't seem to hear him, so Blaney yelled to the other agents, "I want this car and both bodies thoroughly searched. There has to be something that will tell us where the boy is."

Detective Danson suddenly appeared next to Fallon. "There's a real shame. Pete Evans putting his own lights out. He finally did something the town of Cicero can be proud of."

"You know him?" Blaney asked.

"Unfortunately. When I was in uniform, I locked him up more than once. I thought there was something familiar about that voice on the tape."

"He was from Cicero?" Fallon asked.

"Born and raised. The only time he wasn't living here was when he was in the joint."

Fallon grabbed the detective by the arm. "Come on." He led him over to his Mustang. He restarted the car and shoved the ransom tape into the player. "Listen to this and see if there is anything familiar. If, like you say, he never left Cicero, maybe that's something that will tell us where the boy is."

When it finished, Danson said, "Sorry, there's nothing there that I recognize."

"Do you have an idea where he worked?"

"Work? I doubt if he ever worked. If he did, it wasn't for long."

"Did you notice how he described the container that Danny was being held in. He didn't say it was a thing or even a tank, but a 'stainless-steel tank.' He must have had some experience with it to be so specific. And he 'calibrated' the water flow, which would indicate that he probably had been trained how to use it. But the most obvious detail was that he knew the exact radius of the tank. I don't think he'd know that unless he had worked there."

"Do you want me to call the station and have them check for previous employments?" Danson asked.

"I don't think Danny has that kind of time." Fallon yelled to Blaney, "Where's Doc?"

"He's searching the guy in the trunk."

Fallon went around behind the Chrysler and found Mathias Zjorn.

One of the ways the Bureau maintained quality agents in their laboratory was to put them in the field for a few years and then assign them to the lab. With their practical experience, they provided insightful forensic support to the field agents. Zjorn was one of those agents. He had a Ph.D. in applied mathematics and was serving his apprenticeship in Chicago. Six feet tall and slender, his sweeping and imprecise movements made him look gangly. His hair, an inert shade of dark brown, was glossy with gel and carefully cut and combed to appear fashionably disheveled. But his face was far more everyday. A sagging rectangle, it seemed blanched and strained. His eyes were deep-set and had that slightly out-of-focus stare that lifelong eyeglass wearers could never disguise. The flaw was accentuated by contact lenses that made him hold his eyes unnaturally wide and blink too often. He had a tiny hole in his left earlobe that some observant agents suspected held an earring during non-Bureau hours. When his merciless fellow employees challenged a new hairdo or any other attempt at fashion, he always gave a good-natured shrug, indicating that he was simply doing the best he could with what he had.

Fallon and Danson found Zjorn smelling Randy Lee's shoes. He gave a one-word explanation: "Perfume."

"Perfume? Come on, Doc, I need you to concentrate," Fallon said. "The tank that the boy's in, what would you need to figure out its size?"

"What good would that do?" Danson asked.

"You said this guy never left Cicero. The little bit we know about it, it sounds huge. If we can figure out from its size what it's used for, maybe you can point us in the right direction."

"I'll try," Danson said.

"How about it, Doc?" Fallon asked.

"If it's for industrial use, it's some type of cylinder, and a cylinder is just a circle with height. So it's the area of the base times its height."

"We don't know its height."

"Do you know its base?"

"Remember on the tape," Fallon prodded, "Evans said Danny was fifteen feet away, chained to the center of the base."

"That's right." Zjorn stared off as he continued. "But without the height, you can't determine the volume. However, because we know how fast it is filling, the water's rate of flow into the tank can be calculated."

"What will that tell us?"

The Ph.D. closed his eyes. After a few seconds, he took a small notebook and pen out of his jacket pocket. "We know that the water is rising at a rate of one-fifteenth of an inch each minute. And the base of the tank, converting everything to inches is one-eighty squared, times pi, equals 101,736. So you divide that by fifteen, which gives you six thousand cubic inches of water per minute as your rate of flow. A gallon is approximately sixty-seven hundred cubic inches. So close to twenty-five gallons a minute is going into that tank." He looked up and smiled as if the answer should have been obvious.

Fallon hadn't followed any of the calculations, but he knew Zjorn's figures were always accurate. "The bottom line."

"Municipal water is generally thirty to forty pounds per square inch. That converts to fifteen to twenty gallons a minute."

"So?"

"So, if Cicero's water pressure is less than twenty-five, then wherever the boy is being held will have to use a water holding tank to generate that kind of pressure, and there can't be that many businesses in this town with that elaborate a system."

Fallon turned to Danson. "How about it, Walt? It's probably a building that is closed down."

"Cicero is a small town, but not if you're going to try and search every abandoned business in it. I'm a cop; I don't know anything about the water system."

"You must know someone who does," Fallon said.

Danson put his radio to his mouth. "Dispatch, this is Danson. Get me Herb Daniels at home. This is an emergency." He turned to Fallon and Zjorn. "The town water commissioner."

The men checked their watches and waited for the dispatcher to come back on the radio. "He can hear you, go ahead."

"Herb, there's been a kidnapping and a boy's life is at stake. I'm going to put the FBI on and they'll tell you what they need." He handed the radio to Zjorn, who explained quickly about the size of the tank, the rate of flow, and that it was probably in a business that was not active.

The dispatcher said, "He's going to another line to access the water department's computer."

Danson took the radio back and yelled into it, "We don't need anything fancy, Herb."

While everybody waited, Blaney, who had been supervising the search of the car and bodies, came up to the group standing around Danson and said, "We didn't find anything that would tell us where the boy is." Fallon explained to him what they were trying to do.

Finally the dispatcher said, "He's got six possibles. The most likely is the old Sawyer soap factory on Temple Street—"

Zjorn interrupted, "The perfume on the shoes!" He ran over to Evans's body in the front seat of the car, lifted his left foot awkwardly, and smelled it. "Same perfume. It has to be the soap factory." He and Fallon ran to the nearest Bureau car.

Danny Citron had been on his tiptoes the last twenty minutes and the back of his neck was starting to ache from extending it. He tried to hold himself perfectly still because he was only able to breathe through his nostrils. The cold water was starting to cramp his lower legs. He held his breath, and although he was sure the results wouldn't be any different, he tried his foot against the handcuff again. He let his feet go flat again and tried to stretch his lower legs. He exhaled and went back up on his toes. No longer able to say it out loud, he thought, There isn't much time left, Dad.

As the speeding Bureau car approached the Sawyer soap factory, Zjorn, with scientific dispassion said, "I wonder if they figured in the displacement of the boy's mass into the rate of fill."

"Translate."

"If they just set the tank to fill at four inches an hour, that means that it will fill at a faster rate because the boy's body has already taken up some of that space."

"How much faster?"

"Not much—but probably enough."

Their car slid to a stop in the factory's parking lot. Until five years ago, Sawyer had made several quality soap products, but it eventually closed when it became too expensive to continue to manufacture. The building was ideally located for industrial use, but in the years since Sawyer, no buyer had been found.

Fallon grabbed a shotgun from the backseat and, looking for a way in, signaled Zjorn to take one side of the building while he went around to the other.

As Fallon reached the back, Zjorn came running up behind him. "This has got to be it," he whispered, "the water meter is running, re-filling the tank."

"Did you see any doors?"

"Just the overheads, and they look like they haven't been opened in years. When I saw the meters I doubled back."

"Then there's got to be a door between here and the meter." Cautiously they turned the corner, and at the far end of the wall found an employee entrance. Fallon pointed down. Weeds in front of the door sill had been stepped on and were caught under the door. "This is it." He tried the knob, but it didn't open. He took a rifle slug out of his pocket, and as quietly as possible, dropped the shell into the port and chambered the round. Standing back about ten feet, he fired. The blast ripped the lock out of the door and bent its top half inward.

Zjorn kicked it open, and they raced in. There were four twenty-foot-high tanks at one end of the structure. There didn't appear to be anyone else in the building. They ran toward two of the stainless-steel cylinders and each climbed the small metal staircases that wrapped around the outside of the tanks. They both called the boy's name. Fallon's reached the top of his first; it was bone dry. So was Zjorn's.

Fallon started up the third and stopped. He put his hand against the cold steel bulkhead. "I can feel some vibrations." He took the stairs two at a time.

He reached the top stair and looked down. There was seven-year-old Danny Citron. Only the top of his head and his fingers were visible above the surface. Fallon could see that oxygen deprivation had turned his fingernails blue. "Doc! He's here, but he's unconscious. I'm going in. Find a way to drain this!"

Fallon lowered himself over the side, hung for a moment on the edge, then dropped feet first into the four feet of water. The handcuff around the boy's ankle was so tight that it was cutting into the skin while the other end of it was locked around a thick steel loop that appeared to be freshly welded to the tank's permanent structure.

Only for an instant did he consider giving the boy mouth-to-mouth resuscitation; he knew that the water had sealed off the boy's throat so no air could be forced into his lungs until his airway was cleared, and with him underwater that was impossible. Fallon came to the surface and yelled, "Doc, did you find the drain?"

There was no answer, so he dove down to take another look at the handcuffs. He reached in his pocket and took out his keys, one of which was for his own cuffs. It opened most standard handcuffs, but these were cheap and poorly made; the keyhole was a completely different configuration. Again he stood up and yelled, "Doc!" Still there was no answer.

Putting his arm around the boy's waist, Fallon put his other hand under the boy's jaw and tried to get at least his nose above the surface, but the water remained just above it. He dove to the bottom again. The handcuffs held fast against Fallon's efforts to force them open. He thought about trying to shoot them off, but even if he could get his gun to fire underwater, the bullet's velocity would probably be too slow to break the case-hardened chain.

Then he remembered a demonstration in training school. The instructor said that handcuffs are just temporary restraining devices and advised the class not to leave anyone unattended in them for long, because they can be defeated with relative ease. To demonstrate his point, the instructor had taken a thin, stiff wire and pushed it into the juncture where the single strand fed into the double, and it opened immediately. But Fallon didn't have a wire.

He examined the same point on the inexpensive cuffs where the instructor had inserted the wire. The give between the strands was much greater than the brands police officers used. Mentally, Fallon inventoried his pockets. His credentials! His badge was pinned to the front of them. He opened the safety clasp. Shoving the pin into the cuff that held the child's ankle, he could feel it depressing the spring-loaded rachet. He pulled the single strand backward and it swung open.

Immediately, he threw the boy over his shoulder. Suddenly he felt a sucking sensation at his feet. Zjorn had found the tank's drain, but the water was still above Fallon's waist. He jumped up as high as he could and just as he was landing, he jumped up again as violently as possible, causing his shoulder to slam into the boy's stomach. The boy still felt lifeless. He double-jumped again. Still nothing.

About half of the water was now gone and Fallon was able to get more height on his next leap. He felt the boy's limp head slam into his back. Then he heard seven-year-old Danny Citron start throwing up. Fallon let him down and watched as the blue disappeared from his face. He was now choking and coughing at the same time.

Fallon patted him firmly on the back until he stopped. The first thing Danny asked was, "Where's my dad?"

Fallon smiled. "He sent me here to get you."

4

AS SOON AS THE JUDGE ENTERED THE COURTROOM, Kurt Decker sensed something unexpected was about to happen. The jurist's eyes were set with dark purpose, his brow shortened contemptuously. With a quick, ceremony-be-damned collapse, he seated himself behind the bench and lifted the document he was carrying to reading level. Before putting on his glasses, he looked up at Decker. Everyone in the room sat down carefully, not wanting to attract the judge's attention, and waited for the butchery to begin.

Even the assistant prosecutor, who was unable to make any sense of the judge's uncharacteristic display of anger, tried to smile, hoping that justice was about to have one of its rare good days.

But men and their performances did not frighten Decker. He had served a ten-year sentence at Marion, Illinois, the toughest federal prison in the country, the maximum security facility that had been built to replace Alcatraz. In the federal system, inmates were sent to a particular prison based on various factors, anything from space available, to the type and severity of their crime, to the proximity of their family. It could be as arbitrary as the precoffee mood of the assignment officer. But those sent to Marion were there for only one reason: they were the most dangerous men in the United States.

Decker had been sent there to serve a fifteen-year sentence for robbing three armored cars over a two-year period. Once he arrived at the prison, he knew that if he was going to accumulate any good time for early release, he needed to be left alone and not become involved in the unpredictable violence of daily prison life. And to be left alone, experience had taught him, he needed to go on the offensive.

He had learned how to survive prison's unchecked brutality when, at age nineteen, he became an inmate in the Ohio penitentiary system, serving six years for armed robbery. Even at that age he was heavily muscled like his father, but taller and considerably more agile. While his size helped, he soon learned that intimidation was the currency of each day's existence, and unless a man was willing to demonstrate an unbridled aggression, physical strength alone was of little help.

As soon as he was released into the general population at Marion, he made queries as to who was the most feared man incarcerated there. Everyone gave him the same answer: a black Muslim who called himself Kaleel Hallah. The next day, in front of hundreds of other inmates, Decker approached Hallah in the prison yard. In his pocket was a toothbrush that he had melted down into a pencil-point-sharp shank. Decker told the Muslim that he was going to prove that the black man didn't have any heart and handed him the weapon. Stunned, Hallah stood looking at the molded knife. Again Decker told him he didn't have any backbone and to prove it, the black gang leader could have the first three hits with the shiv before he would defend himself. Enraged by a challenge obviously meant to belittle him in front of the other prisoners, Hallah delivered two quick jabs into Decker's stomach. When they slid off Decker's dense abdominals, Hallah used a vicious roundhouse thrust to sink half of the toothbrush into Decker's neck. No sooner had the blow landed than Decker had Hallah by the throat with one hand. With the other, he grabbed his fist and broke three of his fingers. Then using a forearm lock, he fell on Hallah's right arm with his entire body weight, snapping the Muslim's elbow. Decker then stood up, yanked the makeshift knife from his neck, and dropped it onto his opponent's writhing body. While blood flowed from the wound, Decker calmly lit a cigarette.

The entire episode took less than sixty seconds. And during that minute, the prison population learned not only that the black Muslim was no longer Marion's toughest inmate, but that Decker was its craziest. And that was what he wanted. During his ten years there, the legend of Decker's insanity grew with each telling of the story. In the later versions several witnesses swore smoke had come out of the wound in his neck as he took a drag on his cigarette.

So a judge's facial expressions were not about to intimidate Kurt Decker. Although he had been in jail for almost three months awaiting trial for another armored car he had robbed since his release from federal prison, this was only an evidentiary hearing. Next to him, his lawyer absentmindedly flicked the edges of the papers in front of him. Decker reached over and tapped his arm. The lawyer stared straight ahead, ignoring his client.

The judge put on his glasses and made a pretense of rereading the legal document in front of him, occasionally giving a just-perceptible shaking of his head as if frustrated by not being able to find a prosecutorial loophole in it.

Decker turned to his attorney again. "What's going on?" Decker's voice had a natural anger in it that could turn the simplest question into a threat. Finally the lawyer opened his briefcase and handed him a sealed envelope.

Inside was a note written in German:

> Your case is going to be dismissed. If you want to find
> out who your father really was and what kind of life
> you could have, meet me in the bar at the Meridian
> Hotel at 8 PM.

There was no signature. Just as Decker was about to ask his lawyer about the origin of the note, the judge said to the assistant prosecutor, "Do you have anything additional to offer at this time on behalf of the state?"

The prosecutor was confused. The search that was being contested had been clearly legal. That coupled with the judge's demeanor had indicated that the ruling would favor the prosecution, but he had lost enough cases to understand the dismissive tone of the judge's question. "Your Honor, Mr. Decker is charged with an armored car robbery which is extremely similar in its MO to another armored car robbery in which a guard was shot to death for no other reason than the robber's convenience. Additionally, the defendant has previously been convicted of similar crimes, specifically the robbery of three armored cars, and was incarcerated at the federal prison in Marion, Illinois, for the better part of ten years. The state contends that Mr. Decker and his associates, who he has refused to identify, are indeed responsible for this robbery. Not only were some of the canvas shipment bags containing money from the robbery found in Mr. Decker's trunk, a sawed-off carbine that two of the guards described as being similar to the one used by the robbers was found under the front seat of his car."

The judge now spoke with an empathy that seemed slightly labored. "I am aware of all that, but the problem is how those items were obtained. The bank bags were found after the defendant was arrested on the weapons charge, and that was after what appears to be an illegal stop and search of the vehicle he was driving."

"Your Honor, I know there was no search warrant, but because of the exigent circumstances, Mr. Decker's car had to be considered a tool of the crime, therefore making the search allowable. If the detectives had not stopped him, the proceeds of the robbery would never have been found."

With a scolding timbre in his voice, the judge said, "I have considered all these points at length. The search was three days after the robbery; even the most liberal interpretation of the law would strain to qualify that length of time as exigent." He then turned his voice toward the defense table. "Mr. Decker, I have little doubt that you were involved in this crime. However, I am afraid that your attorney is correct—at least constitutionally—about the inadmissibility of the only items of evidence that connect you to the crime. I have to rule that the search of your car by the police was illegal. And since the State of Ohio has no further evidence against you, I have no choice but to dismiss these charges. But mind you, if I ever find you in my courtroom again, I will do everything in my power to see that you never again are turned loose on the outside world." The judge gave one final rap with his gavel.

The lawyer shook Decker's hand perfunctorily. Decker asked, "Where did this note come from?"

"My fee has been paid," was his lawyer's only answer, as if no further explanation were necessary. He closed his briefcase and walked out of the courtroom.

Decker read the unsigned note again. The last thing he needed right now was more trouble, but he knew whoever had arranged his freedom was about to offer him some. It was the only reason anyone would help him. And, because of the amount of money that must have been paid to have his case dismissed, he suspected the proposition would be most tempting. He would have to be careful. Just go and listen, he warned himself. If it isn't perfect, walk away. Temptation and Caution—the criminal's arguing angels.

5

THE MERIDIAN WAS ONE OF THOSE OLD CLEVELAND hotels that had been built around the turn of the century when the city's mills and related industries thrived. But it had steadily declined since the end of World War II, until a few years earlier when it was purchased by a Swedish corporation and renovated to resemble an old European inn. To convince the guests of its authenticity, its interior was filled with mahogany paneling, thick, ornate draperies and rugs, tasteful antique reproductions, and desk clerks who spoke with heavy, unidentifiable accents.

Its lounge was dark and uncrowded, and recorded piano music seeped in unobtrusively. Kurt Decker went straight to the bar and ordered a beer. When he tried to pay for it, the bartender told him that the gentleman in the corner booth had taken care of it. Reminding himself that suspicion was now his greatest ally, Decker took a sip of his beer and walked over to the booth.

Rölf Brunner stood up. His ginger-colored hair was cut short, almost in a military style, but layered in a way that suggested someone with talent had cut it. And the tailored double-breasted suit that he wore looked equally expensive. In the dim light, the man's face seemed perfectly symmetrical, bisected by a narrow, sharp nose. But as Decker came closer, he was struck by the three long scars that crisscrossed Brunner's left cheek and ended at the corner of his mouth. The pale stripes forced the eye to trace them. Anyone who saw them suspected that their source, if ever discovered, would prove the strength of their owner's character.

But because Brunner was meticulous in his grooming and dress, and appeared to have money, Decker concluded that the scars' vulgarity, which could have been reduced, or even eliminated through surgery, was intentional. In prison, Decker had seen men do things to themselves to prove that they were more than what they appeared to be, willing to mutilate themselves with needles, knives, or even to cut off a finger on a dare. For them, tattoos and scars were symbols of rank, and life in prison without them was considered by most a disadvantage. Whatever weakness caused such men to brandish their treachery, Decker understood that more often than not, these weaknesses could make them extremely dangerous.

The German extended his hand coolly. "Mr. Decker." The ex-con took his hand. "I am Rölf Brunner."

Decker held up his beer. "Thanks for the drink. And anything else you may have paid for."

Brunner turned his head slightly and gave a short nod of acknowledgment. "My pleasure. Please, have a seat."

Decker sat down and said, "Now tell me why."

Brunner gave a short grunting laugh. "You Americans, no time for subtlety."

"Subtlety is a scam that just hides what somebody really wants."

"I am sorry—scam?"

"Trying to deceive someone."

Not expecting Decker to be so direct, Brunner took an extra moment to restructure his approach. "You will find that I am not here to deceive you. On the contrary. We can both greatly profit from this meeting. But first I have a favor to ask, would it be alright if we spoke German?"

"*Natürlich.*"

"*Danke.* I do not think well in English. And I obviously do not understand many of your idioms. As you have probably surmised, I am from Germany, and I have come here to make you a proposition."

"Before we discuss what it is you're about to ask me to do, I want to know about my father."

"Again you are to the point. Did your father ever speak of Germany?"

"Only when he was drunk."

"Did he tell you what he did there?"

"He only talked about how the United States and Russia had destroyed what it had once been."

"Do you have an interest in German politics?"

"I don't have an interest in American politics. Besides, anything my father had an interest in, I did my best to hate."

"Well, I work for the German Democratic Alliance party. It is on their behalf that I have come to see you."

"I hope this is the last time I have to say this, but before we talk about my getting involved in your problems, I want to know about my father."

"I apologize. I don't know which is more difficult in America, your language or your impatience. Have you ever heard the name Erich Lukas?"

"Not that I can remember."

"It was your father's real name." Brunner handed him a large envelope. Decker opened it. "That was your father's SS file."

Decker did not know a lot about Nazi Germany, but he had read enough in prison to know the infamous initials. "SS! . . . my father was a janitor."

"You are holding the truth." Brunner's dispassionate tone seemed to prove the statement.

"Did my mother know anything about this?"

"If he did not tell you, his only son, I doubt if he would have told her."

Decker folded back the front cover of the file. Stapled inside was a clear black-and-white photograph of his father at a younger age in a German uniform. Decker didn't know the rank but he could tell that he was an officer. His billed hat was pulled low across his eyes, almost too far, giving him a determined look. The sun came from over his right shoulder, casting a shadow on his face except for his right cheekbone and the jawline immediately underneath it. His head and eyes were turned slightly away from the camera looking beyond the moment, as if he had little time for anything as frivolous as a photograph. He was a man with a mission. Pinned on the left tunic pocket was a thick black cross outlined in white or silver. An identical medal also hung at his throat. "These medals, what are they?"

"The Knight's Cross. Germany's highest decoration for valor."

Decker continued to stare at the fifty-year-old likeness and noticed something he had never seen before in his father—dignity. He couldn't help but wonder what had changed this hero into such a bitter old man. "Why did he change his name?"

Brunner lit a cigarette, tilted his head back, and blew smoke at the ceiling. "He was considered a war criminal."

The German's tone was dismissive, as if *war criminal* were little more than a politically correct term. "What exactly was it that he was supposed to have done?"

"Some Russian prisoners of war that were supposed to have been executed. He was wanted for questioning, nothing more. The Jews, they were looking to blame as many German soldiers as they could. And your father was one of the best known, one of our bravest. They would have the world believe that there were no good soldiers, just butchers. He was beloved in the Fatherland. If they could discredit him, they could further discredit Germany."

Decker drained his beer and Brunner ordered him another. It gave Decker a moment to judge the German's story. The noble warrior in the photograph would not have fled Germany and turned himself into a pathetic drunken janitor because he was wanted "for questioning, nothing more." He decided that the cruel man he had known was completely capable of either ordering his men to shoot the prisoners or, just as likely, doing it himself. Decker started leafing through the pages. "These are just personnel entries: training, shots, the units he was assigned to. There are no specifics about anything he did."

"There's a reason for that. Toward the end of the war, many of the high-ranking officer's files were sanitized so the Allies could not use any of the information against them. I, like many Germans, know a great deal about your father's exploits. He was known as Hitler's commando. Whenever there was an impossible mission, and believe me, no one could come up with more impossibilities than the Führer, many times he called upon your father. If you like I can tell you how he earned his second Knight's Cross."

Decker felt a sudden, unwanted admiration for his father. "Yes."

"During the war, Hungary was a member of the Axis and Admiral Horthy was its regent. When things started going badly, Horthy, although he had pledged his country's loyalty to Hitler a month earlier, started negotiating with the Russians. Hitler was furious and ordered your father to kidnap him. With a small group of men disguised as tourists, he flew to Budapest. But the regent had feared such a maneuver by Hitler and had surrounded himself with heavy security. Your father and his men conducted surveillance of the admiral and soon realized that it was hopeless. However one day, they noticed that his grown son, Miki, Horthy's favorite, was less well-guarded. Although greatly outnumbered, your father and his commandos attacked the Hungarian forces. Your father was wounded, but he continued to throw hand grenades until he and his men could escape with the regent's son. He was flown to Vienna, and after that, Horthy was no longer a problem. And Hitler was more convinced than ever that the Third Reich was invincible. He flew your father to his mountain retreat, Wolf's Lair, the next day and decorated him. He was truly the Reich's hero, the kind of man Hitler wanted every German to become."

"Here he was nobody."

"Surely you must have noticed that your father was much more gifted than the work he did."

Decker stared off into the past. "Once, before he made me quit high school, we got into an argument that ended in a fist fight. He said I was wasting my abilities. I told him that I thought that was pretty hypocritical coming from the smartest janitor in America. I guess I did suspect something."

Both men became silent. Decker took out a cigarette and searched his pockets for a light. Carefully, Brunner reached into his pocket and, holding a silver foil book of matches between the middle knuckles of his second and third fingers, handed them to the American. Decker lit his cigarette and handed them back. Brunner gripped them in the same way and put them back in his jacket pocket. "He was the most bitter man I've ever known. He made everyone around him miserable, especially my mother."

Brunner said, "I am told you have your father's honor."

Decker laughed loudly. "The man I knew had no honor. And if you think I'm going to risk going back to prison because you showed me a picture of some hero I never knew, you've gone to a lot of trouble unnecessarily."

Without hesitation, Brunner said, "My only real concern is that if we do strike a deal, you will honor it."

Decker stood up and handed the file back to Brunner. "I appreciate what you did to keep me out of prison, but I'm not going back because of something my father believed in fifty years ago."

"In that case, would a million dollars inspire your loyalty?"

Decker froze and a smile spread across his face. "A million *U.S.* dollars?"

Brunner nodded. "I assume you would like to know what is expected of you."

"For that amount of money, I'm going to guess somebody is about to die."

Without emotion, Brunner answered, "At least three somebodies." He could see his answer did not intimidate Decker. "And that is just to get us to the starting point."

"The starting point of what?"

"I need you to recover something."

"What?"

"Something worth a great deal of money."

When Brunner did not explain further, Decker thought for a second. "And you don't want to say exactly what it is, because you think I'll go off on my own."

"You'll have to admit, if our roles were reversed, it would be a possibility you would have to consider."

"So, how do we get past this mutual distrust?"

"You could demonstrate your good faith."

"By?"

"There is a man in New York who is one of the three I spoke of. If you could *remove* him from the list, I think we would have a basis for trust."

"You mean you want to have a murder to hold over my head."

"A man in my position is wise to seek collateral."

"That's the kind of collateral I can't get back when our business is finished."

"You have my oath that your deeds in this incident will never come to light."

Decker let out a short sarcastic laugh. "Around here the concept of 'oath' is a little out of date."

Brunner did not want to tell him any more than he already had, but he knew that Decker needed some assurance. "When you learn what is to be recovered, you will see that the consequences for me will be much more dire than something as insignificant as the murder of a few old Nazis. At that point my position will be much more precarious than yours. Simply, our knowledge of each other's crimes will produce a stalemate. And don't forget I am paying to have you commit these murders, which I believe would make me at least as desirable a target of the American justice system as you. And, after you have performed your *down payment*, I will give you one hundred thousand dollars as a sign of our good faith. The balance will be paid upon the completion of your task."

He didn't know what it was that Brunner needed him to find, but with a price tag of one million dollars, it didn't really matter. "I have some people I normally work with."

"One of the reasons these three individuals must die is because they know of the existence of the property you will be trying to recover for me. One man has already been killed for that reason alone. Part of your responsibilities in this matter will be to eliminate anyone else who does. We do not want any additional competition, and we certainly do not want to add your men to that list. Will they follow orders without knowing exactly what it is that they are looking for?"

"For the kind of money you're talking about—absolutely. Besides, they know I could have given them up on the armored car robberies and never did. They'll do as they're told."

"As long as you understand that anybody you use is your responsibility."

"That goes without saying."

"What I mean is that they are your responsibility if they become a problem."

"And who decides when something becomes a problem?"

"Me, of course," Brunner said.

Even with a million dollars for a prize, Decker did not like to be threatened. "Let me ask you something, is it politics that has turned you into a bully, or was it something you've enjoyed your whole life."

Unmoved by the insult, Brunner thought for a moment and said, "As a child, I realized that someone had to organize the weak."

"Is that what you do now?"

"That's what all great men of history have done," Brunner said.

"And is killing necessary to become a great man of history?"

The question was not one that Brunner had expected from a man with Decker's reputation. It caused him to wonder if they understood each other. "Can you kill a man?"

"Given provocation, yes," said Decker.

"And what would provoke you?"

"Someone trying to organize me."

Brunner laughed. "Boundaries noted."

"If I remember right, that was a major problem for the Nazis—recognizing boundaries."

"Oh, we recognize them. It's just that we have never honored them." Brunner handed Decker a small piece of paper. "Meet me at six P.M. the day after tomorrow at this hotel in New York City."

6

EARLY IN HIS ACADEMIC LIFE, JONATHAN GEIST RE-
alized that his desire to become an artist far outweighed his talent, so
he decided to train to become an instructor. But the Second World
War ended those plans. As he agonized over his inevitable conscrip-
tion into the army, one of his professors, who had been put in charge
of warehousing art confiscated from all over Europe, came to his rescue. Remembering Geist's passion for art and his discriminating eye,
he obtained the necessary waivers, and brought him to Linz, Austria.
There he joined dozens of men and women working on what Hitler
had proclaimed would one day be the greatest art museum in the
world. While his friends and relatives were facing the daily horrors of
war, Geist spent his time idyllically cataloguing the Führer's stolen
treasures.

Originally, Geist had been a very small part in the *Führervorbehalt*
plan. As the Allied armies advanced toward Berchtesgaden, he was
hastily summoned to Goering's residence. There he helped display
hundreds of paintings so the *Reichsmarschall* could select the ones
that were to be smuggled out of Germany.

After they were crated and taken away under heavy guard, Geist,
and the others involved, were called into Goering's study. The *Reichsmarschall* personally thanked him for his exceptional service to the
Fatherland and presented the young museum worker with the
Totenkopfring, the SS honor ring. It was engraved not only with the
death head symbol, but with numerous runic symbols that were sup-

posed to reinforce the wearer's "psychic" German virtues. The *Totenkopfring* was coveted by members of the SS, so Geist was greatly honored by the gift. He swore his undying allegiance to Goering and the Third Reich.

Like many former Nazis, Geist had initially fled to the Middle East. But much of the postwar turmoil in Europe had also found its way there. Seeking further relief, he decided to go to America. And he did not go alone. Many of his former associates, under their real or new names, entered the United States in those years, claiming they were escaping the tyranny of the latest threat to world freedom—communism.

Arriving in New York City, he took a job translating technical journals from German into English. It did not pay well, but it allowed him extra time to involve himself in the art scene. Given the postwar chaos in Europe, New York had become the most important trade center for art in the world, and Geist spent a great deal of his time getting to know both artists and gallery owners. When not visiting museums and galleries, he spent long, smoky nights in the cafes and coffeehouses they frequented.

Because of his unparalleled exposure to masterworks at Linz, he was extremely knowledgeable about many forms of European art. Although the market was thriving, it also had the problems that came with a strong economy. Forgeries were becoming increasingly common, so to protect themselves, buyers and sellers alike began approaching Geist for his expertise.

In recent years, he maintained a small office in SoHo in lower Manhattan. He had achieved some status as a broker, and his name was occasionally mentioned in the newspapers in connection with the sale of some costly work. Although he made an adequate living, he was never able to obtain the long-term financial security men of his age dreamt about; he found himself continually anxious for the next deal.

He often thought of the hundred paintings at Berchtesgaden and wondered where they were. Occasionally he would even daydream about being called upon to broker them.

Geist soon noticed that people, for some incomprehensible reason, tended to trust him because he was European. Seizing on this, he exaggerated a continental bearing. He bowed his head respectfully, never allowed himself or his clients to be hurried, and wore dark three-piece suits and a gold pocket watch. He even grew a looping, waxed moustache. His English was heavily accented and scrambled with mutated syntax, but it bore the precision and authority of his native German. Within the art community, he became known as an irrefutable authority and just as importantly, someone who could be trusted.

So it was no surprise that when *Watering Place at Marly* by Alfred Sisley was to be discreetly auctioned, he was contacted by the owner of the gallery where the sale was to take place and asked to put the word out to his more "established" clients. The Sisley was one of the Reserve paintings he recalled packing up at Goering's direction. He called one client, a well-known American playwright who had recently become obsessed with French impressionism and was extremely eager to own anything from that period. He authorized Geist to pay up to three million dollars to secure the painting.

Geist's excitement soared. Could the collection be in the United States? With the reunification of Germany, was someone finally trying to return to power and selling the Reserve to finance the campaign? If so, maybe he could involve himself in the sale of the rest of the paintings, a towering prospect.

When he had been called into the private audience with Goering that night, he was sworn to secrecy and told that if he ever needed to contact someone about the Reserve, it should be the *Reichsmarschall* himself or Hans Trauchmann, no one else. Geist had a brother still living in Germany and sent him a letter containing a sealed note addressed to Trauchmann. In it, he explained that the Sisley was to be sold at a closed auction in New York. If all the paintings were now to be sold, he would appreciate the opportunity to represent the sellers as he was well established in the art business in the United States. Any response should be sent directly to him since his brother had no knowledge of the Reserve.

But the only response he received was a letter in which his brother informed him that he had delivered the note as requested, but Trauchmann had died ten days later of natural causes.

Tonight Geist was going to a show for a new artist. A small gallery was exhibiting the work of a woman who had previously been a martial arts instructor until she discovered, mostly through Buddhist meditation, that she could weld chunks of metal into art; art, Geist believed, that would always be identified by a very small *a*.

The business had become obsessed with the quest for "fresh." America was easily the most bored country in the world and would do anything to find something new, no matter how temporary or pedestrian the focus of its attentions proved to be. He suspected he was getting old and increasingly inflexible. He spent more and more time, as men of his hardening frustrations did, recalling his youth. Nazi Germany—there was tradition, and aesthetics, never to be tempered by the whims of a mercurial culture. Tonight he would go to the showing to hear the buzz about the upcoming Sisley auction. Only a handful of people were going to be allowed to bid, and as one of them he had momentary status in the New York art community. And as long as he had been around it, *momentary* was as permanent as it got.

Tonight's showing, at least during the early part of the evening, would be flooded with former karate students and other equally undiscriminating art enthusiasts who understood welding far better than they understood sculpture. However, he and *his* peers had a sense of protocol and would know not to arrive until all the sport utility vehicles had departed.

Climbing the stairs to his office, he cursed its location and then realized it was his age that made the stairs so steep. He cursed his age. He wanted to check his machine for messages; the playwright was considering upping his limit for the Sisley. Of course, he would not be able to discuss the details of the impending auction at the gallery tonight, but having that knowledge would supply him with an additional ingot of contempt, one of the prized possessions of the New York art scene.

The digital readout on the answering machine showed there were three messages. He removed his suit jacket and sat down with an involuntary grunt. He got out a pencil and paper, but all three calls were hang-ups, the last just ten minutes before. One misdial to his unlisted number was unusual, but three stirred some ancient feelings. As he pushed the rewind button to eliminate the messages, the phone rang. "Hello?" he asked cautiously, not knowing why.

"Herr Geist, please."

It was unusual for anyone to refer to him as *Herr*, and the speaker's pronunciation indicated that he had a knowledge of the nuances of the German language. A long dormant alarm went off in the old Nazi's chest. It had been fifty years since he had felt the leaden butterflies of panic, but they were there now. Without hesitation or thought, he said, "I'm sorry, he's not here right now." When the line went dead, he silently cursed his accent.

He opened a drawer to his desk. In the back under some notebooks, he retrieved a black leather ring box. He opened it and stared at the death head symbol. He had not worn it since the night Goering gave it to him with the instruction that it go to the grave with its wearer.

Not sure why, Geist slipped it on his finger. As if it did indeed enhance his "psychic" German powers, it seemed to release a suffocating fear.

Had he locked the door downstairs? Sometimes it slipped his mind. He cursed his age again.

Then he heard something strange, a vague metal scraping in the lock, like a dentist cleaning teeth with a delicate steel instrument. He challenged the sound. "Who is there?"

The scraping became more insistent. Then . . . a metallic click that Geist had heard a thousand times before—the lock clearing the striker plate. "Who is there?"

The reply, this time, was feet ascending the stairs with the quickness of youth. He picked up the phone and dialed 911. Ron Slade, a tall, muscular man with damp-looking hair, was suddenly before him and ripped the phone from his hand. Before Geist could say anything, a second man, Jimmy Harrison, wrapped a hand around his mouth. Slade spoke into the phone, "Yes, I was wondering if you could tell me the time? . . . well, this is an emergency, I have a date in about an hour and . . ." He looked at Harrison and smiled. "They hung up on me." He motioned Harrison to remove his hand from Geist's mouth. "Maybe you'll be more talkative, Herr Geist."

Before he could answer, the downstairs door opened again and two more sets of footsteps started up to the office. This time they were slow and controlled. Rölf Brunner and Kurt Decker appeared at the second floor landing.

Geist looked at them and then to the other two who had rushed him. "What do you want?"

Brunner spoke in German. "That seems like a fair question. I have been sent by Hans Trauchmann." Geist did not know what to say, but if Trauchmann's name was being used, he knew it had to be about the Reserve. "He wanted us to find out who you have told about the *Führervorbehalt*."

"The *Oberstleutnant* is dead."

Ignoring the old man's response, Brunner said, "Where are my manners? This is Kurt Decker. I believe you have heard of his father, Erich Lukas."

"Hitler's commando?"

Brunner turned to Decker and in a voice meant more to inflame Decker's anger than to congratulate him, he said, "See, I told you your father was a famous man."

Decker took his cue and grabbed Geist's windpipe. The old man struggled briefly and then realized Decker's strength was far superior. Again Brunner asked, "Who else have you told about the *Führervorbehalt*?"

With the oxygen in his lungs waning, Geist clamped both his hands on Decker's wrist and struggled against it for a moment but still found it unmovable. His answer was a gasping choke.

"No one . . . No . . . one!"

Effortlessly, Decker lifted him halfway off the chair and tilted his head up so they could look into each other's eyes. "How do we know you're telling us the truth?"

"Because I am an old man, and I do not want to die."

Decker studied Geist's face, looking for any hint of deceit. "You wouldn't want to go to your grave with a lie on your lips, would you?"

"Please don't kill me, I have some money."

Brunner nodded at Decker to release his grip and said, "This is not about money. Just tell us who you told."

Geist now realized he was going to die. He didn't understand why; he had been loyal. But these men wanted to know who had knowledge of the paintings, and that could mean only one thing, anyone who did was to be eliminated. Geist looked into the eyes of the

man with the scarred face, confirming his fears. If he had told someone about the Reserve, which he hadn't, he would be killed for that.
If he hadn't, he would be killed because he had knowledge of it just
the same. Suddenly, Geist's voice filled with dignity. "I have not broken my oath. Do what you must."

Brunner for the first time understood Hans Trauchmann's wis-
dom. He was right to insist that Brunner kill him before undertaking
the search for the Reserve. It had been a christening, an instruction as
how best to proceed in this search. If Trauchmann had not shown
him, he might have let Geist off with a warning, but now he could
see how dangerous that was—how leaving anyone alive might endan-
ger his mission. Brunner took out a cigarette and a lighter. "You
should be proud of your loyalty and your obvious courage," Brunner
said. "Let me pose a hypothetical situation, if Oberstleutnant Trauchmann suddenly appeared here at this moment, would you still follow
his orders?"

The question caused a momentary rush of survival in the old man.
Maybe there was hope. "Of course. As you have said, I have remained
loyal all these years."

"Then you understand why I find it necessary to carry out his
orders."

Now he realized that Brunner was only toying with him. With a
level of anger that was unusual for him, Geist shot back, "I don't
know. My life has never needed the control that must come from ful-
filling the orders of a dead man."

Brunner laughed. "You old Nazis are a tough lot."

Geist didn't say anything; he had made his final statement. Brunner dropped his cigarette and crushed it under his shoe. He looked
over at Decker and gave him a barely perceptible nod.

Slade, now standing behind the old man, placed a hand over his
mouth. From out of nowhere a knife appeared in the ex-convict's
hand. Without hesitation, it slashed at the old man's throat. Geist
struggled as he felt the sharp edge of steel cut through the loose tissue along the left side of his neck. The blade found the carotid artery
easily, and Geist felt the warmth of his blood run down his neck.
Then he felt his heart start to beat with an increasing hollowness.

Oddly, he thought about how efficiently he was being murdered.

He was being held in such a way that none of his blood was getting on the killer. He must have done it before.

Finally Slade carefully released his hold on the old man, and let him fall to the floor.

Harrison was already wiping down all the smooth surfaces the four men had touched. Slade joined him. Brunner couldn't help but be impressed with their practiced calm. Methodically, they retraced their movements as if they had been memorizing them since entering the office.

Decker spoke in German. "There's your collateral. Now tell me about this *Führervorbehalt*—the Führer's reservation?"

"Reserve, the Führer's Reserve. It is a cache of one hundred paintings, one of which is going to be sold at auction in a couple of days. They were smuggled out of Germany after the war and were intended to finance a new leadership for Germany. I am here to take possession of them."

"Where are they?"

"That's what you're getting a million dollars to find out." Brunner then told him about being summoned to Hans Trauchmann's cell and given all the details of not only the Reserve's existence but of those who guarded its whereabouts.

"Before he died, why didn't this Trauchmann get word to Braune to let you know where Rathkolb is?"

"Braune was ordered by Goering himself never to divulge Rathkolb's location to anyone but Goering or Trauchmann. He is reported to be fanatical. It will not matter that both his contacts are dead. He was given an order and that's it. Besides, he has to die. You will have to *convince* him to tell you where Rathkolb is before you kill him."

"It sounds like you're not planning to make the trip."

"I don't want to be this close to any more of your activities. Besides, I can see that your men are very capable. How will I be able to contact you?"

Decker picked up a pen from Geist's desk and wrote down a name and telephone number on a pad of paper. After wiping off the pen on his shirt, he dropped it back on the desk. Then, so as to not leave evidence of the number's impression behind, he tore the next five pages off of the pad, folded them, and put the sheets in his pocket. He handed the number to Brunner. "She can be trusted. I'll check in a couple of times a day for messages. Now, I think you owe me some money."

Brunner looked down at Geist's body. "I most certainly do. It's in the hotel safe." Gracefully, he extended his arm toward the stairway. "Shall we."

Having finished, Harrison and Slade were waiting at the bottom of the stairs, watching for passersby. Brunner and Decker started down. Halfway, Brunner said, "*Verdammt!*" and started back up.

"Where are you going?" Decker asked.

"I left a cigarette butt up there. I understand there have been cases where they have gotten DNA from them."

Decker continued down the stairs. "Just hurry up."

Brunner walked past the body and picked up the cigarette stub. From his jacket pocket, he pulled out a plastic envelope. Inside was the silver foil matchbook that Decker had used to light his cigarette in the hotel bar. He took it out and tilted it so the light reflected off Decker's almost-perfect thumbprint. Carefully, he placed it on Geist's chest and put the cigarette butt in the envelope. Now he indeed had insurance that could be called in if Decker tried to take the Reserve for himself. Without a name to go with the single print, the police would have to send it through the state fingerprint scanner, but according to the file Brunner had received from Decker's lawyer, Decker had never been arrested in New York.

He turned and hurried back down the stairs.

7

PROOF OF SINCERITY TOOK THE FORM OF A CERTI-
fied check in the amount of one million dollars. That was the entrance fee to the Sisley auction at the small Weisel Gallery on
Manhattan's Lower East Side. Sam Weisel had invited only a dozen
serious collectors for the opportunity to bid on *Watering Place at
Marly*, which had not been seen for over fifty years.

The anonymous seller, through his agent, Robert Pearsay, had
specified that the sale be held in the strictest confidence and if it
became known to the public, would be canceled without warning.
With these unusual restrictions in mind, Weisel meticulously selected those who would be given a chance to buy the Sisley. Not only
did they have to have the necessary financial resources, but, because
of the auction's unique restraints, their discretion had to be as well
established as their credit. Contacting them one by one, he made
them pledge their silence before he identified the painting.

After all the bidders had been invited, Pearsay, a lawyer by training, added the million-dollar earnest-money proviso. Weisel balked,
claiming his clients would be insulted, but Pearsay said the seller insisted on this contingency. Weisel did not believe the attorney, who
had a less-than-sterling reputation in the art business, but since the
gallery owner had no way to contact the seller himself, he was left
with no other choice.

When Weisel recontacted the potential buyers, he was stunned
that they seemed as excited by the demand for such a huge sum as

they were by the possibility of owning the masterpiece. Not only was it an outrageously unique circumstance, its pretentiousness was built in—something, for once, that would not have to be manufactured.

Afterward, it was going to make a great cocktail story, especially now that even more intrigue had attached itself to the sale. It was being whispered around the gallery that Jonathan Geist, one of those invited, had been mysteriously murdered the night before.

Checks in hand, seven men and two women had come to the little gallery. Two more, who had their bank drafts couriered to Weisel, waited anonymously on open phone lines. As the starting hour approached, waiters in white linen jackets served icy champagne and inky caviar.

The one person in attendance who had not presented a certified check was Sivia Roth. She was there as a representative of the International Foundation for Art Research. IFAR sought out stolen works of art with the intention of returning them to their rightful owners. After receiving an anonymous phone call a week earlier, she researched the painting's provenance and determined it had been stolen by the Nazis in 1939 from its owner, an Austrian Jew. She went to see Weisel who, after a brief but wrangling conversation, agreed to help her.

Weisel moved easily from guest to guest, constantly raking the room with his host's smile. Occasionally he let his eyes find Sivia. She seemed much too serious for such an attractive woman. Her dark, glistening eyes cautiously measured the people who had come in hopes of owning the Sisley. In her early thirties, there was an elegant politeness about her. She had a way of holding people with her smile as she listened to them. She was the kind of woman who made men think for the first time that there might be a plan for their lives, but they had made poor choices in its execution to arrive at this point without her. Weisel was in his sixties, and as never before, regretted his age. Looking around the room, he could see she had the same effect on the other men. They would occasionally turn away from their conversations and watch her, hoping to catch her glance.

As Weisel continued to circulate, he could feel the excitement of uncertainty growing. The only person who seemed immune to it was Jason Talsman, a 300-pound bond trader who loved food and art with equal recklessness. He had taken a sip of the champagne and set it down as if he had just been poisoned, and then, with growing hopelessness, sniffed the caviar, which he noted was neither Iranian nor Russian, but American. He telegraphed his suspicions to Weisel by releasing the caviar-laden cracker from his fingers, not caring where it landed.

If you only knew the worst of it, Weisel thought. He raised his voice and said, "Ladies and gentlemen, shall we get started?"

Immediately, a strange calm pervaded the room. There would be only one winner. Everyone sat down, and two uniformed guards walked forward, carrying a draped easel, which they set in the front of the room and then stood off far enough to be unobtrusive but close enough to remind the hopeful of its value.

Sivia had positioned herself behind and to the side of Pearsay so she could watch his reactions during the sale. He gulped his wine and talked with subdued excitement to the bidders on either side of him. She could see that he was a man who did not hide his motivations well, and that pleased her. His Achilles' heel was one of the world's most dependable—greed. And she knew how to exploit that.

Weisel was going through his unveiling dramatics, giving a little history of both Sisley and the painting. A polite murmur went through the crowd when one of Weisel's assistants finally pulled the covering off.

Sivia was familiar with Sisley's work. Although a lesser-known impressionist, he was one of the founders of the movement. A contemporary of both Monet and Renoir, his landscapes were renowned for their delicate serenity. Unlike his more-famous contemporaries, his works had a more spacious and airy look to them. While Monet constantly experimented with new techniques resulting in fragmentary scenes, each of Sisley's pictures were remarkably complete in their effect.

Like most of his paintings, this one was dominated by his rendering of the sky. It was snowy and dark. The scene was vague and melancholy, lacking his trademark clarity and cheerfulness. Although her research had determined the painting was done in 1876, a period when Sisley was at his best, Sivia decided this work was not his best and wondered if that would affect the price.

Then the opening bid came—one million dollars. She glanced at Pearsay, who seemed to be grinning uncontrollably.

Twenty minutes later Weisel declared the painting "sold." Via telephone, the final price had reached $4.6 million. The overweight bond trader jumped to his feet and stormed out as if he had been tricked into watching a bad movie in its entirety.

Since the high bidder was not present, the others came forward to get a close, and perhaps final, look at the painting. Several more bottles of champagne were opened and sipped unenthusiastically. After refilling his glass, Pearsay found Weisel and pumped his hand gratefully. "Congratulations, Sam."

"Thanks, Robert. And congratulations to your client. When you have a moment, I'll need to see you in my office."

Happily, he held up his again-empty glass. "Just let me get a little more of this and I'll be right in."

As Pearsay headed back to the bartender, Weisel signaled Sivia. Five minutes later, the three of them were sitting in Weisel's private office. "Robert, this is a friend of mine, Sivia Roth."

Flush with champagne, and impending wealth, Pearsay could not hold back his burgeoning charm. "A great pleasure indeed. I noticed you during the auction. Did you get a chance to bid?"

Fascinated, Sam Weisel leaned back in his chair. Pearsay had a reputation as an accomplished manipulator, undoubtedly the reason he had been chosen for such a circuitous transaction. Weisel thought he might have to interject himself into the oncoming fray on Sivia's behalf, but he could already see that she held the same advantage over Pearsay that she held over him. She would not need his help; in fact, she seemed eager for the skirmish to begin. She was the hunter, and, for Robert Pearsay, counselor at law, there would likely be no escape.

"I'm afraid I am a bit of an anomaly, Mr. Pearsay. I am a collector without money." She smiled enigmatically, encouraging his curiosity.

"That must greatly limit the quality of what you're able to obtain."

"On the contrary, I have collected some of the world's great art."

Between the champagne and the impending commission, Pearsay had been euphoric, but there was something in Sivia's demeanor that warned him not to celebrate just yet. He felt his combativeness being triggered. He was experienced in starting fights and suspected that this attractive woman was about to become his enemy. Hoping he was misreading the signs, he summoned as much charm as possible and said, "Okay, I give up. How do you do that?"

"Are you familiar with the International Foundation for Art Research?"

"I'm sorry, no."

"We recover stolen art."

Pearsay's commission on the sale was well into six figures. He had spent less than forty hours setting it up. He guessed he knew it was too good to be true, but so many of his deals were. Free lunches were invariably ambushes. But fighting his way out of ambushes is what he did for a living. And he was very good at it. A shudder of adrenaline removed the champagne's vague comfort, and he set his resolve not to surrender his percentage of the sale. He looked at Weisel, who showed no intention of becoming involved. He turned to Sivia. "Then I don't suppose it is a coincidence that you and I are here behind closed doors."

"Your painting was *confiscated* by the SS in 1939."

"That's a shame, but as an attorney, I do know something about the legal ownership of property. And—"

She handed him a three-page document. "That's a court order for the confiscation of the painting."

Pearsay flipped through the pages quickly. "You can't—"

"We have."

"I can also get a court order."

"Possibly, but do you know how many Jewish lawyers would fight you forever for free?"

"I don't care."

"You will when your anger wears off."

Pearsay's mind started gathering speed. "Why didn't you confiscate the painting before the auction? It would have been much easier."

"That's true, but then I would not have had a bargaining chip."

"I don't understand."

"Now we each have something the other wants." Pearsay was still confused. "I'm offering an exchange."

"I'm listening," said Pearsay.

"What is your commission on the sale?"

"Ten percent." He looked at Weisel, now understanding that the gallery owner was on her side. "Minus the twenty thousand that Sam gets for holding the auction. But I'm sure you already know that."

She ignored the accusation of conspiracy. "Then your end is almost half a million dollars. That's a lot of money. If you give me what I want, I won't execute this court order, which means the sale will go forward, and you'll collect your commission."

"And you want . . . what?"

"The name and address of the seller."

"Because of the attorney-client privilege, that would hardly be ethical."

"It's good to see that someone in this world still cares about ethics. Enough to give up hundreds of thousands of dollars."

Pearsay looked at the document without reading it. "This arrangement would be between us?"

"Of course."

"There is one thing I don't understand, Miss Roth. If your foundation is concerned only with the recovery of stolen art, why are you willing to trade this masterpiece for the seller's name and address?"

"I can only say that we believe the person who had possession of the Sisley may have as many as four or five similar works. We think two of them are by Van Dyck and Vermeer, which, in all probability, would prove to be substantially more valuable."

Pearsay's tone now was suspicious. "That seems a little risky. I would think your organization would be a little more bird-in-the-hand."

Sivia lowered her voice and leaned closer. "In a month, a new court order will be issued to the person who purchased the Sisley tonight. But, like you say, that is just between us."

Pearsay smiled. He had a new appreciation of this woman. "And since my fee was from a sale in good faith, it would probably not be subject to revocation."

"That's the way our lawyers see it."

"You are very thorough. But I'm curious how you found out about this sale. We went to a great deal of trouble to keep it quiet."

"My organization received an anonymous call. I guess we have friends everywhere."

"So it would seem. How soon will I receive my commission?"

"If you could provide an address for the seller and we could verify it, I would guess between two and three weeks." She looked at Weisel who nodded his agreement.

Pearsay hesitated, to give the impression that he was wrestling with a moral dilemma. "The man identified himself as Mr. Johnson."

"First name?" Sivia asked.

"He never used one."

"Address or telephone number?"

"Every contact I have had with him has been by telephone only. And he always called me. When I asked him for a number, he said I wouldn't need one. He would contact me."

"How were you supposed to get him his money?"

"He said we would work it out after the sale was made. Obviously he was afraid something like this would happen. I suspect if it went through, he would have instructed me to send the money to some overseas account."

Sivia said, "Mr. Pearsay, I think you are an extremely careful person when it comes to protecting your interests. I find it hard to believe that you wouldn't have learned more about a man who treated you with such caution." Pearsay did not answer. "Remember, our deal is *if* we locate him. Only then will the sale be allowed to go through. Otherwise you're out four hundred and sixty thousand dollars."

The attorney stared at her a moment and decided he had no choice. "Mr. *Johnson*, who by the way speaks with a German accent, shipped the painting by bonded messenger. It was sent to a bank for safekeeping until I had it delivered here tonight. Sam will verify this because he had to send his experts there to authenticate it."

Sivia looked at Weisel and he nodded. She said, "Earlier tonight, I spent a great deal of time inspecting the crate it arrived in, looking for a clue to its origin. If you found any, you're a better detective than I am."

"I'm afraid I'm not quite blue-collar enough for something like that. However, even though bank records are considered confidential, I was able to determine, through a well-placed bribe, that the shipper was a Martin Bach." Pearsay took out a small pocket calendar, extracted a three-by-five card, and handed it to Sivia. "He lives in Des Plaines, Illinois. I looked it up, it's just outside of Chicago."

She copied down the address. "This should be good enough. And if it is, you will be hearing from Sam soon."

Weisel stood up and came around his desk, raising his hand toward the door in a politely dismissive gesture. Pearsay said, "Miss Roth, it has been most interesting. I've almost enjoyed being your victim."

After Pearsay had left, Sivia said, "Do you think he suspects?"

"Does it matter?" Weisel asked sarcastically. "You got the address. Isn't that all that counts?"

"Are you sorry about the auction?"

"I have worked many difficult years to establish myself in this business. I do not feel good about deceiving my customers, especially the ones who were here tonight. They have been very good to me."

"Is that what this is about—profits?"

"It's about integrity. We lied to every one of those people."

"Unless you tell them, they'll never know."

"No? What about Pearsay when he doesn't get his commission?"

"What's he going to say, 'I took a bribe to abandon the lawyer-client privilege'? Not only would he be disbarred, he'd never broker another art deal in this town."

"Everyone who was here tonight is important to me. For God's sake, each brought a million-dollar check. If they ever found out the high bidder was one of your people because you're going to confiscate the painting anyway, I would be through in this business."

"It had to be done. Now when this Martin Bach calls Pearsay, he'll think everything is alright. He won't anticipate our coming."

"*Our* coming?"

"Whoever I can get to help me in Chicago," Sivia said.

"So you'll recruit someone like you did me."

"Like I told the counselor, we have friends everywhere."

"*We?*" Weisel eyes bored into her. "There's more to this than paintings, isn't there?"

"This painting and all the others like it represents what was done to our people. They were murdered so their wealth could be stolen. There are some who are still enjoying that wealth. Don't you think, as a Jew, you should be a little more outraged?"

"You've already used guilt to get me to help you. Please stop dangling it in front of me." He calmed himself. "You seem so driven by this. You are a young woman, you were not even alive when these things happened."

"I'm alive now."

8

SAN CARLOS DE BARILOCHE, A PHOTOGENIC LITTLE
town deep in the Argentine Andes, was founded a hundred years ago
by Germans from Chile. Its climate and rugged high-altitude terrain
had reminded them of Bavaria. When Gerhard Braune first arrived
from Germany in 1945, he found the similarities most appealing. An
even more important consideration for many of the former Nazis
who had relocated there was Argentina's support of fascism.

But that was half a century in the past, and many of the Reich's
officers who had sought the sanctuary of the small ski town were no
longer alive. Five years before, Braune's wife had also died. Now he
lived alone and rarely had guests. But this night, April 20th—the
Führer's birthday—was the one day a year the men of the Third
Reich allowed themselves to gather and celebrate who they had
been.

There were only five of them left now, and Braune was pleased
they had accepted his invitation to come to his house for dinner.
They brought sausages and cheeses, and brandy and cigars. These presents were reminders of the old life, when they were too young to
consider such luxuries vices. Only on this day did Braune allow himself their sweet nostalgia. And it showed. Although he was in his early
eighties, he was extremely fit, with a hard jawline and large, powerful
hands. He still skied, shot skeet, and chopped all his own firewood.

It was almost midnight and the five men, aided by the memories
of their youth and the blur of aged liquor, were still joking and telling

stories. Their intense laughter forced its way into the air and hung awkwardly in defiance of their exile. Braune stood up with his glass. "Gentlemen, a toast." The others stood. "*Auf* Adolf Hitler!"

"*Auf der Führer!*" they responded with military precision and lifted their glasses formally. The resulting exchange of glass-touching pleasantries was interrupted by a knock at the door.

As the others continued to talk loudly, Braune went and opened it. Kurt Decker stood half-shadowed in the light coming from inside the house, smiling. "Herr Braune?"

Braune thought he detected a slight American accent hidden in the stranger's almost flawlessly spoken German. "*Ja.*"

Decker pulled an automatic from under his leather jacket. A silencer extended the length of its muzzle, and Decker touched it against Braune's lips. The former SS major understood its silent order.

Suddenly, Jimmy Harrison and Ron Slade, guns drawn, streamed past Braune. Decker gave them a moment to take control of the others at the table and then motioned for Braune to join them.

The four guests sat at the table with their hands on their heads, obeying the unspoken commands of the intruders. Decker spoke in German, "Herr Braune, I apologize for interrupting your celebration, but I have been sent by Oberstleutnant Trauchmann to request your assistance."

"*Du bist Amerikaner!*" Braune spat out the last word with disdain.

"My father also fled Germany at the end of the war. He was forced to hide in the United States."

"His name?" Braune demanded.

"Lukas. Major Erich Lukas."

Braune's face registered his surprise, but he forced his features back to their mask of indignation so Decker would not gain any sense of advantage. "If you are the son of Major Lukas, the blood of a great soldier fills your veins. Such a man would never conduct himself in this fashion, especially with men as loyal as these."

"If you are as patriotic as you claim, you will aid me in my mission. At Herr Trauchmann's direction, I have been asked to recover the *Führervorbehalt.*"

"I am not familiar with this term, *Führervorbehalt.*"

"Herr Braune, do not take me lightly. *Der Kurator* is starting to sell off the paintings, and I have been commissioned by some of Germany's new party members to recover the Reserve for the financing they will need to take power. I cannot leave without *der Kurator's* location."

"I told you, I am not familiar with—"

Decker spun around and, taking aim, fired a shot at one of the men sitting at the table, hitting him just under the nose. His head jerked back against the high-back chair and a trickle of blood darkened the middle of his upper lip before he fell forward lifelessly. "Now," Decker said, "tell me where Josef Rathkolb is."

Braune responded with silent defiance. Decker put the muzzle of his automatic against the temple of another man sitting at the table. "At your age I wouldn't imagine that you can afford to lose friends at this rate."

"We have seen enough death to know when it is imminent. Since it is apparent that none of us will leave this house alive, I have nothing to say."

Decker could not help but admire the old man's tenacity. He was like Geist, willing to die rather than violate his word. Brunner had been right, Braune was not going to be easy to make talk. "I'll bet you guys were a handful fifty years ago." Decker signaled to Jimmy Harrison, who was standing behind the man who had the gun to his temple. Harrison took a roll of tape from his jacket and stuck two strips over the old man's mouth. Braune's face showed his apprehension. If the man was simply going to be shot there was no reason to gag him. Lowering his gun slowly, Decker fired once into the man's groin. As his hands grabbed at the wound, trying to assess the damage and stem the flow of blood, his eyeballs exploded with pain and he uttered a dull, muted scream.

Decker could see that he was close to finding out what he wanted to know. For the next several seconds, everyone watched in horrible silence as the wounded man writhed and moaned through his taped mouth. Without taking his eyes off of Braune, Decker moved to the next man sitting at the table and lowered the gun to his groin.

Slowly, Braune said, "He's in Chicago, but I do not know where."

Decker fired again, this time striking the gagged and wounded man in the temple. He fell to the floor with the unmistakable thud of dead weight. "I assume you wanted me to reward your cooperation by ending his suffering."

"As an SS officer I took an oath of loyalty, not only to the Fatherland but my comrades, as well. It is evidently something your father forgot to teach you."

Decker laughed. He turned to the Nazi nearest to him and pressed the silencer against his chest and pulled the trigger. "You can't imagine the things my father forgot to teach me." He raised the front sight and shot the last of Braune's guests in the head.

The old Nazi's lips drew back as his jaws clenched in rage. Decker asked, "*Wo ist er in* Chicago?"

"I told you, I don't know where."

"I just killed four men, do you think I am going to settle for *I don't know?*"

The old Nazi straightened himself and said, "And you're about to kill me."

"True, but there's killing and then there's *killllllling.* You decide."

"I don't know anything else."

"You don't know how many times I've used those exact words during interrogations myself. And you know what—every time I was lying." Braune stared straight ahead, trying to appear unaffected by the threat. Decker grabbed his wrist and felt the fear trembling through the old man. "Major, during your time with the SS, did they ever teach you that the two greatest concentrations of nerve endings in the human body are in the feet and the hands? It's something you learn very quickly in prison." Although he did not know exactly what Decker was going to do, his instincts made him try to free his hand from the American's grip. He attempted to yank it away, but without any success.

Decker pulled the old Nazi's hand down to the floor and onto his foot. He fired one shot that passed through both appendages. Braune fell to the floor and curled up, grimacing in pain. "Shall we do your left hand?"

The old man pulled his uninjured hand underneath him. Decker reached down and ripped it free. He held it up in the air and pressed the silencer against it. Braune blurted out, "Okay, okay. The address is in my study."

Decker grabbed him under the arm and half dragged him into the next room. He threw the old man into his chair behind the desk. With his good hand, Braune took out a key ring from a chain clipped to his belt and unlocked a drawer. He took out a large black metal box and used another key to open a small padlock. Inside were three notebooks rubberbanded together. Fumbling with them, he tried to pull the smallest one free. Decker grabbed them from the old man and said, "Which one?"

"The brown one."

Decker took it out of the bundle and handed it to Braune. Holding it against his knee, he leafed through it clumsily. "This is the name he is using—Martin Bach."

Decker looked at the entry. It listed a Des Plaines, Illinois, address and a telephone number. "How do I know this is really him?"

"I could call him and you can listen."

"That doesn't prove he's Rathkolb."

"Look through that book. You can see I call him regularly and then log the call."

Decker leafed through the book until he found the entries. But he took longer studying them than Braune had wanted. "You call him every six months like clockwork. The last time was only two months ago; if you called him now he'd know something is wrong." Braune let his eyes drop, confirming that Decker had discovered the truth. "You are a tough guy, but I think I'm starting to understand you people. You're very thorough, have a plan for everything. So you must have some way of contacting him, in case of an emergency, without spooking him." Braune still wouldn't look at him. "When you won't look at me that tells me I'm right. How about making this easy on everyone including yourself."

Braune raised his eyes to Decker. "There is no such contingency."

The old man's voice was unconvincing. "You're still lying to me." Decker searched the room for a moment until he found what he wanted and then reached over and held up Braune's good hand. Matter-of-factly, he fired a bullet through the center of it. Braune crumpled to the floor, drawing the hand against his stomach,. "How about it, Major?"

Now Braune's tone was more angry than pained. "Never!"

"There's a word that is almost always misused. Let me give you an example of its proper use in a sentence: *Never* say never to a man with a gun." Decker motioned to Slade to help him. They each grabbed a wrist, and with Decker leading, dragged Braune backward to the wall behind him. Five feet off the floor, a long coat rack, made of a rough-hewn timber and a half dozen curved metal hooks, was bolted into the wall. Decker pulled Braune's right hand up to the end hook and forced it through the bullet wound. He motioned to Slade to do the same with the other hand. Slade pulled at the old man's other arm, trying to reach the last hook. "It won't stretch to the end hook," Slade said.

For the first time since entering the house, Decker spoke in English, "The next hook will do. Just so he can't get off by himself."

Slade obeyed, forcing the hook through the bloody wound in the other hand. The three Americans watched in silence as Braune tried to balance himself on his uninjured foot to take some of the weight off his hands.

He went into a rage, trying to overcome his pain. He started a roar that ended with him gathering enough strength to spit at Decker. He missed. Decker said, "I'm waiting."

"There is no contingency," Braune said in a voice that finally sounded exhausted with pain. Decker raised his gun and fired. The knee on Braune's good leg exploded, causing his entire weight to hang from his hands. The old Nazi finally screamed in pain. It lasted for a few seconds and then Decker repeated, "I'm still waiting."

"Please, get me down!"

"First you talk."

Braune hissed through his teeth. "You have to identify yourself with a certain name. Then he will know the message is from me."

"What is the name?"

"First you have to get me down," he said through gritted teeth. "I am afraid you are going to leave me like this."

Decker looked at his watch. He told Harrison and Slade, "We've been here too long already, get him down." The two men lifted him off the hooks and carried him back to the chair.

He stared at Decker. "When you call, tell him I have had a heart attack and asked you to let him know because it doesn't look like I am going to survive. Then tell him that you will be making the six-month calls from now on. He will then ask you your name. And this is what is critical, so make sure you pronounce it correctly—you are Herr Stauffenberg. Once you say the name, he will hang up."

Decker repeated, "Herr Stauffenberg."

"Yes." Braune slumped forward against the desk.

Decker picked up the phone and dialed. He turned to Slade and said in English, "Make sure he doesn't say anything." Slade pulled Braune's head back and clamped his hand over his mouth.

A voice at the other end said, *"Hallo?"*

"Herr Martin Bach, *bitte.*"

"This is Herr Bach." Then, just as Braune had instructed him to, Decker explained why he was calling. "And what is your name, sir?"

Decker could feel the apprehension in Bach's voice. Carefully, he said, "Herr Stauffenberg." The only thing Decker heard then was the line go dead. Something didn't feel right. He didn't know what it was. Bach had responded just as Braune said he would, but after the exchange of words, it seemed there should have been some sort of final response. But these old Nazis were a hard bunch to read. He motioned for Slade to finish Braune. Using the same technique he had used on Geist, he cut Braune's throat and then held him until he bled out. Decker took a last look at him. He had an expression on his face that could be best described as pleased, as if death had somehow been to his advantage.

9

AS HAD BECOME CUSTOMARY ON RAINY OR HEAVILY overcast days, the thick black curtains in the special agent in charge's office were closed tightly. The SAC, Ralph Stamen, had ordered them installed shortly after his arrival in Chicago. Initially, this caused some mild curiosity among the rank-and-file agents until one day Stamen was overheard telling one of his assistants in a tone swollen with command, "If it's going to be dark in here, it's going to be my doing." No further explanation was needed—the "in charge" portion of the new SAC's title was obviously much more a priority than the "agent." The "steer clear" warning went through the office with the speed and hopelessness of amoebic dysentery.

Fallon walked through the cavernous office toward its only source of light, a low-wattage banker's lamp at the corner of Stamen's desk. Its avocado shade released a fixed sphere of light which seemed to provide the SAC with a sanctuary from the darkness.

Ralph Stamen wasn't an attractive man. Although he had an awkwardly thin frame, his face was doughy and constructed without flat planes or straight edges, leaving his features undistinguished, almost erased. His eyes had a limited quality to them and seemed unable to focus on anything past the reaches of the green-tinctured light that encircled his desk. As usual, he sat at the back edge of the raking light, letting the shadows carve temporary drama on his face. It was a practiced pose that left Fallon wondering how a man discovered something like that.

Over the desk, a metallic blue cloud of cigarette smoke rose. Seated in one of the two chairs in front of the SAC was Fallon's supervisor, Pete Blaney. In an attempt to escape the choking air, he sat as far back in his chair as possible. But the effort was proving futile. Sixty pounds over the Bureau weight limit, his oozing girth had come to rest under the chair's arms, locking him into the only possible position.

Stamen took a quick, noisy drag on his cigarette and exhaled quickly, blowing the smoke as far as he could. He waved Fallon into a chair and then gave his cigarette an appraising glance. It was almost half-smoked and he stabbed its tip carefully into the ashtray at least a dozen times, thoroughly extinguishing it, as if he had again made a secret resolution it would be his last. When he was sure it was out, in a final act of mastery, he pushed down on its undamaged length, breaking it in half.

"Boss," Blaney said cautiously, "I think that he just forgot. Right, Taz?"

When Fallon didn't answer right away, Stamen said, "We're all big boys here. One of the things agents are paid for is to remember the smallest of details. This is a pretty big deal: an incentive award and a personal letter from the director. If I were an agent, I would think that was something I'd remember to show up for." Still Fallon didn't respond, so the SAC leaned into the light to make it clear that he was waiting for an answer.

Fallon stared back evenly. His hands, relaxed and motionless, hung from the ends of the chair's arms, as if they, too, were defying Stamen's demand for a response. After a few seconds, the SAC leaned back into the shadows to consider Fallon. He wondered what bothered him so much about this agent. There was something in the way he handled himself, especially in situations like this when he should have been defensive. He was too relaxed, too patient; it had to be an act. But Stamen remembered what Blaney had told him about the Citron kidnapping: the more inflamed the situation grew at the drop site, the more detached and analytical Fallon became. Apparently it was very difficult to pull his strings. Then Stamen realized what was bothering him—Fallon didn't seem to have any strings.

But Fallon wasn't being condescending, either. If any other agent had so blatantly failed to answer him, Stamen would have judged it a clear act of defiance. But even in front of a subordinate like Blaney, he didn't feel his authority was being challenged. Right now, as close to the edge of anger as Stamen was, Fallon's indifference became even more unnerving. With anyone else, he would have demanded an explanation, but there was something pervasive about this agent's calmness, and anyone attempting to violate it promised to expose the pettiness of their ego.

And as he continued to sit silently, there was a vague danger about him. Stamen could feel Fallon's dark brown eyes, with an almost-mechanical dispassion, search the darkness surrounding him, as though waiting to see if a target worthy of assault would appear. Stamen couldn't help but wonder what made him that way; what had he endured that others hadn't?

Again Blaney tried to break the silence. "Hey, I forget stuff all the time. Right, Taz?"

"The SAC knows I didn't forget, Pete," Fallon finally said. The air seemed to go out of Blaney and he slumped down in his chair, surrendering his role as mediator.

Stamen craned his head back, trying to make his neck comfortable against the starched white collar of his shirt, and then adjusted the already straight knot in his tie. Fallon said, "I was sitting on a house, looking for one of my bank robbers."

"That couldn't wait?"

"It could have."

"But you didn't think a news conference was more important?"

"I guess not."

"Come on, everybody likes an occasional pat on the back."

"I've never been much for high fives."

Stamen took a sealed envelope out of his drawer, tossing it across the desk. Fallon picked it up and put it in his inside suit pocket. "Aren't you going to open it?" the SAC asked.

"How much is it?"

"A thousand, minus taxes."

"Now there's no reason to open it."

"Don't you want to read the letter from the director?"

Fallon took out the sealed envelope and touched the corner of it to his temple. "Dear Mr. Fallon, I have learned of your superb performance in the kidnapping case of Daniel Citron. Moreover, I have approved a thousand-dollar incentive award, the check for which is enclosed. During your outstanding investigative efforts—"

"Okay, okay," Stamen laughed without any enthusiasm. "Maybe they are all the same, but most of us like deluding ourself with our own fame."

"Anyone who works for the FBI is probably guilty of that."

"Including you?"

"Including me."

Stamen, pleased with any admission from Fallon, decided to change the subject. "Pete, where are we on the kidnapping, everything cleaned up?"

Eliminating the caution from his voice that had seemed so necessary a few moments before, Blaney said, "I think the only thing left was headquarter's determination on the shootings. Taz has been waiting for a call from them."

Stamen asked Fallon, "Have you heard anything?"

"I'm not sure. As soon as I got in today, the secretary told me to get in here. My message light was on, but I didn't get a chance to see who it was." Stamen rolled his chair back and pointed a palm-up hand at his phone. "Go ahead."

Fallon went around the SAC's desk and dialed his extension. Then, after entering his retrieval code, he hit the speaker phone button and went back to his chair. The voice surprised everyone. "Agent Fallon, this is David Citron, Danny's father. I'd like to have dinner with you tonight if possible. Could you please call me."

Stamen said, "What do you think he wants?"

"Maybe just to have dinner."

"Someone like Citron doesn't *just have dinner.* You have to be careful with someone like him. As far as the Bureau is concerned, he's very controversial."

"It's probably just a thank-you for the kidnapping," said Fallon.

"FBI agents don't run out and have dinner with suspected militants. Who knows what he's up to? You saw all that stuff that came up on him during the kidnapping. You have to protect yourself. If a year from now someone starts making allegations, it wouldn't look good that you were socializing with someone like David Citron."

"Are you telling me I shouldn't call him back?"

"Let me call headquarters and see what they think." The SAC took out an FBIHQ directory and dialed.

"Mr. Hansinger's office."

"This is Ralph Stamen in Chicago. Is he in?"

"One moment, sir."

The SAC pressed the speaker button as Hansinger came on the line. "Ralph, you old flaming heterosexual, what can I do for you?"

"Hi, Bob. I've got you on the speaker phone. One of my agents, Taz Fallon, is here with his supervisor, Pete Blaney. Taz got a call from a guy you have some old Jewish Defense League files on— David Citron."

"Hold on while I pull them up." After thirty seconds, he said, "Okay, I've got him. There's some recent references on him, too. Looks like he's still involved in some pro-Israel activities. Nothing criminal we know of, but definitely connected into Middle Eastern politics. What did he want?"

"His son was kidnapped here a couple of weeks ago. Fallon was largely responsible for the boy's safe return, and now Citron wants to take him to dinner."

"Yes, I remember something about that. Do you think it's more than a way to say thanks?"

"At this point we don't really know, but I wanted to be on the safe side and let someone in officialdom know. Do you have anything new on him we should know about?"

Hansinger was silent for a couple of seconds and then answered a distracted, "No, no, nothing I can see." There was more silence and then he said, "Do you think he feels that he owes us something?"

Stamen looked at Fallon questioningly. Fallon answered loud enough for the speaker phone. "Apparently at least one free meal."

Stamen gave a single shake of his head at Fallon's disregard even for FBI headquarters. "Bob, we don't know. Fallon just received a phone message from him. He hasn't called him back yet. What are you thinking about?"

"Someone like Citron would make an invaluable source. With his

Middle East contacts, he could do us a lot of good. Think there's any chance to bring him on board, Taz?"

Fallon knew the importance of good informants, but he didn't like the idea of trying to take advantage of a personal tragedy to recruit someone. "According to what you have told us about him, he sounds pretty hardcore."

"He is, but the best ones many times are. Why don't you go to dinner and take a run at him. If it doesn't happen, at least we've tried."

The night Fallon had brought Danny back home, he was surprised by his father's reaction. Although he thanked the agents, he seemed extremely reserved, reluctant to celebrate with any real emotion. For the briefest moment, it took Fallon back to the small apartment in Pittsburgh where he and his own father had spent their last six years together. His father shuffling through the door, reeking of tobacco and beer, his face hung in lifeless indifference. The only sounds were those of supper being eaten and then the endless, pale yellow drone of the television set.

But there had been no question about the relief in Citron's eyes; he was genuinely glad his son was safe. Still his restraint puzzled Fallon. Maybe it went back to his days with the JDL when they and the FBI went after each other with a declared vengeance that eventually turned out to be little more than a shadow-boxing match. At first Fallon thought maybe Citron just wasn't the demonstrative type. But this invitation to dinner appeared to contradict that idea. Fallon decided he wanted another opportunity to find out. "I'll give him a call."

While Fallon and Blaney sat there, the SAC picked up the phone so they could no longer hear the entire conversation. "Thanks, Bob. Hey, when is Dollengate retiring?" After he heard the answer, Stamen swiveled away from the two agents and lowered his voice. "I could be talked into it. I've been here two years already . . . I'd appreciate it if you'd keep me in mind. Talk to you soon." Stamen hung up and wheeled around. "Well, Taz, think you can flip him?"

"Tough to call. He was appreciative that night, but I got the feeling that he wasn't the kind of guy who was looking for new friends."

"It would be a real coup for this division."

"I'll have dinner with him." There was a lack of commitment in Fallon's voice.

The SAC said to Blaney, "Pete, can you give us a minute?"

The supervisor, embarrassed by being excluded from a conversation with one of his own agents, lowered his eyes. "Sure."

Blaney closed the door as he left. Stamen lit another cigarette and his demeanor hardened. "When I first met you, I got the distinct impression that you were one of those people who had a need to rebel against authority. But now I'm beginning to see that you simply don't recognize it. That can be a mighty enviable thing—except for the person who happens to be your superior. Then it's not so good. The point I'm trying to make is whether you think I'm in charge or not doesn't matter to me. You do a good job for me and, in turn, I let certain things go—unless I'm slapped in the face. In short, it has to at least *appear* that I'm in charge." Stamen considered pausing for a moment to see if Fallon would nod that he understood, but the SAC knew that if he didn't, what little authority he now held would be lost. "That boy would be dead if it were not for you. Mr. Citron owes you, and the FBI, some reciprocity. Please do your best to bring him in."

After leaving the SAC's office, Fallon found Blaney in his office. "What was that all about?" the supervisor asked.

"He wanted me to be more like you."

"Very funny. Just do me a favor and call Citron."

"And what's in it for me?"

Blaney handed a two-page document to Fallon. "Here's a slow-rolling grounder for you."

Fallon read the title of the case: Unsub(s); Gerhard Braune, et al—victims; FPC. "Foreign Police Cooperation? Isn't that something the Red Cross or SPCA should be handling?"

"You're not too good to work the little cases, are you?"

"Reverse psychology? Boy, I take back every bad thing I've ever said about your management skills."

"It's simple. You know the chief in Des Plaines, don't you?"

"Jack Hasselman, sure. I knew him when he was a Chicago detective. We worked together for three months on that payday Thursday robbery gang."

"That's why I'm giving it to you. Read the rest of it. You've probably heard it on the news the last couple of days. It's a two-call case—

first the phone company and then your buddy Hasselman. It'll give you something to do until you freeload off of Citron."

The electronic communication printout was from an FBI legal attaché in South America. The first word in the title, *Unsub(s)*, meant it was an unsolved crime. In Bureau language, *Unsub* was short for unknown subject. The parenthetic *s* meant the police weren't sure if one, or more, people were involved. Braune, a suspected World War II Nazi, along with four other suspected Nazis, had been murdered in Braune's home in San Carlos de Bariloche, Argentina. Everyone had been killed by gunshot except for Braune, whose throat was cut. Braune had also been shot in both hands, the right foot, and left knee, apparently in an effort to torture him. Nothing of value appeared to be missing from the house. During the murders, a phone call was placed from the house to Des Plaines, Illinois. The number called was listed in the last paragraph along with a request by the Argentine Minister of Justice to obtain the name and address of the person who belonged to that phone and then make discreet inquiries of local law enforcement officials to determine if he or she had any criminal record. Under no circumstances was that person to be interviewed until the South American authorities could complete the initial phase of their investigation.

Although the crime had happened thousands of miles away, and he had been given such a minor role in its investigation, Fallon was intrigued by the case. Halfway around the world and half a century later, someone felt that these former Nazis still deserved to die violently. Fallon could almost see the old men scattered across the floor, puddled in their own blood, the murders cruelly ending their belief that because they had been loyal to their cause, they would be permitted a natural death. He wondered if, like the kidnapping of Adolf Eichmann, it could have been clandestine Israeli forces? But if that were the case, why was the call made to the Chicago area? And he doubted that the Israelis would have found it necessary to torture any of the victims. "Interesting," Fallon said to himself out loud.

"Oh, no you don't. It says 'discreet inquiries only.' I gave it to you because you know the chief out there and that's about as discreet as it gets. I don't know how many different ways I can explain this, but not every case is the Lindbergh kidnapping."

"At a time like this you might find some comfort in the old Bureau adage: Today's international incident is tomorrow's closed case."

"Taz, I'm begging you."

Fallon wagged his eyebrows disobediently.

Reaching across the desk, the supervisor said, "Give it back to me. I'll send it out to the resident agency."

Fallon pulled the document out of Blaney's reach. "Finders keepers."

"This is David Citron."

"Mr. Citron, Taz Fallon."

"Taz, I think you can call me David."

"I just got your message."

"I wanted to thank you again for what you did for Danny. You can't imagine what I feel each time I look at him."

"We're just glad everything worked out." *We're*—Fallon wondered if he wasn't already trying to sell Citron on the FBI.

"I'd like you to join me for dinner tonight. I have something I need to talk to you about."

"Is anything wrong?"

"Not really, but I'd rather not discuss it on the phone. Do you know where Sweeney's is?"

"On lower Wacker."

"Yes. Seven o'clock?"

"I'll see you then."

Fallon disconnected the line. He called the clerk who handled requests for the phone company and gave her the Des Plaines telephone number. While he waited on the line, his mind wandered back to Citron. The tone in his voice—*I need to talk to you* and *I'd rather not discuss it on the phone*—sounded ominous. And again, there was his reluctance to celebrate when his son had been returned safely. He was a man who always seemed to surround himself in mystery. Fallon thought about the communication on his desk. Fifty years later, someone was finding it necessary to kill Nazis. Maybe Jews like Citron feared the comfort of any permanent relief of terror. After all, hadn't they celebrated Passover for three thousand years after Moses

led them from the slavery of Egypt, three thousand years of freedom—before they were sent to the gas chambers by the Nazis.
Maybe that was why Citron held the world at arm's length: someone
had to stand watch.

10

FOR SEVENTY YEARS DARIN SWEENEY'S RESTAURANT
had been difficult to find. Which was exactly what the old gangster
had intended.

During Prohibition, a time in Chicago when the Irish mobsters
were as prolific as the Italians, each gang wanted to be able to retreat
to a place where they could spend evenings without the ever-present
caution their workdays required. Sweeney, a one-time member of the
Irish mob, was commissioned to open such an establishment and instructed that, above all else, its location not be compromised. Lower
Wacker Drive, the subterranean street close to Chicago's downtown,
was chosen. Because of the locale's heavy traffic, it was impossible to
park within a block of it, thereby eliminating the possibility of car
bombs and wheelmen with motors running. The entrance looked
as though it was for either some sort of storage facility or a long-
closed business. There was no sign identifying it, and no windows.
The only known entrance was a single, old-fashioned steel-banded
door painted black.

In succeeding years, Sweeney's son and grandson had run the operation, carefully preserving its history. The food was considered to
be among the best in Chicago, but the establishment was rarely listed
in restaurant guides or mentioned in print, as if no diner wanted to be
responsible for destroying its uniqueness by exposing it to the decay-
ing light of civilization.

At night the entrance was bathed eerily in the green lights that lined Lower Wacker, inviting a transition in time. Once inside, the place conjured up the possibility that at any moment a rival gang might enter to conduct some of their whispered business or gun down an unsuspecting patron. On a good night, maybe both.

Tonight, the latest Sweeney, who acted as maître d', wore a double-breasted chocolate pinstriped suit with the wide lapels of the thirties. The waiters, all in white long-sleeved shirts and black leather bow ties, wore slicked-back pompadours. The interior, lighted almost exclusively by candles melted into the tops of straw-covered wine bottles, was always dark. Conversations, even dinner orders, were usually exchanged in low monotones. All the items on the menu, like some long-standing inside joke, were written in Italian, and the wine, the only available beverage other than water, was a rich Chianti served Prohibition-style in cups from a teapot. There were eight tables with only two sittings each night. Reservations were extremely difficult to get, usually requiring at least three weeks' notice. Since the dinner plans had been made just that day, Fallon suspected that David Citron was a man who knew a lot of people, some of whom were glad to do him a favor.

Before Fallon's eyes could adjust to the darkness, Sweeney walked up and asked if he had a reservation. Although the young owner was in his early thirties, his coarse hair was prematurely gray. It was parted just off-center and combed flat against his head. He was tall with extremely wide shoulders. "I'm meeting David Citron."

"Mr. Fallon?"

"Yes."

"Please follow me."

Fallon followed Sweeney's broad back through the dim, narrow restaurant. When the host finally stepped aside, Fallon was surprised to see that David Citron was not alone. He stood up and shook hands. "Taz, thanks for coming. I would like you to meet an acquaintance of mine from New York. This is Sivia Roth."

The pulsing candlelight fell across her like an intimate silk garment, exquisitely hiding as much as it revealed. Her dark hair, even in the tallowed light, glistened and hung with a geometric precision. Her eyes were dark and exotic, but something about them struck Fallon as less than perfect.

She extended a delicate hand across the table. As Fallon took it, his attention was drawn back to her eyes. Their lower lids, recessed in the valleys above her full round cheekbones, were flat lines, lacking the usual upward curve and causing her eyes to seem smaller, almost as if a mask had been placed over them. Her makeup had been carefully applied to disguise the imperfection, and the more he looked into them, the more difficult they became to read.

He suddenly realized how long he had been holding her hand. She looked up at him with mild amusement. He released her long, slender fingers. "Hi," he said.

"It's nice to meet you, Taz." Her smile was slightly overdone, like that of an experienced salesman. "That isn't short for Tasmania, is it?"

"Actually it's Tazler. But it does have a connection to Tasmania, sort of. I was named for my great-great-grandfather. He was sent from Ireland to Australia in the mid–eighteen hundreds to serve a prison sentence."

"A prisoner? I thought the FBI conducted thorough background investigations on all its people."

"I think they only go back one or two thousand years. Besides, we like to think of the original Tazler Fallon as a political prisoner."

"He was a revolutionary?"

"I think his contribution to the overthrow of the Empire had to do with stealing English money."

"From the British government?"

"No, actually he stole it from a Protestant."

"And that qualifies him as political?"

"It's close enough for an Irish Catholic."

She laughed. "David has been telling me all about the kidnapping. What you did was absolutely unbelievable."

Fallon leaned back in his chair and pushed his hands into his pockets. "Dinner at a great restaurant, beautiful scenery, and now a compliment—if I didn't know better, I'd think I was about to be taken advantage of." He looked at Citron.

Someone else might have been offended by the directness of the statement, but Citron seemed pleased with Fallon's observation. "Sivia is with the International Foundation for Art Research in New York. Ever heard of it?"

"I assume we're getting to the part you couldn't talk about on the phone."

Sivia interjected, "Mostly, we work to recover stolen art objects. Are you familiar with Alfred Sisley?"

"I don't think so."

"He is an important impressionist. We have just recovered one of his works in New York, *Watering Place at Marly.* It was stolen in Austria."

"When?" The single word was demanding, not for a date, but to get to whatever she was trying to avoid.

She glanced at Citron. "In 1939."

The waiter came to the table and asked Fallon, "*Tea*, sir?"

"Yes. I think we're going to need lots of tea. Maybe you'd better leave the pot." The waiter filled all three cups with the dark red wine and set the container in the middle of the table. Fallon thought about the five dead Nazis in Argentina and the phone call to Des Plaines. "I may not know much about art, but I do know that in 1939, the Nazis occupied Austria. Would they have anything to do with the painting?" Again his tone was more demanding than inquiring.

"Yes, it was stolen by the Nazis. It was one of nearly half a million works of art the Nazis stole from their owners, especially if they were Jewish." Her words, though controlled, had an unmistakable anger to them. He assumed it was toward the Nazis and not his questions, but he wasn't sure.

Citron said, "Sivia called me from New York and said she needed help. And did I know anyone I could trust?"

"David, I'm not sure you understand all the nuances of being appreciative. See, I find your son and then *you* owe *me* a favor. But maybe I'm wrong—that's not just a Christian concept, is it?"

Citron gave a brief smile of apology and blinked his eyes once slowly to acknowledge Fallon's point. "I know. But this is very—"

Sivia placed her hand lightly on Citron's. "I'm afraid this is my doing. I needed some help and out of desperation asked David to approach you. And I say 'out of desperation' only because I'm not sure my problem can necessarily be solved within the strict confines of the law. I am sorry if this appears to be deceptive. We planned to tell you everything as the night went on. I apologize for my lack of candor."

Fallon could see that being apologetic did not come naturally to this woman, and he wasn't sure that candor did, either. He took a sip of wine. "I assume what we are about to discuss is not something that the average FBI agent would want to do."

"The Sisley was one of at least three paintings taken from the same Jewish family. There may be as many as five. This is the first time since 1939 that anything has been known about any of them. We are hoping the individual who sold this one is still in possession of the others."

"After all this time, isn't that pretty unlikely?"

"Two of the others are by well-known masters, Van Dyck and Vermeer. If either were ever on the open market, they would have drawn a crowd, and we would have heard about them. As we did with the Sisley."

"And if they weren't on the *open* market?"

"Granted, they could have been sold to private collectors. But if that were his method then why would he sell the Sisley at an auction? Besides, we have to investigate any possible lead. I would assume you work the same way."

"Why not use official channels? I would assume your organization worked with the government on things like this before."

"Yes, we have. And more often than not, that has worked well. But when we deal with an individual who we suspect has more than one work of art, and we jump over all your hurdles, that person is, by the drawn-out nature of the process, warned. Almost without exception, we are unable to recover any additional paintings."

"So you're here in an officially unofficial capacity?"

"Actually, I'm here in an unofficially unofficial capacity. The foundation doesn't know that I'm doing this. They have strict rules about following procedure, especially when it comes to the federal authorities."

Fallon glanced over at Citron. His face was unreadable. "And your best guess about me is that I don't."

"It's just that you can look for a painting for years before getting one fleeting chance to gain possession of it. So when I saw an opportunity for at least two more, I decided to abandon the type of procedure that has been unsuccessful in the past."

"What exactly is it that you think I can do for you that the entire U.S. government can't?"

"I have tracked the seller of the Sisley to Chicago. With your help, I was hoping we could somehow determine where the other paintings are located and seize them before they can be moved."

Fallon laughed. "And how would we *determine* where they are?"

"David told me that during the kidnapping, the entire FBI went one way and, with some personal risk, you went the other. I'm sure a man as resourceful as you could come up with something."

He stared at her for a moment. The way she had said *man* had distracted him, ever so slightly deeper in tone, throaty, a single word as seductive as her eyes. He suspected it was not the first time she had used the technique. "You're not used to hearing no, are you?"

She reached across the table and put her hand on his. "Will you help us?"

Involuntarily, Fallon's thoughts turned to FBI headquarter's request that he try to recruit Citron as a source. Fallon turned to him and, wanting him to know exactly what was being proposed, bluntly asked, "What does the FBI get out of this?"

Citron, with some ceremony, folded his hands on the table in front of him. "I assume that your lack of subtlety is intentional, so let me be equally direct. I could never compromise my involvement in any of the things that might interest the FBI. What I do, I do to protect future generations. I don't think you are the kind of man who would ask me to trade that away?"

"I had an obligation to ask."

"I appreciate your honesty. The little I know about you tells me that you and I carry the same contempt for injustice, and at times that can be a terrible burden. Mine is very selfish. I limit my efforts only to the well-being of Jews, and when necessary, can offer my religion as justification for my actions. You, on the other hand, must serve everyone equally and therefore have no such defense. Knowing this, it is unfair to ask for your help. But history has taught me to be unfair when necessary. The Holocaust will continue until the survivors and their heirs get back what was taken from them. And I don't think you're a man who would let that happen."

Fallon was surprised by the slight flush of emotion that he felt from Citron's appeal. Although he found the possibility of tracking down art stolen by Nazis irresistible, he felt uneasy about the intentions of this woman. He should say no: he wanted to say no, but that knot started tying itself in his stomach again, and he knew he had little choice. "Are we talking about something illegal?" He tried to make the question sound like he still needed convincing, but doubted that he was deceiving anyone.

An enigmatic smile drifted up slowly from the corners of Sivia's mouth and Fallon realized that she understood him far better than he wanted her to. "There's illegal, and then there's illegal," she said.

"Since that's a defense I've used more than once, I don't find that very reassuring."

"The truth is that we don't know what lies ahead. We're not *planning* to break the law."

Citron said, "Anytime this becomes uncomfortable, you can walk away. There will be no hard feelings, and no one will know. Not from us, anyhow."

Their proposal was intentionally vague, which meant they suspected there could be more risk than they were admitting. But he was hooked and, if he was reading them right, they knew it. "There is one small problem from the start, David. If I tell them you turned me down, I'll probably be ordered not to have any further contact with you. And I'm sure I'll be given the same instructions regarding Sivia. So, if anyone asks me, I'm going to tell them that you're under development, and I have to help Sivia to fully gain your confidence."

"It's reassuring to know that I am so well thought of by your employer."

Fallon said to Sivia, "Give me what you have on the seller."

"His name is Martin Bach."

"Martin Bach! On Lansing Street in Des Plaines?"

"Yes. How did you know?"

"You've heard about the five Nazis who were murdered in Argentina."

"On the news, yes."

"The night they were killed, someone called from the victim's house to a suburban Chicago number. The Argentinean government has asked the Bureau to make some preliminary inquiries. Just before

I left to come here, the phone company identified the subscriber as Martin Bach."

Sivia sat silently, connecting the two events in her mind. "That means that Bach is somehow tied to the Nazis in Argentina."

"But why would anyone want to kill five old men? According to the police down there, the owner of the house was apparently tortured before he had his throat cut."

"Six," Sivia said without emotion.

Fallon said, "What do you mean?"

"A sixth Nazi has been killed. There was a man in New York, Jonathan Geist. He had his throat cut the night before the Sisley auction."

"Did he have any connection to the Sisley?" Fallon asked.

"He was supposed to bid on it," Sivia said.

Fallon thought for a second. "Could this all be about the other paintings?"

Sivia said, "It could be; the Sisley is worth at least four million dollars."

"You said it was one of at least three paintings. If Bach has just two more—did you say Vermeer and Van Dyck—what would they be worth?"

"Each would sell for at least as much. But probably much more."

"That's more than a million dollars a murder, which beats union scale," Fallon said. "Since the Nazi in Argentina was tortured, maybe they were trying to find out from him where these other paintings were."

"Who are *they?*" Citron asked.

"I don't know. But it's starting to look like the sale of the Sisley triggered something more than Sivia's investigation."

Sivia said, "But why the phone call?"

Fallon stood up. "I don't know, but I'm not going to find out sitting here."

"Where are you going?" Citron asked.

"To Bach's." Sivia stood up and started pulling her coat on, but Fallon stopped her. "Whoa. I'll let you know when I need you to come along."

"You can't be sure that anyone is looking for Bach besides us. All this stuff is just conjecture. Look at it from my standpoint—what if you go out there and get into his house, and he realizes who you are? By the time you got back there with me—if there are any paintings—they'll be gone."

Fallon knew she was right. It had been his experience that the harder something or someone was to find, the fewer the chances for capture or recovery. If Sivia could identify any paintings in Bach's possession as those taken by the Nazis, he would simply commandeer them, if need be, at gunpoint and let the lawyers sort it out later. "I have a feeling this is a waste of breath to ask, but if I take you along, will you agree to do exactly as I say?"

She smiled and said, "You're the boss."

"That's very reassuring. How about a compromise—you can come, but you wait in the car until you're needed."

"You've got a deal." She turned to Citron. "Thanks for everything, David."

"Yeah, David, thanks for everything," Fallon said.

Citron smiled briefly. "You will be careful?"

"If I were going to be careful, I'd be home by now."

11

ROBBING ARMORED CARS WAS NOT AN OCCUPATION for the casual criminal. Those who chose its high-risk/high-reward rush were more than men who committed armed robbery for a living; they were at the absolute end of their frayed commitment to civilization, like the degenerate gambler who has finally moved up to betting a thousand dollars a pass at the crap table, or the terminally addicted drug user who has to now shoot cocaine and heroine speedballs to find out if he is indeed mortal. With each crime they raced a little faster toward whatever was beyond the farthest edge of self-preservation. Kurt Decker and his crew were such men.

If it weren't for the Federal Correction Institution at Marion, Illinois, Decker, Ron Slade, Jimmy Harrison, and Del Brantley would never have met. Brantley, the last to be paroled, was out of prison for only one month when the four of them robbed an armored car and killed a guard. But after they robbed a second one, Decker was arrested. By the time the charges against him were dropped, all three of his men were in need of money and, even more, Decker's ability to find the big score. When he told them he had found one but warned killing was going to be involved, Slade was the only one to react. He smiled and said, "So what's the downside?"

A stolen metallic green Pontiac Bonneville four-door sedan pulled up in front of the Des Plaines address that Gerhard Braune had identified as belonging to Martin Bach. Decker told Slade, "Go see if the door is a problem."

Slade returned in less than a minute. "One dead bolt. The short wrecking bar will open it faster than a key."

Decker looked around the quiet, suburban street and decided the risk was minimal. He had tried several calls to the residence and no one had answered. It was dusk and although a few of the houses on the block had lights on, Bach's residence was still dark. "Go ahead. We'll be right up behind you."

"Should we put masks on?" Slade asked.

"No. It would be too obvious if one of the neighbors spots us going in," Decker said. "But everybody take one with you just in case."

Slade went around to the trunk and sorted through a long canvas bag filled with a variety of weapons and burglary tools until he found a short crowbar. He also pulled out four ski masks and handed them to the others. He hung the curved end of the pry bar on his belt and walked with a contained eagerness toward Bach's front door while holding his arm stiffly over the tool.

Once he reached the porch, the other three men got out and walked casually up behind him. The timing was just right. As the others reached the top stair, they could barely hear the short, muffled sound of metal being wrenched away from wood. They followed Slade into the house as if the owner, seeing them come up the walk, had opened the door to greet them.

Because of Slade's experience with such entries, Decker was able to shut the door completely. Other than the marks on the jamb, which were hardly noticeable, there was no sign of forced entry. Decker pointed at Harrison and then toward the second floor. Without a word, Harrison drew a gun and started up the stairs. With the same silent order, Brantley was sent down into the basement. Decker headed for the kitchen while Slade took up a position by a front window so he could watch the street.

Decker found Martin Bach. He was lying on the floor next to the kitchen table and appeared to have been dead for at least a day. His face was bloated, pink and blue. On the table where he must have been sitting before he collapsed was a handwritten note. The black angled formal script had been learned a long time ago in a place other than the United States. It read:

For fifty years, I have lived with the fear that Jewish injustice was stalking me. I have now been warned that it is at my threshold. This is Beneath contempt. Now, with my comrades in New York and Argentina being assassinated, Every person I encounter, I must consider my executioner. I have decided to put an end to this Thing. By taking my own life, I will not only ensure the honor of my death, but more importantly, prevent their revenge. Unfortunately There does not seem to be an alternative.

It was unsigned and Decker wondered if the man who authored it couldn't decide whether to use his real name or his alias. Either way Decker had evidently found *der Kurator*.

Also on the table was a hand-crafted walnut box. On the lid was engraved *Meine Ehre heisst Treue*. Decker opened it. Inside, sitting on a dark blue satin cloth was a black-handled steel dagger with the SS lightning bolts and an eagle perched above a swastika. Engraved along the blade were the same four German words that were carved into the lid of the box. Decker assumed it was a ceremonial weapon, just the thing to haul out for an occasion such as a suicide. Above the knife was a short rectangular depression, which held a small brass cylinder that looked like a rifle cartridge, except the slug end was covered with a screw cap that made it waterproof. Next to it was a glass vial, small enough to fit inside the metal cylinder. Its small knobbed end had been broken off so its contents could finally be used. Apparently it had been kept in the brass tube all those years. A few drops of a thick clear liquid were still inside. Decker picked it up and carefully brought it toward his nose. The unmistakable odor of bitter almonds made him jerk his head back.

Slade came up behind him. "That Bach?"

"That'd be my guess."

"What happened to him?"

"Looks like a cyanide cocktail."

Slade noticed the box and dagger. "Same words on the box as the knife. What do they mean?"

"'Loyalty is my honor.' I think it was the motto of the SS."

"What's the SS?"

"Go back and watch the street. And now that we know this guy isn't going to surprise us, turn some lights on."

Decker carefully picked up the suicide note by its edges and saw that there were two newspaper articles under it. One reported the death of Jonathan Geist in New York, and the other the sensational murders of five Nazis in Argentina. He reread the suicide note. Evidently Bach thought the Israelis were responsible for the murders in New York and Argentina and were coming for him next. Well, Decker thought, at least you were right about being next.

Brantley came back upstairs from the basement and barely glanced at the body on the floor. "Nobody in the basement." Harrison walked into the kitchen and reported the same for the second floor.

"Either of you see any paintings?"

"Nothing that looked any good to me," Harrison said and shrugged his shoulders to explain that his ignorance of fine art was somehow not his fault. Brantley just shook his head.

"Go look again. In all the closets and everywhere else, and if it isn't cocker spaniels playing poker, bring it down here so I can take a look at it."

Both men disappeared and Decker sat down on the chair that was last occupied by the man who now lay dead on the floor. Decker took another look at him and noticed Bach's red goatee. His hair was white but the goatee was an unblemished red, almost as if it were a false beard. He reached down and gave it a tug. It was real.

He turned his attention back to the note and reread it. Although ornate, the handwriting had a harsh, jagged precision to it, almost like the tracing of a polygraph pen. He had seen this style only once before: it had belonged to his father. Every letter was drawn with the pride and patience of an engraver.

Then he noticed something odd—four of the words that shouldn't have been were capitalized. If he had not been exposed to his father's handwriting, he would probably never have detected the flaws. Rathkolb had further disguised the errors by placing each of the four words at the beginning of their lines. Decker began to wonder if the Nazi had some other purpose in doing so.

He found a small pad of paper and pencil in a drawer and wrote down the four words: Beneath Every Thing There.

He looked at it for a moment longer and then called Slade over. "What do you make of this?"

Slade considered it briefly. "Beneath everything there is what?"

"No, these words were capitalized and they shouldn't have been."

"Maybe because they're at the beginning of the line."

"Then why not capitalize all the lines?"

"Hey, you know what, Deck, the guy made a couple of mistakes. You'd probably do the same thing if you're about to kill yourself. You're making this a lot more complicated than it is. That's the problem with taking all those college classes in the joint, you're always looking for the hidden meaning in things. We're here to rob some expensive paintings, and you're correcting a dead guy's English."

"No, there's more to it. There's a reason for these mistakes."

"Fine, you figure it out. You're the one always reading and working on those puzzles." Slade wandered back to the window.

Was it a puzzle, Decker wondered. And if it was, did it have anything to do with the Reserve? *Beneath Every Thing There* . . . what could it mean? He wrote the words again, this time along the left edge of the paper.

Beneath
Every
Thing
There

For a moment he didn't see it, but then the vertical column of capital letters caught his eye.

B-E-T-T: *Bett* was the German word for bed. Decker shot to his feet. "Of course!" He yelled to Slade, "Come on," and headed to the second floor.

There were two small bedrooms upstairs. One was sparsely furnished and used for storage. Harrison stood in its closet, throwing things off the shelf. The other was where Rathkolb slept. Decker said to Slade, "Lets move the bed."

Slade gave him a questioning glance. Decker still had the pad of paper in his hand and held it up. "It's telling us where to look. The capital letters spell out *Bett*, which is German for bed. And the words *beneath every thing there* tell us to look under it."

The two men quickly tossed the mattress to one side, followed by the box spring and then the frame. Decker grabbed the area rug that was slightly larger than the bed and pulled it back. Two of the tongue-and-groove oak strips that had been part of the floor were sawed through and replaced with a piece of plywood that measured six inches by eight inches. It had a small hole the diameter of a finger drilled through one end. The saw marks appeared to have been recently made. Decker pulled up the plywood.

Inside was a small cloth-bound notebook. Decker took it out and opened it. Two words were written on the first page: DIE VORMUNDE. "The Guardians," Decker said out loud. On each of the next six pages were a series of letters. The first contained a total of fifty letters:

MRSFI CXYMG DOBQT QXMAZ BSODL

QHNRU KPQCE TOAJU ZQUDB BZEID__ __

The rest contained only ten each:

SVJFDNREPT__ __
UATWMODLVN__ __
SVMIJQNSUX__ __
YGNEVLSZPD__ __
IBPKMFJQBZ__ __

Decker lapsed into deep thought, trying to make sense of the codes. He didn't hear Taz Fallon's car pull up outside.

12

FALLON PUSHED THE GEARSHIFT INTO PARK AS HE watched for movement inside Martin Bach's house. Light came through the windows on both the first and second floors. A car was parked directly in front of the house, not in the driveway like most of the other cars in the neighborhood. "It looks like he may have company. Do you have any idea what he looks like?"

"No, but he has to be in his late seventies or early eighties."

"Then hopefully he won't be able to outrun me."

"Don't take these people lightly. It doesn't take a great deal of speed or strength to pull a trigger."

Fallon was surprised at the expert tone to her voice. "Maybe you should go to the door."

"Just be careful," she said. "What are you going to say to him?"

Fallon opened his briefcase and took out a thick stack of business cards he had collected during his ten years as an agent. Shuffling through them, he found the one he wanted: *Allan Jackson—Worldwide Realty.*

"That's going to be you?"

Fallon looked at Bach's house. "That house is probably worth maybe a hundred and fifty thousand. I'll be representing a California couple, who, because it reminds the wife of the house she grew up in, is willing to offer as high as two hundred thousand dollars, if it is in good repair, but I'll need to look around before bringing them by."

"Something like that actually works?"

"That's the nice thing about this scam, even if you do run into someone who is smart, you can usually depend on greed to overcome logic. The only problem is that if this isn't who we want, the real Allan Jackson is going to be getting some outraged phone calls for the next couple of days wondering where the buyer is. As far as the paintings go, what should I be looking for?"

"Vermeer and Van Dyck were seventeenth-century painters, so if you see any three-hundred-year-old original oils, you can pretty much assume we're on the right track. If something appears questionable, tell him that the house is perfect and you have the buyer out in the car. You might even be able to get him an offer tonight. Then I can come in and take a look. Also you should look for any hidden storage areas."

"It took me a lot of years to become this devious, how come it took you just a few minutes?"

"I've always been susceptible to my immediate environment," she said. "What do you plan on doing if the paintings are there?"

"I'll badge him, and we'll just take them."

"Isn't that illegal?" Her tone was slightly accusatory.

"If my understanding of the Constitution is correct."

"And you don't have any problem with that?"

"I thought you found me irresistible because of my willingness to violate the Bill of Rights," he said. "You're going to have to choose right now, righteous indignation or aiding and abetting."

"I just wanted to see where we were heading."

"Don't worry, I won't beat him in front of you." He snapped his briefcase closed. "Stay in the car." He got out and slammed the door loudly in case Bach was watching. Fallon didn't want it to look like he was trying to sneak up on him. As he walked toward the house, he took a closer look at the car parked in front.

Inside the second-floor bedroom, Slade and Decker were busy rifling through drawers, looking for anything that might be the key to the code in the Guardian book. They both heard the car door, and without stopping his search, Decker nodded at Slade to take a look. The ex-con peeked out the shaded window. "Somebody's coming."

"Who is it?"

"A suit."

"Cop?"

"Can't tell. Doesn't dress like one. But he walks like one."

Decker walked over to the window and watched Fallon approach the house. "Get downstairs and tell Brantley to be quiet. If this guy doesn't get an answer, he'll have to leave. Just in case, put the masks on."

Very quickly, and with surprising stealth for his size, Slade made his way downstairs to warn Brantley in the basement. Then he hid out of sight of the front door. Decker went in the other bedroom and told Harrison that they had a cop coming up the driveway.

As part of his real estate act, Fallon walked straight up to the door and rang the bell. He held his briefcase in front of him with both hands on its handle and smiled disarmingly. He listened for someone approaching, but no one came. Something was wrong. The lights were on, and a car was parked in front. Fallon stepped back and held his breath, trying to detect any motion across the interior floor that sometimes can be felt in the porch flooring. At the same time, he watched the glass in the nearest window for any movement that could be caused by doors opening or closing inside the house. The stillness continued its warning.

Then he noticed the fresh jimmy marks on the doorjamb. With his fingertips only, he pushed gently and the door swung open with a slow, ominous creaking. He was ready to continue his realtor hoax and yell, "Hello, Allan Jackson, real estate broker, here," when he heard a faint but familiar, double metallic click—the safety of an automatic handgun being switched off. Quietly, he set down his briefcase and drew his own nine millimeter, hitting the safety in response. "Come out, come out, wherever you are," Fallon yelled into the house.

There was no answer. Fallon stepped inside the tiny foyer and listened. Nothing. He started cautiously toward the direction the clicks had come from.

Slade was pinned against the kitchen wall, gun in hand, hoping that Decker would make the first move because he was afraid Fallon was about to find him. And once Bach was spotted dead on the floor, the shooting would begin.

Suddenly a voice came down the stairs. "Can I help you?"

Surprised, Fallon yelled up, "I'm looking for the owner."

"I'm the owner," Decker said.

Slade heard Fallon take a couple of steps toward the upstairs, which would put the cop's back toward him. He wondered if Decker was trying to draw him over into that position so Slade could get a clean shot at him.

Fallon asked, "Are you Marian Bach?" deliberately giving the wrong first name.

"Martin Bach. What do you want?"

"To talk to you."

"Who are you?"

Fallon knew he wasn't talking to Martin Bach and that, in all likelihood, he was dealing with more than one intruder. It had always been his philosophy that if someone was going to shoot at him, he wanted that person to know exactly who he was. "FBI."

There was a brief silence which, experience had taught Fallon, would be followed by false indignation. "You are in my house illegally."

"You're absolutely right. If I were you, I'd call the police."

Slade spun around the wall and aimed his gun at where he thought Fallon would be standing. His target had vanished.

In the basement, Brantley could hear both Decker and Fallon. He also assumed that Slade was about to take out the agent. They didn't need his help, and there was a good possibility that more cops were on the way. Since his primary skill within the crew was as a driver, he decided to get out of the house and make sure the car was ready. At the far end of the basement, a door led up to the backyard. Using the driveway to skirt the house, he worked his way to the street. As he kept an eye on the front door, he got behind the car and gave a brief, shrill whistle.

Sivia saw Brantley come around the house. Stunned by the sight of someone in a ski mask exiting the house that Fallon had drawn his gun and disappeared into, she suspected that being caught in the car might not be the best tactical decision. Cautiously she got out and stood half-crouched behind it.

But Decker had recognized Brantley's whistle, and when he looked out, he saw Sivia get out of the car. He opened the window and pointed at the FBI vehicle. Then he grabbed his wrist decisively. As soon as Brantley looked over and saw the top of Sivia's head, he understood Decker was signaling him to take the woman hostage.

He circled around the back of the Bureau car and, before she saw him, grabbed Sivia, putting the muzzle of his gun in the small of her back. Once Brantley had control of her, Decker yelled down to Slade, "Where is he?"

Because Slade didn't know Fallon's exact location, he didn't want to answer and give away his own position. That left him with only one choice: he had to take the FBI agent out himself. Slade had been through the first floor and there was only one place that Fallon could be—the dining room. Slade walked cautiously toward it and readied himself to open fire.

As he walked by a closet, he did not hear its door open because Fallon pulled up on the knob to take the weight off the hinges to keep them from squeaking. Suddenly, Slade heard the unmistakable sound of Fallon thumbing back the hammer of his automatic, inches away from his head. He didn't move a muscle, and Fallon knew that wasn't a good sign. If someone in that position was about to surrender, his arms would go limp and the shoulder and neck muscles relaxed simultaneously. Slade was thinking about whirling and firing. Fallon whispered, "That's right, you can beat me. Go ahead, I'm begging you." Slade was stunned. If he tried to turn and fire, he'd never live to see the man who had killed him. He let his gun hit the floor.

Fallon had him get on his knees and then yelled up the stairs. "Oh, *Mr. Bach*, your friend would like to tell you where I am now."

With the barrel of his gun, Fallon prodded his prisoner to answer the gang leader's last question. Slade called up, "He's got me."

"And is he embarrassed," Fallon finished.

Fallon was about to pull off Slade's mask when Decker called down, "Hey, FBI, you should take better care of your dates."

Fallon was a couple of feet from the front door and pulled back the thin shade. Across the street, he could see another masked man standing behind Sivia, her face white with fear. He jerked Slade to his feet and pushed him to the door. Slade yelled, "He's taking me outside."

Slade stumbled through the front door with Fallon behind him.

Brantley pushed Sivia between himself and the agent. Fallon started moving off to the side, toward the gang's sedan, not wanting to get caught in a crossfire when whoever was upstairs came out. He got behind the car's back end, using it as a shield to cover his back.

Decker and Harrison came out the front door, moving toward Brantley and the woman, while keeping the guns trained on the agent. When the gang leader got close enough, he put the muzzle of his weapon against Sivia's temple. "Talk about a Mexican standoff," Decker said. "But it looks like I've got the advantage. Three of us with guns. And then your girlfriend here. And you with all those rules you have to pay attention to."

"You're forgetting, your car is over here. You have no other way out. And I have to believe that the police are on the way."

"I don't know, this is a pretty sleepy neighborhood. I doubt if anyone called them."

Without looking, Fallon lowered his nine millimeter and fired twice into the ground. "I'll bet they have."

"I guess that makes us pretty even. How about a trade?" Decker moved his gun behind Sivia's ear. "Before the police get here and innocent bystanders are killed."

Fallon looked at Slade and then Sivia. "Well, yours is definitely cuter, but I'm hoping mine will be a great conversationalist."

"Trust me, he's got a very limited vocabulary."

"Okay, call me shallow, I'll take the good-looking one."

"The first thing we need to do is get to our car, so if you don't mind . . ." Decker held his gun up and made a stirring motion to indicate that the two groups should change places. Slowly, he, along with Sivia and the other two men, circled toward their car. Fallon, keeping Slade between himself and the others, moved to the Bureau car. As soon as Decker reached the sedan, he motioned for the other two men to get in. Brantley got behind the wheel and started the car with a roar. Decker said, "That just leaves our little swap."

"Whenever you're ready," Fallon said.

"Okay, everybody walk slowly."

Slade started toward Decker. At the same time, Sivia began moving with obvious restraint, forcing herself not to break into a run. When she reached Fallon, he pushed her down behind the hood of his car.

Slade reached the sedan and slid into the backseat. Fallon and Decker lowered their guns at the same time. They stared at each other. "Maybe I'll see you again sometime," Decker said, his tone threatening.

"I'd like that. Why don't you give me your number." Decker raised his gun and pointed it at Fallon.

Fallon stood there defiantly. Decker smiled. "Some people are more of an obstacle dead than alive." Fallon knew that he was referring to the manhunt that would follow the killing of an FBI agent. Decker fired a single round into Fallon's front tire. Then he stepped into his car and took off.

Fallon put his arm around a shaken Sivia and said, "And you thought art history was going to be boring."

13

THEY HEARD THE REASSURING SOUND OF SIRENS. With the description of the carnage in San Carlos de Bariloche in the back of his mind, Fallon ordered Sivia to wait on the front porch while he checked the house.

Since he had seen the entire first floor except for the kitchen, he headed there first. The body was visible from the doorway. Walking around the table, Fallon read the note. Then he squatted down and examined the corpse.

"Martin Bach, I presume," Sivia said.

Fallon was surprised that she wasn't bothered by the body. "I thought I asked you to wait outside."

"You *demanded* that I stay out. Big difference. Besides, I thought you should know the police are just about here." Nodding at the corpse, she said, "Did they do that?"

"I don't think so. He's been dead for a while. He left a note, it looks like a suicide," Fallon said. "We'd better wait outside."

As the first police car slid to a stop, Fallon held up his credentials before any more guns could be aimed at him. He told the uniformed officer that he had interrupted a home invasion and the owner of the house was dead of an apparent suicide. The men who had broken into the residence fled northbound. After supplying the sedan's color, model, and license plate, he gave the heights and weights of the four men, which the officer relayed by radio to all their units and the surrounding departments.

Fallon radioed the FBI office. The night supervisor said he would scramble some agents. An unmarked police car with a red light held magnetically to its roof came speeding up. A detective got out and introduced himself as Tom Dale.

Fallon told him about Bach and the confrontation with the four men. Then he provided the details of the Nazis being killed in Argentina and New York and how the phone call to Bach's residence had led him there. "So there's a good chance these guys are responsible for the other murders?" Dale asked.

"Right now they're at the top of my list."

"Do you have any idea who they are?"

"None. But I can tell you one thing, they weren't new at this. They were definitely hard-core. The leader had to give very few orders. They were careful not to let any names slip, and no matter what happened, no one panicked. I'm going to guess they've spent some time on the inside, and not on white-collar convictions."

As the two men started toward the house, Dale asked, "Any idea what they wanted here?"

"If Argentina is any indication, they may have come to kill Bach. At least that seems to have been *his* thinking." Fallon led the way into the kitchen and pointed to the suicide note. "Apparently, he thought someone was coming to kill him and decided to beat them to the punch."

Dale studied the note for half a minute and then examined the broken vial. "Probably cyanide. *Looks* like a suicide." The detective knelt down and examined the old man's face. "I'd say he's been dead at least two days." He stood up and looked at the open box. Without touching anything, he bent over and examined the dagger. "Think this guy was a Nazi, too?"

"If he wasn't, he missed a great opportunity."

"The woman outside—your partner?"

"She's with a New York–based organization that searches for stolen art. She recently recovered one of a group of paintings that was stolen by the Nazis in 1939. The last person known to have any of them in his possession was Bach, so she came to Chicago hoping to question him about the others."

"How much are they worth?"

"According to her, millions."

Dale whistled. "Do you think these guys found any of them?"

"The only thing they carried out of here was their guns."

"Could the paintings still be here?" Dale asked.

"If they are, they're pretty well hidden. These guys had time to search before I got here."

"Maybe we should have a good look around."

The uniformed officer who had been first to arrive came downstairs and said, "Looks like they found whatever they were searching for upstairs in the bedroom."

Dale said, "Call for the crime scene officer and then make sure no one else comes in."

Upstairs, Dale and Fallon peered into the empty compartment in the floor. "Whatever was in there, it was smaller than paintings. Any ideas?"

"Money, jewels, I don't know," Fallon said.

"After we thoroughly search the house, I'm going to need you and the woman to come to the station and give me a formal statement."

As they started down the stairs, they heard the precursor tones of an argument at the front door. It was Peter Blaney, who lived less than fifteen minutes away. Dale signaled the uniformed officer to let him in. Fallon introduced the two men, and Blaney asked, "What happened?"

Fallon said to the detective, "Why don't you go ahead with your search while I brief my boss."

When Dale headed for the basement stairs, Blaney asked, "Who's the woman?"

"A friend of Citron's. He asked me to give her a hand." Fallon then explained about the Sisley and the other paintings, and how once he discovered that the trails from the auction and from Argentina led to Bach, he wound up confronting the men who were probably responsible for the killings.

Blaney shook his head "You were specifically instructed not to come out here."

"Pete, you have an amazing grasp of the small picture. What was I supposed to do, let these guys stroll in here and kill him?"

"You should have checked with me first."

"And what would you have done? You would have had me contact him."

Blaney thought for a moment. "Okay, I would have. It's just when you're responsible for people and they wind up in dangerous situations, you try to figure out how things could have been done differently. Just promise me if there's a chance in a million that you'll run into this crew again, you'll get some help on the front end."

"Don't worry."

Blaney lowered his voice to a whisper. "Any luck recruiting Citron?"

He didn't like deceiving Blaney, but Fallon knew that if he were to continue working with Sivia it was necessary. "He said if we could help Sivia with her paintings, he would be in our debt. That's why she's here."

"Well, I guess it's alright. Just don't drag her in front of any more of these freaks taking up the trigger slack on one another. She is a civilian." Suddenly, Blaney's dormant investigative instincts kicked in. "You *are* being straight with me, aren't you? That's an awfully good-looking woman."

Grinning, Fallon said, "Peter—"

Blaney held up his hands. "Just be in the office early tomorrow. And remember what the SAC wants to hear."

After changing the tire, Fallon and Sivia drove to the Des Plaines Police Department, where Tom Dale took their statements. After nearly two hours, the detective said, "I think we're about done here. Is there anything you need from us?" the detective asked.

"Did you get anything at the house?"

"Not really. A few latents, probably Bach's. The gun you had the guy drop had some partials on it with the serial number filed off. I'll send it up to the state police lab. They'll probably be able to raise the numbers, but as thorough as they were, I'd be surprised if it wasn't stolen." He picked up a folder that was marked *Martin Bach Scene* and leafed through it. "The only other things we removed were that glass vial we thought was cyanide, the note, and the two newspaper articles about the Nazi killings. Because it was apparently a suicide and not a murder, we have to limit our investigation. We've had some legal problems lately taking things out of residences without the family's permission. So unless it's something directly related to the death, we leave it behind. We're trying to find relatives now. None of the neighbors know of any, so if we can't find someone in twenty-four hours, we'll go back and see if there's anything else we need. Were you looking for anything in particular?"

"Not really," Fallon said. "What did the neighbors have to say about Bach?"

"Kept to himself, never had much to say. Had lived there forever. One of the original people on the block. Retired from Chrysler. For this community, he was pretty generic."

"Would it be alright if I took one last look around the house?"

"I don't think Mr. Bach will mind. Just don't remove anything." Dale located an envelope at the back of the folder and took a key out of it. "The dead bolt was damaged so we padlocked it to be on the safe side. Just drop the key at the front desk when you're done."

"What about the license plate I gave you?"

Dale shuffled through the growing mound of paper on his desk until he spotted a sheet of yellow teletype paper. He glanced at it and handed it to Fallon. "Stolen yesterday in Calumet City. I'll put out a BOLO on the car with a hold-for-prints if found."

"Just make sure to include that these guys are armed and extremely dangerous."

"Anything else?"

"Yeah, that they're not likely to surrender."

14

WHEN FALLON AND SIVIA PULLED UP AGAIN IN FRONT of Bach's house, he said, "I suppose we're going to argue about you staying in the car."

"Why would I do that, it worked out so well the last time."

"I'm going to go out on a limb here and guess you're not married."

"Meaning no man will be able to stand me that long?"

"Meaning, in a partnership there should be a spirit of cooperation."

"And your definition of a partnership is you giving orders and me following them."

"Why is it that suddenly I feel like *I'm* married?"

"What are we doing here? Bach is dead. There apparently are no more paintings. And I've been held hostage once today, which is pretty much my limit."

"Good, then you can wait in the car?"

She got out and said, "Sizing up people quickly isn't one of your strong points, is it?"

Once they were in the house, Fallon said, "I'll take the basement."

"What am I looking for?"

"Unless the police missed a hidden storage area, the paintings aren't here. We know your friends in the ski masks didn't have them when they left, so maybe Bach hid them somewhere else and left a clue where they are."

"And maybe Bach just didn't have any other paintings."

Fallon thought about the way she had stared at Bach's lifeless body on the floor. "One of those Nazis in South America was tortured. That led these guys to Bach. He had to have something they wanted. I thought you would be a little more tenacious. I assume you do want to find those paintings if they exist."

Inexplicably, Fallon's observation ruffled her composure. "Alright, I'll take the upstairs."

Fallon headed downstairs. The basement was small, taking up only about three quarters of the area of the house's first floor. The usual mechanical items such as a hot water heater and furnace were located at one end. Old newspapers were tied in neat bundles and stacked at the other. In the middle of the floor was a large workbench. Its entire top was made of glued planks of hardwood that had been carefully planed to a flat surface. There were a number of hand tools: planes, mallets, brace-and-bit, two back saws, a coping saw, and a dozen assorted gluing clamps. In the only drawer were wood screws, finishing nails, and metal dies, the kind used to hammer letters and numbers into wood. There wasn't any wood stock in the basement, not even scraps or sawdust from recent projects, which made the single item on the bench that much more curious—an empty picture frame. It was painted an antique blue. Fallon turned it over. On the back was a small gold foil sticker. In black letters, it read: THE RHINE ANTIQUE GALLERY with a Near North Chicago address and phone number.

When Fallon returned to the first floor, he found Sivia sitting at the kitchen table, staring at the boxed SS dagger, her disdain obvious. She noticed Fallon. "What's that?" she asked pointing at the picture frame in his hand.

"Found it in the basement. What do you think?"

She examined it carefully. "It's a fairly expensive frame. Custom made." She ran her finger along the inside edge where the painting would fit and said, "Doesn't look like there was ever anything mounted in it. From what I've seen, the few things he has on the walls wouldn't warrant anything of this quality." She turned it over and after seeing the gold sticker said, "The Rhine Antique Gallery? Sounds German. Do you think it belongs to another one of these people?" She pointed at the wooden box on the table.

Fallon glanced at the dagger case. He went to the sink and picked up a dish towel. After closing the box's lid, he used the cloth to wipe the silver fingerprint dust off of the dark wood. "Notice anything funny about this?"

She raised the lid and then looked at the dagger, as if it were continuing proof of some atrocity. "I don't find anything funny about it at all."

"Don't you think it's a little big?"

"It's a big knife."

"I don't mean long-and-wide big, I mean deep."

This time she examined the box a little more objectively, closing the lid and then opening it again. It was deep, but with the lid closed it didn't look out of proportion to its overall length and width. "It's hard to say."

The dagger rested on a bed of purple velvet. Picking the knife up, Fallon placed it on the table. He explored the bed with the tips of his fingers. He could feel some sort of molded backing shaped to hold the dagger and its sheath snugly in place. At both ends, he found a recessed area and lifted out the fabric with its backing. He picked up the box, placing one hand inside and one on the outside bottom. There was a difference of about an inch and a half. Judging by the thickness and weight of the lid, it appeared that the bottom was not solid wood.

Tapping it with a knuckle, he said, "It's hollow." He examined all four sides, which were joined with dovetail joints. The bottom likewise was solid and seamless except for a small, carved diamond-shaped recess. Fallon looked back at the dagger and realized that the silver tip at the bottom of the sheath was the same shape. He inserted it into the opening. When nothing happened, he turned it clockwise and then counterclockwise. He heard a tiny metallic click. On two hidden interior hinges, the inside bottom panel swung up. He lifted the false bottom and found two documents.

The top page was a long series of numbers and letters in groups of five. The second document was handwritten in German. Sivia looked on in fascination and immediately recognized the signature at the bottom of the first sheet—Reichsmarschall Hermann Goering. "My God. It's from Goering himself."

"I'll check at the office tomorrow, but it'll probably have to go back to Washington for translation."

Sivia was quiet for a moment and then said, "That's right, not everybody you wiretap speaks English, do they?" The way she had pronounced *wiretap* indicated that she didn't see a whole lot of difference between some of the FBI's techniques and those used by men like Bach.

"A couple of hours ago you were begging me to violate this guy's rights, so save the self-righteousness for the next ACLU meeting. Sure we have translators. We have foreign embassies and consulates. We have organized crime figures who speak only Italian. Then there's the South American drug dealers. Of course we wiretap phones. And sometimes we just need a document translated. I didn't hear any complaints when some of our translators prevented those terrorist bombings in the New York subways."

"Okay, okay, I'm sorry. Are we done here now?"

"As soon as I drop off the key. I'll take you back to your hotel. Where are you staying?"

"The Blackthorn."

"That's not far from the antique gallery where the frame was made. Maybe we should take a look at it on the way. At this time of night no one should be around."

"Do you think there is a connection?"

"I don't know. Like you said, Rhine Gallery sounds German. I suppose there could be another Nazi or two around."

"Have you ever heard of the Office of Special Investigations? It's in the Department of Justice."

"I don't think so."

"According to them, between 1948 and 1952, ten thousand Nazis entered the United States. With Chicago's size, there's probably more than a few of them here."

"All the more reason to take a look at this place tonight."

After reassembling the dagger case, Fallon carefully placed each of the documents into clear plastic evidence envelopes from his brief-case. He decided to take the picture frame with him and padlocked the front door as they left. Dale was no longer at the station so Fallon left the key with the desk sergeant. He got on the Kennedy Express-way and drove to the Near North Side.

The Rhine Antique Gallery was located on a street corner in what appeared to be an old neighborhood bank building. The entrance was on an avenue zoned for business, while the intersecting street was a series of long, shaded residential blocks. It had been built in more formal times when people viewed deposits and withdrawals as something to be proud of, and were willing to walk to and from the bank to prolong the ceremony.

The structure itself was a two-story cube faced in flat, gray granite. The second floor appeared to have been converted to an apartment. Muted light seeped from behind the curtains covering one of its windows. It was almost midnight. "I'll be right back," Fallon said.

He stood in front of the shop trying to find its hours, but none were posted. If there were any lights on inside the first floor, he couldn't see them. At a lower corner of the window, in black and gold letters worn by years of sunlight, was a sign: THE RHINE ANTIQUE GALLERY—SALES AND RESTORATIONS—MARVIN AND HILDA RISCH, PROPRIETORS.

The objects in the windows were dull not only in color, but presentation. A painting was perched on a rudimentary easel, an especially lifeless still life. Vases and urns were randomly placed, as if they were there to catch ceiling leaks rather than to attract customers.

Fallon walked around the corner to the rear of the building. There was a door with a mailbox hung next to it. Handprinted across it was the name *M. Risch*. There was also a doorbell.

He went back to the car, opened the trunk, and took out the picture frame. He looked up at a light on the second floor and said, "I think that's the owner upstairs. Same name on the mail box and the store window."

"Isn't it kind of late?"

"Do you think those four guys from Bach's house took the night off to go to a lodge meeting?"

Sivia got out of the car. "You just have one speed, don't you?"

"If we can get someone to answer the door, I'm going to give them the impression that you're also an agent. They'll be more likely to talk candidly if they believe we're both with the government."

"Great. Now I'm lying about being an FBI agent."

"Relax, if you're a good girl, when we're done, we'll go wiretap some Republicans."

Fallon rang the bell. There was no answer. He pushed the button again. They could hear an upstairs door open and an older man's voice yelled down. "Who is there?"

"Mr. Risch?"

"Ya."

"We're with the FBI." Sivia gave him a rebellious glance. He held his hand up so he couldn't see her face. "We'd like to talk to you."

"The FBI? What have I done?"

"Nothing, sir. It's about one of your picture frames. It's come up in one of our investigations."

"Come around the front of the store so I can see your identification before I let you in."

Fallon stood at the front of the shop, and as he waited, watched as Sivia peered anxiously through the window. "Even if this Risch is a Nazi, that was a long time ago. The fact that he's willing to open the door for the FBI probably means he hasn't murdered anyone in months." Now Fallon could see something moving around amongst the shadows, working its way through the inventory toward the door.

Finally, a rather elegant man in his eighties stepped up to the door and appraised his visitors. The pajamas and dressing gown he was wearing gave him an old European dignity, but his face was worn out, as though he had been taken to his limit for too long. While time had rounded his spine and shoulders and left him with a shuffling gait, it was easy to picture him as taller when he was a young man. He had survivor's eyes: cautious, measuring, accurate. Fallon held up his credentials, and immediately the man opened the door.

"I am sorry to be so cautious. It is a symptom of getting old, I'm afraid. I am Marvin Risch, the owner. How may I help you?" Despite his age, Risch's voice was firm, authoritative, and had a graveled German accent.

"I'm Taz Fallon and this is Sivia Roth." Holding up the frame, he said, "Sorry about the hour, but we're trying to find out about this."

With a trace of vanity, Risch ran his hand along its smooth length verifying the workmanship and then glanced at the label on the back. "Is there a problem with it?"

"Not really, we're just trying to find out its history."

"Please, come in where you can be more comfortable."

As they followed Risch, Fallon began to see that he had been wrong about the shop being cluttered. The more his eyes searched the rows of objects, the more organized everything appeared to be. Each section of the floor was arranged like a room in a house. If someone wanted to decorate a living room, there were two or three areas set up with all furnishings necessary. The motif flowed from wall to wall. It was all quite ingenious, room setting after room setting. Risch suggested they sit in one of the living room areas because there wasn't enough room in his tiny office. He sat on a striped satin wingback chair and waved them to a matching couch across from it. "Would you like me to make some coffee?" Risch asked.

"Thank you, no. If you can tell us about the frame, we'll let you go back to whatever you were doing before we barged in."

"I am glad to help. I get so few visitors since my wife Hilda died."

"We're sorry," Sivia said.

"Yes, it is hard to believe it has been almost a year now. Seems like yesterday. She was a wonderful person. She loved this shop. We opened it when we came from Germany. She had a great deal of artistic talent. The woman could restore anything. Me, I was a goldsmith when I was young but I lost my taste for it during the war. Here I was content to just make frames and take care of the bookkeeping. This business provided us with a wonderful life together. This country has been very good to us. There I go, talking just to hear myself. That's what Hilda used to say. I'm sorry, you came about this frame. What exactly do you need to know?"

"Do you recall who you made it for?" Fallon asked.

"Yes, Mr. Martin Bach."

"Could you describe him?"

"Not a big man, about my size but stout. I would guess in his seventies. White hair, and a funny little red beard."

"Would you still have his address?"

"It should be in my records."

"May we see them?"

"Certainly. It'll just take a moment. Are you sure I can't get you something to drink?"

"We're sure, thank you." The office was adjacent to where they were sitting and Fallon could see Risch as he went behind his desk to an ancient black metal filing cabinet. The old man attempted to open the top drawer but the face on it was bent inward slightly, causing it to stick. On the third yank, it popped open, throwing Risch slightly off balance. He leafed through some folders, finally pulling one out. He brought it back to where they were sitting and opened it. "Martin Bach," Risch said. "He ordered seven frames over a three-week period. They were all made within the last two months."

Sivia asked, "What kind of paintings were they?"

"That's the odd thing, I never saw them. He just brought in the dimensions. This frame was the first one I made for him. He came back to me and said it was too small, so I asked him to bring in the painting so I could measure it precisely. He seemed nervous about that and asked me to show him how to measure the painting, which I did. I offered to take that one back and refund his money, but he said that was alright. Then he laughed and said he would use it as a guide as how not to measure the next one."

"Were all the frames the same size?" Sivia asked.

"No. All completely different. Different sizes, different colors."

"Was that unusual, for a customer not to bring in the painting, just order the frames?" Fallon asked.

Risch sensed he was not being told something. "May I ask why you are not asking Mr. Bach these questions?"

"He's dead."

Stunned, Risch said, "No." He smiled sadly. "He seemed like a nice enough man. Was it his heart?"

"It appears to have been a suicide," she said.

"That's awful. He did seem a little nervous when he would come in—but suicide?"

"Sometimes circumstances change," Fallon said. "Did he say what he was going to do with whatever he was framing?"

"Let's see. He said he was going to sell one and make presents of the others."

Sivia said, "Mr. Risch, do you know which frame he was going to sell?"

"Yes. He said he wanted the one for sale to look expensive, to help the price. It was gold, with ornate beading on the two long sides."

"Do you have the dimensions?"

Risch flipped a couple of pages in the file and said, "Sixty-three by ninety-one centimeters."

She looked at Fallon. "That was about the size of the Sisley. And it sounds like the same frame." She asked Risch. "Were all the frames measured in centimeters?"

Again Risch leafed through the pages. "Yes."

Fallon could see an excitement in her eyes. "Is that important?"

She seemed to ignore his question, and asked Risch, "Do you have a copying machine?"

"Yes, a small one, in the office."

"Would you mind if I copied the file?"

"Of course not."

"I also need to make a long-distance phone call. I have a credit card."

"Don't be silly. Someone as pretty as you can use my phone to call wherever you like. And such a beautiful Jewish name—Sivia. Let me show you where everything is." Once they were in the office, he said, "May I call you Sivia?"

She was caught off guard. "Yes, sure."

"Sivia, you are not with the FBI, are you?"

She felt herself blush. "How did you know?"

"Agent Fallon is a law enforcer. The way he asks a question while his eyes are like a lie detector. You are a beautiful woman, too surprised by the things you discover here tonight. For Agent Fallon, it is all routine."

Sivia smiled contritely. "We thought you would be more cooperative if you were under the impression that we were both from the FBI. Actually, I'm with the International Foundation for Art Research." The old man nodded his head in recognition of the name. "You've heard of us?"

Risch pulled up the left sleeve of his bathrobe, exposing a tattoo on the outside of his forearm. It was a linear series of hand-drawn numbers—137188. They were in a crude handwriting, its carelessness an indelible insult to their bearers. The tattoo's blue ink had faded with the passage of decades and the decreasing elasticity of Risch's skin. "Treblinka. Being a Jew, and in this business, it would be hard not to know of your organization."

Sivia had seen these tattoos before, but they still stunned her. She took a moment and then said, "The Sisley I mentioned was stolen by the Nazis in 1939. Last week, Bach tried to have it quietly auctioned at a small gallery in New York. From the description you gave us, it was probably in that gold frame you made. But there was no sticker on it."

"They are easy enough to remove."

"I'm sure he did. He went to great lengths to keep his identity secret."

"Then Bach was a Nazi?"

She was quiet for a few seconds. "I'm sorry, can you wait here a moment? I need to talk to Agent Fallon."

"Certainly. In the meantime, I will copy this file for you."

Sivia sat on the couch next to Fallon and lowered her voice. "That the measurements of those seven frames were all in centimeters means that the paintings Bach wanted framed were all painted in Europe. American canvases are in inches. European are in centimeters."

"Which means he had at least six more European paintings."

"Six more stolen paintings."

"That seems logical," Fallon said. "The only problem is finding them."

"There's got to be something to tell us in those documents you found. Why else would they be in code and hidden like that?"

"I'll see about getting them translated and decoded in the morning."

"You're the one who said the competition wasn't taking the night off. Let's have Risch translate them."

"Risch? I thought you were worried about him being a Nazi."

"He's a Jew. And he's no dummy; he figured out I wasn't with the FBI."

"Okay, he's not one of them, but do we really want an outsider knowing about this?"

Sivia's voice hardened. "He's *not* an outsider. He's a Treblinka survivor. That's really what all this is about."

"Did he *tell* you he was at Treblinka?"

"Yes . . . and then he showed me his tattoo."

For a moment, Fallon seemed embarrassed by his mistrust. "Sorry, but it's my job to be cynical."

"Anyone ever tell you that sometimes you do it a little too well?" she said.

"I've heard the complaint before."

"And it's *my* job to remember what happened to people like him. Now, can we have him translate the letter?"

"Okay," Fallon said, his tone not completely convinced. "But he's not going to be able to decode the second page."

"That should make you happy because then he won't know everything you do."

In an intentionally defiant tone, he said, "It does."

While Fallon went out to his car to retrieve the documents, Sivia went back into the office. "Mr. Risch, what I am about to ask you to do can go no further. I can't explain everything to you, but as a Jew I'm asking you to trust me."

"I understand."

A few minutes later, Fallon came back in and handed the plastic envelopes to Sivia. She said to Risch, "Martin Bach was a Nazi. He may have had a hand in channeling art, stolen by the Nazis, into this country. At his house, there was an SS dagger in a wooden case. Hidden inside were two documents. At least one of them is in German, and we need you to translate it to save us time. Again, it is critical that you not say anything about this."

Risch seemed to understand that she was repeating the request for confidentiality to reassure the FBI agent, someone who did not understand the bond between Jews. "It is an honor to help in such a matter. I should have seen who Bach was. His accent, he was German and maybe inside I knew he was the right age to be a Nazi. But one of the reasons we came to this wonderful country is so we could forget and try to start trusting people again."

Sivia handed him the letter signed by Goering. Immediately he noticed the signature at the bottom and looked shocked. "Goering?"

"It appears to be," Sivia said.

He turned his attention back to the sheet of paper. "In this business, I have learned about old documents and this one appears to be genuine. See how the ink has oxidized to a rust color. That takes many years." He read it carefully to himself and then out loud, translating it into English. "To the loyal members of the Third Reich, the bearer of this letter is Major Josef Rathkolb, who is working directly at my orders in a matter that is of the utmost importance to the future of Germany. If necessary you should be willing to offer your life to protect the—" Risch hesitated. "I'm not sure the meaning of this word—*Führervorbehalt*. Literally translated it means the Führer's Reserve." He looked at both of his visitors.

Sivia was lost in thought. Fallon said, "It doesn't mean anything to me. Sivia?"

"I'm sorry what was it? The Führer's Reserve? No, I've never heard of it."

Fallon said, "Is that all of it, Mr. Risch?"

"Then just Goering's signature." Risch handed the document back to Sivia. "I'm such a fool for not seeing who this Bach was. You must allow me to help."

"I'm not sure what you can do," Fallon said.

"I've been in this business for almost fifty years. I have associates and friends in the art business in many places. Maybe I can help you find these other paintings. Do you have any idea what they are?"

Sivia answered, "Not really."

"Then who the artists are?"

"Two of them are possibly by Vermeer and Van Dyck, but we're not sure."

Fallon asked Risch, "Can you think of anything else Bach might have said?"

"Like I said, my memory is not what it once was, but now, because of who Bach was, I will dream of him, and things will come back to me. This has happened before. May I have your card?" Fallon took one out and handed it to him. "Don't worry, I will remember. I will be of some help."

"We appreciate the help you have already given us. If I'm not there when you call, just leave a message."

Sivia handed him the coded document. "I don't suppose you can help us with that."

Risch scanned it briefly. "No, it is an Enigma machine code." Both Sivia and Fallon gave him a questioning stare. "The Enigma coding machine. That's what these groupings of letters appear to be. When I was at Treblinka, I was eighteen and one of my duties was as a messenger. I saw the communications being encoded and decoded almost daily. At the time, the machine was very sophisticated, but once the Allies broke it, the Nazis, in their typical arrogance, refused to believe that anyone could have figured it out. It was an important factor in Germany's defeat. It is one of the most famous failures of the Second World War."

Fallon said to Sivia, "Our lab has a cryptography section. I'm sure they won't have any trouble with it."

Risch stared off into the distance. "I wonder why Bach picked me."

"Maybe he simply saw The Rhine Antique Gallery in the Yellow Pages and hoped that if you were from Germany, you would be accommodating."

"My God, I wonder if he noticed my tattoo and that was what made him cautious."

"Possibly. In his suicide note, he said he feared his past was catching up with him."

"For fifty years this tattoo has been an awful reminder of the camps, like its job was to keep the horror alive in me until I was dead. Maybe, after all those nightmares, it finally caused some fear in those who were responsible."

15

ONCE THEY WERE IN THE CAR, FALLON ASKED, "WHO is Josef Rathkolb?" She glanced at him briefly and then looked at her hands. "Come on, I saw your reaction when Risch read his name."

"In the Nazi hierarchy, he was known as *der Kurator*. He was in charge of collecting Goering's art."

"Were Bach and Rathkolb the same person?"

"Possibly." Then she contradicted herself. "I don't know—probably. Rathkolb, I think, was wanted for war crimes connected with gathering art."

"Why didn't you tell me about him?"

"I didn't know that Bach would turn out to be this world-class villain. I thought he was just someone who could have possibly wound up with a few paintings that were taken sixty years ago. Our research showed only that they were taken at the same time, not who took them. When I found out it was Martin Bach selling the Sisley, I searched his name and came up with nothing. I just assumed he was someone we had never heard of before. There was no way of realizing that it was an alias of Josef Rathkolb's."

"Then why were you reluctant to tell me about him just now?"

"Because I'm trying to figure out what all this means. Especially the Führer's Reserve. It sounds like something that the Nazis thought was very important to their future." She hesitated for a moment and then looked at Fallon. "To be truthful, I wasn't sure that the FBI would understand its importance. At least not enough to give it the priority needed."

"So you were thinking about cutting me out of this."

Sivia knew that without Fallon it was unlikely that she would ever find the Reserve, whatever it was—if it really existed. And that should have been obvious to him, but apparently it wasn't. Earlier she had witnessed him face possible death without batting an eye, but he had an irrational fear of being excluded from this investigation. She had seen it in the restaurant, too. As intuitive as he was, he had to see the personal risk he was being asked to take on. But he accepted, and in such a blatant manner that Sivia was sure he really had no control over the decision. "I was thinking about cutting out the United States government, specifically the FBI."

"Excuse me, didn't you come to me?"

"When I say the FBI, I'm not talking about you. I wouldn't have known any of this without you. I need your help. It's just that I don't want *the* FBI to find out about this because I have a feeling we're seeing only the tip of an iceberg."

"You're guessing. For all we know, the Führer's Reserve could be some more paintings, or it could be a case of Hitler's favorite brandy."

"I doubt if even Goering was delusional enough to think the well-being of Germany was dependent on a few bottles of liquor. Rathkolb was his collector. He describes this Reserve as 'of the utmost importance to the future of Germany' and asks everyone to defend it with their lives. It's much more likely that he was talking about a significant cache of stolen art."

"I hate to keep bringing this up, but Goering has been dead for fifty years. Wouldn't a large stash of paintings, or at least some of them, have come to someone's attention by now?"

"Like I told you at the restaurant, with the Sisley surfacing so noticeably, despite efforts to the contrary, we would have known if other significant works came on the market. Even if they had all been sold discreetly, after six decades there would be second and third owners who would have put them on the open market because they would have assumed, after changing hands that many times, the paintings were legitimate. We would have seen some of them by now. And most importantly, it was Rathkolb trying to sell the Sisley, not someone who had bought it from him years earlier."

"Why can't I go to the bosses and make sure it becomes a priority for the Bureau?"

"No offense, but that's probably the worst thing you could do. Remember those statistics I gave you from the Office of Special Investigations, about the ten thousand Nazis that came here in the late forties and early fifties? Of those, only forty-four have been deported in the last half century. *Forty-four.* And I've been through this with governmental agencies before. The one irrevocable rule is that the bigger a case is, the more political it becomes. Can you deny that?"

Fallon couldn't. Once Washington became involved, every decision was made by committee, which invariably became a nondecision. Chances were, before he would be allowed to accomplish anything, the men he had faced earlier that night would have found the Reserve, sold it, and be living luxuriously in some country that didn't have an extradition treaty with the United States.

Sivia said, "If the FBI did recover the Reserve, by the time the art worked its way through the system and got back to the rightful owners or their heirs, it would have little or no significance in their lives," she said. "I'm begging you, don't let them know about this. We can look into it and find out if such a collection does exist, and then make a decision."

"On one condition; that I won't have to pry any more information out of you. There's enough to deal with here."

A little too quickly, she said, "Agreed."

"I got a feeling this isn't going to be our last discussion on the topic, but I'll give you the benefit of the doubt for now. We'll take this to the next level without letting the Bureau know all the details. As far as they are concerned, I'm working on a murder case with a small possibility of recovering a few more paintings. That way the resources of the Bureau will be available without the politics."

"And if your superiors find out?"

"This would be a very dull job if I did only things my bosses knew about."

"Then what do we do next?"

"You go back to your hotel, while I try to find the crew who beat us to Bach's house."

"This alliance is shaky at best," Sivia said. "On top of dealing with you, I am also risking my job by not telling *my* superiors about any of this. If you think I'm not going to be with you every step of the way to protect my interests, you're making a mistake."

"It's a matter of safety, nothing more."

"In other words, I'm a liability."

"Don't get me wrong, I know you probably hang out only at the toughest sections of the Guggenheim, but these guys—"

"There's a lot more to this than waving guns."

"Like?"

"Like that coded message. How long will it take your lab to get it decoded and translated?"

"With a rush put on it, maybe two days."

"But now you can't send it to the lab, because if you do, Washington will know about the Reserve. So if you're going to keep this from them, you have to give up a number of your agency's resources. I can have that message decoded by noon tomorrow. Whether we do this together or not, I'm not going to sit in my hotel room or anywhere else. Either accept my help or consider me a competitor because whatever this Reserve is, I'm going after it."

Fallon pulled out the coded document and took a moment to consider Sivia's ultimatum. "Let's go find a fax machine."

Naperville, Illinois, was approximately thirty miles south of Martin Bach's house in Des Plaines. At the Motel 6, Kurt Decker was about to make a phone call from his room to Cleveland. He had just sent Del Brantley to O'Hare airport to steal another vehicle. Before leaving, Brantley, knowing the police had probably gotten their license plate from the FBI, stole fresh plates for the short trip. Decker wanted the car dumped at O'Hare for a couple of reasons: first, Brantley had to steal a new car and there was always a large selection at airports. Secondly, when the abandoned car was found, they hoped the Bureau would assume that the gang had boarded an airplane, and the FBI would stop looking for them in the Chicago area.

After Brantley found a Chevrolet Caprice four-door that suited their needs, he left the Pontiac two rows over and then changed its plates back to the ones the police knew about, making it easier to spot. He drove to the parking attendant's booth, took the ticket from the Chevy's visor, and paid it. Five minutes later, he was headed south on the Tri-State Tollway.

Decker dialed. "Darla, it's me."

"Where are you?"

"Still out on that job interview."

"How's it look?"

"Pretty good, but it's going to take a little longer than I thought."

"Are you alright? Just saw something on the news about some federal trouble out that way. Anywhere near you?"

"It was pretty close, but we're okay. Any calls?"

"The gentleman who helped you with your court case wanted you to call him."

"Is he still in Cleveland?"

"He said he was where he met you for a drink."

"I'll talk to you later." Decker called the Meridian Hotel and asked for the alias Brunner had given him. "Mr. Danker's room."

"Hello."

"*Bach ist tot,*" Decker said.

"*Gut.*"

"Yeah, but we didn't kill him. He was dead before we got there. Suicide, cyanide I think. He left a note. Said he had been warned."

"Warned? By whom?"

"It didn't say. Who else knows about this?"

"Not anyone who could warn him." Brunner thought for a second. "Maybe when you called him from Argentina. What did you say to him?"

"Just what Braune told me, that he had a heart attack, and I'd be making the calls in the future."

"Did he give you any recognition code?"

"Just to tell him I was Herr Stauffenberg."

"Stauffenberg! That was the warning. It was designed to expose anyone without a knowledge of Nazi history. Colonel Stauffenberg was the man who plotted the assassination of Hitler and left the bomb that wounded him. Anyone from the party would have immediately recognized it as a warning."

Decker thought back to that night in San Carlos de Bariloche and how much pain Braune had been in, and still he had not betrayed his oath. He reminded himself that Brunner was from the same origins, another reason to treat him with caution. "There are other problems." He then told the German about the coded note leading to the Guardian notebook.

"Yet another clue only for Germans. And it's coded you say."

"Yeah, I'm no expert, but I understand the basics. As best I can tell there are two coding systems: the first entry is fifty letters broken down into ten sets of five, the other five are simpler, each is a single group of ten letters."

"I know nothing about codes. Read them to me while I copy them down." When Decker finished, Brunner said, "I'll call these back to my friend overseas and see if he can help. It may take a while. Is there a number where I can reach you?"

"I'll give you the number here, but we're a pretty hot item right now. Just go through Darla."

"If you find it difficult to stay there, why do you remain in that city?"

"I have to assume that Rathkolb kept the Reserve close at hand."

"That makes sense," Brunner said. "This is becoming complicated, but I don't have to remind you how important it is to me."

"About as important as a million dollars is to me."

16

THE NIGHT BEFORE, AS EXHAUSTED AS FALLON WAS, he couldn't get Sivia out of his thoughts. He was confused as much by the inconsistency of her intentions as he was by his attraction to her. Normally, he would never allow himself to consider getting involved with anyone unless the asset column clearly listed one item first: trust. And whatever he now felt for Sivia, trust was not part of it. There were too many incongruities. After they had found Bach dead, she seemed to have little desire to search for the other paintings that might have been in his possession—until Risch had translated the Goering letter, revealing the existence of the Führer's Reserve. And then she seemed just as interested in Josef Rathkolb as the art. And who were these contacts she was so confident in?

It was almost 9 A.M. when he got to the office the next morning. Mat Zjorn was sitting at Fallon's desk. He had the telephone to his ear and was turned toward the wall. Fallon waited a moment for him to respond to his arrival, but there was no movement or conversation on the phone. Then Fallon heard a low, shallow snore. Zjorn was asleep and using the phone as a prop. "Doc." Fallon grabbed his shoulder and shook him. "Reveille, Doc."

Zjorn spun around with a start. He gave his eyes a second to focus before deciding where he was. "Taz."

He was obviously hung over. His eyes were wet and red, and his breath gave off the last esters of decomposing alcohol. A ruby stud dotted his left earlobe. Fallon flicked a finger across his own lobe, and

Zjorn, realizing it was still there, quickly removed it. "Let me guess," Fallon said, "you found a new topless bar last night."

Zjorn smiled uninhibitedly. "Someone has to support the arts." And then in a voice with a trace of new-agent awe, said, "Heard about the gun-pointing at the OK Corral. How was it?"

"I've never felt more alive as a person. Now, please get out of my chair. And why are you here? You've got your own desk to drool on."

"Today's your lucky day."

"Something in your demented smile tells me that those words couldn't be farther from the truth."

"That's right, thrill seekers, I've been assigned to help you with the Nazi murders."

"I hate to crush your youthful enthusiasm, but it doesn't look like there are going to be many women involved in this case," said Fallon.

"Are there any at all?"

"So far only one. And although she's on our side, she insists upon keeping her clothes on."

"Where do they get these women? I told Blaney this was a bad idea."

Fallon opened his briefcase and took out the teletype containing all the information about the stolen Bonneville. "Here. As long as I'm stuck with you, call down to Calumet City and see what they can tell us about this car."

"This the one they were driving?"

"Yes. Des Plaines put out a message to hold it for prints and notify us if it's recovered. When you talk to Calumet City, see if there were any stolen cars recovered in the same area. Especially from points east."

"Why east?"

"These guys have hit in New York and South America, so chances are they're not local. The fact that Cal City is on the eastern edge of the state and a long way from Des Plaines would indicate that, after crossing the Illinois line, and not wanting to drive around in stolen out-of-state plates, they'd dump what they were driving and pick up something with Illinois tags. Maybe we'll get lucky and find out where they're from."

"Now see, that's why I'm the gofer. I have yet to develop your great criminal mind."

The phone rang. Fallon pulled Zjorn out of his chair. "Go get some coffee, Doc." He sat down. "Fallon."

"Agent Fallon, this is Sergeant Sadowski at the Cook County sheriff's office. I'm assigned to the airport detail at O'Hare. I just talked to the Des Plaines PD. They said that I should call you about this Pontiac they entered in NCIC. One of our patrol units found it a couple of hours ago in the long-term parking lot."

"Have you had a look at it?"

"Yeah, just now."

"Did they leave anything behind that might help us identify them?"

"It's clean as a whistle. I can't be sure, but it looks like they wiped it down. Even took the ashtrays."

"Did Des Plaines say they were going to process it?"

"Yes, they did."

"Then just release it to them. Do you know how many cars were reported stolen at the airport since last night?"

"Hold on, I'll get the morning report." A couple of minutes later, Sadowski came back on the line. "Just three."

"Can you let me have their descriptions?"

The first stolen car was a Mazda Miata, only two seats, so Fallon discounted it. The other two were a Chevrolet Caprice and a Lincoln Continental, both four-doors, both large enough to carry four men. Fallon thanked him and hung up.

The phone rang again. "You finally made it in." It was Blaney. "I'm in the SAC's office. We need to see you."

We didn't sound good to Fallon. It probably meant that his supervisor was at least pretending to be in agreement with Stamen, discussing the previous night's events and probably Fallon's mistakes. He thought again about the lies he was about to tell.

Fallon went over to Zjorn's desk. The Ph.D.'s eyes were still having trouble focusing. Fallon clapped his hands twice, startling him. "Doc, I need you to come to life."

"I'll call Calumet City. Just give me a minute."

Fallon handed him the information on the three cars stolen from the airport. "They found our Pontiac at the airport. Overnight, there were two fresh steals that could belong to these guys. I need you to send out a BOLO to all the departments in the tristate area, asking them to contact us immediately if they recover either the Chevy or the Lincoln. Forget about the Mazda for now." Zjorn still looked confused. "Doc, are you with me?"

"I got it, I got it. Be on the lookout for the Chevy or Lincoln. I got it."

Again, the curtains were drawn in the SAC's office. He and Pete Blaney sat in the bubble of light at the far end. Stamen said, "Taz, glad you could join us." His tone was a delicately mixed amalgam of kidding and scolding. "Where were you at eight-fifteen when the rest of us working stiffs reported in?"

"Sleeping."

Stamen gave a hard, single-syllable laugh. He picked up a cigarette, and his face went temporarily flat in the white flare of his lighter. "Pete's been filling me in on last night. Do you think those guys are good for the murders in Argentina?"

"Probably."

"How about the art broker in New York?"

"Possibly."

"And Bach was a suicide?"

"It appears he somehow knew these guys were coming, and that he was on their short list. The note he left indicated he thought they might be Israelis."

"Do you think that's a possibility?"

"These guys weren't Israelis, they're hard-core habituals."

"Do you have any idea what they were after?"

"The best guess is those paintings this woman from New York is looking for."

"How much does she think they're worth?"

"The Sisley just sold for over four million, but she doesn't know who the other artists are. If they do exist, more than likely, they'd be worth millions, too."

"'FBI Recovers Priceless Art Stolen by Nazis'—you've got to admit it has a nice ring to it. We kept America safe from them during the Second World War and we're still doing it. Think this crew is still around?"

"I don't know. I just got a call from the airport. The car they were in last night has been recovered out there."

"So they're gone."

"Maybe. Or maybe that's what we're supposed to think. It was dumped in the long-term parking lot. That's the best place to steal another one because there's a better chance it won't be reported for a while. Besides, I got the feeling last night we interrupted them, that they had unfinished business."

"Is there anything else we can do? I can give you some help if you want."

"Right now we have to wait for their next move. Pete has assigned Mat Zjorn to give me a hand. That should be enough for now. If I need more, I'll let someone know."

"Well, I'd like a little more of a full-court press, but I'll trust your instincts. *For now*," Stamen said. "How did it go with Citron?"

Rarely in Fallon's ten years as an agent had he witnessed a lie escape the scrutiny of time, especially one as unprotected as he was about to tell. But, for some reason, he didn't mind lying to this man. "When he asked me to help the woman, I told him I needed to know what the Bureau was going to get out of it. He's no fool. I'm sure there's been more than one attempt by other agencies to recruit him. He told me that if I could help her, he would consider some type of reciprocal relationship."

"Was he talking about us paying him for information in the future?"

"He's got too much money, and integrity, for that. I think the only thing he wants from us are favors we can accomplish for the causes he believes in."

"You'd think rescuing his son would be enough to put him in our debt."

"He probably figures that was our job. If we hadn't done it, he would have never even considered talking to us. Now we're looking to trade favors. I think he sees the paintings as a test case to find out if we're sincere about holding up our end of any exchange of information."

Another blue-gray cloud billowed from the shadows as Stamen dutifully stabbed the cigarette into the ashtray twelve times before snapping it in two. "Alright, I guess it won't hurt to give the appearance of helping the girl. It's all part of our case anyway." He reached for another cigarette. He sat in silence without lighting it. "Why am I getting the feeling that you're holding something back?"

Fallon smiled. "You wouldn't if you saw the girl."

Stamen laughed. "Just keep her as far away from everything as possible unless you need her art expertise. We won't score any points with Citron if she has another go-around like last night."

"If you met her, you'd see that's easier said than done."

The SAC pushed his unlit cigarette out into the ashtray and broke it in half. "Just don't let Citron, or her, wind up working you."

17

FALLON SAT DOWN AT HIS DESK AND LET THE SAC'S last words run through his head. Was Sivia working him? Did he already know, down under those layers of suspicion, that she was, but could only maintain his relationship with her by letting it continue? For now, he decided he didn't really care. He picked up the phone and dialed her hotel room. There was no answer.

"Taz." Fallon turned around to find Zjorn standing there. "I called Calumet City. They didn't really have much on that Pontiac, but yesterday they found this car abandoned a half mile away." He handed Fallon a printout describing a vehicle stolen in Bay Village, Ohio, two days earlier. "I looked up Bay Village on the map. It's a western suburb of Cleveland, bordering on Lake Erie. The sergeant at Cal City said the ignition had been punched, and there wasn't a gum wrapper left behind. They even stole the ashtrays."

"That's them, they took the ashtrays out of the Pontiac, too."

"I've never heard of that before. They must have had some intense forensic training."

"The prisons are full of experts. Did you call Bay Village?"

"Just got off the phone with them. They have no suspects. I asked if they had found any stolen cars in the vicinity. Since it's a small bedroom community, stolen cars turn up in a hurry. They haven't had one in almost a month. So maybe our friends are from the Cleveland area."

"Did the message go out on the steals from the airport?"

"I did that first."

"Good. Now just keep your fingers crossed that someone spots them before they switch cars again."

A half hour later, Fallon tried Sivia's room again. This time she answered. "I tried you earlier."

"I was probably in the hotel gym," she said.

"Any luck with that letter?"

"As a matter of fact, yes. That friend of mine knows someone at NSA's Museum of Cryptography near Baltimore. They have an Enigma machine, but without the setting, it would be too time consuming to decode it, so they ran it through one of their computers. She just called me back. It's done, but it's in German. So she's making some discreet calls to find someone to translate it."

"Why don't we have Risch do it?"

"I thought you didn't want him knowing all our business," she said.

"He was the one who knew it was an Enigma message, and more importantly, he has an understanding of these Nazis."

"That's true. And who knows what else he might come up with."

"Why don't you call your friend back and have her fax it to you the way it is. With it written in German, we won't have to worry about some hotel clerk getting curious."

"That makes more sense."

"Call Risch and I'll pick you up in an hour."

When Fallon pulled in front of the Blackthorn, Sivia got in the car and handed him an envelope with the hotel's crest on it. He took out the single folded page typed in German. In the upper right-hand corner was the date 14 Oktober 1946. "If this thing is fifty years old, I hope it'll still be of some help."

Sivia said, "Actually that's an interesting date. Goering was supposed to be hanged on October 15, 1946. Just hours before, he committed suicide by taking cyanide."

"I guess he *was* Rathkolb's role model."

Fallon continued to examine the letter. The only other item he could decipher was Goering's name typed at the bottom. He had not expected any great revelations about the text of the message, but he was looking for clues as to the origin of the electronically transmitted document. Fax machines usually typed in along the top of the page the sender's number and some sort of identifier plus the date and time. At the very top right-hand edge of the Goering letter, typed in a faded font distinguishable from that of the text, was the current date, and a transmission time of 12:27 P.M. Also the notation *Page no. 1*. Fallon let his eye trace back along the edge to the left side. It was blank. Looking closer, he could just distinguish the slightest right-angle gray shadow. It was caused by using a piece of paper to cover an item on a page before photocopying it. The fax had been duplicated to erase its identifiers.

Sivia began to wonder why Fallon was taking so long to examine a letter that was written in a language he didn't understand. "Anything wrong?"

She was wearing an ankle-length pale yellow dress covered with bright spring flowers. Her black hair was pulled back and still slightly damp at the temples. "Your hair's still wet. Do you want me to turn the heat on?"

She smoothed a damp spot. "No, it's fine. I've been running late all morning." She noticed that he was gazing at her and she felt a blush warm her face. She turned forward and looked out the windshield. To distract him, she asked, "Are you originally from here, Taz?"

"Ah, Pittsburgh. A small town just outside."

"Do you still have family there?"

"No, I'm the last of this particular strain of Fallon."

"No brothers or sisters?"

"Not that are willing to admit it." The comment was meant to be funny, but there was no humor in Fallon's tone.

"Have your parents been gone long?"

"My mother when I was eleven, my father six or eight years ago."

"Your mother must have been young."

"Hit by a car on the way to the store. They never did find the driver."

"And your father?"

"Irish suicide."

"Irish suicide?"

"He finally drank himself to death."

"Sounds like he died of a broken heart."

"I'm sure that's the way the Brothers Grimm would have written it up." His face now unreadable, Fallon leaned over and turned the FM radio on. The station was playing jazz and he set the volume just loud enough to discourage conversation. Sivia felt the car accelerate slightly.

She stared out the side window. Apparently Fallon didn't like his father. Not knowing the exact date of his death, and the obvious reference that his dying of a broken heart was a fairy tale, left little doubt that they had not gotten along. Whatever their relationship was, Sivia suspected that Fallon's unwillingness to give into any emotion was traceable back to his father. Ultimately, everyone played to the same hidden audience—one or both of their parents.

They watched as Marvin Risch shuffled toward the door, his face flushed with anticipation. "Sivia. Agent Fallon. Come in, come in, please. I have made tea." He directed them to the farthest end of the shop where a dark red cherry table was surrounded by six matching Windsor chairs. In the center, a cast-iron trivet held an antique silver teapot. Steam wafted from its delicate *S*-curved spout. Next to it, a dish was covered with an assortment of cookies. Risch was dressed in a jacket and tie. With an almost-forgotten elegance, he poured tea into small, delicate cups covered with iridescent flowers that had been painted a hundred years earlier. In his trembling hands, they rattled against their saucers like old dry bones.

Sivia said, "Marvin, this is very nice."

"Thank you for indulging an old man's whims. But you have more urgent business, no?" She handed him the hotel envelope. After taking the single page out, he scanned it briefly. Pulling down on the lapels of his suit coat, he adopted the more official demeanor of someone whose expertise was critical to the investigation. He went over to a tall yellow pine secretary, picked up a pad of paper and a pen, and sat back at the table. "Because it is not so long, I will write it out for you." It took him less than five minutes to translate the entire text. He shook his head in disgust and pushed the page across the table to Sivia. After reading it, she gave it to Fallon.

14 October 1946

Dear Josef,

Unfortunately, I am to be hanged tomorrow for, among other charges, crimes against humanity. But my life is of little consequence when compared to the perpetuation of the Fatherland. We have forged the correct path and must find strength in our misfortune just as we did after the First World War. In time Germany will rise and again lead the world.

This is why everything we have planned is now so vital. By default, you have become the sole guardian of Germany's destiny. Although this responsibility is monumental, there are many of our former comrades who live in close proximity to you. The person who will smuggle this letter out is also forwarding dossiers on those individuals in your area. Maintain a knowledge of their whereabouts, and if you should ever need their assistance, present them with the authorization letter I gave you the night you left Germany. They are honorable soldiers who will not question orders.

I have requested a firing squad so I might die from my enemy's bullet like an honorable soldier, but this request has been denied. But I have managed to secrete, during this entire incarceration, a little something so I may disappoint those who would tighten a rope around my neck. This final writing will be encoded and sent through Braune in South America. I pray it finds you.

Hermann Goering
Reichsmarschall

Sivia noticed that Risch was still staring at the fax he had translated. She reached over and put her hand in his. "Marvin, I'm sorry if this has upset you." He stared ahead and sipped his tea. She turned to Fallon. "We'd better go."

Risch said, "No, it's alright. Please finish your tea."

"Are you sure?"

"Yes, I'm fine. It just took me by surprise." He picked up the cookie plate and held it out to her. "Too many memories."

She chose one and took a bite. "You're not going to tell me you baked these yourself, are you, Marvin?"

Still somewhat distracted, he smiled weakly. "Only if you like them."

Fallon watched as Sivia carefully brought him back to the present, dissolving the memories that had welled up in his eyes. She made him laugh and touched him with her graceful fingers, occasionally squeezing his forearm as if it were a heart in need of rhythm.

They had stayed almost an hour. When he walked them to the door, Sivia thanked him, and kissed him on the cheek. "You make me feel a hundred years younger," he said.

After watching her with Risch, Fallon understood that the Nazis, more than art or anything else, had stolen dignity. In her own elegant way she had returned some of it to Risch today.

They drove in silence for a while before Fallon asked, "How much can this Reserve be worth?"

"Evidently as much as Goering felt would be necessary to finance fascism back into power. But as shrewd a collector as he was, I doubt even he could have guessed how much art would appreciate."

"How many paintings do you think we're talking about?" Fallon asked.

"How can you gauge something like that? The Sisley plus the six frames make at least seven. But Goering had thousands to choose from, so it's certainly possible there are more."

"So if there are—say, twenty-five—all of the quality of the Sisley, then we're talking about a hundred million dollars?"

"Depending on the artists, it could be twice that, even more."

"So this isn't farfetched."

"Unfortunately no," she said. "It looks like someone may be trying to fund a new Nazi Germany."

18

IT WAS 2 A.M. WHEN THE PHONE RANG IN DECKER'S room. He let it ring again while he cleared the sleep out of his mind. "Yeah."

"Kurt?"

Recognizing Rölf Brunner's voice, Decker answered in German. "I assume you had some luck with the list?"

"It would seem so." Brunner had phoned Arnulf Mueller, and as Hans Trauchmann promised, he was eager to help. Brunner had given him the codes and asked if there was anyone who could decode them. He had called back just minutes before. "Sorry about the hour, it's the difference in time between here and Germany. My contact called one of the codes specialists who served in Goering's *Forschungsamt*. They were very good at it. During the war they broke the codes of dozens of countries. He recognized the first one right away because it was fifty letters. That was the minimum number needed when using the Enigma machine. It was—"

"I know what it is."

"Good. Much of cryptography is computerized now, and since some of its software has the Enigma configurations in it, he was able to find the key without any problem. He says the first entry is a ten-digit number."

"What about the other five?"

"I took notes. Let me find his exact words . . . here it is. The first is a straight translation from the Enigma machine. The other five have their own coding system. Without the key, it would be virtually impossible to break them. To decipher any code, at least eighty letters are needed to establish its pattern. And since we don't have that many, you'd have to find the key to decode the system."

Decker had opened the notebook containing the Guardian codes and looked at the fifty-digit clue that had now been reduced to ten numbers. "What did he say about the two dashes at the end of each of the clues?"

"He said it could be anything. Possibly it is something to be filled in when the codes are broken, but he has no idea what."

"Rathkolb was pretty smart. If you have the Enigma machine, he'll lead you to the first clue. After that, you have a whole new puzzle. Like the note at the house, it had two separate systems in it."

"I'm sure that he thought only the Nazis would think to use an Enigma machine to decipher the clues."

Decker leafed through the other pages. "Did they say anything about the other clues having ten letters apiece?"

"Yes, each one of them is probably also a series of ten numbers, quite possibly they are telephone numbers. If that is the case, it is probably a simple replacement code. In other words, something like W is one, A is two, or whatever. You'd just have to find the key."

Decker asked, "If these Guardian codes are six different people's phone numbers, do you think they each have an equal number of the paintings?"

"It's possible, I suppose. Maybe Rathkolb didn't want to do what you Americans call putting all the eggs in one basket."

"Give me the first number." Brunner read it to him. "I'll call you right back."

Decker dialed the ten digits. It rang four times before a sleepy voice answered. "*Hallo?*"

"Is Tony there?"

"There *ist* no Tony here."

"I'm terribly sorry." Decker hung up and called directory assistance. "Yes, could you tell me if this is a valid area code—four-one-one."

"Checking . . . yes, sir, that's for southeastern Wisconsin, generally in the Milwaukee area."

Decker disconnected the line and redialed Brunner. "I called the number and an old man with a German accent answered. It's in the Milwaukee, Wisconsin, area, which is less than two hours from where I am now. I'll leave first thing in the morning."

"How will you get the address?"

"Don't worry, I'll get it."

"When you do, remember, outside of our little circle, the fewer who speak of the Reserve, the better."

"I'll call you when I get the next step figured out."

Decker called Cleveland and, after giving Darla the Milwaukee number, told her what to do with it in the morning. Then he went to the room next to his and tapped on the door. He heard the faint sound of an automatic handgun's slide being released, chambering a round.

Jimmy Harrison's voice asked through a closed door, "Who is it?"

"It's me." After Harrison let him in, Decker said, "Have Del get a fresh car, we're going to Wisconsin first thing in the morning."

When Fallon arrived at work the next morning, Zjorn was waiting for him. "Looks like Naperville found that Chevy we put the message out on. About an hour ago."

"I don't suppose anyone was in it."

"Abandoned. It's being towed into the station right now."

"Grab the evidence kit. I'll meet you in the garage."

At the Naperville Police Department, a young uniformed officer introduced himself. "I'm Tom Yancey." They shook hands. "Do you want our evidence tech to process the car?"

"Thanks, but we'll take care of it."

"Mind if I watch?"

"Not at all, but it's just as boring when we do it." Yancey laughed. "Were you the recovering officer?"

"Yes, sir."

"Where did you find it?"

"In the downtown business area."

Zjorn was pulling on a pair of evidence gloves and asked, "Tom, have you touched anything on the car, inside or out?"

"Ah, the only thing was when I cupped my hand against the windshield so I could read the vehicle identification number."

"Good." Zjorn opened a jar of silver fingerprint powder and dipped a brush in. He held it above the windshield where Yancey had touched it and tapped the brush twice. Powder fell lightly onto the glass. Too much could obliterate the delicate patterns. Because fingerprint ridges were curved, Zjorn touched the brush carefully to the surface and started moving it in a circular motion to highlight the print. After thirty seconds, he stood back and cocked his head to see the light at an angle. "Did you use your right hand?" Zjorn asked.

To assist his recollection, Yancey raised his right hand toward the car. "Yes, I did."

Zjorn nodded approvingly. Because the officer remembered this small detail, he would clearly have recalled any further contamination of the car. "What'd these guys do?" Yancey asked.

"We think they're good for some homicides."

After dusting the door handle and not finding any prints, Zjorn got into the car slowly, being careful not to touch any smooth surface where a print may have been left. "Taz, did you see the ashtrays are gone?"

"That was the first thing I noticed. This has to be our crew." He examined the steering column. "They punched the ignition."

"Yeah, nothing fancy," Yancey said. "Do you think they're from around here?"

"Our current best guess is the Cleveland area."

"What do you think they're doing around here?"

"That's a good question. Are there any hotels or motels close to where you found the car?"

"There are two: the Traveler and a Motel 6."

Fallon watched Zjorn for a while. His face had smudges of silver powder where he had wiped away sweat. He was checking everywhere: the steering wheel, the rearview mirror, the seat adjustment knob, the radio, and even the metal seatbelt fittings. He knew that the more difficult the surface was for him to reach, the better the chance that it wouldn't have been wiped clean. Zjorn contorted his body under the dash and seats. "You getting anything, Doc?"

"Not yet."

Fallon asked the police officer, "Do you know the people who run those motels?"

"Sure, we're always answering calls there."

"What do you say we go talk to them while Doc finishes the car?"

Fallon and Yancey rode over to the Traveler Motel in the police-man's patrol car. After Yancey introduced him to the manager, Fallon asked about the four men and the cars they had been driving. No one fitting their descriptions had stayed there the last couple of nights, so they headed for the Motel 6. As soon as they walked in, the desk clerk greeted the cop. "Hey, Tom."

"Allen, this is Taz Fallon. He's with the FBI."

"Yes, sir. What can I do for the United States government?"

"I'm looking for four white males. May have been driving a metal-lic green Pontiac Bonneville or a dark blue Chevy Caprice. Would have stayed here last night, maybe the night before."

"I think they were here. Kind of a tough bunch. Didn't go out much and when I did see them, they wouldn't have much to say. Didn't want maid service. One of them would go get carryout for all of them." Fallon gave the clerk their heights and weights. "Yeah, that sounds like them. Each had a different room, insisted they all be next to one another."

"When did they leave?"

"Checked out early this morning, before I got to work."

"Have their rooms been cleaned?"

He leaned over and looked at a worksheet on a clipboard. "Yep, all four."

"Did they make any phone calls?"

He turned to a computer keyboard and typed. After a few sec-onds, he said, "Yeah, some calls to Cleveland. Want a printout?"

"I would appreciate it. Did they receive any calls?"

"Not while I was on duty."

The manager handed Fallon the list of phone calls. All the rooms had been rented and paid for by Ronald Hunter. Two different Cleve-land numbers had been called a total of five different times. There was also one call to Wisconsin. "Do you know if anyone would have seen them leave? We'd like to get a description of the car they were driving, if possible."

"I can ask around."

Yancey said, "If you hear anything else, Allen, call me."

"I'll check with the others and let you know."

By the time Fallon and Yancey got back to the police department, Zjorn had finished processing the stolen car. "Anything, Doc?"

"Not even a smudge. How'd you do at the motels?"

"We may have gotten lucky. I've got to get back to the office and call Cleveland. I'll fill you in on the way."

As they drove, Fallon told Zjorn about the telephone calls from the motel. "It's probably a good bet that whoever this Ronald Hunter really is, he's from Cleveland. The first car was stolen in Ohio outside of Cleveland, and now these calls."

"What about the call to Wisconsin?"

"I don't know. Take a look at that printout from the motel. The clerk said they checked out early. What time were the calls this morning?"

"There were two calls made within a couple of minutes of each other, around two-fifteen A.M. One to Milwaukee, and one to a Cleveland number with the last four digits seven-oh-oh-oh; sounds like a business. Then there's a call to another Cleveland number at about two-thirty."

"It sounds like those calls triggered something. When we get in, I'll call Cleveland. You take Wisconsin."

"Debbin."

"Jack, Taz Fallon."

Jack Debbin was almost sixty years old. The mandatory retirement for agents was fifty-seven. When asked how he continued to get the yearly age waivers, he would lower his voice and confide that J. Edgar himself had marked it in his file, and, to secure the favor, Debbin only had to dance with the Director only once. While agents of his generation were usually transferred to a number of different field offices, Debbin had spent his entire career in Cleveland, another unexplained irregularity of his employment. And, despite his age, he steadfastly maintained his assignment to the fugitive and bank robbery squad, which was normally manned by younger agents who liked the action. He found in their youthful zeal a camaraderie that invariably disappeared with experience.

As a result, he enjoyed a senior agent's status with the young members of his squad. They would ask him for his investigative insights—many of which came from phone calls to his well-informed sources—and, in return, he would make them play handball. He played at one o'clock, every day at the local YMCA, no matter what was going on. And on Friday afternoons, he held court at a local tavern. The exact location was always kept confidential until the last moment to "evade the evil eyes of management," and the entire squad, minus the supervisor, would meet there for stories and a few beers. Like the mandatory handball appointments, no excuses were accepted. Through these tactics, he was able to maintain the atmosphere of the Bureau he had joined thirty-five years earlier. Agents from other divisions who had worked a case with Jack Debbin knew whom to call when something out of the ordinary needed to get done in Cleveland. "Heard about your recent kidnapping. Murder-suicide is a nice way to close a case. Unfortunately, I don't think Ohio has criminals sophisticated enough to grasp that kind of subtlety."

"Actually, I think you've got at least one group that might qualify." Fallon told him about the Nazi murders and how the trail had led to Cleveland and Wisconsin. "How's your office contact at the phone company?"

"By the book, nothing without a subpoena or court order. But I've got old friends who, not unlike myself, have worked their way down to menial stations in life. What exactly do you need?"

"First, I need subscriber information for a couple of numbers."

"Let me have them."

After he read them to Debbin, Fallon said, "Can you also ask him for any long-distance calls *from* those phones?"

"Hey, I said this guy's an old friend, not that we're having regular sex. Hold on while I go to a different phone."

When Debbin came back on the line, he said, "Taz, one belongs to a Darla Kincade on the West Side, and the other comes back to the Meridian Hotel, which is just a couple of blocks from the office here. The calls to the Meridian went through the switchboard, so we won't be able to tell who was called unless they made outgoing calls to the same numbers."

"Anything to Wisconsin?"

"Nothing."

"Can you run a check on Kincade and see who her male felon friends are? The only name we've been able to come up with here is Ronald Hunter. He used it to check into the motel where these calls came from. I'm sure it's a phony."

"I'll run it here. And I suppose you'll want me to shuffle over to the Meridian and find out what I can there."

"Doing a good job eventually becomes its own punishment. The call to the hotel was made around two A.M. this morning." After he gave him the Illinois number, Fallon asked, "How often can we check Kincade's outgoing calls?"

"How often do you want it checked?"

"A couple of times a day?"

"You're running up quite a tab here," Debbin said. "I'll call you twice a day and leave them on your voice mail if you're not in."

Everything in Cleveland was starting to tie in. With a little of Jack Debbin's sleight of hand, more answers would be coming. But the Wisconsin call was starting to bother Fallon. Its proximity to Chicago, Josef Rathkolb's home, was too close to ignore.

19

AS THE STOLEN CHEVROLET CROSSED THE WISCON-
sin border, Kurt Decker studied a map of the area. He still didn't
know the name or address that belonged to the phone number that
had been decoded from the Guardian book, but its 414 area code
covered southeastern Wisconsin. "When we get to Route 50, head
east to Kenosha. It's about twenty miles south of Milwaukee, just
across the Illinois border. No use going any farther until we find out
exactly what city this guy lives in."

Del Brantley said, "How're you going to get that phone number
broken down?"

"If it's a listed number, it's easy. Remember Vinny Caps in the
joint?"

"Yeah, sure."

"He made a lot of big scores in Detroit's suburbs. His peak season
was winter. He'd rent a Lincoln or Cadillac while the rich people
were away. Usually he'd do it the morning after a snowfall so he
could see who really wasn't home. Then to be doubly sure, he had an
uncle who was an accountant with General Motors. He gave Vinny
the GM account number for this R. L. Polk outfit, that puts out these
crisscross directories. You know, if you have an address or phone
number without a name, you can look it up and find out who it belongs to. GM uses them a lot, calls them every day from all over the
world, so nobody would be able to detect an extra one from Vinny.
He'd give them the address and they'd supply the name and phone

number for the house he was looking to hit. Then when he was going to make the place, he'd call from the car to make sure no one was home. He was a good thief. Had some big scores. He gave me the account number when we were inside."

"It couldn't have been too perfect if he wound up knowing us."

"R. L. Polk can give you a lot of information, but they don't have a listing of the houses with silent alarms."

From the backseat Jimmy Harrison said, "We could stop at the local library and use their Polk's. That's what I used to do when I was ripping houses."

Decker said, "At best, that information is at least six months old. But when you call their office it's up to the minute. Besides, nobody sees your face on the telephone." Decker went back to his map. "Stop at the first motel you see. Just to be on the safe side, let's stay away from the chains. They're on national computer systems; one call to their headquarters, and they can alert them all." Brantley could see a sign for a motel in the distance and got in the right lane to exit.

The Chevrolet pulled into the Blue Water Motel. There were only two other cars in the lot. Directly in front of the office was a drained swimming pool. Decker went in and rented four rooms for the night.

When he came back to the car, he handed everyone their keys. "Nobody get lost. I gave Darla the number last night and she was calling Polk's first thing this morning. And Del, go get some Wisconsin plates for the car."

Decker threw the deadbolt on his door and lit a cigarette. He pulled the curtain back and studied the driveway. If anyone came looking for him, they would have to stop at the manager's office, which was directly across from his room. Then, he checked for an escape route. There was a small window in the bathroom. It had a horizontally sliding glass panel that had been painted so many times it would no longer open, but, if necessary, he could break it out easily. He sat down on the bed, took another drag, and called Darla. "Any luck with that item?"

"Yeah, he was listed. It's in a town called Whitefish Bay. His name is Eugene Steinmel."

Decker wrote down the address. "Any word from our overseas client?"

"Nothing."

"Okay, I'll call him."

Decker dialed Brunner's hotel room in Cleveland. "Hello."

"It's me."

"*Wo bist du?*" Brunner asked.

"Just outside of Milwaukee," Decker answered in German. "I'm about to call on that customer. We're arranging transportation right now."

"*Sehr gut.* Is there anything I can do?"

"The person we're going to visit is Eugene Steinmel. I don't want another Colonel Stauffenberg problem. Does that name mean anything to you?"

"Steinmel? No, I have never heard it. Would you like me to call my contact in Germany and see if it is of any consequence? Unfortunately, it will take at least a half day. Can you wait that long?"

"I've never been very good at waiting. We'll be leaving soon. I'll let you know what happens."

Decker took out his automatic and checked the clip. He jacked a round into the chamber and set the safety. Then he peeked out the window again. He was anxious to get to this guy Steinmel. In fact, to get done with everything. He kept thinking about that FBI agent, how calm he was, even with a gun pointed at him. Decker knew he was not going to be allowed many mistakes.

Forty-five minutes later the blue Chevrolet, bearing stolen Wisconsin plates, pulled up to the door of Decker's room and beeped once. They all quickly loaded into the car and Decker told him to head north along the lake.

The phone rang at Fallon's desk; it was Mat Zjorn. "Taz, I've hooked up a conference call. This is Bob Tomlinson in Milwaukee. His squad handles foreign police cooperation cases. I filled him in on what's happened so far."

"Bob, I've got a phone number these guys called in Milwaukee, could you see if it's in your crisscross?"

"That's just a short walk down the hall. Fire away."

A couple of minutes later Tomlinson came back on the phone. "It's listed to Eugene Steinmel, up in Whitefish Bay, that's just north of the city."

"Sounds like a good German name."

"Yeah, we've got more than a few of them here."

"Every one of the victims in this case has been an older German male who was a Nazi fifty years ago. Can you run a driver's license check and see how old he is?"

"Hold on."

Five minutes later, Tomlinson said, "He's eighty-four years old." He paused. "Do you think he could be their next target?"

"It's a possibility."

"Do you want me to go out and interview him?"

"The problem is if he has the paintings, you'd probably spook him into moving them. Let me go and get this art expert. We'll get up there as fast as we can."

"Should I meet you there?"

"Maybe you'd better get some loose surveillance on the house."

"Okay. When you get in the area, I'll be on the radio if you need directions."

"I'm on my way," Fallon said. "And Bob, if you do spot these guys, be careful. They like combat."

20

WHEN TOMLINSON GOT TO THE ADDRESS IN WHITE-
fish Bay, a car was already sitting in the driveway, a four-door Chevrolet. He drove by, trying to appear casual as he noted the Wisconsin
plate. Jimmy Harrison, stationed at the window, watched as the agent
slowed down to read the tag. "Del," he called quietly over his shoulder. "What kind of car did you take that plate from?"

Brantley walked over to the window and watched as Tomlinson
drove up the street, turned around in a driveway, and parked three
quarters of a block away under the shade of a half-bloomed red
maple. "I got lucky; they're off a Caprice but a year newer." He
watched the FBI agent for a moment and then said, "I'll let Deck
know."

Kurt Decker sat in the kitchen in front of Eugene Steinmel, who
was tied to a high-backed wooden chair. On the table next to them
was a painting wrapped in heavy brown paper, the front of which had
been torn to verify its contents. "Where are the rest?"

Steinmel, whose face had already begun to swell from the blows
that were inflicted to bring him under control, winced as he spoke.
"That is all he brought."

"What did he look like?"

"He was old like me. Maybe a little younger. White hair. But a red
beard, very red."

"Do you mean a goatee?"

"Yes, on the chin, yes."

Brantley came in and said, "Deck, I think we got a problem. A car just cruised by and copped our tag. I got a feeling he's a fed. He parked up the street, like he's waiting for help."

Decker yelled so he could be heard through the small house. "Ron, are you done?"

Slade came back into the kitchen. "I couldn't find anything."

Decker asked Brantley, "Did you finish, Del?"

"Give me a second. I've got one more closet I want to check."

"Make it quick." Decker turned back to the old man. "What instructions did he give you with the painting?"

"He just said to keep it until someone came to get it. That's all. He showed me a letter from Reichsmarschall Goering. It said I was to follow his orders."

"Goering died a long time ago. Why would you follow his orders?" Decker asked. Steinmel didn't answer and lowered his eyes.

Picking his spot, Decker slapped him across an existing bruise. When he raised his hand again the old man said, "Stop, stop. I fled Germany after the war because I was told I was wanted. My real name is Johann Volkner. This Rathkolb somehow knew. I am too old to go back."

"Do you know who else this man was giving paintings to?"

"I didn't know there were any more."

Brantley came back into the room with a report on the closets. "Nothing."

Walking to the window and peering out, Decker asked Harrison, "See anybody else?"

"Not yet."

He went back in the kitchen and studied the old man for a moment. "My father was Erich Lukas. Do you know that name?"

Hope became apparent on the old man's face. "He was a great soldier."

Decker raised his silenced automatic and fired once, hitting the old Nazi in the bridge of the nose. The force knocked over the chair he was tied to. Decker picked up the painting. "Everybody's calm when we walk to the car. Just keep your heads down so he can't get a good look at our faces."

Brantley left first and started the car, then the others came down the stairs at a controlled speed. Once they were in the car, Decker said, "We'd better slow this fed down. Put your masks on." Once they covered their faces, Brantley backed out of the driveway.

From where Tomlinson had parked he could see the men as they exited the house. One of them was carrying what appeared to be something the size of a framed painting in front of his face. Tomlinson started to reach for the radio but decided they were too close. He would have to wait until they pulled away.

The Chevrolet backed out and drove toward Tomlinson. He had made the right decision not to try to radio for help. At Decker's direction, Brantley pulled up next to Tomlinson's car. Slade, now masked, rolled down the rear window, and from a distance of six feet, pointed a shotgun at the agent. "Throw your keys over here." Tomlinson did so, and Slade lowered the barrel and fired once, blowing out the front tire. The Chevy screeched off.

When Sivia and Fallon reached the outskirts of Milwaukee, he radioed the FBI office and was given directions to Steinmel's house. He was told that Tomlinson was already at the location, and there had been a shooting.

The house was surrounded by police and FBI cars, an emergency medical van, television trucks, and reporters. Fallon, with Sivia close at his side, badged his way past the uniformed cops. A reporter saw the badge and yelled a question at him, which was indecipherable. Once inside, he was directed to the kitchen where Bob Tomlinson was watching the paramedics examine the old man's body. One of them folded his stethoscope and stood up. "That round took out the back of his skull."

Tomlinson glanced up. "Taz?"

Fallon stuck out his hand. "Yes, this is Sivia Roth."

Tomlinson nodded at her, but she was unable to take her eyes off the bloody corpse on the floor. Fallon said, "Let's find some place to talk."

The Milwaukee agent followed them into a small den. "You weren't kidding about these guys. I was the better part of a block away watching the house and they spotted me. I didn't even know they were in here. I saw a car in the driveway with local tags. I ran it and it came back to the same kind of car. At that time they hadn't been reported stolen so I didn't know what I had."

"Did you get a good look at them when they left?"

"No. They kept their faces down, and by the time their car pulled up next to me, they were all wearing masks. But one of them was carrying something."

"A painting?" Sivia asked.

"It could have been; it was about the right size. Looked like it was wrapped with some kind of heavy brown paper."

"Have you searched the house?"

"I haven't, but I think the uniforms have been through it." Tomlinson called over to a sergeant who was handing something to another officer. "Hey, Bill, did you guys find anything?"

The cop yelled back, "Not that you would call fascinating."

Fallon asked, "Mind if we poke around?"

"Poke away."

It was a small house and Fallon and Sivia took their time. It was old, but in meticulous condition. Built in the thirties, all its smooth, hard plaster walls eliminated the possibility of storage areas secreted behind paneling or wallpapered surfaces. After half an hour, they found themselves back in the first-floor den. Fallon glanced into the kitchen and saw that the body had been removed. He said to Sivia, "I didn't see any indication that this guy was a Nazi."

"He has to be. Why else would he have one of the paintings? That's what this is all about—art stolen by the Nazis, given to Nazis for safekeeping. But I don't understand where these Americans fit in, especially if, as that letter said, the retrieval of the Reserve is to fund a new Germany."

"That is a good question, but right now I'm more concerned with who their next target is."

"How are you going to figure that out?"

"That phone in Cleveland is the only way we can track them." Fallon looked over at an evidence tech who was dusting the telephone. "Is there another phone in the house?"

"No, this is it."

He said to Sivia, "Let's get out of here and find a phone."

Outside, Tomlinson was talking to a detective. Fallon said, "Can you start running some background checks on Steinmel. Get his credit and phone records. I'd be especially interested in anything that comes back to the Chicago area."

"That's no problem. I'll call you as soon as I have anything."

"Thanks. If you don't need anything from us, we're going to head back and try to figure out where these guys are going next."

They shook hands. "If it's Milwaukee, please call another agent. I'm out of spare tires."

As soon as they pulled away, Sivia dug in her purse and handed Fallon a cellular telephone. "You can use this."

After giving Zjorn the details of what had happened, Fallon said, "I need you to call Cleveland and talk to Jack Debbin. Get an update on the tolls on that Kincade woman's phone. And ask him if they can trap and trace incoming calls."

"Where are you?"d

"We're heading back. I'm on a cellular. Hold on while I get the number." Sivia recited it and Fallon repeated it to Zjorn. "Call me if there's anything new."

As they were exiting onto the Kennedy Expressway an hour later, the phone rang. "Taz, there was only one additional long-distance call. To Detroit at nine this morning."

"Detroit?"

"I called an agent I know there. He ran it down. It's for R. L. Polk, you know, the cross directories. Anyway, a woman called them. It was to get Steinmel's address."

"How did he know that?"

"For billing purposes, Polk's logs every call. At nine-oh-two they received a query from a woman using a GM account number asking to identify a phone number that came back to Eugene Steinmel in Whitefish Bay, Wisconsin."

"So they had a phone number for Steinmel but not his address."

"That's what it looks like. I had them put a stop on that account number. If they use it again, we'll be notified right away."

"Good. What did Debbin say about trapping that Cleveland phone?"

"He said it's not possible unless you're willing to violate the federal wiretap statute."

"I was afraid of that," Fallon said. "What about the call to that Cleveland hotel?"

"The Meridian Hotel. Yeah, Debbin was able to identify the guy through a call he made to the Motel 6. Used the name Jon Dankers. Paid cash. Debbin said it was probably an alias. And the local address he gave when he checked in was a phony. Oh, and the name, Ronald Hunter—nothing."

"Sounds like a lot of dead ends."

"Need anything else?"

"No, I think we've done everything we can do for now. I'll see you in the morning."

Fallon handed the phone back to Sivia. "No luck getting a trace on the calls?" she asked.

"Even if they were able to do it legally, tracing an interstate phone call is difficult. It takes a while, and all the calls so far have been extremely short."

"Did I hear right, they found Steinmel through a phone number?"

"That's what it sounds like."

"What are we going to do now?"

As he glanced over at her, she gave him a relaxed smile. "Are you on an expense account?" he asked.

"I could probably fake something."

"Then you can buy me dinner," Fallon said.

"I take back everything I've ever said about FBI agents not being chivalrous."

21

IN KENOSHA, DECKER SAT ALONE IN HIS ROOM AT the Blue Water Motel, examining the painting that he had killed another former Nazi to get his hands on. He could barely make out the artist's signature in the lower right corner. It was either Cranach or Cranack. It was a picture of two old men in armor alongside three young naked women and it looked old, very old. The figures were uncomplicated in both body and facial expression. He found it unattractive, and that bothered him, because it was supposed to be priceless, and he didn't understand why. Of the many things in his life he had chosen to ignore, art had probably been the easiest. But this small cracked painting was worth more than all the armored cars he would ever rob. And ninety-eight more of them were out there somewhere waiting for him.

On the back was a small, thick swastika, perfectly stamped in black ink, irrefutable evidence of the Reich's eternal ownership. Next to it, in what looked like red pencil was written *Si 21*.

Using a pocketknife, he carefully pried the painting from its frame, which was an unflattering green and appeared to have been recently constructed. The number 42 was stamped in the back of the top cross piece. He wondered if it was the key to the codes. But since the codes were all in letters rather than numbers, how could forty-two be the key to the twenty-six letters of the alphabet? He thought about it for a while, and after trying several combinations, wasn't able to find any connection between the two.

Abandoning the 42, he turned his attention to the Si 21. He searched the five Guardian codes for Si, thinking it might somehow translate into twenty-one, but that two-letter sequence did not exist in the fifty remaining coded letters. The only conclusion he could draw was that not all of the markings were necessarily relevant to the codes. Some, like the swastika, were obviously incidental to the Nazis taking possession of the work. He called Brunner's hotel in Cleveland and was told that he had checked out. He dialed Darla. "It's me."

"Did you go to Milwaukee?"

"Yeah."

"Everything alright?"

"We made some progress. Did that client call you?" Decker asked.

"Yes. He's in Chicago now. Here's the number."

After writing it down, Decker said, "In case I miss him and he calls, tell him we got the first piece of that shipment."

"The first piece?"

"I told you before, you're better off not knowing. If he does call, just tell him I'm having trouble locating the rest. I may need his help. We'll be staying here tonight but coming back to his location tomorrow morning. If he can, he should give me a call. Here's the number."

"You doing alright?"

"I keep running into the competition. I don't know how they're keeping up with us. You haven't gotten any unusual calls or visits, have you?"

"No, I haven't been out of the apartment since you left, but I'll keep an eye out when I do."

"Okay, did the client say when he would be at the new number?"

"He should be there now."

"I'll talk to you in the morning before we leave."

Decker hung up and punched in the number Darla had given him. It rang in Brunner's room. "*Hallo?*"

"*Wie geht es?*"

"Good, you got my message," Brunner returned in German.

"I got more than your message."

"You have found them!"

"I have one. That's all Steinmel had. Unlike your friend in Argentina, he was most anxious to talk. Said that one was all he had been given."

"Was it Rathkolb who gave it to him?"

"It was him alright. White hair and that bizarre red goatee."

"What does the painting look like?"

"It's by either Cranack or Cranach. It's small, no bigger than a sheet of typewriter paper. A couple of guys in armor and three naked women. Looks pretty old."

"Cranach. It's five hundred years old. And very valuable." As soon as the last sentence was out of Brunner's mouth, he regretted it. He did not want to distract Decker with any temptation that might cause him to abandon his search for the entire Reserve for a quick profit. "That is, if you can find the right buyer, or any buyer at all."

Even in another language, the distrust in the German's voice was obvious. "Let me explain something to you, Brunner. I'm a very quick decider. If I was going to rip off this painting, we would not be speaking right now. I don't know much about art, but I know this is valuable. So, if I was going to go that way, you would have never seen me, your hundred grand, or this painting again. This deal is my retirement package. You can ask my partners, my lawyer, or my bondsman, when I make a deal, I never look to renegotiate."

"You have my apologies. This is all new to me."

"I hope you don't mean keeping your word."

"You know what I mean."

"Then we will not have this problem again."

"I shall not initiate it," Brunner said.

"I guess that will have to be good enough for now. What do you want me to do with this?"

"Where are you?"

"About an hour or so north of you."

"Can we meet so I can take it off your hands?"

"Not tonight, I don't want to move until early tomorrow morning. We have to get some fresh transportation."

Brunner paused. "I understand. Is there any indication about the next Guardian?"

"There are a number of things that could be the key." Decker didn't elaborate.

"Well, what are they?"

"I'm not sure they mean anything."

"Just tell me what they are."

"On the back of the canvas is a stamped swastika with a notation written in pencil. It's a capital *S* followed by a small *i* and then the number twenty-one."

"That is significant. It is definitely part of the Reserve. Paintings collected for the Third Reich were stamped with a swastika. The penciled notation simply means that it was confiscated from someone whose last name began with *Si*, like Silverman or Simon, and that the Cranach was the twenty-first work taken from that person."

"Then that isn't the key to the code?"

"I don't know. It could be, I guess. I will check with my contact and see what he can find out."

"There is something else . . . "

"Yes."

"On the back of the frame, the number forty-two is stamped along the top."

"That sounds like part of a code. Do you think it could be the key?"

"I played with it but couldn't make anything work."

"Let me contact Berlin, maybe they can figure it out. Call me when you get back here tomorrow," Brunner said and hung up.

Decker examined the frame again, searching for any other information that Rathkolb might have hidden. He took out the Guardian book and reexamined the first code, the one that had contained fifty letters decoded by the Enigma machine. The double blank at the end seemed to be waiting for something to be written in, so he penciled in the 42. It satisfied a vague disorder he had felt since he first saw the blanks. But if that was where those markings fit, what was the key?

When Fallon and Sivia pulled up to her hotel, she told him to leave the car with the valet.

"Valet parking at the Blackthorn, exactly how much money does IFAR have?"

"IFAR? Barely shoestrings. David Citron got the room, he knows someone here."

"He seems to know a lot of people." Fallon's observation was more a question than a statement. But Sivia either missed the nuance or chose to ignore it.

"I guess he does. Do you feel like eating any place special?" she asked.

"It's your credit card."

"It's been a long day, do you mind if we eat here?"

"If you'd rather skip it—"

"No, it's just that I've had enough traveling for one day."

"Here is fine."

"Why don't you come up. There's just something about dead bodies and inhaling fingerprint dust that makes me want to take a shower. I won't be long. You can help yourself to the mini-bar."

The room was a small suite on the twenty-fourth floor. After Sivia disappeared into the bathroom, Fallon sat down at a large desk and called for his messages. "Taz, it's Jack Debbin. My contact at the phone company called just before he left for the day. There were no more toll calls as of five P.M. Eastern time. I'll get back to you in the morning."

Fallon could hear Sivia's shower running. He got a bottle of beer from the mini-bar and loosened his tie. He stared out the window. A few early sailboats bobbed through Lake Michigan's gray waters.

As he was finishing a second beer, she reappeared wearing a short, beige sheath dress. As she walked to a front closet to retrieve her shoes, Fallon noticed for the first time that she was slightly pigeon-toed, giving her a teetering gait. She put on a pair of high heels and walked back toward him. To compensate for her turned-in feet, she lengthened her stride, causing her body to sway from side to side with an added sensuality. She seemed to be completely recharged. "Ready?"

Fallon shook off the vague inertia of the alcohol and put his jacket on. "Ready."

The restaurant had a series of darkened booths spaced against winding walls, calculated to give the diners as much privacy as possible. In the distance, piano music played warmly. On top of each table was a small shaded lamp that barely gave off enough light to illuminate the white linen tablecloths. Most of the people appeared to be couples, so when the maître d' seated Fallon and Sivia, he gave them an appraising glance and then smiled conspiratorially to tell them they had chosen the right place for a late, intimate meal. Both of them suddenly felt the need for a cease-fire.

Sivia ordered a glass of wine, and Fallon stayed with beer. She said, "Was your phone call productive?" Thinking she had been in the shower when he made the call, he looked at her quizzically. "There's a phone in the bathroom. I saw the light."

"It was Cleveland. There were no more long-distance calls from that number today."

"Do you find it odd that they had a telephone number for Steinmel but not his name or address?"

"Wherever Rathkolb hid the Reserve, I'm guessing he didn't want someone to stumble across it by leaving names and addresses," Fallon said. "The thing I'd like to know is exactly how many paintings are involved."

"I've been giving that some more thought. I'm convinced there has to be more than six. Many of Goering's art purchases were well documented. We know that even with his heavy-handed discount, the most he ever paid for a single painting was twenty or thirty thousand dollars. That was considered a lot of money then, but I don't think six paintings would have provided him with the kind of future he saw for himself. He was a man who was used to living out his delusions of grandeur, a man who needed box cars to move his art collection. I just can't picture him being satisfied with seven lousy paintings, no matter how valuable he thought they might become. Especially when thirty or forty are almost as easy to conceal and transport as seven."

"No matter how many there are, we're still left with the problem of finding them."

"Any ideas?" Sivia asked.

"There's only one way I know of . . . and you're not going to like it."

"Try me."

"Get a wiretap on that Cleveland phone."

She smiled slowly. "Funny how ethical that suddenly seems. Will you be able to do that?"

"Contrary to public perception, it is one of the most difficult things to get approved in the Bureau. Approval goes all the way up to and including *the* attorney general. Somebody has to go out on a limb. And stopping a group of men considerate enough to kill a bunch of old Nazis isn't exactly out-on-the-limb territory. But I'll make a fool of myself tomorrow and try."

The waiter came again and they ordered dinner. She said, "But if you did get a wiretap, wouldn't that increase the possibility of the FBI finding out about the Reserve?"

"Probably."

"And then if they find out you knew about it, wouldn't your job be in even more jeopardy?"

He laughed. "Only if we don't recover it."

Their meals arrived and Sivia ordered another glass of wine. Fallon switched to coffee. "So what got you interested in art?"

"My mother was kind of an art nut. When I was young, we lived in Manhattan and she was forever dragging me to the museums and galleries. Back then, we couldn't afford to buy anything so she collected *intellectually*. It really was fun, talking about all that wonderful art and then all the bohemians I got to know. When I went off to NYU and took my first art history course, I had already seen firsthand a lot of the stuff the professors showed slides of. I realized how well I had already been educated, so art history seemed like a natural. How about you, what did you major in?"

"A three-and-a-half-year quest for the elusive C average."

"You didn't like college?"

"It was alright. But I looked at it as something I had to get out of the way."

"You finished in three and a half years?" Fallon nodded. "Well, I guess you did alright."

"It was a matter of economics and sleep deprivation. I worked two jobs to cover what the GI bill didn't pay."

"You were in the army *before* you went to college?"

"That's right, you're having dinner with an enlisted man. And it was the marines."

"What *was* your major?"

"Believe it or not, philosophy."

"That's surprising."

"It still surprises me. Most of it was over my head."

"I didn't mean it that way. Every philosophy major I've ever met is constantly quoting all their favorite mentors, looking for the secret of life."

"Maybe that's why I stayed with it—I was looking for the meaning of life."

"Have you found it yet?"

"I didn't even realize I was looking for it until just now."

She laughed. "I think you're putting me on. I'll bet you were serious about it at the time."

"You're not asking me to start quoting all those old, dead guys, are you?"

"God no," she said. "But I am curious, did you have a favorite philosopher?"

"I suppose I'd have to say Socrates. He has my undying gratitude for never recording any of his thoughts, which left very little to be read."

"If I remember right, he also carried out his own death sentence rather than compromise his beliefs."

"I suppose twenty-five hundred years ago someone would have found that admirable, but it's hardly the direction I'd choose for myself."

She smiled. "Maybe you already have."

After they finished eating, the waiter put the check down in front of Fallon. Without looking at it, he handed the waiter a credit card. With a trace of protest, Sivia said, "This is supposed to be my treat."

"It's okay. If you're worried about any sort of obligation, we're going by Midwest rules, which state that the male can have no after-dinner expectations unless his date has both an appetizer and dessert. You had only the appetizer." He leaned back and, with an intimacy she had not heard in his voice before, said, "Unless you want to break the rules."

Her eyes glinted mischievously. "I know New Yorkers are thought of as being indulgent, but I've never been the kind of girl who has dessert on the first date."

22

IT WAS NOT LIGHT YET WHEN BRANTLEY KNOCKED on Decker's door. "I'm going to look for another car. Anything special?"

"I think you better get two. We'll split up for the ride back down to Chicago, in case they're looking for four men in a car. I'll take Harrison with me. We'll go first. Give us an hour head start."

"Where're we going to meet?"

Decker walked over to the bed and picked up a map book. "Here."

"Evanston?"

"Yeah. At the Northwestern University library. I think I've been neglecting my fine arts education."

Brantley nodded at the painting sitting on the cheap motel desk. "That thing worth a lot of money?"

"Only if you can sell it."

While Harrison drove south, Decker studied the German masterpiece. He memorized its limited colors, the small breasts of all three women, their hairstyles, their jewelry. He also took note of the old men in the armor. The intricate armor greatly contrasted with the nudity of the young women. The men's faces were bearded and more detailed than the women's. A twisted tree ran up behind them and one of their horses was tied to it. At the top of the tree, a small Cupid aimed his arrow at one or all of the women.

He held the canvas up to the light and pored over the five-hun-

dred-year-old brush strokes. He became intrigued by its lush background and vistas, its contrasted subjects, and most of all, its silent
unsolvable meaning. It was presented in a language he had never
known, but now wanted to learn.

Harrison followed the signs to the university. After another five
minutes, and directions from a student, they pulled up in front of the
library. "How long are you going to be?"

"A while. As soon as the others get here, go with them in their car.
I'll meet you at six tonight at that truck stop we ate at the night we
left."

Before Decker got out, he slipped the frameless painting into a
large valise. He got out and waited for some students to head toward
the entrance. When a blonde coed wearing a green nylon backpack
arrived, he struck up a conversation with her and continued it as they
walked inside.

In a seldom-trafficked alcove of the library, where most of the
light was defused by the dark, slick patina that oak paneling acquires
after the better part of a century, Decker sat behind a half igloo of
stacked art history books. There was something about this place, with
its acrid mustiness and subdued conversations that he liked—its per-
manency, its sense of belonging. For a moment he watched a square
shaft of white sunlight that angled on to the floor. A galaxy of dust
particles briefly floated through its warm illumination, like the students before they disappeared into the unknown world beyond. Even
though they may never come back, it was a place they would always
think of as their own.

Not exactly the stark college experience he had in prison, but for
him, getting a degree under those impossible circumstances had been
absolutely necessary. The most pragmatic reason was that when it
came time to be considered for parole, the board always looked upon
the accomplishment most favorably. However, he suspected what
motivated him, far more than early release from prison, was that it
would be another way to show his father, even though he was dead,
that he had been wrong. His father made him quit school at the age
of sixteen to get a job. And once he did, the old man's drinking increased to the point where he never worked again. Decker would
have left home right then but he knew he had to remain to protect

his mother. She had always been a convenient target during his father's binges, and many times would take a beating that had been meant for her rebellious son. Although the old man remained physically superior during those times, Decker was big enough to get between him and his mother. Three months after he was sent to the federal prison at Marion, she died. He couldn't help wonder if it wasn't his fault. It was the only thing he truly regretted in his life.

He read about the German Renaissance painters, in particular those from the north. Lucas Cranach the Elder had painted before and after 1500. He was most famous for his portraits of kings, emperors, and even Martin Luther. Artistically, it was one of the most important periods for the country, and most prolific. Considering Hitler's obsession with the superiority of German bloodlines, it was understandable that Cranach was one of his favorites.

And Goering had been right to choose him as one of the Reserve artists. Cranach had held up well over the last half millennium. His precise, small portraits and mythological scenes like the one in Decker's valise were full of exceptional detail. Even in Cranach's lifetime, the provincial aristocracy considered them collectors' items.

Decker couldn't find a photograph of the painting he had, and while none of the color plates of Cranach's other works were detailed enough to reveal the artist's brush strokes, there was a definite similarity in the subject matter and detail.

Although his purpose had been to find out what made these paintings so valuable, he was surprised by the intensity of Cranach's images. By today's standards they were stiff and unnaturally staged, but they somehow had a contemporary appeal. And that was reflected in the current market. Some of the newspaper articles he retrieved from the library's archives gave auction prices of a few other German Renaissance paintings. In recent years, not one of them had sold for less than a million dollars.

Additionally, he found a lengthy magazine article about the looting of art by the Nazis. Dozens of works that were scattered throughout Europe after the war were now being contested as stolen objects. Decker started to slip the magazine into his valise, but then realized if caught, he could wind up arrested. He went off in search of a copying machine.

For the next hour, he stared at the Cranach, which leaned against the books in front of him. He had hoped to find the name of the painting, as it might provide the answer to the code. But if it was in these massive archives, he hadn't come across it. He studied the markings on the back again.

Where was its secret? What was the key to the second Guardian? He took out a blank sheet of paper and wrote on it:

42

Si 21

卐

Cranach

Again, he looked for ways the 42 could be used to unlock the first clue. After a few more unsuccessful minutes, he drew a line through it. Si 21 had been explained by Brunner. He lined it out. Could it somehow be the swastika? Did any of its arms point to any particular number or letter?

The way he had written it, the Nazi symbol was directly over the C in Cranach. All of a sudden the swastika became a guiding star. The C, was that it?

He got out the Guardian book. He turned to the second page and copied the clue *SVJFDNREPT.* Then, down the side of the sheet, using the C as a starting point, he wrote *C-1, D-2, E-3, F-4, G-5, H-6, I-7, J-8, K-9, L-0,* then started over: *M-1, N-2* until *Z-4.* Any one number, because of the ten-digit repeat, was represented by two or three letters. The number 3 could be *E* or *O* or *Y.* He quickly translated the letters into numbers: *7084226348.* Was this a phone number? It was so ingeniously simple, and yet, without the key, completely inaccessible.

He found a phone booth near the library entrance and took out the directory; 708 was the area code for Chicago's southern suburbs.

That had to be it. Each painting had its own key built in: the first letter of the artist's last name. The next Guardian's location could not be decoded without possessing the previous painting.

Decker grabbed his bag and headed for the door.

23

WHEN FALLON ARRIVED THAT MORNING, ZJORN WAS scanning an avalanche of computer printouts. "What's all this, Doc?"

"I was trying to trace that Chevy they were using up in Wisconsin."

"How did you get it identified? It had stolen plates."

"That's the problem. Tomlinson wasn't even sure what year it was, but I had the Illinois and Wisconsin state police do some off-line searches overnight. You wouldn't believe how many cars are stolen and recovered every day." Zjorn gestured to the stacks on his desk.

"You're sure full of energy this morning." He looked at Zjorn a little closer. "Looks like you got all eight hours of sleep last night."

"I'm resting up for tonight." He raised his eyebrows mischievously.

"Let me guess, it's double coupon night at one of your topless bars."

"The Lap Dog is not a topless bar. It's a gentlemen's club. A retreat, if you will, from the pressures of being a straight white male carnivore."

"Exactly what pressure are you and your fellow *gentlemen* under?"

"Do you think it's easy faking all this political correctness. Playing the sensitive male. Women owe us."

"If they owe you, why do you pay them to grind on your lap until your fly is welded shut?"

"These women are artists, and I am their patron. There are forces on this earth you obviously do not understand—"

Fallon held up his hand. "Before you start on that 'curative powers of breast tissue' lecture again, I've got to see Blaney."

Fallon found his supervisor in his office, leafing through a filing cabinet. "Pete, I need to run something by you."

"I hope it's good news. The SAC has been calling over here every two minutes, asking about the Nazi killings."

"There *is* a way to take these guys off."

Blaney pulled a file out of the drawer and sat down carefully, letting his girth settle comfortably over all the available space on the chair. "Every time I hear a teaser that loaded with drama, I'm terrified. And that you're making me ask for the details tells me I'm definitely not going to like whatever you've come up with."

"Just keep an open mind."

"Boy, are you in the wrong place. With less than ninety days to retirement, you couldn't find a more narrow-minded person. In fact, let me be downright bigoted and say no before I become subpoenable."

"It'll take a wire on a phone in Cleveland."

Blaney started laughing. "Sorry, Taz, for a minute there I thought you were serious."

"Come on, Pete. Think about it. There's no other way."

"You've got coverage on the phone in Cleveland. And R. L. Polk in Detroit."

"We don't know if they'll use Polk again. And we're only getting her outgoing calls."

"I don't know why I'm letting you give me indigestion over this. Go see the assistant United States attorney. It's his call." Blaney smiled cryptically.

"What?"

"Do you know who the duty AUSA is this week?" Fallon shook his head. "Phillip Wayburn."

Fallon closed his eyes in disappointment. "Well, I've got to try. Maybe he'll understand how urgent this is."

"Urgent? I don't think that arrow is in his intellectual quiver."

Historically, the small offices from which the United States attorneys issued their prosecutive authority had never been considered particularly lawyerly. They lacked the slick, subtle aura of financial success of the private firms, the diplomatic air of the always-in-progress hard sell.

Other than the occasional dusty-framed proclamation of legal ethics that both gravity and abandoned idealism had sent askew, the walls of the governmental work spaces were unadorned and unrepaired, reflecting a long line of previous tenants who treated them as a career holding cell, a twelve foot by twelve foot filing cabinet needed only long enough to gather the ink of experience that would complete their resumés for the big firms.

But Phillip Wayburn's office was different. The walls, instead of being painted one of the government's narcoleptic pastels, were Burnt Sunset orange. Wayburn had broken the first commandment of civil servants—*Never spend your own money*—when he and his wife, who often prefaced her credibility with "my husband is a lawyer for the government, and he says . . . ," had spent the better part of a weekend doing the redecorating themselves. Across those carrot-colored planes hung professionally framed degrees and family photos. From a long-forgotten stockroom, he had seized an oversize walnut desk. On its surface, a large circular burn mark was barely noticeable under an oversize potted plant. On its front edge sat an engraved brass name plate without abbreviation: ASSISTANT UNITED STATES ATTORNEY PHILLIP E. WAYBURN.

Ever fearful of exposing in open court the personal shortcomings that he skillfully learned to manage through self-denial and avoided decisions, Wayburn had quickly developed a reputation for being nonconfrontational, not an endearing quality to agents who, because of less-than-air-tight cases, tended to gravitate toward AUSAs who were not afraid to "run back punts without their helmets."

Conversely, good news was a warning for him, the prelude to a sucker punch. The sunnier things became for Wayburn—a condition he interpreted as proof of the planet-wide conspiracies against him— the greater his urge to go underground became. As a result, agents, ever ready to tag the enemy, nicknamed him "Punxsutawney Phil." For AUSA Wayburn, unlike the famed Pennsylvania groundhog, it was a good bet that spring would never arrive.

Fallon tapped on his door twice and walked in. Wayburn stood at his window, which opened onto an airshaft, watering a cactus. He wore a dark, lifeless suit that despite his huge waistline hung on him loosely. "Phil, you got a minute?"

The assistant federal prosecutor had a big round baby face with tiny black eyes that now darted around the room as if Fallon had walked in armed with an AK-47 and wearing a postal uniform. "Ah, yeah." He looked at his wrist though it did not have a watch strapped to it. "I've got about two minutes before I'm due at a meeting."

"Okay, I'll just give you the headlines then." Without telling him about the Reserve, Fallon summed up the murders of all the Nazis and how everything was connected to the telephone in Cleveland. "The only way we're going to be able to stop these guys is to get a Title Three on that line."

Wayburn's head snapped back at the words *Title Three.* "A wire? Do you know what kind of probable cause that would take?"

There it was—*probable cause.* The AUSA's one-size-fits-all tourniquet used to cut off agent requests. Although probable cause was little more than common sense, attorneys described it as something so arcane that only they were capable of deciphering and deciding its intricacies. The agents who had dealt with Wayburn had come to the conclusion that the only PC he would accept was the signed confession of a dead man, and then only because dead men usually didn't need prosecuting. Fallon said, "I just gave you more probable cause than you usually get."

"Yeah, but you're talking about a Title Three. Do you know how long it took them to put together the wire for the Antonucci case? Almost a year."

"That was some fringe mobsters, booking bets. I'm talking about people dying."

"Exactly. The Antonucci affidavit was a hundred and thirty pages. And you're talking about an emergency installation which has much more stringent guidelines—rock-solid probable cause. Can you sit down and document a hundred pages of irrefutable evidence? If you could, it would take so long that these people would probably be in custody by the time you were through."

"I'm willing to put the work in."

For a moment, Wayburn seemed cornered, but then relief wrinkled the outer corners of his eyes. "What am I thinking about? This isn't even in my jurisdiction. You'll have to get the Cleveland United States attorney to authorize this. It would be their wire. Do you think they'll want to go through all that angst for a Chicago case?"

"I know it would be Cleveland's wire, but I have to get a preliminary decision in this district."

"The legal complications would be monumental. Even if the Cleveland USA wanted this, which I doubt, it would take a minimum of a month. From what you have told me, these people are working very fast. In a month, they'd probably be long gone."

Fallon had no response. He realized that what he was proposing was so illogical that even Punxsutawney Phil's rejection seemed to be the correct decision. Not only would the federal prosecutor in Cleveland be reluctant to put that much effort into a case clearly beneficial only to Chicago, but the FBI there would have to supply agents to man the wiretap. Agents hated working a wire on their own cases; another office's would be absolutely intolerable. Why hadn't he foreseen these problems? Without warning, he recalled a brief image of Sivia, in the beige sheath dress, walking past him with her long, swiveling strides.

When he got back to the office, messages from Bob Tomlinson in Milwaukee and Sivia were on his voice mail. He called Tomlinson first. "Taz, I've been going through some of Steinmel's papers the police took from his house. One of the things I found was his lawyer's name, so I called him to let him know about the murder. He asked me if I had contacted Steinmel's sister yet. When I told him no, he said as far as he knew, she was his only living relative. Her name is Elga Melling. She lives just west of Chicago. I thought you might want to interview her."

"I'd better. Maybe she knows something about the other paintings. Who knows, maybe she was given one. Let me have the address."

He hung up and called Sivia. "The Milwaukee office came up with a sister of Steinmel's. She lives in Oak Park. I don't know if she has any involvement in this, but I'm going out to interview her. Interested?"

"Absolutely."

*   *   *

As Fallon and Sivia drove west on the Eisenhower Expressway, she said, "Did you have a chance to ask about the wiretap?"

"I talked to my supervisor and the assistant United States attorney. They both suggested I seek therapy."

"Do you still think it's the best way to catch them?"

"As far as I can see, it is. I just hope it's not the only one."

Elga Melling's house was not unlike her brother's. A brick bungalow with dark brown trim, it was small and meticulously kept. As Fallon and Sivia walked up the driveway, he could see an extensive flower garden in the backyard next to a one-car garage. He rang the doorbell and a stern-looking woman in her seventies answered it almost immediately. Fallon held up his credentials. "Elga Melling?"

The woman looked at him judiciously and then turned her analytical stare on Sivia. "Yes, I have been expecting you. My brother's lawyer called," she answered with a heavy German accent.

Sivia said, "We're sorry for your loss."

"Come in."

There was an unhappiness in the old woman's face, not just from something so recent as her brother's death, but the kind that etched itself deeply over decades. Fallon said, "We are trying to find the men who killed your brother. Do you know why he was murdered?"

She looked at them as if they were completely different people from the two that she had let into her house. "You are not here about my brother's real identity?"

Fallon had searched for enough fugitives to understand what had caused the sister's question. "Your brother was wanted?"

She took a moment to decide whether to trust them. "I'm sure you will find out anyway. Yes, my brother's real name was Johann Volkner. He was a guard at Dachau. He was a good man until the war, then they stole his *Seele*, how you say—soul. The higher-ups told him at the end that he was wanted and they would help him escape to America. They gave him papers with a new identity. He could never understand this because he was just a corporal, and these were staff officers who, until then, didn't even know he existed. And now they have murdered him."

"How do you know it was the Nazis who killed him?"

"A few weeks ago, a man came to him and said he knew my

brother's real name and that he was wanted for war crimes. At first Johann denied it, but the man had a large ledger. He said there appeared to be many names in it. The man read detailed facts about my brother's military service and even had an old photograph of him. Then he showed him a letter from Hermann Goering. It was an order to do whatever the man told him to."

"What did he want him to do?" Fallon asked.

"To keep a painting."

"Keep it until when?"

"He told Johann that someone would come and get it. He didn't say who."

"Did he say when?"

"No. And my brother was so frightened, he did what he was told. He called me as soon as the man left."

"Did he know the man's name?"

"It was in the letter from Goering but he couldn't remember."

"Did he describe him?"

"The only thing he said was that he had this strange-looking red beard that seemed to be dyed, because all his hair was completely white."

"Did your brother say anything about any other paintings?"

"No."

"Did you or your brother know any other Germans who served in the war who are now living in this country?"

"I don't. If he did, he never told me."

Sivia said, "What did he tell you about the painting?"

"When it was given to him, it was all wrapped up in brown paper and he was told not to open it, but he did. It was of some men in armor and naked women."

"Did he say who the artist was?"

"No, not that I remember."

Although Sivia tried to force complacency into her voice, it revealed urgency. "What about that ledger? Did he say anything else about that?"

Fallon thought that was a strange question from someone who was supposedly interested only in recovering paintings. The old woman answered, "No."

Fallon asked her, "Did he say anything else?"

"One thing that now seems odd. He said the painting was old, the paint was cracked. And it smelled."

"Smelled?" Sivia asked. "Like what?"

The old woman looked at them with her unhappy eyes. "Death."

24

IF NOTHING ELSE, AN EX-CONVICT LEARNS TO APPRE-
ciate his freedom. Kurt Decker thought of criminals as a minority
who need more freedom than most, fewer rules, less regimentation,
and ideally, no one giving them orders. It was the reason they broke
the law rather than swim along in the mainstream. And Decker saw
himself as someone who needed more freedom than most criminals.
He hated taking orders, a legacy, he was sure, left him by his father—
Hitler's commando, hiding in the United States with no one left to
give his drunken orders to but his wife and son. Nothing angered
Kurt Decker faster than being told what to do. So when Brunner had
insisted that he bring the Cranach to his downtown Chicago hotel
room, it did not sit well with him. But one of the first lessons he had
learned in prison was if you want something bad enough, you have to
let the man think you're working his agenda.

And at this point, Decker found that especially true since he was
developing his own agenda. He had the key to the Guardian codes,
and he didn't see any advantage in sharing it with his employer.
While he wanted to go after the next painting on his own, he knew
he had to keep Brunner involved a little longer because he was still
going to need his help.

He knocked on the door to the German's room. It was on the
concierge level of the New Brunswick Hotel. A bellman had to insert
a key in the elevator panel to allow Decker to ride to that floor. The
suite had a bedroom large enough to hold a couch and two easy

chairs, a sitting room with its own dining area, and a bathroom that was bigger than Decker's entire motel room. "Come in, come in," Brunner said, never taking his eyes from Decker's valise.

"Nice *room*," Decker said with more than a touch of sarcasm.

Completely distracted by the object that was about to turn dreams into certainty, Brunner answered, "Yes, yes, thank you. On the table, if you please," waving in the direction of the dining area.

Decker took his time lifting the case up on the table and unzipped it with the tease of a stripper. Finally the painting came out, wrapped in the original brown paper.

Brunner clawed at it carefully, a rush of emotion running through him. No longer was his quest a fool's treasure map—it had become a priceless reality. The torch was being passed to him from Hermann Goering. But he could not ignore the painting's power, which had increased in the hundreds of years since Cranach's brush last touched the canvas. It ignited Brunner's fantasies on more than one level. "Magnificent!" The comment was meant less for Decker than whatever saint was charged with the protection and advancement of evil. Brunner was now savoring the conspiracy.

"Check out the back," Decker offered.

Brunner carefully turned over the work and inspected the markings on the canvas and then the frame. "Forty-two—that certainly appears to be part of a code."

Decker took a moment to calculate his response. He did not want to give any indication, verbal or otherwise, that he had found the solution to the codes. "I don't know why but I get the feeling it's supposed to go in the two blanks at the end of the first clue. Did your people have any luck with the second Guardian clue?"

"I talked to them about it a short while ago. They still haven't been able to find the key."

"Well, I can't do anything more without it."

Brunner continued to stare at the painting. "I suppose not."

Decker sat down at the table and took out a pad of paper. "Let me play with it for a while." He started writing the letters of the alphabet along the left edge of the paper and then listed long sets of random numbers next to them. He wanted to clutter the sheet with so many sets of numbers and letters it would be indecipherable. For the next half hour, he filled page after page, flipping each one over noisily. He got up and brought the phone book back to the table. Checking one of his scribbled lists against the area codes, he said disgustedly, "That's not it."

Brunner picked up a pad of the hotel's blue stationery and made a halfhearted attempt to find the answer himself. When he grew bored, he placed a call to Germany. The conversation was guarded, but Decker heard enough to understand that it was party business.

At the bottom of his fifth page, amidst a jumble of letters and numbers, Decker finally wrote the telephone number he had deciphered earlier. As proof of its epiphany, he held the pad of paper at arm's length for a moment and studied the numbers, as if they were creatures never before encountered on earth. When he felt Brunner's attention in his peripheral vision, he grabbed for the phone book anxiously. He ran his finger down a page, stopped, and bolted to his feet. In formal German, Brunner spoke into the phone, "I'm sorry, I'll have to call you back" and then hung up. "What is it?"

Decker didn't take his eyes off the page of scribblings. "Get on the extension, I've got a possible." Brunner went to a second phone that sat on a small table. Decker dialed the number, and a female voice, thickly Germanic, answered, "*Hallo?*"

"Is this JB's trailer rentals?"

"No, you have the wrong number."

"Is this four-two-two-six-three-four-seven?" Decker asked, intentionally changing the last digit.

"No, this is four-two-two-six-three-four-eight."

"I'm very sorry. I must have dialed the wrong number." Decker hung up and looked at Brunner.

"That's got to be it! You've found the key."

Decker let the joy on his face wilt into confusion. He flipped through the pages on his pad, almost frantically, as though looking for a suddenly lost child. Then he turned them in the other direction more slowly. Then the other way again. "I don't know how I did it."

"What!"

"It must have been dumb luck." He continued to look through the pages.

"Never mind. For now it's enough. Give me the number again, I'll call our contact. Maybe he'll be able to break the code, now that you have found a solution."

Decker cursed himself. A code expert would be able to easily decipher the clues now that he had a model. But Brunner had heard only the last seven digits when Decker asked the woman what her number was, so he couldn't risk trying to change them. "Four-two-two-six-three-four-eight."

"And the area code?"

The only hope he had was to give him an incorrect area code. The Chicago area had five of them. The one he had just dialed was 708, which was generally for the southwest suburban area. "Seven-seven-three," he answered, giving the three-digit prefix that was the closest numerically.

Although Brunner had detected a slight hesitation in Decker's answer, he gave no indication of noticing it. "Good. Now you can go after the next painting."

"I can't do anything until tomorrow. Darla won't be able to get the number broken down until after nine A.M."

"You'll let me know as soon as you get it?"

"That's what you're paying me for."

After Decker left, Brunner picked up the television remote and turned the set on. He followed the instructions on the screen to bring up the itemized bill for his room. The last phone call listed was area code 708. Decker had lied to him. There could be only one reason for that. Suddenly he felt very alone, very much a foreigner. He picked up the phone and dialed a number in Berlin that he had hoped he would not need.

25

IT WAS AFTER 9 P.M. BY THE TIME THEY LEFT ELGA Melling. Heading downtown along the Eisenhower, Fallon used Sivia's phone to get his messages. Jack Debbin had called again. There were no new toll calls made from Darla Kincade's phone in the last twenty-four hours.

Fallon said, "I can't get those seven frames out of my mind. Why only seven if there are more paintings? I think Steinmel's sister was being truthful with us about him only being given one painting, so we can be fairly certain the Reserve wasn't divided equally among the remaining six people."

"This is starting to sound like one of those bizarre word problems that everyone hated in high school algebra."

"Not everyone." He took the next exit.

As topless bars went, the Lap Dog was considered a cut above the competition. Some rumors credited its popularity to mob ownership. But Fallon knew that was not true because organized crime only got involved in a successful business to bleed it dry. The reason for its profitability was simple: the Lap Dog paid better than the other bars and therefore could truthfully boast that its dancers were unrivaled in both beauty and cup size.

Fallon pulled into the parking lot. Sivia glanced at the club's sign. "I'm going to guess this isn't the Museum of Science and Industry?"

"It depends on your definition of industry. You can wait in the car, if you want."

"And miss another great cultural opportunity?"

"I'm looking for someone who may be able to make some sense of all this."

"And who's that?"

"An agent. He's kind of a genius at math. Actually, he's the one who figured out where Danny Citron was. He's been helping me with the case."

"He knows about the Reserve?"

"No, but we'll need to tell him. He can be trusted—unless you decide to take your clothes off."

"I assume that isn't the slogan on his business cards."

The doorman, a 250-pound block of stone, solemnly guarded the entrance. Fallon flashed his credentials. "We'll just be a minute; we're looking for someone."

"Are you expecting trouble?" he asked.

"Not the kind you're thinking of."

"Just let me know if you need a hand."

Fallon nodded his appreciation and took Sivia's arm. As soon as they stepped through the door, some testosterone-fueled radar went off. A number of male heads turned and their eyes ran up and down her body with the subtleness of wet tongues. Unintimidated, she said to Fallon, "This would be a great place to open a drive-thru sperm bank."

"Yeah, that's just what this country needs is another generation of these guys."

The bar was packed and Fallon stood on his toes trying to spot Mat Zjorn. He had never been to a topless bar with Doc but had heard stories about how manic the Ph.D. in applied mathematics became once exposed to the deadly combination of alcohol and female skin.

There was a commotion at the front of the stage. Two of the Lap Dog's more top-heavy entertainers were down to their G-strings, and the song for their third and final act, "Rocket Man," had just started up. From the crowd, a customer was lifted up and pushed onto the stage. It was Doc.

A low male cheer went up. Zjorn raised his hands in the air as he watched the hips of his "backup" dancers and fell into rhythm with them. He was wearing a cotton crewneck sweater and pulled it off with a single, explosive motion. Another cheer went up.

Fallon searched the crowd for the first wave of the bouncer's counterstrike. Not only were they paid to keep the dancers' space unviolated, most of them fantasized about being the girls' heroes. And here was a chance to show what they could do.

Three of them worked their way—not so gently—through the enthusiastic rows of men. Before they could reach the front of the stage, Zjorn had flung his trousers into the air, which brought another roar, followed by a rhythmic chant that he do the same with his boxer shorts. Once the bouncers gained the front row, one of them signaled the DJ to cut the music.

After a disappointed groan, the crowd fell silent. The employee who had ordered the music stopped nodded at the grinding Ph.D. with surprising graciousness, hinting that this confrontation had occurred before, and it was now time for Zjorn to step down. With as much elegance as a man in boxers and black knee-high socks could muster, Doc turned to his fellow hoofers and kissed each of their hands. He raised his arms to the crowd for one last inspirational cheer and, with the abandon of an errant fan at a rock concert, dove head first into the arms of the bouncers.

With two of the black-shirted employees holding him by the elbows, Zjorn and his clothes were channeled toward the front door. As they passed Fallon and Sivia, Doc said, "Taz, I think I've found a new career." Then he noticed Sivia. "Yeow! You must be new here."

As he was hustled out, Sivia said to Fallon, "I'm going to guess that J. Edgar doesn't know about this one."

Fallon said, "Right about now, I'm probably looking pretty good to you."

Under the bored supervision of the doorman, Zjorn stood outside, teetering on one foot, trying to find the leg hole in his pants. Fallon and Sivia walked up to him. "Doc, you've got to get some new hobbies."

Zjorn looked up and couldn't take his eyes off of Sivia. "Calling this a hobby is an insult. I like to think of it as an obsession."

"This is Sivia Roth. She's from New York."

Forgetting about his trousers, Zjorn released them, and as they fell to the ground, he kissed her hand the way he had the dancers'. "That's too bad. I thought you were one of the employees." He looked at her chest. "It's certainly an understandable mistake."

"Oh, you mathematicians."

"You know that I am a mathematician? So this is to be about my mind and not my body?"

"I'm afraid so."

Zjorn let a disgusted *pfffff* escape from his lips. "Then let us find coffee."

Once Zjorn got himself dressed, the three of them walked next door to a twenty-four-hour restaurant. They found an isolated table and everyone ordered coffee.

"Doc, are you sober enough to do some thinking?"

"Only amateurs have to be sober to think. The only distraction my mind will have to overcome is this smoldering creature you have brought with you. But let's give it a try."

Fallon then told him about the documents they had found and their suspicions about a larger cache of paintings. "We're trying to figure out where this guy Rathkolb hid them, or at least, what kind of clues he left."

Zjorn took a sip of coffee, and without another word, leaned his head back and closed his eyes. After a few minutes, Sivia looked at Fallon in inquisitive silence, wondering if the Ph.D. had fallen asleep.

Finally Zjorn started moving his head in a figure-eight motion. After a dozen or so of the looping configurations, he began to hum in an off-key whine, like a centuries-old chant used by monks to flush demons from their hiding places in the monastery rafters, or in Doc's case, his head. Suddenly he opened his eyes and, with a voice full of clarity, asked, "How big do you think this cache is, Sivia?"

"I don't know exactly, but we think Goering was planning to finance a new Nazi party with it."

"What would masterpieces have sold for during the war?"

"Of course it depended on the work, but on average, twenty to thirty thousand dollars."

Zjorn sipped at his coffee. "Let's say that Goering was able to pursue his dream to become Führer. And for the sake of argument, the seven paintings would have been worth a total of a hundred and fifty thousand dollars. In the late forties, would that have been enough money to bring him to power?"

"I'm not a political historian, but if I had to guess, I'd say it would take at least a couple of million."

"Well, if seven are worth a hundred and fifty thousand, then two million would be roughly eighty paintings. Of those, we know seven were framed, one of which, the Sisley, has been recovered. Rathkolb apparently divided the rest of them into two groups—the six that he distributed to the old Nazis and the mother lode, which, if my math is correct, should be in excess of seventy paintings."

"Why would Rathkolb do that?" Sivia asked.

"That's a good question, and the only way to search for an answer is by examining the actions of our friends from Cleveland. I think we can assume they went to Rathkolb's house expecting to find the entire Reserve. And since you were there, we know they were unsuccessful. But they did find something small concealed in the bedroom floor. Because of their call to Polk's we know that at least part of that was a phone number. A phone number that led them to Milwaukee and the probable recovery of a single painting."

Fallon asked, "Do you think they have phone numbers for the other five?"

"I don't think they have a list of six phone numbers simply because they would probably have had Polk's identify them all during the first call. Why call six times when you're using an illegally authorized account number? No, it sounds like what they found hidden in the floor is in some sort of code, one which can only be deciphered one clue at time."

Sivia said, "We found one document that was encoded on a German machine called the Enigma. Could that be the key to the clues?"

"I am somewhat familiar with the Enigma machine. If it was used for all of the clues, they would have broken all six codes at once, and again, requested Polk's to identify all of them. But there is a high probability that the rest of the clues, when broken down, will also be phone numbers because nothing can pinpoint a person's location in fewer characters. Something like a Social Security number, while it has only nine characters, would be virtually useless because governmental privacy laws make it extremely difficult to find out who it belongs to."

"So what does all this mean?" Sivia asked.

"Since Rathkolb had time to finish hiding all of the paintings before committing suicide, we have to assume that he intended to distribute only those six. It's my guess that he hid them like the classic treasure hunt where each clue leads to the next."

Sivia said, "And when the six are recovered, they will lead to the larger cache?"

"That'd be my guess."

"So whoever finds the sixth one will have the location of the Reserve," she said.

"Either that or all the frames together would give the location, like the parts of a jigsaw puzzle."

"There are no other possibilities?" Fallon asked.

"Not that have any probability."

"If you need all six paintings to find the answer, and we each wound up with some of them, could either of us find the Reserve?" Sivia asked.

"I couldn't say until I saw the clues. But it would be my guess that the paintings are the key, not what was hidden in Bach's floor."

"Do you think that the final location is something with six letters or numbers, like a—"

"I don't know. Off hand I can't think of anything with six characters that could lead you to such a specific location. But, it could be six or six hundred. Whatever the number, it's probably divisible by six. If we can recover one of them, maybe I can figure out something a little more useful."

Sivia said, "Thanks, Doc. You've made sense out of a lot of bits and pieces."

Fallon swallowed the last of his coffee. "Come on, we'll take you home."

Fallon pulled up in front of an apartment building on the Near North Side. Zjorn got out of the backseat and bent down at Sivia's window. "If this man does not treat you with sufficient debauchery, I can be reached twenty-four hours a day."

She looked at Fallon and then back at Zjorn. "You'd better give me your number."

He swayed for a few seconds before he dug his hands into his pockets. He yanked out a wrinkled business card. After trying unsuccessfully to read it, he handed it to Sivia.

She glanced at it. "'Kendall Ross, Producer. Hollywood Pictures'? Does that actually work?"

"In a topless bar? You'd be surprised how few things *don't* work." He held out his hand. "May I have it back?"

He smoothed it between his fingers before jamming it back in his pocket. "If you should need me, Taz has my number." He did a shaky about-face and, listing aport, walked to his apartment building, finally angling himself through the front door.

Fallon drove up to the front of the Blackthorn Hotel and turned off the engine. Sivia turned toward him slightly. "Well, I'll give you one thing, Fallon, hanging around with you hasn't been boring. Since being introduced to you, I've been to a topless bar. Had my personal numbers for observed dead bodies go off the charts. And being a key figure in a hostage exchange? What can I say? Get out the good scotch. I don't know if I'll ever want to go back to New York. I'm surprised you don't have to beat women off."

"I've been told I have a gift."

She laughed and then stared at him for a moment. When David Citron had introduced them at the restaurant, Fallon had surprised her. She was expecting someone in a white shirt and wingtips, at best an intermediary of governmental policy and caution, but instead she saw soft brown tweed and reckless, coffee brown eyes. He had accepted the risks of her proposal with an easy confidence, as if he preferred to act against the safety net of the Bureau's rules and procedures. Trouble was comfortable for him, a place where he operated best.

She had felt something stir that night and warned herself to keep in mind why she was there. The purpose of her trip left no room for personal involvement. She had tried not to let it happen, and even though they both went out of their way to argue at every turn, something had been steadily growing between them.

She leaned over and kissed him lightly on the mouth. When he didn't respond, she pulled back, a little embarrassed. "Sorry, Taz, I got the impression you liked me."

He looked straight ahead. "I do like you . . ."

"But?"

"But there are things you're not telling me. It's hard for me to interpret this."

"Interpret a kiss? Let me *interpret* it for you. It means I like you and am willing to take a chance by demonstrating that. I'm physically offering you an emotional connection. Something you're apparently afraid, or unable, to do. A kiss is supposed to be enjoyed, not analyzed. I've never met a person more in control of his emotions than you . . . no, I take that back, you don't control them, you extinguish them. How is that humanly possible?"

He went into that calm shell she hated and smiled mechanically. "It must be a genetic flaw."

This was not the first time he had used humor to avoid uncomfortable questions, especially about his family. And he had just made another veiled reference to his father. She removed all the emotion from the question she was about to ask so she could better detect any in his answer. "Are you saying your father was the same way?"

After a pause, he said, "You mean, didn't he like kissing women? No, I'm pretty sure he was straight."

"Please don't try to distract me with jokes. Why is it that you can't talk about your father?"

"Believe me, there's nothing to talk about," Fallon said, his voice finally beginning to show some irritation.

So that was it. His father had somehow stripped the emotion out of him, or at least had carved it into an enemy. "Will you please tell me about your father?"

"I've done just fine not talking about him—or to him—since I was seventeen, why should I start now?"

"Everybody has *genetic flaws* traceable to their parents. I could tell you stories about my mother—"

"I have a friend, a nice guy, but he occasionally likes to complain about how difficult it was growing up with money. I guess we all have a need to feel sorry for ourselves. But take my word for it, you and I don't come from the same place."

"And wherever you come from, is it what leaves you so cold and empty that you personally need to right every wrong?"

"At least I'm not doing this because I'm riding around in a limousine full of guilt. Or because I'm bored."

"And I'm not doing this because I had a lousy childhood!"

Fallon stared through the windshield and his voice sounded as though he was somewhere else. "Like that friend of mine with the money is always saying, there's all kinds of lousy."

She got out of the car and slammed the door.

HAVING RECEIVED THE SECOND GUARDIAN PHONE
number from Decker the night before, Darla Kincade called R. L.
Polk at 9 A.M. Fifteen minutes later her phone rang. "Did you get it?"
Decker asked.

"Ah, hi. Yes, it's listed to Luther Schwend at Seventy-two Haverhill Lane in Tinley Park, Illinois."

"Thanks, baby. I'll call you tonight."

"I miss you."

"Yeah, I'll call you tonight."

He dialed the motel's switchboard and was connected to Del Brantley's room. "Get everyone moving. We're leaving in five minutes."

Fallon sat at his desk trying to find anything he might have missed
that would lead to the next painting. But his mind kept returning to
the argument with Sivia the night before. He could see her face, its
exceptional symmetry twisted with anger. The car door kept slam-
ming with the insistence of a distant drum, refusing to go unnoticed.

"Taz!" Zjorn came hurrying over. "Detroit just called. About ten
minutes ago a woman using the same GM account at Polk's called in
a new phone number. It comes back to a Luther Schwend at Seventy-
two Haverhill Lane in Tinley Park."

"Come on." Fallon went into Blaney's office. "Pete, it looks as if
they are about to hit in Tinley Park."

"Did you get this from Detroit?"

"Doc just got the call. They queried the number about ten minutes ago."

Blaney picked up the phone. "I'll get SWAT moving."

"I don't know if there's enough time. We'll head out there now."

"No, you won't. The last two times out these guys didn't think twice about killing FBI tires. The way they keep leaving dead Nazis everywhere, I don't think they would hesitate to move up to agents. You'll wait here until SWAT can be rounded up."

"Just tell them to hurry." He checked the time. Hopefully the opposition wasn't on their way there yet.

A few minutes later, Blaney appeared at Fallon's desk. "Saddle up, SWAT's meeting us at the Tinley Park PD *now*."

As they neared Tinley Park, Decker realized that his crew had become silent. They sensed that what they were about to do was not without its chances. Usually they didn't stop to consider consequences, but the last two times the FBI had shown up, and that wasn't exactly a confidence builder. But they had less fear of the FBI than of failure. All the defeats of their lives were boiling to the surface, warning them that another could be at hand.

Decker remembered feeling the same apprehension on the way to Milwaukee, and an agent had appeared shortly after they arrived at Steinmel's house. Had there been a second list at Rathkolb's house they missed? The trail, with its initial clues disguised with German handwriting and words and Enigma codes, was obviously left for someone who understood the old ways, someone like Brunner, so he doubted that *der Kurator* would have left more than one path to the Reserve.

That meant the FBI had somehow figured out Steinmel was one of their targets. The only way they could do that was by tracing Decker's movements. It had to be R. L. Polk. Maybe Polk had discovered he had been accessing their records by using GM's account and called the FBI. Technically, it was fraud by wire, a law, federal prison had taught him, that the FBI had primary jurisdiction over. If he was right, there were probably agents on their way to Tinley Park. But he had to chance it. Failure to obtain the next painting would break the chain of clues that somehow led to the Reserve, and if that should happen, there was no way to reestablish it. He checked his watch. It had been less than an hour since Darla called Detroit. The government couldn't react that fast . . . or could they?

As they neared the block that Schwend's house sat on, Decker said to the others, "I've got a bad feeling about this. We've got to get in and get out. Nothing pretty. Del, take a ride around the block. We'll pick out a spot where you can wait with the car so if something goes wrong, we can get out the back." He glanced at Slade. "Ronnie, take the carbine just in case."

Fallon was surprised how quickly the SWAT team had assembled. He supposed it was because the call came first thing in the morning before its members had scattered to the demands of their normal agent duties. And with two shootings in the last five days, they had stuck a little closer to their radios than usual.

A dozen men in dark jumpsuits stood around the Tinley Park police parking lot, cinching up their thick bulletproof vests, double-checking magazines, and testing radios. A marked Tinley Park patrol car with two officers in the front seat waited.

Blaney came over to Fallon. "Everyone's just about ready. The marked unit is going to lead the way over there and provide a uniformed presence, then SWAT, then you, Doc, and I in my car."

The SWAT agents started getting in their cars. Zjorn was putting two small wads of cotton in his ears when he noticed Fallon looking at him. "There's nothing worse for a hangover than a shootout."

Del Brantley pulled up in front of 72 Haverhill Lane. The street was lined with modest single-family dwellings, some brick, some wood frame. The midmorning air was still damp with dew. As soon as the three men got out, Brantley drove away. Slade walked with an M-1 carbine low along his leg. Harrison carried a small crowbar in a similar manner. The front door was opened with a quick, low crack and they were inside the house almost without breaking stride.

Decker heard light, shuffling footsteps on the second floor. Snapping his fingers once, he alerted the other two men. With Slade watching the street, Decker motioned for Harrison to cover the stairs in case somebody came down unexpectedly.

Quickly, Decker searched the first floor, but found no one. Then from the second floor, he heard an old woman's crackled voice say something in muffled German. A single male grunt was the only response.

As Decker and Harrison were about to start up the stairs, Slade, in a strained whisper said, "Deck, cops!" The gang's leader peeked out of the window and saw a marked police car sitting in the middle of the street a half block away. A number of other cars were lining up behind it.

"*Wer bist du?*" Decker spun around to see an old woman in her eighties, a laundry basket in her hands, on the landing. After the initial shock of finding strangers in her house, she noticed the guns. First her eyes and then her broad, sagging mouth went wide with fear. Before she could scream, Decker's silenced automatic spit once, striking her in the chest. She sat back on the stairs behind her as her eyes rolled upward. After teetering for a moment, with the basket still clutched in her hands, she tumbled forward in perfect somersaults, her dead body as lithe as a young gymnast's. Decker sidestepped her as she crashed past him. He took the rest of the stairs two at a time. Reaching the top, he heard a man's thick accent, "What did you say, Greta?"

Moving quickly toward the voice, he found Luther Schwend coming out of the bathroom. Decker pressed his gun to the old man's throat. "The painting!"

"Greta?"

"Gone. The painting?"

"Under our bed."

Decker pushed the old man hard into the room and threw him on the floor. "Get it!"

Schwend pulled out a painting-size package, wrapped in the same brown paper as the one they had taken from Steinmel.

Decker tore open the paper. It was a portrait of a woman. He turned it over. The swastika was there with *Ka 7*. In the top cross piece of the frame was stamped *19*.

Schwend had gotten to his feet and was standing against the wall. Taking two quick steps over to him, Decker turned the muzzle of his gun upward and, holding the painting as far away from the old man as he could, fired a single shot up through the old man's lower jaw.

Abruptly, Slade's carbine opened fire. Decker looked out of the bedroom window that faced the street and saw the long line of cars halt as their occupants bailed out to use them as cover. Slade's volley had bottlenecked the law enforcement convoy. And their narrow column would allow Slade, firing from a single point, to keep them all from flanking the house, at least temporarily.

Some of the SWAT team opened up. A few rounds shattered a front window and door. Decker, caught midstaircase, dove over the railing, carefully tossing the painting ahead of him. As soon as he hit the floor, he said, "Ronnie, give them the rest of the clip and let's get out of here." From his position on the floor, Slade thrust the muzzle of his carbine through the window and blindly emptied his weapon with three bursts.

All three men ran in low profile toward the back door just as a heavy burst of return fire came through the windows and walls.

From his vantage point behind the last car, Fallon could see that the initial shots from the house had been taken at too great a distance to be effective. If they had been intended to cause casualties, they would have waited until the officers and agents were closer to the house. Instead, they were meant to be a delaying action.

He ran to the same side of the street as Schwend's house. The shots had come out of the first floor. Skirting the neighboring houses, Fallon shielded himself from the sniper's field of fire. When he reached the residence next to Schwend's, he cut up the driveway and across the backyard. Carefully approaching the house, he saw the back door standing open. The SWAT commander yelled for a cease-fire so his men could start evacuating people from the neighboring houses.

Quietly, Fallon vaulted over the fence and drew his automatic. He listened for a moment and when he didn't hear anything from the house, walked up the stairs and stepped inside.

The first thing he found was Mrs. Schwend's body. He checked the rest of the first floor before heading upstairs. In the bedroom, his eyes followed the wet trail of blood down the wall to Luther Schwend, his neck extended to a strained length, his chin forced tightly against his chest.

Fallon went back downstairs and yelled that he was coming out. Cautiously he stepped through the front door. "They're gone."As if he had said "cut" on a movie set, everyone released from their defensive stances.

The first one to reach Fallon was Pete Blaney. "That was real smart," he said. Then he nodded past the door.

"Two dead. Probably Schwend and his wife."

"Any signs of a painting?"

"Not that I saw, but I doubt if these guys would have silenced Schwend unless they had it."

"They sure don't believe in leaving witnesses." Blaney asked one of the police officers to follow him inside.

Fallon went to look for any hidden storage areas. He examined the different rooms, their walls and floors. One of the bedroom closets had a ceiling access panel, so he pulled himself up through it and wandered around for a few minutes, stepping carefully from joist to joist, searching for anything out of the ordinary.

By the time he was done, the agents had cleared the house and were out in the clogged street removing all their cumbersome equipment. There were now twice as many police officers and detectives. Television reporters, who routinely monitored the police bands, were starting to show up in their vans. Blaney stood in the street talking to the SWAT commander. "Stay close to your radios, I think we're going to see these guys again." He asked Fallon, "Anything in there I need to know about?"

"I get the feeling that they were expecting us. They had the right weapon to stop us. And it was in the most advantageous spot. When I ran into them the first time, they had their car parked right out in front. The same thing in Milwaukee. But here, they had it hidden in the opposite direction of the gunfire."

"Yeah, usually we learn from the criminal," Blaney said. "Normally, it's the best way to catch them. But it looks like this crew is learning from us."

"I think I've got an idea how to teach them the wrong thing."

27

KURT DECKER SAT ON THE FLOOR OF HIS ROOM AT the Renaissance Motor Inn. Five feet in front of him, tilted against the faded wallpaper, was the work of art he had just taken from the Schwends. For the better part of thirty minutes, he had been staring at it, making occasional adjustments to keep it in natural light.

Despite his hours at the Northwestern University library, he was unable to tell, by style, who the artist was. It was a drawing of a woman from the waist up, in a long-sleeved V-neck dress with puffy shoulders. He was, however, pleased that he did recognize the medium, pastels. Some of the strokes seemed amateurish, as if a child had hurriedly used crayons to fill in the less-focused areas of the drawing, especially the sleeves of her dress. But the artist's real genius became obvious in the woman's face. In sharp contrast to the crude strokes that represented the clothing, her attractive face was drawn with just a few fine lines and dusty, pale smudges rendering the woman's features with near-photographic clarity. Decker studied the drawing for a few more minutes, trying to discover how its creator had performed such a miracle.

He remembered reading that great art could not be understood by analytically dissecting the color or line or form, but rather, needed a judicious eye that accepted the entire work and was capable of interpreting it emotionally and intellectually. He wondered if it was something a person like him could ever learn.

But for now, his inability to recognize the artist by technique didn't really matter. At the top of the work was a name, presumably that of the drawing's subject, Gabrielle Diot. Under that were several other words scribbled in another language. But, most importantly, just above her left shoulder, scrawled with shopping-list carelessness, was the artist's name—Degas.

Decker was certain of one thing: it had to be worth a fortune, much more than the money that Brunner would owe him. But the German politician was probably right; finding a buyer was not something Decker would be able to do without the risk of being caught. The paintings would have to be sold directly to buyers, rich buyers willing to trade their discretion for a substantial reduction in price. And these were not people ex-convicts, staying one small step ahead of the law, were likely to meet. He picked up the phone and dialed Rölf Brunner's hotel.

"I've got the second item that you ordered."

A little too quickly, Brunner asked, "Who's the artist?"

The German's question probably meant that his contacts in Berlin had broken the last-name code. If they had, he knew that Decker gave him the wrong area code. But it didn't matter whether Brunner trusted him or not, because even if the German could find someone else to hunt down the Reserve, it meant that he would have to kill Decker and his crew as part of the switchover. And if he were capable of something like that, he wouldn't have needed Decker in the first place.

But Decker never assumed an opponent weak. He treated them all with the same degree of distrust. Conversely, deception had always been Decker's most trusted ally, so he said, "Ah, I think it's . . . " Decker hesitated a moment as he deliberately mispronounced the artist's name, "Dee-*gazz*."

Although they were speaking German, Brunner corrected him, "*Day*-gah." This time Brunner was careful not to be too enthusiastic. "Very good. And did you get to meet the previous owners?"

"Briefly, but if you're thinking about any further contact with them, they went out of business."

"Well, that happens. When can you make delivery?"

During the conversation, Decker had moved directly in front of the pastel. He did not want to give it up. He had relinquished the

Cranach, and it still bothered him. Of course the paintings were worth a great deal of money, but there was something else. He, an ex-convict, was in sole possession of an extremely coveted piece of art. In the motel's squalid setting, the Degas, like a kidnapped prince, rose above its surroundings and even the vulgarity of its capture. He simply liked being in its company. But, for the time being, Decker knew his best interests would be served by appearing committed to their agreement. "The item belongs to you. Just tell me where and when."

"Not here," Brunner said. "I don't know if I'm becoming paranoid, but with all that has been happening I feel the need to become a little less stationary."

Evidently Brunner wanted to put an additional, untraceable link between them. Decker decided he wanted a similar advantage. "With the FBI on my tail, I'm feeling the same way. It may be best if we don't know each other's exact location. Then if something happens to one of us, the other can't be traced through telephone calls."

"Then how would we communicate?"

"I'll get some beepers. When we need to talk, we'll page each other and then call the number in Cleveland. Darla can hook us up on a three-way conversation. That way she won't know where we are, either. And it'll be in German so she won't be able to understand what's being said."

"That makes sense. But for now, what about the Degas?"

"Stay at your hotel until I can get the beepers."

"How long do you think it will take?"

"Not long, a couple of hours," Decker said. "One last thing, did your contact find the key to the code?"

"I think it's best if we discuss that in person."

When Fallon returned to the office, there was a message from Sivia. She had heard about the shooting on the news and wanted to be sure he was alright. And then her tone deepened—she was sorry about last night.

She answered on the first ring. "Hello." The single word was quick, expectant.

"It's me."

"Are you alright?"

"Everyone's fine. They were just trying to slow us down."

"Good." Her choice of word was more subdued than her tone. "Did they get the painting?"

"As best I could tell."

"Then we're not doing too well."

"There should be four more chances. We only need to find a way to get to one of them first."

"That's exactly what I need to talk to you about. Do you think we could have lunch?"

There was something uncomfortable in her voice. "Is your hotel okay, where we had dinner the other night?"

"Sure. In a half hour?"

"Sivia . . . "

"Yes?"

"I'm sorry, too."

By the time Fallon arrived, Sivia was already seated. The waiter led him to what seemed to be the most remote booth in the restaurant. As he sat down next to her, the waiter handed him a menu. She smiled and said, "I would have ordered for you, but I didn't know what was really good after a shootout."

"How's the chicken here?"

A short scale of musical laughter escaped from her. "I'm sure you were very courageous."

"So what do we need to talk about?"

She reached over and the tips of her fingers touched the back of his hand. "I want you to know that I'd never do anything to hurt you, Taz. Never. But there is a great deal at stake here."

"I'm really not that easy to hurt."

She studied him for a moment before saying, "I've done something. It's illegal. And I know if I tell you about it, you'll either have to report me, or become involved."

"How illegal?"

"Very," she answered. "But it can't work without you." Her words were no longer imploring but had started to harden into small, insistent pellets.

"I got a feeling I don't want to hear this."

"That's up to you," she said, although she knew he would not be able to disengage himself from the search for the Reserve at this point.

He took a sip of water and then said, "Okay, what is it?"

Her hand squeezed his appreciatively. "During my work, I meet a great many people. Some of them, as I'm sure you will not be surprised, are private detectives working as freelancers for insurance companies who need stolen art recovered. I have been able to help a number of them, and since IFAR is a nonprofit organization, I have always let them claim any reward due. So I am owed favors and probably seen as a good bet for future cases. I've worked with one of them a couple of times. He has all the latest equipment, so I—"

"Put a wire on the Cleveland phone."

"It was that obvious?"

"Do you know what they do with FBI agents who break the law?"

"I'm going to guess they go to prison."

"And, although I don't like to think of myself as especially self-destructive, I completely agree with that. You're talking about me risking my freedom so some people can become wealthy by getting back their paintings."

"This is not about the value of the art, or the money. It's a matter of justice. As long as one painting stolen by the Nazis remains unreturned, it means they are still winning. It's just as David Citron said, the Holocaust goes on."

The bitterness of her response was finally providing Fallon with a glimpse through the latticework that surrounded Sivia Roth. "Angry indignation is not the best way to recruit felons?"

"*Recruiting* isn't necessary if you can find people who are more concerned with justice than themselves."

He stood up and tossed his napkin on the table. "You really are good at this, aren't you?"

As she watched him go, she knew he could walk away from her, but never from the hunt for the Reserve. Something inside of him was turned the wrong way, some imbalance that he was compensating for. Whatever it was, she knew it wasn't possible for him to quit, not now.

Then suddenly, for the first time in her life, she hated that she understood these things about men.

28

A LIGHT RAIN HAD CLEARED OUT THE BROOKFIELD Zoo parking lot. Decker sat low in the black Camaro, his automatic accessible under the seat. He had picked the location because, with all the signs leading to the zoo, Rölf Brunner would have little trouble finding it. In the distance, a silver Lincoln Town Car drove into the lot and slowed to a searching speed. When it got close enough, Decker tapped his horn once. The Lincoln pulled into the space next to him.

For a few seconds, both men stared at each other through the glass of their door windows, preferring the barriers over the conversation that was about to take place. Finally Brunner's window came down with a motorized precision. In response, Decker lowered his and said, "Open your trunk." He hit the release in his own car, then got out and took the wrapped Degas and placed it carefully in Brunner's. As soon as he opened the Lincoln's passenger door, he noticed the new-car smell. "I assume this is a rental."

"Yes, why?"

"You didn't use your own identification?"

"I'd like to think I'm a little smarter than that."

"I just wanted to make sure." He handed the German a beeper.

"Any problems getting the painting?" Brunner asked.

"Not really."

"The television said there was shooting with the police."

"Just a diversion."

Brunner nodded his head absentmindedly at the explanation. "Even though you gave me the wrong area code for Schwend, my friends in Berlin have broken the Guardian codes."

"Really." Decker's voice, totally void of inflection, left Brunner wondering if the single-word answer referred to the phone number error or that the code had been broken. "And what is it?" he asked without a hint of curiosity.

"I think you know it's the first initial of the artist's last name."

Without looking at him, Decker nodded his head solemnly, and again Brunner couldn't tell if the American was acknowledging his suspicions or affirming the ingenuity of the code. "When will you go after the next painting?"

"First thing in the morning," said Decker.

"I thought you would be anxious to do it now."

"The FBI almost beat us there today. I've got to shoot a different move. It's going to take a little longer." Decker could see the suspicion in Brunner's face. "Or would you rather I rush right in there and get caught. Then you would be on your own."

If Decker's tactic caused any apprehension in Brunner, it didn't show. "Do what you have to do. Were there markings on this frame also?"

"In the same place . . . the number nineteen." Brunner opened a small black notebook and turned to a page that read SVJFDNREPT _ _ and wrote *19* in the two blank spaces.

Decker said, "So you think that's where those numbers go, too."

"For now, it's as good a guess as any."

"Any idea what they mean?"

"Not yet."

"It must be another code that tells where the Reserve is."

"It could be."

Decker could see that Brunner did not want to provide any more information than was necessary and decided to end the meeting as quickly as possible. "The number for your beeper is printed on its clip. Give me your book and I'll write mine down." When he was done, Decker said, "I'll call you as soon as we get the next location."

Decker exited the lot and headed west. Almost a half mile behind him, another rented car made the same turn.

*   *   *

When Fallon returned to the office, his message light was on. Jack Debbin from Cleveland wanted him to call right away.

"Jack, it's Taz. I hope this is good news."

"Yeah, I heard about the old guy and his wife, but maybe this will improve your day. It looks like we've got your little band of marauders identified. We went out to our sources regarding this Darla Kincade, and one of the guys on the public corruption squad has someone who knows her, or more accurately, her boyfriend. Ever heard the name Kurt Decker?"

"I don't think so."

"He's a local antihero. Banks, armored cars, home invasions. He just beat an armored car robbery case that looked dead bang. But the judge suspiciously dismissed it on some very shaky legal ground. If Decker did dollar-bill his way out, it couldn't have been cheap. No one around here thinks he has the juice to push something like that off the table. He must have tied up to a heavyweight somewhere."

"That makes sense. How else would a Cleveland stickup man get involved in murders from here to Argentina over some paintings that were stolen in Germany before he was born?"

"Even though your crew only has four individuals in it, we've come up with five possibles, Decker and four other guys he does scores with. I'll vigit their photos as soon as we're done." The Video Imaging Graphics Information Transceiver instantly scanned photographs and digitally transmitted them to the receiving office's computer monitor. Then as many copies as desired could be printed out.

"That's great, Jack," Fallon said. "And as long as you're on a roll, how about your friend at the phone company?"

"I just checked with him, nothing in the last twelve hours."

"Let's hope that doesn't dry up. It's the only way we're staying competitive."

After receiving the five photographs, Fallon went to Blaney's office. As usual, the supervisor was wedged into his chair, reading incoming mail. "It looks like Cleveland may have identified our crew." He dropped the stack of photos on the desk.

Blaney shuffled through them quickly. "Do we know which four are ours?"

"Not really. But this one," Fallon tapped Decker's photo, "is supposed to be the boss."

Blaney picked it up and read the description Debbin had penned at the bottom. "Kurt Decker. Thirty-eight years old. Six foot two, two twenty-five. Looks like a load."

"So far I think that's a pretty fair assessment."

"Think we can give these to the media?"

"There's no doubt in my mind these guys are our subjects, but we can't prove it. And I'm afraid if their faces are flashed all over, they'll just disappear until the heat's off. We'll have gained nothing."

"So you just want to wait for them to kill someone else?"

"Spreading their photos around isn't necessarily going to get them caught, but it will make them that much more cautious. And right now I don't want that. Instead, I've got an idea how to make them come to us. Do you think SWAT would like another shot at them?" asked Fallon.

"As bad as they made us look this morning, absolutely."

"We'll pick a spot where we can take them off without endangering any civilians. Then I'll have Detroit give R. L. Polk that location so when Decker or his girlfriend call in the next number, no matter where it is, they'll be given the address we're set up on. Besides having them come to us, they'll be giving us the number of the person with the next painting."

"You must have had a very twisted childhood."

Fallon pulled Decker's photo out of the pile and studied it for a moment. "Now if he'll just cooperate and call."

29

JUST BEFORE 9 A.M. THE NEXT MORNING, DECKER sat in his room, thumbing through the local telephone book looking for a German-sounding name. His search ended when he spotted *Gruber, Meyer.* After writing down the address in northwest Chicago and the number, he called Darla.

"I need you to make another call to Polk's."

He gave her the phone number that was listed to Meyer Gruber. She asked, "You want me to call now?"

"Yeah, and do it on a three-way hookup. I want to listen."

"Is there anything wrong?"

"I'll know better after you call."

She dialed the Detroit number. Once she gave the General Motors account number, the woman who answered seemed to become rigid, her responses metered and exact. Darla read off the ten digits. After a few moments, the woman gave the name Friedrich Volker with an address, which, although different from the one Decker had gotten out of the phone book, was also in northwest Chicago.

So that *is* the way they've been tracking us, Decker thought. And it was pretty clever of them to substitute their own location, trying to set him up. He was also impressed that since the agents didn't know which area code would be queried, they must have given Polk one false address for each of the five possibilities.

The R. L. Polk employee hung up and Darla said, "Did you get that?"

"It's a phony."

"They're on to us?"

"They're on to Polk's. Maybe that account number isn't good anymore, I don't know. We'll have to get this one some other way."

"Do you think they can trace that call back to me?"

"It's interstate, it takes too long."

"Are you sure they know?"

"I'm going to find out."

"Kurt, I don't like this. Can't you leave this one alone, I'm worried."

"Just do what you're told. And stop whining, I've got enough problems to deal with here."

She started to cry. "It's just that I miss you."

Decker hung up.

FBI SWAT was set up on the address the clerk at R. L. Polk had given Darla Kincade along with the name Friedrich Volker. Once Fallon and the team leader started making plans, they realized that they would need five contingency addresses, depending on which area code the requested number came from. When they finished, the SWAT team staged itself at a point that was as close as possible to the geographic middle of all five locations. Each was near an expressway, with the farthest being less than twenty minutes away.

It had been decided that SWAT would take care of Decker and his gang, leaving Fallon and Zjorn to confront the person whose phone number Darla Kincade had called into Polk's—Meyer Gruber. Hopefully they would be able to convince Gruber to cooperate and, if Rathkolb had given him a painting, to turn it over.

As they neared the address, Zjorn asked, "How are you going to get inside?"

"I'm hoping once we explain the consequences of dealing with Decker rather than us, he'll beg us to take the painting."

They parked in front of the house. "Doc, take the back just in case."

"Sure, but who am I trying to stop?"

"We'll take anyone with a painting under their arm."

As Zjorn walked toward the back of the house, Fallon rang the bell. A few seconds later an attractive woman in her early thirties appeared at the door. "Can I help you?"

Fallon opened his credentials. "Yes, I'm looking for Meyer Gruber."

"FBI? Meyer's my husband. Is there a problem?"

"Your husband? Do you mind if I ask how old he is?"

"Thirty-four, why?"

"Is there another Meyer Gruber, maybe his father?"

"No, his father's name was Gunther. He's been dead for many years. The only Meyer I know is my husband. What is this all about?"

Fallon sensed something was very wrong. "This may seem like a strange question, Mrs. Gruber, but have you or your husband received a painting from anyone in the last six months?"

"No."

"I'm sorry, I evidently have been given the wrong information."

Once they were back in the car, Zjorn asked, "What happened?"

"These are the wrong people." He picked up the radio mike and called Blaney. "Have you got anything?"

"Zero."

"He must know we're onto Polk's. We're at the Gruber address, and it looks like it was a setup."

"Why would he do that?" Blaney asked.

Fallon hesitated. *Why would he do that?* "Of course," he said out loud. He looked through the windshield, scanning the neighborhood. He peered into the rearview mirror. A black Camaro that had been parked a block and a half behind him pulled into the street and drove slowly toward him. Fallon was sitting on a one-way street with his back to the oncoming car. He jumped out and drew his automatic. The car stopped at an intersection less than thirty yards away. Aiming his gun at the driver, Fallon recognized Kurt Decker from his photo. Above his front sight blade, he watched Decker smile at him. The ex-con knew the law: police agencies could not fire at fleeing felons, especially those who were only *suspected* of breaking the law.

Slowly Decker turned right into the cross street. He continued to smile at Fallon, letting the FBI agent know he had lost again. His car, moving barely faster than an idle, disappeared from view.

Fallon jumped back into the Bureau car. Turning around in a

driveway, he started up the one-way street the wrong way. At the intersection, he made the same turn as Decker but the black car was gone. Fallon drove a couple of blocks but could find no trace of him. He radioed Blaney again. "You can break it off. Decker was here to see if we were onto him. I'll bet he got Gruber's number right out of the phone book. Unfortunately, he won't be calling Polk's again."

"Want us to come over there?"

"It wouldn't do any good, he's just a vapor trail now."

They listened as Blaney talked to the SWAT team commander. "You copy, Sierra One?"

"That's fourteen, we're breaking off."

Zjorn said, "How'd he know?"

"Probably when we showed up at Schwend's, he realized the only way we could have known was through Polk's."

"Do you think he knows we're watching the girl's phone?"

"After the way he just made a fool out of me, I wouldn't underestimate him about anything. But he knows how we normally do things, and hopefully thinks because we haven't run out and confronted her, that we're not aware of their connection. From the calls on her phone, it's obvious that he needs her help to find these paintings. And he's careful not to let her call him, so he probably thinks that even if we were aware of her, we could not trace him through her phone. He's been around enough to realize that we could never get a tap on it in time." That is, a legal tap, Fallon thought. "Let's just hope that Cleveland comes up with something we can use."

"And if they don't?"

"Then I'm afraid someone else is going to die."

"Hallo," the old man's voice answered.

"Good afternoon," the woman said pleasantly, "this is Detective Christina Grohmann. I am an investigator with the Winter Haven, Florida, Police Department. How are you today?"

"I do not understand. You are the police, in Florida?"

"Yes, sir. In Winter Haven."

"Why do the police in Florida call me?"

"There's no problem, sir. We've arrested some people down

here who were running a boiler room operation. Do you know what that is?"

"No."

"It's a confidence game, where the perpetrators try to defraud senior citizens out of money. Getting them to invest in phony business deals."

"I know nothing about this."

"Don't get the wrong idea, we know you're not involved. We arrested a group of them a couple of days ago. In their papers were numerous phone numbers that appear to belong to people who might have been cheated by them. We're calling all the numbers to find out who has sent them money. Have you been contacted by anyone and asked to invest in either gold coins or oil leases, guaranteeing you a thirty percent return on your investment?"

"No."

"Well, consider yourself lucky. I've called—let's see—seventeen people on my list and you are only the second one who has not been contacted by them. I'm going to give you my name and telephone number so you can let me know if you are contacted in the future. Sometimes they sell their list of names to other criminals. Have you got a pencil and paper?"

"One moment, please. "She could hear the old man's chair slowly scrape across the floor as he got up. A few seconds later, he said, "Yes, go ahead, please."

She spelled her name for him and gave the nonemergency telephone number for the police department. "Oh, I almost forgot. They just had your phone number listed. I'll need your name and address for our records, in case you have to call us back, we'll know who we're talking to."

"Yes. It is Edgar Lech. I live at Three-twelve Lincoln."

"And what city is that, Mr. Lech?"

"Buffalo Grove."

"Illinois?"

"Yes."

"Thank you for your time, sir." When she hung up, Kurt Decker said, "That was perfect, baby."

"Did you get it all?"

"Yeah, the connection was good. And I think the old guy enjoyed talking to a fine young *Mädchen* like Christina Grohmann."

"You'll call tonight and let me know how it went?"

"I'll call when I get hooked up with my German friend on the three-way. We can talk then. Right now I'd better go introduce myself to Mr. Lech." He hung up.

30

FALLON KEPT TRYING TO CONVINCE HIMSELF THAT if he could find Decker and his gang before Sivia actually got the illegal wiretap information from the private investigator in Cleveland, she somehow wouldn't be guilty of breaking the law. Of course he knew he was deluding himself. The recorder was already in place, making her as guilty of criminal conspiracy as if she had installed it herself. He wondered how his thinking had become so illogical, but then he remembered that night in the car and the waxy-fruit taste of her lipstick.

He spent the remainder of the day reviewing criminal records for Decker and his four gang members, looking for a way to find them. He had Zjorn call the police departments all over the country that had arrested the men in the past, along with the prisons where they had served their time, trying to identify any of their known family or associates. If such people lived in the Cleveland area, maybe the gang members were exchanging calls with them. As these names surfaced, Fallon fed them to Jack Debbin, who in turn had their phone records searched. By the end of the day, when the Cleveland agent's source officially had to log off his computer, they had failed to uncover even one long-distance phone call to Illinois. The one positive piece of information he developed was that Frank Lassiter, one of the names supplied by Debbin as a member of Decker's crew, was in an Arizona prison. That left Fallon with three names—Delmer Brantley, Ronald Slade, and James Harrison—in all likelihood, the other men behind the ski masks.

It was almost five when Fallon's supervisor, with uncharacteristic speed, hurried over to his desk. Handing him a message slip, Blaney said, "Looks like Decker found his next victim without Polk's help." Fallon looked at the name and Buffalo Grove address. "The police are there now. The owner, Edgar Lech, is ten-seven, single gunshot wound to the back of the head."

"Did they say how old he is?"

"Seventy-nine. And the neighbors described him as a 'nice old German guy.' Take Doc and give the locals what we got."

A block away from Lech's, they could see several vehicles, including TV trucks, parked haphazardly around a house. "Looks like standing room only," Zjorn said.

When they got out, one of the reporters recognized Fallon from the Schwend murder scene and shouted, "Agent, why do you think someone is killing all these old German people? We've been told they're all Nazis. Is that true?"

Fallon gave no indication of hearing the question and pushed through the crowd. At the door, they flashed their credentials for the uniformed officer and were directed to the detective in charge. Fallon explained about how he believed this murder was probably related to the other Nazi killings.

Unlike the random search of a blitzkrieging burglar, Edgar Lech's house had been searched with a purposeful efficiency. Drawers were left unopened, but doors and cabinet fronts had been left ajar, mattresses overturned, and in the basement, a panel, which had been discreetly screwed into the wall, was pried open, revealing a compartment capable of holding a large object. On the floor in front of the opening, Fallon found a torn piece of brown wrapping paper. He remembered that Bob Tomlinson had seen what he thought was a painting wrapped in the same material when the gang left Eugene Steinmel's house in Wisconsin. And Steinmel's sister had reported the same thing. Decker had the third painting.

Back in the kitchen, a uniformed officer was dusting the telephone and the surrounding desk for latents. A small pad of paper had the name Christina Grohmann with a phone number. "Nine-four-one," he said to the cop. "Do you know where that is?"

"Somebody checked, it's in Florida."

"Did anyone call this Christina Grohmann?"

"We haven't had a chance yet."

Fallon could see where latents had been lifted off of the phone. "Done with this?"

"All set."

Fallon dialed the number. "Winter Haven Police, can I help you?"

"This is a police department?"

"Yes, sir, Winter Haven. Can I help you?"

"This is Taz Fallon in Chicago, I'm with the FBI and I'm at a murder scene. Next to the phone, someone has written your number along with the name Christina Grohmann. Does she work there?"

"What was the name?"

"Christina Grohmann?"

"Sorry, I've never heard the name before."

Fallon thanked him and hung up. Zjorn asked, "She *doesn't* work there?"

"It must be part of a pretext they used to get Lech to tell them where he lived. I'm guessing that it was Darla Kincade who called." If it had been her, that meant Decker still felt her phone was safe. Fallon looked over at Edgar Lech's rigored body, his face destroyed by the bullet's exit wound. He knew he had no choice but to call Sivia.

Halfheartedly, Darla listened to the conversation, though she did not understand one syllable of the growling, jumbled German dialogue between the two men until a familiar name caught her ear—Toulouse-Lautrec.

"This is good—Toulouse-Lautrec," Brunner continued in his native language. "Have you calculated the next location yet?"

"No, we just got back. Besides, I didn't know whether to use *T* or *L*."

"You take the *L*," Brunner suggested, "and I will take the *T*."

The phone was silent for a few minutes and then Decker said, "It must be *T*; my area code would be eight-one-two and that is in," Decker scanned a phone book, "Indiana, way down in southern Indiana."

"Just a minute," Brunner said. "Is Six-three-oh a Chicago area code?"

"Yeah, it's straight west of the city, what's the rest of the number?"

After Brunner had read it to him, Decker said, "I'll make the call, but that must be it."

"When can I get the painting?"

Decker hesitated for a moment. "I got to tell you, I'm not crazy about driving around making deliveries with an item in my trunk that can get me convicted of murder. Besides, the time can be better spent getting the next one. Then I can give them both to you in one drop."

If Brunner did not like Decker having one painting for very long, the idea of him having two in his possession was even less appealing. "That was not our arrangement, I need that item tonight."

"It wasn't our arrangement that the FBI would be waiting around every corner, either. We need to be logical. The longer this takes, the less likely we are to be successful."

Brunner knew there was nothing he could do at the moment, but he had already started to develop a contingency plan. And it wouldn't work if he and Decker began bickering, or worse, competing for the Reserve. "Okay, you are probably right. How soon do you think it will take to get the next one?"

"The scam that Darla ran today worked well, but if she is supposed to be a cop, we can't have her calling at night. It'll have to wait until first thing in the morning."

"You will call me as soon as you have secured it?"

"Yeah. But in the meantime, you'd better get that hotshot friend of yours in Berlin to figure out what this two-digit code on the back of the frames means, because if we can't figure that out, nobody's going to find the rest of these paintings."

"Give me the number from the back of this frame."

"Twenty-six."

"I will contact him as soon as we are through."

With his contempt for Brunner growing, Decker said in English, "Well then, I think we *are* just about through." He doubted that, in the language so foreign to Brunner, his subtle warning would be detectable.

After the German hung up, Decker said, "Darla, are you still there?"

"I'm here."

"I'll call you at nine tomorrow morning with a number so you can do your Winter Haven bit."

"Kurt, this is about stolen paintings, isn't it?"

"How'd you know that?"

"I heard him mention Toulouse-Lautrec."

Decker's men knew they were after six paintings, but he had been very careful not to give them any indication of the existence of the Reserve. But Darla was no fool. If she started piecing it together, it could cause him problems he didn't need. "Baby, don't you even think about this. When it's over, you and I will be living any place in the world you want and doing whatever we want. And there'll be no more of this ripping and running. It'll be just you and me."

"I just couldn't handle it if you had to go back to prison."

Neither could I, he thought. Neither could I.

31

WIRETAPS, WHILE EXTREMELY DIFFICULT TO OBTAIN legally, offered two invaluable tools to law enforcement. First, the information gathered, in the voices of the criminals, is considered so accurate, so irrefutable, that its evidentiary value usually holds the weight of a confession. Second, there was no greater source of instantaneous intelligence. Crimes could be prevented, individuals arrested, and lives saved. Information obtained from the wiretap that Sivia had arranged, while it could never be used in a court of law, would be just as accurate and timely. It was, unquestionably, their best chance to catch Decker and his crew before they struck again.

But it was illegal. And while Fallon was willing to accept the consequences to save lives, on a personal level, he could not deny that breaking the law, no matter how well justified, was an act of surrender, an abandonment of something he was supposed to believe in. Each time he thought about this resignation, a struggle to resist rose up in him—and then he remembered there were only three more paintings. And their owners, at least for now, were still alive. He dialed Sivia's number. "It's Taz. They've got the third painting."

"Did they kill anyone?"

"That's why I'm calling. I can't stop them without that information from Cleveland."

"It'll be alright, Taz. He's being very careful."

Fallon hesitated a moment. "How're you doing it?"

"The woman in Cleveland lives in an apartment building so he said it was just a matter of getting into the juncture box, whatever that is. He put a recorder on her line. Once a day, he collects the tapes and plays them on the phone for me. I record them off of my phone and then he erases his tape. He says it will hurt the sound quality a little but the chain of evidence, if it were to become that, is nonexistent."

"What time is he going to call you?"

"He said it would be better if he didn't go in until around eleven at night when everyone is in bed or watching the news. No later than midnight is what he promised."

"If he's arrested, is there any chance he'll give you up?"

"No."

"Why?"

"He likes me."

"Likes?"

"Maybe more than that."

"Okay. But one word of caution, if you tell anyone about this, we will probably go to jail."

"I understand."

"Good. And so everyone's protected, each time your friend does this, instead of just erasing the tape, have him physically destroy it. I'm sure, with my luck, that sometime between our indictment and trial, the FBI lab will come up with a way to reconstruct erased conversations."

"Anything else?"

"Yeah, convince me I'm not a fool."

Sivia's phone rang at a few minutes past midnight. After listening for a few moments, she pushed a button on the tape recorder and said, "Go ahead." Ten minutes later she turned off the machine and said, "Thanks, I'll talk to you tomorrow" and hung up.

Fallon rewound the tape and then pushed the play button. A computerized voice gave the date and then the area code and number of the phone that was being taped. Fallon was glad to see that Sivia's friend was being careful not to identify the tape with his own voice.

The first segment was Darla's call to R. L. Polk. It was followed by her ruse with Edgar Lech. And then finally, the three-way conversation between Decker, Darla, and the unknown German.

"There's nothing there in English that's going to help us," Fallon said.

"Any ideas?"

"Since this isn't exactly court authorized, I can't call our language people to translate it."

"How about Risch?"

"One of the first rules to committing a felony is to keep to a minimum the number of people who know about it."

"If you're worried about him turning us in, I know he won't. When you had me call him to see if he would translate the Enigma message, he told me about his time in Treblinka. The Nazis had found out that he was an accomplished goldsmith. Almost daily, the soldiers brought him gold and ordered him to make them trinkets. He knew where the metal was coming from. Sometimes it was in the shape of teeth and fillings with blood and tissue still stuck to it. But he wanted to survive, so in addition to following orders, he siphoned off minute pieces of the gold and used them to bribe the guards for extra food or medical supplies. He feels that he used his fellow Jews' deaths to keep himself alive. He has more guilt about that than he will ever be able to outlive. He could never inform on us, not only because what we are doing is right, but because I am a Jew and he could never betray another one."

"Call him."

It was almost 9 A.M. when Stefan Rochlitz's phone rang. "Hello," his wife, Berta, answered in a heavy German accent.

Darla Kincade had expected a man to answer. She felt momentarily confused. "Good morning, this is Detective Christina Grohmann. I am an investigator with the Winter Haven, Florida, Police Department. How are you today?"

"I am good; what is this about?"

Decker immediately noticed that the conversation did not have the give-and-take like the one with Edgar Lech. With him, there had been a compulsion to exonerate himself. That was the way the pretext was designed: to force any person, whether guilty or innocent, into a position where they felt it was in their best interest to tell the caller everything they wanted to know. To do that, the individual had to believe that some sort of jeopardy existed, that he or she was in danger of being defrauded. If done right, after some initial reluctance, they were basically begging Darla to take their names and addresses to protect their own future interests.

But something in the old woman's responses was different. Her voice sounded hurried yet controlled. When Darla finally asked for her name and address, she rattled it off faster than the rest of her answers, giving the impression that the completion of this final segment was a source of relief. Then Darla was smart enough to ask her husband's name, "just for the record." This seemed to confuse her. After a pause, she said, "Stefan Rochlitz."

After Berta Rochlitz hung up, Darla said, "Kurt, did you get it all?"

"Yeah, I did. Did you get any bad vibes from her?"

"No, what's wrong?"

"I'll call you later." Lost in thought, he eased the phone onto its cradle.

Less than two hours later, Decker and his crew in two freshly stolen cars neared the address for Stefan Rochlitz and his wife in Naperville, Illinois, forty miles west southwest of downtown Chicago.

Signaling for the second car to pull over, Decker got out and walked back to it. He looked at the two men as if trying to choose one. Finally he said, "Jimmy, when we get there, I want you to go to the door. See if this Rochlitz is there. If he is, just take him back inside, and we'll follow you in."

Slade, who was driving, asked, "You want me to park behind the place in case there's a problem?"

"No, let's just try it this way."

"Then you're not expecting trouble this time?" Slade asked.

Without answering, Decker got back in his car and let the others take the lead. He told Brantley, "Give him a block lead, especially when he pulls up to the house."

Slade eased the car up to the house. Harrison, concealing a carbine under his long coat, walked up to the front door. He knocked, and when there was no immediate answer, he looked around for Decker.

Once the gang leader saw this, he reached into the backseat and, from under a blanket, pulled out a twelve-gauge pump shotgun. He jacked a round in the chamber with such conviction that Brantley, sensing that things were about to get rougher, fastened his seat belt.

Decker watched as Harrison again reached for the doorbell. For a moment his hand hung frozen in the air. He took a quick step backward as he fumbled under his jacket, attempting to bring his weapon into a firing position. His hands were moving at a speed that indicated panic rather than technique. The muzzle of his weapon hadn't quite broken the horizontal plane when the glass of the storm door exploded with a soft *thrrrrrip!*

In a violent jerk, Harrison's body was thrown off the porch and landed on the lawn with a lifeless thud. From the car at the curb, a burst of automatic gunfire erupted. Slade then got out to go to Harrison's aid, but immediately an intense volley of gunfire was returned from the house. Cars at both ends of the street screeched into gear. Slade realized Harrison was dead. He scrambled back into his car and floored it.

Hearing more tires, Decker spun around and saw a car bearing down on them. "Get us out of here," he told Brantley. He leaned out the window with the shotgun and fired two rounds at the oncoming vehicle. Brantley had no choice but to drive toward Slade and all the government cars that were trying to pin him in.

Slade drove up on the lawn to avoid an FBI car that was trying to ram him. Brantley decided on a different tactic. The Bureau car chasing Slade stayed in the street paralleling him. Brantley headed straight at it as Decker leaned out the window and aimed the shotgun at the advancing government agents. Finally the Bureau car swerved and ran up on the lawn. Brantley sped past them, taking the first available turn.

As he accelerated, Brantley could see there was only one car chasing them now. They were about four blocks from the expressway. Decker spotted a dead-end street. He yelled at Brantley, "Turn right!"

"It's a dead end!"

"Turn right!"

Brantley slid around the corner and the closing Bureau car overshot it and had to stop and back up to make the turn. Then the agent accelerated before he realized there was no way out. At the end of the street, Brantley had already turned around. Both cars now faced each other like knights covered in hammered steel. Decker said, "Punch it."

As Brantley stomped the gas pedal, Decker climbed halfway out and sat on the window frame and took careful aim at the oncoming FBI agents. He fired once, hitting but not shattering their windshield. There was time for one more shot before the two cars collided. Decker decided which way they were likely to swerve to avoid the collision and then fired at that side's tire. The shot exploded the driver's side tire, transferring all the traction to the right tire. The government vehicle veered sharply to the left. The agent was already pulling hard on the wheel. Once the tire collapsed, the car rolled over violently.

When they reached the expressway, Decker said, "Head north, we'll have to find another motel."

"What about Slade?"

"He's got my beeper number."

"What about Harrison?"

Decker looked at him coldly. "There's a simple rule in this business: the more destructive we become, the more likely we are to be destroyed."

32

DURING THE DRIVE BACK FROM THE ROCHLITZ RESI-dence, Fallon and Sivia listened to the SWAT shootout along with the subsequent chases on the Bureau radio. She said, "I can't tell what's going on. Everybody is talking at once."

"Generally, the more chaotic the transmissions are, the worse it's going. It sounds like one of them has been shot and killed, and my guess is the others are in the process of getting away."

"How can that happen?"

"We have to err on the side of caution. And Decker was probably suspicious. Mrs. Rochlitz was pretty shaky on the phone. But we got the painting, and they didn't kill anyone. For us, that's not a bad day."

The night before they had gone to Risch's apartment with the tape of the conversation between Decker, Darla, and the unidentified man. Risch invited them upstairs and made coffee, then disappeared into a bedroom. Because the quality of the twice-recorded telephone call was poor, he had to listen to it a couple of times. He came out with a handwritten translation that included the phone number that Darla was to call the next morning. Fallon then dropped Sivia at her hotel and hurried back to the office. He called in his supervisor and the SWAT team commander. The three of them spent the rest of the night devising an arrest plan that included finding an unoccupied house to direct Decker and his gang to.

Early the next morning, Fallon picked up Sivia and proceeded to the Rochlitzes' house, which was a good ten miles from the address they had given Decker. Stefan Rochlitz answered the door. Fallon identified himself as an FBI agent and then introduced Sivia as being from IFAR. As soon as Rochlitz heard Sivia's name, he glared at her. Half a century had failed to calm his hatred for Jews. "Josef Rathkolb gave you a painting to keep," Fallon said. "It is stolen property. We are here to confiscate it. I know confiscation is a concept that people like you and Rathkolb are familiar with."

"I don't know what you are talking about." He smiled, enjoying his lie.

"I assume you have heard on the news about a group of men killing older German immigrants. The people being murdered are those who, like yourself, have been given paintings. If you turn this painting over to us there will no longer be any reason for you to be murdered."

Without hesitation Rochlitz said, "Get out of my house."

Unintimidated by the old man's violent stare, Sivia thought about Eugene Steinmel, who was also known as Johann Volkner and the ledger Rathkolb had used to remind him of his past. "Is Stefan Rochlitz your real name?"

The old man's eyes narrowed. Sivia was about to threaten him with an immigration investigation when his wife walked into the room with a package wrapped in paper. The former Nazi gave her an enraged look before retreating up a nearby stairway. "We do not want the trouble this brings," she said, handing it to Sivia. "I am sorry, but he lives in the past."

As Sivia unwrapped the package to verify its contents, Fallon informed Berta Rochlitz that she was about to receive a call from the man who was responsible for the recent murders, and the purpose of his call would be to obtain her address. The only way to stop him was for her to help the FBI apprehend him. Although she was very uncomfortable with the idea of trying to be deceptive on the telephone, she realized she had no other option.

Fallon briefed her on what to expect during the phone call and rehearsed her as much as possible. Because of the old woman's nervousness, Fallon was worried that Darla, or Decker, if he was listening, would become suspicious. But Fallon, too, had no other choice.

As soon as the phone rang, Mrs. Rochlitz stiffened, and then proceeded, as Fallon had feared, to respond to the caller's questions with short, stiff answers. He could only hope that whoever was listening at the other end would not become suspicious enough to avoid the trap. The moment the call was completed, Fallon called the office and told them to notify Blaney that it looked like Decker was on the way.

For the next half hour, Fallon and Sivia interviewed the old woman, trying to find a connection to the other paintings, but she related the same story they had heard from Eugene Steinmel's sister. Bach had brought the painting and told Rochlitz to keep it until someone came for it. She refused to say anything about a ledger or her husband being threatened with his past, but neither Fallon nor Sivia had expected her to. Fifteen minutes after they left the Rochlitzes, they listened as the shootout between Decker's gang and the SWAT team began.

Now, the chaotic transmissions on the radio had dissolved into routine chatter. None of the Bureau units were in pursuit any longer, and Fallon suspected that Decker had gotten away.

During one of the lulls in the radio traffic, Sivia said, "Have you thought at all about when they were discussing the artist's name and how they turned that into a phone number."

"I really haven't had time."

"They said, 'Toulouse-Lautrec . . . have you figured the next location yet?' Then the other said, 'I didn't know whether to use the *T* or the *L*.' Then they each took a letter and came up with possible phone numbers. Remember Doc told us that whatever they found under Rathkolb's bedroom floor was in code and that the unscrambling of each clue was probably dependent on the previous one? It sounds like the first letter of the artist's last name is the key."

"That makes sense. If you're right, we'll have to make sure no one knows who this artist is. By the way, who is the artist?"

"Matisse. And it is in excellent condition."

"Then, without that name, Decker's through because he can't decode the next clue." When she didn't respond, Fallon looked over at her and could see her apprehension. "That isn't good news?"

"Yes it is, but then how do *we* find the Reserve?"

Fallon started to slow down. The house that fifteen minutes earlier had been the site of the SWAT shootout was now surrounded by activity. Yellow-and-black plastic tape cordoned off the front yard, near the center of which lay Harrison's body. Fallon had to park almost a half block away. As he started to get out, he spotted the SAC talking to the SWAT team commander. "That's a question we'll have to try and answer later," he said to Sivia. "For right now, how about waiting in the car? I've got some lies to tell, and I don't want to do that in front of people I like."

"Well, since you asked so nicely this time, I guess I could forego the pleasure of seeing another corpse."

The SAC stood over Jimmy Harrison's body as one of the SWAT team members searched it. The SWAT agent said, "Nothing except eight hundred and thirty dollars in cash. No wallet or keys."

"Did you get both of those plates on the air?" Stamen asked.

"Yes, sir. I put them out on our channel and had the radio room call the state and locals."

Stamen noticed Fallon. "How did it go with Rochlitz?"

"You can put him down as one vote for the Holocaust, but his wife seemed to understand the connection between art and death. And once Sivia let them know they might have some immigration problems, the wife became extremely patriotic. She was pretty shaky on the phone with Decker's girlfriend, so if they were hinky, that's probably why."

"Blaney said you were going to use Rochlitz's real name. Would Decker have known the difference?"

"It looks like there's some sort of connection with Germany. We didn't know if Decker, once he got the name, could check to see if Rochlitz was a former Nazi or not. We knew we could give him a false address, but didn't want to chance a phony name."

"Did Rochlitz have a painting?"

"Come on, I'll show you." They walked back to his car and Fallon opened the trunk. He pulled away the thick brown paper. Stamen bent over to get a closer look. "What's it worth?"

"Let's ask the expert." Fallon went around the car and opened the door.

"Sivia, this is the special agent in charge of our office, Ralph Stamen."

The SAC extended his hand with a forced gentleness, and in a voice threaded with his best charm, said, "It's so nice to finally meet you."

"And you," she answered smoothly. Though only two words, Fallon recognized their tone and could see the effect they were about to have on the SAC; she was about to add his scalp to her collection.

"Taz was telling me you were responsible for recovering the painting. That's very impressive. Maybe we should be offering you a job," Stamen said. "I hope you won't be offended, but to my uneducated eye, it seems a little crude."

"In other words, you're asking me what it's worth."

"Yes, I guess I am."

"Well, Mr. Stamen, you can rest easy. This is a very important work on several levels—"

With his voice still straining with sincerity, he interrupted her. "Do you know what causes men my age to have midlife crises—beautiful young women calling them *mister* or *sir*."

Her head rolled back with a gentle laugh and she put her hand on his forearm. Purposely, she left it there a little too long, and he kept his arm awkwardly still so she wouldn't remove it. Then she let her hand fall away slowly, dragging the tips of her fingers, giving the impression that she regretted the separation. She said, "Well, Ralph, let me see if I can't give you a crash course. As you may know, my organization has as its primary purpose the tracking and recovering of stolen art objects. While there are some that we know little about, this one is rather well known. It is by Henri Matisse—"

"I've heard of him."

"Yes, he's a very important twentieth-century artist. He was a central figure in the Fauve movement, which was short-lived but greatly influenced German expressionism. That's important because it demonstrates why Hitler was so anxious to obtain works by Matisse. This particular painting is entitled *Oriental Woman Seated on Floor* and it was stolen by the Nazis from one of the largest collections in Europe. It belonged to Paul Rosenberg, a French dealer and collector, who had more than four hundred paintings confiscated simply because he was a Jew." Carefully she turned the painting over. "See the *Ros 213*. That means it was from Mr. Rosenberg's collection and it was the two hundred and thirteenth work taken from him. Now, due to your efforts, this one can be returned to his heirs."

"You were going to tell me how much it's worth?"

"Of course any object is worth only what it can be sold for. At a recent sale, a Matisse of similar quality went for five-point-five million dollars. So, for your purposes, I would think a fair estimate would be between five and six million. Possibly more. If you have no objection, I'll start making arrangements to ship it back to our offices in New York so it can be returned to the Rosenberg family." When he didn't immediately answer, she put her hand on his arm again and said, "It'll mean a great deal to them."

Stamen finally took his eyes from her, and she watched as his pupils flitted aimlessly, trying to resist the comfort he was feeling. The only words he could manage were, "I don't know."

"It'll give them some sense of justice," she said. "That is what the FBI's supposed to be about, isn't it?"

He looked at her and then turned away. "Justice in this day and age is a very complicated process. It—Sivia, I'm sorry, but I'm going to have to get some direction from Washington. I can't just turn over something so valuable without some sort of authorization. It would be suicide." He took out a cigarette and lit it with a noisy drag.

Stamen bent over and inspected the Matisse again. As he did, Sivia, to remind Fallon of her prediction of Department of Justice foot-dragging, gave him a I-told-you-so look. Then she said, "Ralph, I understand you have procedures, but there is one thing I must insist upon: No one can know that this painting is by Matisse. Taz and I are of the opinion that the name of the artist is part of a code system that will somehow lead Decker to the next painting. We don't know exactly how it works, but if we're right, without the name Matisse, he won't be able to find his next victim."

Stamen said, "It's the least I can do for having to delay you with all this red tape. You have my word." He then turned to Fallon, and in a less charming voice, said, "Codes? This is pretty complex, how did you find Rochlitz before Decker?"

Fallon wanted to give Stamen the impression that there were things that he had not told Sivia. He said, "Sivia, I'm sorry, but you're going to have to excuse us."

Fallon and the SAC headed back toward the house. "It was done through a legally gray area," Fallon said. Stamen exhaled a labored, smoky sigh, then dropped his cigarette on the ground. "Decker has a message drop in Cleveland. One of the agents there, who is a friend of mine, has been monitoring the toll records, unofficially. After the last victim, Edgar Lech, was killed, this agent found that Lech had been called prior to his murder. Unfortunately the information didn't become available until it was too late to do anything about it. Then late yesterday, he saw another call to the Chicago area and called me immediately. This time it was to Rochlitz."

"And it gave you enough time to set all this up."

"That's right. At Lech's house we found some information he had written down that made it look like Decker's girlfriend used a pre-text call to get the address. So we figured they would do the same thing with Rochlitz and planned this accordingly."

"What did he say about how he got the painting?"

Fallon reminded himself not to divulge the name Josef Rathkolb because it was too entangled with the existence of the Reserve. "According to his wife, a man identifying himself as Martin Bach brought it to him about six weeks ago and told him that someone would be coming for it."

"Did she know about any of the others?"

"Nothing. Bach showed up out of nowhere and gave him the painting for safe keeping. End of story."

"What was he told to do with it?"

"Just to hold it until someone came for it. He wasn't given a name."

From an inside pocket, Stamen took out another cigarette, touched his lighter to it, and drew in deeply. "Too bad the rest of them got away."

"The important thing is that he can't find his next victim."

The SAC took another long drag on his cigarette and rather than flipping it with his fingertips, he threw it with an overhand motion, as if this time his silent promise to quit was irrevocable. "You've done a good job here, but I can't have you using these *unofficial* channels of investigation. Are we clear?"

"I think so." Fallon understood the SAC didn't want him to stop using the Cleveland source, just stop telling him about it.

A voice that Fallon vaguely recognized called from the crowd. "Ralph, can I get an interview?" Fallon turned around and recognized one of the local TV reporters, Chad Nelson. He had interviewed Stamen on numerous occasions, and when citing an "anonymous federal source" in his reports, few agents had any doubts who was leaking the information. The SAC signaled Nelson that he would be with him in a moment.

Stamen said, "I'd better go do this. Anything you want me to say?"

"Just don't give up the artist's name. And I wouldn't say anything about the victims being Nazis. There's no way for us to confirm that right now. You don't want to provide any ammunition for a lawsuit. If you're going to say anything about the painting just say it's valuable; it was stolen, and the FBI, along with IFAR, recovered it."

"Do you think it's time we let everyone know who we're looking for?"

Fallon knew if pictures of Decker and his crew were put all over the news, even if they didn't leave Chicago, conversations on Darla's phone would be much more guarded. And since Fallon couldn't tell the SAC about an illegal wiretap, he had to find another way to discourage him. "We still don't have any hard evidence. Besides, our biggest advantage at this point is that Decker still believes that we don't know his true identity. If we spook him and he takes off, we'll never see those other paintings. It looks like they already have three, and Sivia thinks there may be two more that we can recover. If each one is as valuable as the Matisse, we'll be looking at an additional recovery of tens of millions of dollars, plus all the good press about us tracking down art looted by the Nazis. That will be a great story—if we can pull it off. We just have to be patient."

"That *sounds* good, but you said yourself that this crew won't be able to find their next victim without the artist's name. We have to come up with some plan of attack."

"There is something I think might work. These guys stay in motels. Give me ten agents to start canvassing motels with their photos. It shouldn't take more than a couple of days. Maybe we can catch them while they're laying low. If that doesn't work, then we can give it to the media."

"Okay, two days." Stamen straightened his tie and pulled at each of his shirt cuffs. He waved to Chad Nelson to come inside the yellow-tape perimeter. As Fallon started to leave, the SAC said, "Can I show the painting without giving the name?"

"If Sivia can identify the artist, I'm sure others can, too."

"Okay, but don't leave yet. You know how these reporters can ask more questions than one man can answer."

Chad Nelson came bounding up with his cameraman. "I appreciate this, Ralph." He pumped his thumb back over his shoulder. "Who's the good-looking female agent I saw you talking to?"

"Actually she's a civilian. She's with an organization out of New York. An expert on stolen art."

"Stolen art! Is that what these killings are about?"

"At this point we can't be positive." He looked at Fallon, who stood within earshot and then with failed humility said, "But as a result of our investigation, a priceless masterpiece has been recovered today."

"This is great. None of the other stations will have this. Do you think I could do an interview with your art expert, too?"

"Sure." Stamen sent one of the SWAT agents to get Sivia. Then, as the interview was about to begin, he gave Fallon a short, mandating glance that he should be signaled if he was about to say anything inappropriate.

Including Chad Nelson's lead-in, which contained his assurances that the viewer was indeed witnessing another Channel 7 exclusive, the SAC's interview took less than five minutes. Stamen, remembering Fallon's lawsuit warning, answered questions with the usual governmental caution, masterfully avoiding even the most marginal questions. He explained how the FBI believed that the recent string of murders of elderly people of German ancestry was being committed by the same group of individuals. As yet, their identities were unknown. Today, one of the men had been killed in a shootout with agents. His fingerprints would be sent off to Washington for possible identification, a process that should take less than a week. Additionally, a valuable stolen painting had been recovered with the assistance of the International Foundation for Art Research. And no, he didn't know if the painting was the motive behind the unusual murders.

Chad Nelson waved his microphone across his throat, signaling his cameraman to stop taping. "That was great, Ralph. I really appreciate it."

"You sure? I thought I was a little stiff."

"You were fine, trust me. Now, how about the girl?"

Stamen walked over to where Sivia was standing with Fallon. "Sivia, Chad would like to interview you also."

Fallon was surprised at how uncomfortable the invitation made her. She blushed slightly and her eyes widened. "Oh, no, I couldn't."

Stamen said, "I thought you said there were two more paintings waiting to be recovered. An appeal by you just might get someone to call in. You're perfect, you're not connected with the government so they don't have to worry about answering any uncomfortable immigration questions, and you can give them your civilian phone number to call in New York. In fact, tell them there is a substantial reward for the paintings, no questions asked."

"The foundation is nonprofit; we don't have money for anything like that."

"Don't worry about it, the Bureau will underwrite any reward, as long as we're in on the recovery."

As a final appeal, Sivia looked at Fallon. He shrugged. "It doesn't sound like a bad idea."

Although still reluctant, she said, "I guess it'll be alright."

Stamen walked her over to Nelson and introduced them. After lining her up for the camera, the reporter gave another lead-in, again announcing the exclusiveness of his broadcast. Then he said, "I'm here with Sivia Roth who is with the International Foundation for Art Research. It is a New York-based nonprofit organization that tracks and recovers stolen art. Miss Roth, can you tell us what led you to Chicago and the stolen painting you and the FBI recovered today?"

"As is the case with so many of the art objects we are able to recover, my office in New York received an anonymous call stating that an especially important painting, *Watering Place at Marly*, by the impressionist Alfred Sisley, was to be auctioned at a local gallery. We researched the piece and found it had been stolen in 1939. Further tracking of that particular work and others taken at the same time led us to Chicago."

"And as a result, you, along with the FBI, recovered a second painting today."

"That's right."

"Who is the artist of the painting you recovered today?"

"Because of the ongoing FBI investigation, I'm afraid I can't be any more specific."

"Can you tell us if it is valuable?"

"Yes, it is."

"Would you have any idea to its exact worth?"

"Again, I'm afraid I can't be any more specific."

"Do you expect to recover more paintings?"

"There may be others. If anyone has any information regarding the whereabouts of stolen paintings, they can call our office in New York City. Directory assistance can give you the number, and all calls are handled as confidential. We're a private agency. Again, it's the International Foundation for Art Research." She glanced at Stamen. "There is a sizable reward for information that leads to the recovery of any of these works."

"Miss Roth, let me play the devil's advocate here for a moment. You have offered a reward but if I have one of these priceless paintings in my possession, what is going to keep me from selling it on my own? It has to be worth more than the reward."

"As the auction in New York proved, selling a painting by a master is an extremely arduous task, even if it *isn't* stolen. The person who tried to sell the Sisley did everything possible to keep it secret, but IFAR found out about it nonetheless. Without exception, something like this attracts a crowd. The art world is a lot smaller than most people realize."

Recognizing a setup for a closing line, Nelson turned toward the camera. "Well, Sivia Roth, I'm sure art lovers everywhere today are glad that you're such an integral part of that small world, because through your efforts, the larger world, the one the rest of us belong to, has regained a masterpiece." Nelson let his trademark expression of humble sincerity settle across his features, holding it until his cameraman's light went out. "Sivia, that was great. You're a natural. If you get any calls that work out, I'd appreciate it if you'd let me know. The station loves when they can put that kind of stuff in their promos."

"I'd be glad to."

Stamen, who had been just off-camera, came over and said, "And just let me know if you need any reward money."

She extended her hand. "Thanks for everything, Ralph."

Fallon said to the SAC, "If you're all set, I'm going to take Sivia back to her hotel."

As soon as they were out of earshot, Nelson said, "Ralph, I appreciate the story."

"Do you think the network will pick it up?" Stamen asked. "Never hurts to have Bureau headquarters see on their own television sets what we're accomplishing out here."

"Every time one of my stories makes it to the network news, it— let's just say that I'd like nothing better than to see this on the network, but I think it's missing that one little bit of sex appeal."

"Like what?"

"Like the artist's name."

"Chad, I can't."

"Ralph, I don't know about you, but I don't plan on spending the rest of my career in Chicago."

As Fallon pulled away, Sivia said, "I'll add that to my list of growing complaints about working with you."

"Hey, you heard Chad Hairspray, you're a natural."

"Oh, then I stand corrected, that *was* a lot of fun."

"Hey, after seeing that, I'd call you if I knew where the paintings were."

"Yes, but you're not Decker."

"And Decker doesn't have the Matisse."

She didn't answer right away. Then she said, "Does that mean we're starting to win *now*?"

"I don't know. Usually when you get a break like this, you can feel things starting to fall into place. I don't sense that happening. We've broken the trail of clues and, by all rights, Decker should be through. But every time it looks like we're about to go one up on him, he comes at us from a different angle. We should have arrested him today, but again, he was a half a step ahead of us."

"We still have our advantage in Cleveland."

"That's the strange thing about this case, no one ever seems to gain an advantage. Someone should be winning, but so far we've spent all our time trying to take each other out. Something else is going on, something we're not seeing."

33

THE TRY FOR THE FOURTH PAINTING HAD BEEN A disaster. Harrison was dead and they had lost the only link to the next Guardian. Decker wondered if the hunt for the Reserve was over. At this point, it was extremely tempting to take the hundred thousand dollars along with the Toulouse-Lautrec and abandon Brunner.

The Toulouse-Lautrec—there was something about this painting—even more than the others. The scene was the interior of a music hall where a man and woman were about to start dancing. In the background, other patrons drank and danced, even some of the band were visible in the upper right-hand corner. He immediately recognized the artist. He remembered reading that, because of childhood injuries, Toulouse-Lautrec was little more than a crippled dwarf, who found some solace in the alcohol and prostitutes that were the lifeblood of the scenes he depicted. Although the colors used were dark and, to Decker's untrained eye, off a shade or two, he found them strangely comforting.

He got up and switched on the noon news. The lead story, as he knew it would be, was the shootout in which Harrison was killed. He wanted to see if anything would be reported that would tell him how the FBI had discovered Rochlitz's identity. Somehow they had anticipated him, and if he were to have any chance of recovering the Reserve, he needed to find out how it had been done.

The reporter at the scene was interviewing the head of the Chicago FBI, who announced that they would send the dead man's fingerprints to Washington to identify him. Decker knew once they discovered who Harrison was, it would not take long to figure out who the rest of them were.

Conditions were becoming more difficult. Although he didn't have the key to the next Guardian, he was going to have to find a way to get it. And he still didn't know what the number codes on the back of the frames meant. Maybe if they could be broken, he would not need the last three paintings to locate the Reserve. After failing to beat the FBI to Rochlitz, it was the only possibility he had left. Brunner was going to have to put more pressure on his contacts in Germany. As he reached for the phone, the same reporter started interviewing the woman he recognized as the one they had taken hostage briefly outside Josef Rathkolb's house. It had marked the beginning of his troubles with the FBI.

As the reporter gave her name, the camera moved in for a close-up. Decker did not remember her being that attractive. She seemed comfortable on camera and had an elegance about her, the kind that had its beginning generations before. Like the painting in front of him, her eyes held a deeper, unspoken meaning. He turned to the dancehall scene again. And then she told the reporter that she couldn't give the name of the artist of the recovered painting. His head snapped back toward the television. Decker knew she could have only one reason for ducking the question: they had figured out that the artist's name was the key. But how?

She now gave the name of her organization, International Foundation for Art Research and that there was a reward. Decker wrote down the name.

When she was asked about selling stolen paintings, she said it was difficult because the art world was a lot smaller than most people realized. As the reporter was signing off, the camera kept her in the shot. As Decker watched her, he finally understood why Toulouse-Lautrec appealed to him. Her face was so close, yet completely untouchable. It gave him an insight into the artist's agony, into his exemption from the mainstream. Although born into aristocracy, his disabilities forced him into a seamy world. The dancehall had no windows, no natural light. The dark colors that had confused Decker were simply distorted by the tawny glow of gaslight. The air was stale and suffocating. Nobody smiled; everyone was indifferent, and not a single person looked in the artist's direction. In retaliation, he trapped them all within the boundaries of his work, just as he was confined to the body that fate had disfigured. Life was full of prisons, the worst of which were inescapable because they had no doors or locks.

There was a knock at the door. Decker grabbed his automatic, then he heard Ron Slade's voice. "Deck, it's us." He stuck the gun under the pillow. When he opened the door he was surprised to see Del Brantley with him.

Decker said, "Ronnie, you made it. Good."

Slade glared at him. "What was that about, sending me and Jimmy out there like that while you stood off? You knew it was a setup, didn't you?"

"I thought it was a possibility. What other choice was there? And you're getting a hundred grand a piece for a couple of weeks' work. Tell me some place that you would make that without me. The down side is occasionally you get killed."

"Funny thing about getting killed, it's real hard spending that money afterward."

"Are you taking a walk?"

"Oh no, we've got too much invested in this." Slade glanced over at Brantley. "We want a bigger cut."

"Okay, you can split Jimmy's hundred K."

"No. A hundred and a half isn't going to do it. We've been kept in the dark about what we're looking for, and that's okay, because that's the way you want to do this. We don't need to know everything. You can run the show as long as we're taken care of. But the way you staked Jimmy out in the open like that . . ." He glanced over at Brantley to ensure they were still united in their defiance. "We want three apiece."

"Which means I only get four. And that's only if we find the end of the rainbow. Otherwise we're not getting another dime."

"Deck, I've been with you during enough scores to know that with all this fancy art laying around, you aren't going down for a flat million. This stuff is worth a lot more, and you're always looking to move up. That's why you went to that library. So either agree to this, or kill us, because three hundred is our absolute lowest number."

Anger hardened Decker's face. He sat down on the bed and considered the weapon under his pillow. But he knew he needed the two men. Finding the Reserve would be difficult with their help and probably impossible without it. Adjustments could always be made later. "Three hundred it is, but we've got to be the only ones standing at the end. That means you have to do what I say without any second-guessing, even if it kills you."

Slade and Brantley nodded at each other. "We're in."

Decker's pager went off. It showed Darla's number, which probably meant that Brunner had seen the news and was calling for a three-way hookup through her phone. "I've got to make this call." The two men left without another word.

Darla answered cautiously, "Hello?"

Decker started speaking German. "Brunner, you there?"

"Yes."

"I think it would be wise if we didn't discuss any specifics. I'm not so sure about this line anymore."

"I understand. I have just seen the news. You did not get the fourth item."

"I was directed to the wrong location. Our competitors have it."

"And I still do not have number three," Brunner said.

"If I were you, I'd worry more about us now not being able to find number five. Without the one today, we may be finished."

"That was your miscalculation. You will have to find a way to regain the advantage."

"I don't suppose you would have any suggestions how."

"Improvise. I believe that is what I am paying you for."

"You paid me to find someone and retrieve your property. You didn't say anything about running through a minefield blindfolded. The only way to get around today's loss is to get your overseas friends to break down the information on the back of the items we've already obtained and find the final location. Maybe if we know what those things mean, we can leapfrog to the end."

"You do not think they represent another phone number?"

"It looks like there's going to be twelve digits, so I doubt it."

"Okay, I will make a call and see if I can expedite an answer," Brunner said. "Did you get a name for this last customer?"

"The name I was given was Stefan Rochlitz."

"Okay. Now, what about the third item, I would like to have it tonight."

"You saw the news, you know how hot we are right now. I can't move."

"I am tiring of excuses. I want that piece tonight."

"Just call your friends. If they don't find that answer, none of this is going to matter." Decker hung up the phone before Brunner could say anything else.

Since his dueling society days, Rölf Brunner took a great deal of pride in his self-control. The first time he was slashed across the face and had to endure the wound's searing pain while he completed the courtesies of the ritual, he found control at such moments was as powerful a weapon as any sword. Anger should serve only its owner and never be allowed to warn its enemy. He would deal with Decker, but not before it was completely to his advantage.

But first he needed to call Berlin. Decker was right about decoding the numbers on the back of the frames. The solution to that puzzle would lead them to the Reserve. As he waited for the connection to be completed, Brunner felt a deep admiration for the men of the Third Reich. Hans Trauchmann had devised a way for him to track down the Reserve after fifty years, even providing the name and telephone of a man like Arnulf Mueller to handle any problems that arose. And Mueller, although he was in his eighties, had responded with energy and an amazing ability to accomplish the seemingly impossible. From the contacts in Cleveland who got Decker out of jail, to the Enigma translation, to breaking the Guardian code. And he was equally in awe of Rathkolb. Although finding the Reserve had become a nightmare, *der Kurator*'s meticulous planning would certainly keep it from falling into the wrong hands. "*Hallo.*"

"Arnulf, it is Rölf. How are you?"

"I am good. Where have you been, I have been trying to contact you, but they said you checked out. And you told me not to call that Cleveland number unless it was absolutely necessary."

"The project I am working on is in dire circumstances. It is not advisable for me to stay in one location too long. I hope you were trying to call me about the second code."

"Yes, I believe you will be pleased. We have figured out what the twelve numbers are. When you have all twelve digits, we think you'll have the longitude and latitude of the location you are seeking."

"Are you sure?"

"Fairly positive. Precise locations given in longitude and latitudes are twelve digits, unless the longitude is over ninety-nine degrees. But for the part of the world you are in, there would be only twelve. The latitude is traditionally given first. The north latitude for Chicago is forty-two degrees. The number on the back of the first frame was forty-two. To know for sure, the fourth number, if the location you are seeking is in your part of the United States, would have to be in the eighties or nineties. Do you have the fourth number yet?"

Brunner sighed audibly. "No, we don't. The opposition has beaten us to it and is keeping it secret. Would we need all the numbers to pinpoint the site?"

"Twelve digits will bring you within a hundred feet."

"What we are looking for will probably be stored in some type of building."

"Then a hundred feet should pinpoint it exactly. But if you are missing any of the coordinates, the likelihood of success decreases exponentially. I am afraid without the fourth set, it would be impossible. Along the forty-second parallel, the location could be anywhere from Chicago to southern Russia."

"Hopefully we will be able to obtain all of them. In the meantime, is there something we could be doing to identify the other Guardians? Without the fourth item, we cannot find the fifth or sixth. Do you think there could be any relationship between these men that might help us determine who the remaining people are?"

"Do you have any additional names?"

"The fourth one is named Stefan Rochlitz."

"I will make some calls. Give me your new number."

After he hung up, Brunner's thoughts returned to Decker. Apparently, the American, driven by greed, was developing his own plan. As Brunner had feared all along, Decker wanted to take possession of the Reserve. And the only way that could happen was for Brunner to die. He did not find that a very appealing option for Germany, or himself.

Decker had too much freedom, too many options. One way to stop that was to give him an unsolvable problem, something which would make the immediacy of the million dollars much more appealing than traveling the long, difficult road necessary to cash in on the Reserve. He called directory assistance in New York City and asked for the number for the police. When asked which precinct, he said whoever would handle murders in Manhattan. After being connected to a homicide detective, he struggled to minimize his accent and said, "The man who killed Jonathan Geist is Kurt Decker. He lives in Cleveland and you can find him at this telephone number."

After reciting Darla's phone number back to Brunner, the detective asked, "Could I have your name, sir?" Brunner hung up.

Although Decker and his gang might eventually be linked to all the murders, the evidence against them right now was mostly circumstantial. But the matchbook with his thumbprint planted on Geist's body would supply the New York City police with irrefutable proof of the American's involvement in that killing. So the police would now be actively hunting for Decker on a murder charge.

Additionally, the police would be watching Darla to determine his whereabouts, greatly reducing her ability to help him. During their three-way phone calls, it was obvious to Brunner how little regard Decker had for her, but she was an indispensable tool for him. Limiting her assistance would also limit Decker's options.

Brunner went to the closet and took out the few items of clothing he had unpacked and started putting them back in his suitcase. It was time to move again.

34

IT WAS ALMOST 6 P.M. BY THE TIME FALLON HAD FIN-
ished assigning search patterns to the ten agents who were to contact
motels looking for Decker and his crew. Zjorn was sent to man an
auxiliary radio in the major case room where he could keep track of
everyone's progress. Next to Fallon's desk sat the Matisse, still
wrapped in brown paper. He and Sivia had only glanced at it before
prepping Rochlitz's wife for the incoming call from Darla Kincade.

As Fallon started filling out the inventory sheets that accompany
all evidence, he uncovered the painting. It was staggering that an
amalgam of a few pennies' worth of canvas and oil paint created seventy years earlier could now be worth millions of dollars. He took a
moment to study it and, if for no other reason than its unique colors,
found it attractive. But he suspected that his decision was based
largely on Matisse's reputation rather than any innate sense of art appreciation.

Once the paperwork was completed, Fallon needed to safely store
the painting. Evidence that had a high monetary value was kept in
the SAC's safe, which was actually a small room with a combination
lock door. The secretary who was normally in charge of securing such
evidence had left at five and told Fallon she would leave the combination dialed into the door. A short spin was all that would be necessary to gain entrance. Every morning she unlocked it and then left the
dial in that position to expedite her routine trips in and out during
the day.

Fallon entered the room and switched on the light. Deciding to leave the painting on an empty shelf, he grabbed it with both hands and noticed that the brown paper had come unfolded. For the first time, he noticed the number on the back of the frame—88. Four perfect circles, cut into the wood with some sort of numbering instrument. He unwrapped the painting completely and searched for any other numbers, but there were none.

On the phone call tape that Marvin Risch had translated, Decker said something about another code. Fallon went back to his desk and took the transcript out of his briefcase. Scanning it, he found where Decker asked about the "other code" and gave the German the number 26. Was the 88 part of another code?

The phone rang. "Taz!" It was Sivia in a state of controlled panic.

"What's the matter?"

"Have you seen the six o'clock news?"

"No."

"Chad Nelson announced that the painting was by Matisse!"

"How did he know?"

"All he said was that it came from an undisclosed source."

"Since you, me, and Stamen are the only ones who knew it was Matisse, it doesn't take a lot of imagination to come up with a suspect." Even though the evidence was substantial, Fallon couldn't conceive of any career need that would cause Stamen to leak information so critical to the investigation. But the need to be promoted was one Fallon had never understood.

"What are we going to do?" she asked.

"There's only one thing we can do, wait for the midnight call from Cleveland. I checked with Jack Debbin again. He said there weren't any outgoing calls from Darla to Chicago, but we know from the tape that Decker is still calling her. But even if she knows where he is, he probably doesn't let her call him. It's probably a precaution they use whether they're suspicious or not. But I've found something else." He explained about the number on the back of the frame, and then reminded her about Decker's taped reference to another frame number that might be part of a second code. "Did Risch say anything to you about numbering the frames he makes? Maybe it's a cataloging system."

"He didn't say anything to me. Framemakers don't normally do anything like that."

There was a pause and then Sivia said, "That frame you found in Rathkolb's basement, the one that led us to Risch, was there a number on it?"

"No, that's right. So the numbers couldn't have been stamped into the frame by Risch. Rathkolb had to put them there."

"They must be part of the second code Decker was talking about. Remember, Doc predicted each of these paintings might be a clue to the Reserve's location."

"If that's true, then even if they get all the others, they'll still be missing part of the answer," Fallon said. "Unfortunately, there are two more people out there who could die. Decker might be on his way to the next one right now, and we have to wait until midnight."

"There is a way we can cut some of the delay out of it," Sivia said.

"How?"

"You're not going to like it."

"There's a surprise."

"I can have my friend in Cleveland call us directly at Marvin's. That way we can get it translated immediately."

Fallon said, "You want him to be one step closer to what we're doing illegally? I think he is already in possession of more evidence than they'll need to convict us."

"We haven't had any trouble yet."

"*Yet* can be a mighty big word. It's the reason the statute of limitations is five years in federal cases."

"Pick me up at eleven-thirty. We can argue about it then."

Brunner had checked into the Crown Hotel located in the transient south end of Chicago's Loop. His room was about three hundred dollars less a night than the other hotels he had been staying at, but no one would think to look for him there. Not only was his room rundown, but his fellow guests were equally distasteful. The old building's walls were unpainted, thin and uninsulated. Conversations, whether between two people or a one-sided delusional soliloquy, were carried out with equal combat. Fortunately the exact words, distorted by the small amount of building material that did exist, were unintelligible. Only their rage was apparent to the German. It seemed to be a necessity of the American lexicon.

Brunner switched on the television to offset the room's lonely squalor. On the back of the set was a steel eyebolt through which ran a thick, silvery, case-hardened chain. At the other end, it was threaded through another eyebolt that had been cemented into the floor. A few inches away were the remains of a smaller bolt, the loop of which had been snapped off. *Americans.*

The six o'clock news was in progress. Brunner turned up the volume carefully, making it just loud enough to drown out the last of his neighbors. He started to unpack when he heard Chad Nelson's voice. It was part of an interview Brunner had seen during the noon broadcast. A woman from New York was talking about the painting Decker had failed to recover. She carefully explained that, because of the FBI's ongoing investigation, she couldn't disclose the identity of the artist. Brunner started to change the channel when Nelson came on live and said that despite the woman's refusal to answer his question, he had learned exclusively the painting was by Matisse. Brunner hurried to the phone and paged Decker. Then he dialed Darla's number.

When she answered, he asked, "Is he there?"

"I'm here," Decker said in German.

"Did you see it?"

"See what?"

"The news. The six o'clock news. They said who the artist was—it's Matisse."

Decker said, "Earlier the girl said they couldn't give out that information. Why would they do it now?"

"The reporter said the information came from an 'undisclosed source.' "

"Why would the FBI be that careless? This could be another setup."

"One of the reasons Germany lost the Second World War was because Hitler refused to believe that the Allies would do anything as obvious as invade Normandy."

"You may be right, but let's not discuss any specifics on this line, just in case," said Decker.

"So now you will be able to go after number five in the morning."

"I'm not waiting. Last time it cost me one of my men. As soon as I break down the number, I'm going. In the meantime, you better get ahold of your overseas friends and come up with the key to all this." Decker sensed something in Brunner's silence. "Or have you already heard something from them?"

Brunner thought about how the Reserve's longitude and latitude were inscribed on the back of the six frames. "No," he lied. "I was just about to call them again. Call me when you have completed the fifth leg, maybe I will have something by then."

Emil Ziegland's phone rang. His real name was Hals Lepter, a former SS captain assigned to Bergen-Belsen, the first concentration camp liberated by the Allies in 1945. The British troops found 10,000 un-buried bodies, along with 40,000 starving and dying prisoners. Lepter had fled Germany just days ahead of the Brits. "*Hallo?*"

"This is Detective Christina Grohmann. I'm an investigator with the Winter Haven, Florida, Police Department. I'm sorry to be calling so late, but this is somewhat of an emergency. How are you tonight?"

"Is there a problem, Officer?"

35

IT WAS AFTER 11 P.M. WHEN FALLON WALKED INTO the major-case room. Zjorn was listening on the phone, taking notes. As soon as he hung up, he ripped the page off the pad. "That was Melrose Park. They're at a fresh homicide. Victim's name is," Zjorn glanced at the sheet, "Emil Ziegland. A eighty-one-year-old German male. One shot between the running lights." Zjorn handed him the note. "Said they thought it sounded like the other killings on the news and wanted to notify us."

"Anyone get a plate?"

"Of course not. You going out there?"

"I'm working on something else. How are you doing with the motels?"

"They're working their way through the list but nothing yet." Zjorn pointed to a large freestanding blackboard. "Those are the ones we've contacted. Without counting them, I'd guess seventy to eighty so far."

"Just tell them to be careful. If Decker just hit, he's probably changing his location again. We don't want any of our people wandering into him or his crew."

"And what is the 'something else' you're working on?"

"Doc, you're a loyal friend, but you're already carrying around more of this than you should be. The best way for me to show my appreciation is by not telling you."

*   *   *

"Darla, does Karen downstairs have three-way calling?"

"Yes she does."

"I'll call you there in five minutes."

"Is everything okay?"

"Just go."

Because of the late hour, Darla was already wearing a long T-shirt that served as her nightgown. She went into the bedroom and put on a pair of jeans, then to the closet to find a blouse. One of Decker's flannel shirts hung on a hook. She slipped into its warmth, hoping to smell some trace of him but then remembered having washed it. On the top of his dresser was a bottle of cologne she had given him for his last birthday. He rarely wore it, usually only when they went out. She dabbed a little on the shirt with a single fingertip and then headed to Karen Wilson's apartment.

When the phone rang, Darla answered, "Is anything wrong, Kurt?"

After killing Emil Ziegland and obtaining the fifth painting from him, Decker wasted no time in decoding the telephone number of the sixth, and last, Guardian. As suspicious as he had been about being set up with the identity of Matisse as the fourth artist, the FBI was nowhere around when he went to Ziegland's house. Now that he was a step ahead of them, he realized he would be foolish to wait to get the last painting. Any delay would only give the FBI a chance to catch up. "I need you to make one more call and I was afraid to give the number on your phone. Write this down, then call and give them your Winter Haven routine. This is the last one, baby."

She took down the number and then reconnected Decker into a conference call. "Kurt, hold on while I dial."

Once the call went through, there was a double tone, and then a recorded message announced that the number had been changed.

Decker swore. "This guy must have gotten hinky from all the news coverage about these old krauts being murdered. There's nothing we can do now. Unless my employer gets lucky. You'd better get back to your apartment in case he calls."

Still angered, Decker slammed down the phone. After a few moments, he dialed the operator. "May I help you?"

"Yes, ma'am. A friend of mine gave me this number and when I call it, I get a message that it's been changed. Could you give me the new number?"

"What is the number, please?" Decker read it to her, and after a few moments she said, "I'm sorry, sir, at the subscriber's request, the new number is unlisted."

"What name do you show?" Decker asked.

"I'm sorry, I'm not allowed to give out that information." He slammed down the phone again.

Propped up against the headboard of the second bed in his room were the last two paintings. Unbelievably, the latest one was a Renoir. The trail of clues was getting more difficult to resist. Decker suspected this, like everything else in Rathkolb's plan, was intentional: the more difficult the search became, the larger its promise grew. He started pacing back and forth in front of them. Maybe this was going to be his only payoff. That wasn't all bad, a Toulouse-Lautrec and a Renoir. They must be worth a fortune. In the terms of his life, several fortunes.

Suddenly, a sense of powerlessness closed around him. Who was he kidding? He couldn't sell the paintings. Even if he did find someone willing to take them, he'd be lucky to get a penny on the dollar. To sell something as one-of-a-kind as a looted masterpiece, you had to know serious private collectors, people with a great deal of money and a desire for art so strong that they were willing to keep the acquired work secret. Clearly not the kind of people that Decker knew.

He sat down on the same bed as the paintings and lit a cigarette. Right now, they were his. He was the collector. The Renoir's colors were brilliant, especially the blues from which the light seemed to pour, as if the oil in the paint was a source of energy. It depicted an attractive young woman, leaning on her elbow. Her face, although beautiful, was a study in indifference. Her mouth held a hint of disdain for what she was being put through; there were more important things in her life.

Her detachment reminded Decker of Sivia Roth, who also appeared as though she were being kept from what she really wanted to be doing, her beauty incidental to her purpose. He wondered if she was aware of the Reserve's existence. Or was she just looking for a few paintings?

Absentmindedly, he sat staring at the paintings, tapping his ashes on the floor. He had only one option. Taking a last drag on his cigarette, he opened the door and flicked it into the motel's courtyard.

He paged Brunner to Darla's number, waited a few minutes, and then dialed it himself.

"Did you get the fifth item?" Brunner asked.

"Yes, but there's a problem."

"Who is the artist?"

"Did you hear what I said?"

"You do not call me unless there is a problem. Who is the artist?"

Decker felt the anger spread through him like a brushfire. But now was not the time, he reminded himself. In a flat, unemotional tone, he said, "Renoir."

"Excellent," Brunner said. "Now what is the problem?"

"I tried to call the sixth customer but his number has been changed, and it's unlisted."

"What are you going to do?"

"I'm afraid that was my question to you. I've gone as far as I can."

"Give me the fifth customer's name, the one you just met with."

"Why do you need that?"

"The names are suddenly very important. When you paged me, I was finishing an overseas call. There has been an interesting development. The first two Guardians—Schwend and Steinmel, whose real name is Volkner, were in the same SS unit. They are checking on the others now. Possibly, if they are all connected, they may be able to come up with the last one by the process of elimination."

"Emil Ziegland," Decker said.

"And the number on the back?"

"I don't think it's wise to discuss that on this phone." Then in English, he said, "Darla, are you there?"

"Yes, Kurt."

"Where I last talked to you, I'll call there in five minutes." Then to Brunner, he said in German, "Hang up. I'm going to page you to a different number."

As soon as Karen Wilson let Darla into her apartment, the phone rang. It was Brunner. There was a second ring on the line and she connected Decker. "Are you there?" he asked the German.

"Yes."

"The number on the back is twenty-nine. But we're missing the fourth and sixth clues. I don't know how important they are, but if your people can figure out the code, maybe we won't need every one of them."

"I have a feeling that we will," Brunner said. "If you can get number four, we will have five of the six pieces. Then maybe the last one will fall into place."

"Get number four! It's gone, unless you think I could shoot my way in and out of the federal building and kill any FBI agents who get in my way."

"My paying you one million dollars makes that your problem. We do not have any idea where number six is, but we do know the exact location of number four. Do whatever you have to do."

"You must be crazy. Until you get that code broken, we won't know if the fourth one means anything," said Decker.

"I want you to get number four."

Decker's temper started to flare again, but something was wrong. He replayed the last part of the conversation in his head. Brunner's insistence that he try and get the Matisse away from the FBI didn't make any sense, especially since they didn't know if it would be significant to the location of the Reserve. Unless . . . "You know something you haven't told me. They've broken the code, haven't they?"

It was now apparent that Decker was not going to try to retrieve the Matisse from the FBI unless he was told why the numbers on the back of its frame were one of the most critical clues. And it didn't matter what Decker knew at this point, or if a few paintings were lost, because Brunner's alternate plan was now in place. "Yes, they have."

"Why were you keeping that from me?"

"Your reluctance to bring me the paintings in your possession does not exactly encourage trust. I was going to trade the key to the code for them."

"Then why are you telling me?"

"Because I could see that there was no way to convince you to get the fourth frame number without telling you. I just have to trust that when the time comes you will turn over all the paintings."

"You're right. Without a very good reason, I wouldn't even think about going after the Matisse," Decker said. "What is the key?"

"Do you know anything about longitude and latitude?"

"The basic stuff, the world's divided into degrees. Parallels are north and south; meridians, east and west."

"That is right. But the important thing is that any precise location in this part of the world is expressed in twelve digits."

"Six paintings, two numbers apiece, twelve digits," Decker said.

"Exactly, and the area that we are in, the north latitude, which is always listed first, is forty-two degrees."

"The number on the Cranach."

"Yes, and that means the fourth set of numbers is the western longitude, without which, the Reserve could be anywhere in the world along the forty-second parallel. Now you can see why getting the Matisse is so necessary. Or at a minimum, the numbers on the back of its frame."

"Even if I knew exactly where the FBI stored the painting, the building has armed guards and agents in their offices twenty-four hours a day. There's no way."

"Hitler sent your father to Hungary with a few men to kidnap the head of the country and bring him back to Germany. That, too, was an impossible mission, until your father showed up back in Germany, wounded, with the man's son. But as you are always so quick to point out, you are not your father."

36

IT WAS ALMOST MIDNIGHT WHEN THE PHONE IN Marvin Risch's apartment rang. He handed it to Sivia. She turned on her recorder and said, "Go ahead." Fifteen minutes later she took the suction cup microphone off the receiver and said to the caller, "We're at a crucial point with this. Would it be possible to get this service tomorrow morning? . . . Can I get a call here by noon? . . . I appreciate it." She hung up. "He's going to make an entry tomorrow morning sometime after nine, whenever the building traffic quiets down. If it's alright, Marvin, he'll call us here around noon."

Risch said, "You are always welcome."

She held up the recorder. "It's almost all in German." She handed it to Risch. "Can you translate it as it plays? Time is very important."

"Certainly. If you will tell me what you are looking for, I will skip over everything else."

Fallon said, "They have just killed a man named Emil Ziegland. They probably took a painting from him. If so, they will use the name of that artist to decode a ten-digit number which will be a telephone number, probably in the Chicago area. We are interested in that number or the subscriber's name."

"So you can stop them," Risch said.

"Hopefully. And of course, we're interested in any other information that might lead to their whereabouts."

Risch smiled at Sivia. "I understand. And afterward I will write out a full translation."

"That would be great." She took a sip of the coffee Risch had made for them.

For a few seconds, Risch fumbled with the recorder, trying to recall how to rewind it. Fallon reached over and pushed the button. "Thank you," the old man said. "Electronics I'm not so good at." Once it was rewound, Risch pushed the play button with twice as much force as was needed to start it. Again a computerized voice reported the date and phone number intercepted. After a snatch of conversation, Risch said, "They discuss that the FBI recovered the latest painting, and because of that, how finding the next one will be impossible. Is that the kind of information you're interested in?"

"Yes it is, Marvin," Sivia replied.

He played some more. "They are now arguing about getting someone overseas to break a code that's on the back of the items already recovered. Evidently, they feel it is the key to, what they call the 'final location.' And if they can find the answer, maybe they can 'leapfrog to the end.' "

Fallon asked, "They've talked about some numbers stamped onto the back of the frames you made. We found some on the Matisse. Was that your work?"

"No. What color was that frame?"

"A dark, burnt red. Why, do you think that was important?"

"I don't know. Bach, or whatever his name was, had me paint each one a different color. That must have had some purpose."

"I'm sure you're right, but for now let's see if there is anything else on the tape."

"Sorry, each day I seem to get more easily distracted. I promise, only conversation about phone numbers, names, and locations." He turned the recorder back on. "They feel that the final code has twelve digits and for that reason could not be a phone number." He listened a while longer and said, "I think this is a later call. They saw the news and now know the artist is Matisse, and the one man says as soon as he figures out the number he's going to get the next painting. They are being very guarded in what they say, very suspicious of the phone. Then there's a call in English." Risch turned up the volume and the three of them listened as Darla Kincade made her pretext call to Emil Ziegland. The old man accepted her warm assurances that everything was alright, never suspecting that she was asking for his address so he could be murdered.

Fallon watched as Risch resumed his work on the next conversation and was surprised that the elderly antique dealer didn't seem to have any reservations about helping break the law. Maybe it was the guilt from surviving the extermination camp. Or more than likely, he had come under the spell Sivia seemed to cast over every man she encountered. Maybe it was a bond that only Jews understood. Whatever it was, Risch undertook his part in the felony with as little concern as if he were dusting his antiques.

Letting the machine run while he spoke, Risch said, "The fifth painting, it's a Renoir . . . good news, the phone of the sixth man has been changed to an unlisted number. They say they now have no way to find him. Then the American gives the other man the name Emil Ziegland. This is important because someone has matched up the first two men who were murdered as members of the same SS unit during the war. The German says his people are going to see if they can't determine the sixth name through the process of elimination." Then, as the tape ended, Risch said, "Bad news. They were talking about the number on the back of a painting and decided to finish the call on another phone."

"Did they give the other number where that call was to be made?" Sivia asked, indicating to Fallon that she would not hesitate to have a tap placed on that line, also.

"No, I'm sorry, they didn't," Risch said.

Sivia stood up and extended her hand to Risch. "Marvin, we've kept you up far too late. Thanks for all your help."

He cradled her hand in both of his and held it while he spoke. "Anytime. You're a light in the darkness of my December. I'll have the entire translation for you by the time you come tomorrow afternoon."

When Sivia and Fallon were back in the car, she asked, "The way they switched phones worries me. Do you think they know we're recording them?"

"The organized crime squad once had a bug in a suspect's car. Every time he got in it, the first thing he said was 'I know you cops are listening.' He had no idea there was a wire. It's just criminal para-

noia. Because we beat him to the Matisse, Decker is being cautious
about what he says on Darla's phone. Logically, it *is* the only way
we could have gotten to Rochlitz before him. But the fact that he's
still using that phone to handle routine communication means he
isn't sure. But for anything specific that might tip us off to where
they are, or the location of the Reserve, they're going to use a different line."

"So what can we do now?"

"It looks like a stalemate. Whatever that code is, they're missing
two clues and we're missing four."

"If they figure out the key to the twelve-digit code, will four be
enough?"

"Whoever laid out this maze was pretty thorough. I'd be surprised
if anyone will find the Reserve without all six pieces. Anyway, tomorrow we'll unleash the media and see if the good citizens of Chicago
can help us find these guys."

"So all we can do is wait."

"I don't know about you, but I haven't had any sleep in forty
hours. I'm going to do my waiting in bed."

Fallon's Bureau car pulled up in front of the Blackthorn Hotel.
The parking valet came out and opened Sivia's door. She said, "Feel
like a beer?"

Fallon looked at his watch. "Is the bar still open?"

"That's the nice thing about a mini-bar, it never closes."

As they rode up the elevator in silence, Fallon, for the first time
since they met, felt alone with her. Her perfume reached over and
pulled at him. She glanced over and smiled. Her eyes were without
their usual weighty knots of a hidden agenda. When she took her
room key out of her purse, he took it from her hand. As he did so, he
moved against her. She didn't move away.

In the room, Fallon took off his jacket and threw it across a chair.
He unclipped his holster and slipped his weapon underneath the
coat. Sivia said, "Imported or domestic?"

"Whichever's closest."

After taking out a beer, she poured herself a glass of wine. She
came over to the couch, handed him his drink, and sat down. He
opened the can and touched it to the lip of her glass. "My father,"

he said. It was not a question or the beginning of a statement, but rather like an introduction to a lecture. The two words were being thrown out to see if an audience existed.

"Yes," she said. "I'd like to know about him."

"Why?"

"Because our parents have a lot to do with who we are."

"And who do you think I am?"

"I'm not sure. On the one hand, you refuse to be manipulated by anyone, but on the other, your work manipulates you. Take the Reserve—you're actually breaking the law, risking your job and possibly your freedom. The way you avoid talking about your father, I figure he has something to do with what drives you to those extremes."

"It sounds like you already have me figured out. In fact, I think you've known where my buttons have been for a while. Like when you told me about the tap in Cleveland—you did that because you knew I couldn't walk away, at least not for very long."

"I'm sorry, but I didn't see any other way. You said it yourself, we weren't going to find them without it."

Fallon took a sip of beer and set the can down on the coffee table in front of him. "I told you my mother died when I was eleven. She was a warm and kind person, but *he* treated her like a lowly employee. Sometimes I still wonder why she married him. Maybe because she was born with a severe stutter. At times it became so bad that the contracting of the speech muscles would cause her face to contort into these painful grimaces. It made her extremely shy. Maybe she married him because she thought she couldn't do any better. I don't know. But the bottom line was that he felt absolutely no responsibility to the family other than to bring home a paycheck. Everything else, and I mean everything, was left for my mother to do. After she died, it was all passed on to me."

"At eleven years old?"

"Oh yeah. The shopping, the cooking, laundry, everything."

"That's an awful lot to ask of a child. What happened when you did something wrong?"

"He'd just glare at me. That was enough. When you're that young, all you really want is your parent's approval. And the funny thing was, no matter how badly you were treated, you assumed it was normal. You have no other reference point, you think this is the way it must be everywhere."

"Did he ever hit you?"

"I wish he would have. At least it would have meant that he knew I was around. He completely ignored me. It wasn't unusual for him to go a week without speaking to me. And when he did, it would be only to ask if I'd done something like pay the electric bill."

"I can't believe after your mother died, he wouldn't be more of a father, especially to a son."

Fallon's eyes were unfocused with memory and anger. "He wouldn't even hand me the money. He'd come home on Friday night to that little basement apartment and put enough cash to pay the bills in an old pair of work boots in his closet. The less he had to do with me the better. You said I don't control emotions, I extinguish them. I made myself that way around him; I wanted to deprive him of my having any emotions, to show him I could be as cold as him, that I had no feelings for him, and there was nothing he could do to provoke them in me. It was the only way I had to get even."

"What about other things, like school?"

"For the first couple of years, I did okay. It was my only link with being normal. Besides, I was eleven years old. I needed to get his approval anyway I could. I thought if I did well, maybe I'd get some recognition from him. Once, when I had gotten almost all *A*'s, I made him his breakfast and put my report card next to his coffee with a pen so he could sign it and see how proud he should be of me. After he left for work without saying a word, I looked at it. He hadn't signed it. I never showed it to him again. I just forged his signature. I think the teacher knew, too. After a while, I think everybody knew."

"Well, at least you did well in school. A lot of people would have used it as an excuse not to do anything."

"In time that broke down, too. In high school, when all the other kids were playing sports, dating, hanging out, I'd go home to do the laundry and wash the floor. Needless to say, the rage started building up. When I finally decided I had enough, I went out for football. At first I thought it was great, I was actually being encouraged to hit people. And that felt so good. I guess a little too good. I didn't make it halfway through the season before I was thrown off the team for fighting. And if the players on the other team wouldn't fight me, I'd start on my own. A couple of weeks later I was arrested in a stolen car."

"What'd your father do?"

Fallon laughed. "There was a detective there, Jack Rymill. He knew my mother in high school. We ran into him once and she told me how he had always stuck up for her when the other kids teased her about her stutter. After I was brought into the station, he came into my cell and told me that he called my father and told him if he came and got me, I wouldn't be charged. My father told him he wasn't coming. Jack talked to me for an hour, which in cop time is about a year. He said he had seen too many other people on the same path, and there was only two places I could wind up—dead or in prison."

"Did that scare you?"

"I guess it did, because I started opening up to him about my father and what it was like living with him. That was something I never told anybody. There was something about Jack, he had a way of seeing inside of people, and knew what was really bothering them. Right then, I felt closer to him than anyone since my mother died. At one point, he put his hand on my shoulder and it felt like everything that was wrong was being drawn out through his hand. I guess that's how much I must have really been in need of any adult male connection. Some nights when I'm unable to block all this out, I can still feel that touch."

"Did he let you go then?"

"Couldn't. Or at least that's what he told me. I think he knew if he just cut me loose, I'd be back with bigger problems. He left me in the cell for a couple of hours before he came back and got me out. I was scared to death it was to turn me over to my father. Right then I decided if it was, I was never going back to that apartment. Instead Jack took me to a restaurant for this huge breakfast. It was so big I couldn't finish it. Then he asked me if I wanted a way out. I asked him if he meant the car. He said he was talking about everything. I said, sure. Then he told me he thought my only shot was the marines. I laughed, *the marines*. But he just kept drinking his coffee while I thought about it. He knew I'd realize I had no choice. He had already arranged everything. He had a lot of friends. One of them was the Marine Corps recruiter. Together they spoke to a judge, and that afternoon I was on a bus to Parris Island." Fallon laughed. "It took a while, but eventually those drill instructors beat some sense into me. Later he told me he had destroyed all the paperwork from the arrest. He never made a big deal out of it but I suspect he did it at some risk to his job."

"What about your father?"

"I never saw him again. It's funny, when you're in boot camp, the DI's make you write home and tell your family what a great time you're having. I didn't have anyone to write to, but that was not acceptable to the marines, so I started writing to Jack. In his first letter, he said he had gone to tell my father I was in the Marine Corps. My father showed his trademark gift for language by closing the door in his face. I think from that moment on, Jack realized he had no choice but to become my surrogate father."

"Do you still talk to him?"

"He died three years ago January."

"I'm sorry, Taz."

"I guess he's the reason I became an agent. When I graduated, he drove all the way to Quantico to see me get my credentials. He tried not to show it, but I think he was really proud. I don't know, maybe I'm imagining that, trying to find something to fill in some of the holes."

"If he went all the way down there, I'm sure he did feel some special connection to you."

"That night we went out to dinner, and I thanked him. I told him everything I had I owed to him. It was hard to do because it was very emotional, and as you've seen, those moments don't come easy to me. But now that's he's gone, I'm glad I did."

"I'll bet he was touched."

"I suppose he was, but he was always working me, trying to get me to let go of things. He told me there was a way I could pay him back. He said a policeman learns to be distrustful quick enough, but my father had already caused too much of that in me. What I needed was to learn to trust people. If I didn't, I was never going to be truly happy. I promised him I'd try." Fallon had been staring off into the distance of time past as he spoke. He picked up his beer and took a long drink. "So there's my relationship with my father. And as far as my need, as you put it, 'to right every wrong'—well, I guess I'm still trying to get his attention."

"And what about your promise to Jack to trust people?"

"People, especially the ones that come with this job, don't make it easy."

"Like me?"

He touched his fingertips to her face. "I wouldn't be telling you this if I didn't want to trust you."

She leaned over and kissed him. This time he kissed her back. She stood up, undid three buttons, and let her dress drop to the floor.

At a little after 3 A.M., Darla Kincade's phone rang. All she could manage was, " 'Lo." A few seconds of silence were followed by an older man's voice with a heavy German accent, "Ist he dort?"

"What? Who is this?"

There was more silence. Then, "Ist he dare?"

Finally Darla understood the question. "Is who here?" There was no response. Now wide awake, she sat up. "Are you looking for the German gentleman?"

"Ya."

"He's not here."

"Haben hist Telefonnummer?"

"I'm sorry, you're going to have to repeat that."

"Hist Telefon."

"His telephone number?"

"Ya."

"No, I don't have it, but I can get him a message." Again, there was silence. "He's working with my friend. If it's something important, I can let him know."

"Call your freund."

"Okay, hold on." She paged Decker.

Less than a minute later, he rang in. "Did you just beep me?"

"I got this creepy German guy on the phone. I think he's looking for your employer."

"Hook us up." Decker heard the line click in. "Hello?"

"Sprechen Sie deutsch?"

"*Jawohl.*"

"Are you Herr Decker?"

"Yes."

"I am looking for an acquaintance of mine. I tried the last place he was staying, but he is no longer there. He also gave me your number."

Decker remembered Brunner saying that he had given his contact Darla's number in case of an emergency. Maybe he had found out something about the last Guardian. If he had, it would be to Decker's advantage to have sole possession of the information. "He's unreachable until morning. You can leave a message with me."

The voice hesitated again. "Do you know what he wanted us to find for him?"

"The last Guardian."

"If you know that, I'm sure it is alright if I leave this information with you. The name you are looking for may be Conrad Linge. The last address we had for him was Seventeen Central Road, Deer Park, Illinois."

"I'll make sure he gets this."

Without another word, the caller hung up.

Darla asked, "Kurt, you still there?"

"I'll call you later." He pressed the button disconnecting the line and then dialed the room next to his. "Del, get Slade, we're going to work."

37

CONRAD LINGE'S HOUSE WAS LOCATED ON A BACK road, a half mile from his nearest neighbor. Less than a hundred yards away, cloaked by the rural night, sat Kurt Decker. He was still thinking about the call he had received an hour before. There was something about it that didn't seem quite right. It was almost too easy. The picture of Harrison being blown off the porch flashed through his head. As he had with the Matisse news leak, he wondered if the FBI had manufactured this call to set him up out here in the boonies. It was a perfect location for an ambush. But there was no way they could have known about the sixth Guardian. Still, he couldn't be positive, so he decided to be cautious. "Okay, Ronnie, you wanted the big money. Here's where you earn it."

"Why do you say that? This looks like it couldn't be any easier."

"That's exactly what's bothering me." Decker had seen Slade under prison conditions, a place where all masks were eventually lowered, and knew how to motivate him. "I'm probably being a little paranoid, but this could be a setup. So if you want to pass, we can pull out."

"And do what, hustle for nickels and dimes until they lock us up again? No thanks. You want me to go to the door? I don't care, I'll go."

"Del and I will wait in the car until you're inside." Decker realized that if Linge was, in fact, the last Guardian, it might be to his advantage if Brunner didn't find out for a while that he had gotten the sixth painting and more importantly, the last coordinate. "If this is our target, don't make a mess. I don't want anyone to find him for a couple of days."

Brantley eased the car up to the front of the house and turned the lights out. Slade got out and walked up on the porch. He knocked loudly and after a few seconds, a light went on in a second-floor window. Half a minute later, through the locked front door, the voice of an old man said, "What is it?"

"There's been an accident." Intentionally, Slade hesitated to let the drama build. "Are you Conrad Linge?"

"What has happened?"

"I'm sorry, I can't hear you through the door. Are you Conrad Linge?"

The door was unlocked and opened a crack exposing a chain lock. "Yes, I am."

As the two front doors of the car opened, Slade kicked the door, snapping the chain and knocking Linge down. Before he could get to his feet, Slade rushed in and clamped his hand over the old man's mouth.

A quarter mile beyond the house, unnoticed by Decker and his crew, two men in a car watched them through a night-vision scope.

Fallon opened his eyes and glanced at the clock on the nightstand. It was almost 7 A.M. He closed them again and let the warm pressure of Sivia's body take over his senses. She was half-draped across him, her head resting lightly on his chest. His arm encircled her and his fingertips came to rest on the sharp edge of her hip bone. Her hair, now tangled, held a different smell than it had the night before. Its sweet synthetic odor had been replaced by the raw, spicy musk of intimacy, sweeping him back into the darkness that had surrounded them as they physically explored and exhausted each other. Unexpectedly, within Sivia's passion, Fallon had detected the slightest trace of inexperience, which made her even more desirable, if that were possible.

Not that he was all that experienced himself. He wasn't. But the women he had dated were predictable. Their intimacy, practiced and mechanical, left little of the mystery that was supposed to make sex so exquisitely haunting. The entire process, and its measured steps, seemed somehow insincere, doomed from the start. But because of

Sivia, he was beginning to understand it wasn't the other women who had caused that shortfall, but rather his own tangle of inhibitions. Now, laying there, he felt as though he had finally been disconnected from the burning touch of his childhood.

He rubbed her upper arm slowly, and she purred, *mmmm*. Then she said, "Whatever you are about to suggest, the answer is *no*."

"*Now* that word finds its way into your vocabulary."

Fallon slid from under her and got up. She asked, "Where do you think you're going?"

"To work. You remember—paintings, illegal wiretaps, dead bodies."

Sivia pushed her arms over her head into a body-long stretch, and then punctuated its release with another *mmmm*, this time the utterance came from down in her throat. She sat up and the sheet fell away from her. "You don't have to go this early, do you?"

He looked at the perfect curve of her breasts. "Give me a break here, I'm trying to get my pants on."

Her voice became throaty and intimate. "You will be careful?"

"I haven't got enough testosterone left to be anything else."

Six members of the Cleveland Police Department's fugitive squad sat in their cars watching Darla Kincade's apartment building. The midnight shift had received a call from a New York City detective requesting their assistance in the arrest of Kurt Decker. Such requests, no matter who they came from, were handled as obligingly as possible depending on circumstances and manpower, which usually meant that the leads got covered within a week or two. But ever since the armed robbery and murder charges had been dismissed against Decker, the Cleveland police, as good cops did everywhere, kept his name inside their heads as someone who was worthy of a little more of their attention the next time around.

As they were taking up their surveillance positions, the officers spotted a car with New York license plates outside the back entrance. Because Decker was wanted out of New York, they decided to watch it as well as the building. Fifteen minutes later, a man came out and started to get in. From their mug shots of Decker, they could see it was not him, but there was always a possibility this man was an accomplice. Two officers, holding drawn weapons down at their sides, approached him and asked for identification. He said he didn't have any, which set off the usual alarms. When asked what he was doing in the building, he said he was looking for a friend, but he had the wrong building. Another excuse they had heard before; the alarm sounded a little louder.

One of the cops said, "You being from New York, you're probably not aware of it, but we have a city ordinance against using criminal clichés, and you've just used two in a row, so now I've got to give you a little pat down. Turn around and put your hands on the car." They found no wallet, but instead, a set of lock picks and a small but expensive tape recorder with a tape still in it. The cop searching him smiled. "Uh oh."

"I want my lawyer."

"There's a surprise."

Because they didn't know what they had, the sergeant in charge of the crew made the decision to go to Darla Kincade's apartment and attempt to arrest Decker. He feared that if the wrong person had seen the commotion with the nameless man from New York, they might, given time, warn Decker.

Darla had just finished showering and was drying her hair when the heavy pounding on the door startled her. Peeking through the peephole, she saw a policeman holding up a badge. Although she hadn't said anything, he had seen her shadow move across the other side of the tiny opening. He stepped to the side and announce loudly, "Either you open it, or we will."

"What do you want?"

"We have a warrant, open the door."

"For what?"

She heard a shotgun chamber a round. "Now!"

After she fumbled to unlock the door, two of the cops were past her and their sergeant had her by the arm. "Where is he?" the sergeant asked, his tone one of practiced menace. His shoulders were exceptionally broad, like those of a one-time athlete, but too many years of sitting in a cruiser and on a bar stool had caused them to bow forward. His stomach hung over his belt, reflecting equal neglect.

To most people he would have been imposing, but Darla had lived with Decker for too long to be intimidated merely by size or gruff words. Although she knew who they were looking for, she said, "Who?"

From the way she calmly asked the one-word question, the sergeant knew Decker wasn't there. He was surprised that her face was so plain. Most big-time stickup men liked their women flashy. But then he noticed through her loose-fitting robe that her figure was anything but plain. She saw his glance and pulled on both lapels to wrap her upper body more securely. Then she cinched the belt even tighter. This defined her silhouette even more. Finally she folded her arms across her chest and an air of defiance set in. The sergeant realized he had to go on the attack. "You know who—Kurt Decker."

"He's not here." She looked over her shoulder and saw the first two officers starting to look through the rooms. "Do you have a search warrant?"

The sergeant took a moment to scan the room and was surprised how clean and well-decorated it was. "Better than that, we've got a murder warrant."

"Murder?"

"That's right, your boyfriend cut an eighty-year-old man's throat in New York." The two cops who had been searching came back into the room and signaled that Decker wasn't there. "Where is he?"

"I want to talk to a lawyer."

"That's been a very popular request today."

The sergeant knew it was always a gamble to hit a residence without being certain the fugitive was inside—and now he had lost. Decker would be warned. And since there was no proof that Darla was aiding him, nothing could be done to induce her cooperation. The big cop started on the usual warning about harboring a fugitive, and she immediately sensed the shift in power, her rights were overtaking his authority. "You have searched my home illegally, and I want you out of here, now." The sergeant felt obliged to make one last appeal, but before he could get started, she said in a louder, but equally controlled tone, "Get out."

38

AFTER LEAVING SIVIA, FALLON HEADED FOR THE office. He found Zjorn in the major-case room. In front of him were the Yellow Pages of three suburban directories opened to the *M*'s. Lost in thought, he was drawing lines through the motels that were listed on the blackboard as CONTACTED. "Any luck?" Fallon asked.

Zjorn stared at Fallon for a moment, as though he couldn't recall who he was. "Oh, hi, ah, no, nothing yet. How'd you make out last night with your 'one last thing'?"

"Less than perfect."

Zjorn stood up and dropped his pen. "So now we'll be going with the media blitz."

"I guess so, but I need your undivided attention before things around here get too crazy."

Zjorn sat down on the chair behind him. "As long as it's more challenging than lining out the names of cheap motels, I'm ready."

"I've got some more information on the Reserve code."

"Like what?"

"Last night, I found the number eighty-eight on the back of the Matisse frame," Fallon said.

"As far as we know, there are still only six paintings, and the Matisse is number four?"

"That's right."

"And you don't know any of the other numbers?" Zjorn asked.

Because the information had come from the wiretap, Fallon decided not to tell him about the number 26, at least not yet. "No."

"Do you have any new information that would indicate that these six clues do *not* lead to the Reserve?"

"No."

For the next five minutes, Zjorn sat staring at the space between himself and the wall. There was an orange on the desk in front of him. It was starting to shrivel and appeared to have been there for at least a week, probably left over from someone's lunch. He picked it up, and walked over to a wall covered with a cork board. A map was dotted with location pins, the kind with tiny red plastic spheres at one end. He pulled one out, surveyed the orange, and, with some precision, jammed it in. He handed it to Fallon and smiled. "Anything else?"

Fallon considered the orange for a moment and then said, "No, this will pretty much do it."

"You don't see it, do you?"

"No, no, I got it: fruit, masterpieces. I didn't go to the University of Chicago like some Ph.D.s, but I see the connection: oranges equal art."

"Okay, I'll explain it. Like the commercial says, Don't think locally, think globally. You're thinking Chicago, but you have to remember these paintings have come a third of the way around the world. Rathkolb wanted whoever was sent from Germany to be able to locate them regardless of language or cultural differences, which includes the metric and standard measurement systems. And to do that, they had to quantify the location in a universal language. The problem is reducible to one fairly simply question: What twelve-digit number gives an exact location in the world?"

Fallon looked down at the orange. "Longitude and latitude."

"Chicago's longitude, the fourth coordinate of six, is roughly at eighty-eight degrees west. The fourth set of digits is eighty-eight, the same as your frame."

"That means we're five coordinates short."

"But more importantly, it leaves Decker one very critical clue short. Since he can't get ours, the only logical way the Reserve can be located is if we can find him and get his."

A trash can sat ten feet away. Fallon threw the orange into it with a hollow thud. "Unfortunately, Kurt Decker hasn't been considerate enough to follow what you describe as *logic.*"

It was funny, Darla thought, that more than the prosecutorial threats of the police, she feared Kurt Decker's displeasure. When he was angered, whether it was her fault or not, he treated her with an exhausting contempt. Her mother had been the same way, unable to abandon the man who had slowly, but thoroughly, destroyed her. Not that Kurt was like her father. Max Kincade had been an abusive man who would take a belt to his wife with little or no provocation. Finally, to escape the fifteen-year marriage, her mother committed the ultimate act of divorce by closing herself in a bedroom closet, cinching the belt he beat her with around both the clothes rod and her neck, and then simply sat down. Since the act could be reversed simply by standing up, it was a clear indication of her commitment to separate herself from her husband. Darla had been the one who opened the closet door.

But Kurt Decker would never hurt her; he never had. He was strong in so many ways and, when times were good, very generous. Whatever deal he was working on now caused him to anger easily. But she knew that when it was finished, he would realize how unshakably loyal she had remained and would treat her accordingly.

As soon as the police left, her impulse was to contact him immediately. But because she was afraid he would criticize her for reacting emotionally, she tried to think like him. The police knew about her phone, so she would have to call him from Karen's. As she started toward the door, an idea struck her. She *would* use her phone, but to place long-distance calls, all to people who did not know Kurt Decker. If the police were monitoring the toll records, they would be chasing so many false leads, there wouldn't be enough time left to look in the right places. For the better part of an hour she made as many out-of-state calls as she could. Then she took off for Karen's.

When Darla answered her friend's phone after paging Decker, he said, "Is that guy calling me?"

"No, Kurt. The police were here. They have a warrant for you, for *murder.*"

"The police? Not the FBI?"

"The Cleveland police. Said it was for murdering an old man in New York City."

"Did they say anything about Chicago?"

"No, nothing."

"It won't be long before they put it together. I can't imagine how they connected me to New York."

Now that she had him on the line, her wild-goose chase idea seemed a lot less clever. She was almost afraid to tell him. He was there right now, able to yell at her for doing something she had no expertise in. Had she done the right thing? If not, she'd better tell him now. "Kurt, I hope I didn't do anything wrong, but after the police left, I made a bunch of calls from my phone to people who have nothing to do with you, you know, in case they checked the records, they'd be chasing their tails for a while."

"No, that's fine," he said without enthusiasm. "I've got to figure some things out; I'll call you later."

As she hung up the phone, she couldn't help but smile. He said she did "fine."

39

WHEN FALLON PULLED UP IN FRONT OF THE BLACK-thorn Hotel, Sivia was talking to the doorman. She was wearing an off-white dress that was gathered at the waist with a belt. Small black buttons ran down the front and along each cuff. At first glance, the garment didn't look expensive to Fallon, but as she started walking toward the car, he noticed that the material hung dramatically from her hips and shoulders, revealing the subtlety of its design. When she got in the car, he saw that the buttons were hand-carved. He could only imagine the cost. It was yet another difference between them.

He said, "It looks like Doc has figured out the code on the back of the frames," and then explained about the longitude and latitude co-ordinates.

"That's great. We already have two."

"And unfortunately, Decker has three."

"One of which we have. Plus we have one that he doesn't."

"Hopefully that will be enough to keep him from the Reserve."

"Maybe there'll be more on this tape."

"That may be a little optimistic?"

"I'm feeling *very* optimistic."

"Is there something you're not telling me?"

She leaned over until her lips touched his ear and whispered, "I got lucky last night?"

Her tongue gave off the slightest rattle, almost as if the heat of the words was causing her to lisp. A charge of sexual electricity flashed through him. He wanted to tell her he was the one who was lucky; he wanted to take her back to her room and convince himself what he was feeling was real. But he was afraid he would find out it wasn't.

He pulled the Bureau car out into traffic and headed toward the Rhine Antique Gallery.

When they arrived, Risch had a fresh pot of coffee waiting and offered them something to eat. "No thanks, Marvin," Sivia replied. "As soon as this call comes in, we'll be out of your way."

"You could never be in my way."

She smiled and asked, "Do you mind if we watch the news while we wait? There's something we want to see."

Risch got up and turned on the television. The twelve o'clock news was just starting and the lead story was about the search for Kurt Decker and his gang. They were wanted for questioning by state authorities in connection with the murders of several elderly Chicago-area German immigrants, the anchorwoman said. For the last twenty-four hours, FBI agents had been canvassing motels in the greater Chicago area, looking for the fugitives. Anyone with information regarding their whereabouts should call the Chicago office of the FBI. The number was electronically printed across the bottom of the screen. There was no mention of the New York murder warrant that had been issued for Decker.

Using the remote to turn down the volume, Risch asked Fallon, "This is the man whose voice I hear on the tape?"

"That's him."

"And who is the other voice?"

"We don't know. Is there anything you can tell us about him by the way he speaks German?"

"The one you call Decker, his German is almost flawless, but if you listen closely, you can tell he is an American. But the other, he is definitely German. The way he speaks to Decker, I would judge that the American is working for him. But their arrangement appears to be straining. You don't know the German's connection to the paintings?"

"Just that he's trying to find them. The only specific information we have about him is what you have translated for us. My guess is that he wants to take them back to Germany for who knows what."

"How many paintings do you think there are?"

"We can't be sure, but right now we believe at least eighty."

"My goodness. If they are of the quality of the Matisse you have told me about, they are worth tens of millions of dollars."

"More like hundreds of million," Sivia added.

Fallon's attention was back to the TV. Decker's photo was being shown again. "Marvin, could you turn up the volume?"

When he did, the anchorwoman said, "I've just been handed this update. A warrant has been issued in the state of New York for Kurt Decker, the man wanted in connection with the murders of the elderly German immigrants in the Chicago area. He has been charged with the death of Jonathan Geist, an eighty-year-old German-American who was self-employed as an art broker. Mr. Geist was found in his Manhattan office with his throat cut. Decker is a convicted felon who has served time in federal prison for robbing two armored cars. Additional robbery and murder charges against him were recently dropped in the city of Cleveland. The Cleveland police, when contacted, would only say that they were conducting an investigation to locate the suspect."

Risch lowered the volume and asked Fallon, "Did you know this?"

"I thought he was responsible for the murder, but I didn't know a warrant had been issued."

Sivia said, "Taz, do you think he'll still use that phone?"

"Now that he's being looked for in Cleveland, if anything is said on that line, it's going to be pretty sterile."

"Then this call we're waiting for may be our last chance."

Fallon looked at his watch. "Shouldn't he have called by now?"

"He did say before noon. Marvin, do you mind if we wait a while longer?"

"Now we'll have a little something to eat, yes?"

Kurt Decker sat staring at himself on the television. The cheap motel set seemed to dissolve his features, using less than a dozen shades of gray to mark the edges and recesses of his photographed face. For an instant he allowed himself to believe that it was not detailed enough for strangers to recognize him, but then he thought of the Degas that he had foolishly turned over to Brunner and how, in just a few strokes, the artist had left no doubt of the identity of the woman in the portrait. He, Brantley, and Slade were all recognizable from their mug shots, no matter how dated or poorly reproduced. They had to move again, but checking into another motel around Chicago, in light of the FBI's ongoing canvass, would be inviting capture.

A new face came on the screen, a female reporter was now talking about the upcoming boating season. She was broadcasting live from Burnham Harbor on Lake Michigan. As the camera swept along endless rows of boats, she explained that many of the larger ones were being prepped for the upcoming season.

Decker called Brantley's room. When he answered, Decker asked, "Have you ever stolen a boat?"

Fallon and Sivia had waited almost three hours for the call from Cleveland, but it never came. They made their apologies to Risch and left for Sivia's hotel. As they drove along Lake Shore Drive, Fallon's supervisor came on the Bureau radio. "Can you give me a land-line right away?"

Fallon asked Sivia for her cellular and dialed Blaney's number. "What's up, Pete?"

"Are you alone?"

Fallon looked over at Sivia. "Yes."

"We got a call from the office in Cleveland. NYPD got paper on Decker for the Geist murder and called Cleveland to execute it. This morning they went to his girlfriend's apartment to put the grab on him. Of course he wasn't there, but they arrested a guy coming out of the building. He was carrying lock picks and a fairly high-tech tape recorder. On the tape were two males speaking German. They were able to figure out that one of them was Decker. Once they saw it was an interception of communications case, they called us. Some agents interviewed this guy but he refused to say anything. And he didn't have any identification. They searched his car and found a hotel room key. They checked it out and there were several calls to Chicago. They got a hold of us and asked us to break down the numbers. One of them came back to Sivia Roth's hotel. We checked her outgoing calls and there were some back to this guy's number. And both of them had called a number in New York, which had been previously identified by our office there as belonging to a subject named Alan Singer. He had come to their attention earlier because he was heading a new Jewish militant group called *Brichah*. It's supposed to be named after some organization that smuggled Jewish refugees out of Europe and into Palestine immediately following the Second World War. They were also involved in identifying and assassinating SS officers responsible for Nazi atrocities. God only knows what this new group is about. I didn't know if you were aware of any of this or what your relationship is with this woman, but I wanted to give you the heads up. The SAC is going crazy. He wants to see you right away."

Unemotionally, Fallon said, "Thanks, Pete," and disconnected the phone.

Sivia asked, "Good news? Bad news?"

"I think this one is pretty much bad news."

"What happened?"

"Seems I was the last to find out, but your friend in Cleveland was arrested, and the Bureau now knows about you, and Alan Singer, and *Brichah*."

Fallon's words tightened around her heart like an angry fist. "Taz, I—"

"Please don't say anything unless you're going to start telling me the truth."

She didn't speak for a few seconds. "I don't know what you've been told, but *Brichah* is not some far-flung terrorist organization— it's little more than an idea. I told you the stats on the government reluctance to extradite Nazi war criminals. Some of us who were offended by the injustice of these people being able to live here so freely got together to see if something more couldn't be done."

"The original *Brichah* assassinated Nazi war criminals, what do you mean by *more?*"

"Whatever you think of me, you know that I would never be a part of any killing. We were a small group that had visions of righting the historic wrongs that our parents and grandparents suffered. Rathkolb was the first person we tried to do anything about. I suppose we fantasized about finding people like him, and when we did, somehow they would just wake up one day in Israeli custody. I don't know how, we hadn't thought that far ahead. There was never any intention to kill anyone. We took the name only for a sense of identity."

"What about IFAR, is it a front for *Brichah?*"

"No, they don't know anything about this. The foundation does great work and gets very little credit. And now I suppose I'll have to resign."

"And Citron?"

Sivia took in a deep breath, then let out a sigh of surrender. "David is well-known for his sympathy with all Jewish causes and has a deep network of contacts. He's known as a man you can go to if you have a problem. Around the world there are many like him. When we found we needed help in Chicago, he was called. Other than introducing me to you, he has no connection with this at all." Her tone then changed from apologetic to defiant. "Whether this group exists or not, the Reserve still needs to be found."

Fallon pulled up in front of her hotel. "You don't get it. This isn't about *Brichah*, it's about you using me. I knew something was wrong from the start. There were too many things that didn't make sense, but I let it go because I felt something for you. Obviously, I've made a mistake."

"When I first met you and thought Rathkolb was still alive, I *did* intend to use you. But when I saw him dead, I realized just how terrifying revenge is. I was glad he killed himself because I just wanted out. But then we found out about the Reserve. That's my job—finding stolen art. It was no longer about Nazis but about looted paintings. My *Brichah* contacts were in place, so why wouldn't I use them," she said. "Right now I can see how this must look, but I was not using you."

"Then why do I feel so betrayed?" Sivia didn't say anything. "And now if you will get out of the car, I'll go and pay the price."

"What about the Reserve, and all these murders?"

"I'd say my time left with the Bureau is going to be about as long as it takes me to get to the SAC's office. Someone else will be assigned Decker. And since the FBI doesn't know about the Reserve, that is now your problem exclusively." Large, clear tears started to fill her eyes. His voice was now chillingly unemotional. "Don't you get it? I'm no good to you anymore, so just get out of the car."

She climbed out and then turned back to him. "Don't sell yourself short, Taz. Even if I wasn't involved, you would have taken the same chances, because no matter what happens to you or me, what we did was right." She closed the door and walked into the hotel.

"Burnham Harbor, harbor master's office."

"Hi, this is Jeff Jackson. I'm a technician with Seven Seas Navigational Systems in Boston. One of your mooring holders there—just a minute, let me check—a Mr. Easterling, has contracted us to install our new R-two-eighty navigational system on his boat, the *Lost Weekend*. He told us that he spends the winter in Florida, but we forgot to find out when he'd be back up there in Chicago. He has to be aboard during installation so we can train him in the new system's use. The number we have for him isn't working."

"Hold on while I check." After a couple of minutes, the assistant harbor master came back on the line. "Yes, sir. He's due back here two weeks from tomorrow."

"Great, that'll fit my schedule perfectly. Thanks for your help." Kurt Decker hung up the boat's telephone. "We've got two weeks," he announced to Slade and Brantley. "How much gas do we have?"

Brantley said, "She's full up."

"Any trouble with the locks?"

"I just kept searching the nicer boats that looked like they weren't in use until I found one with the key hidden. Most of them hide keys. This was only the third one I checked."

"Well, you picked a good one. Three bedrooms, kitchen, shower, TV, a couple of cellular phones that even have caller ID. And according to the papers you found, the owner's only up here for about three months a year. How many feet is this?"

"As close as I can figure—about forty. It's got twin diesel engines. Should move pretty good."

Decker gave Slade a hundred-dollar bill. "Both of you go get some food, but leave five minutes apart. Find some hats and sunglasses. Ronnie, you go in the restaurant alone. You guys don't need to be seen together."

As Brantley and Slade each left, they scanned the marina for anyone who might recognize them. They were unable to see the two men in the slate gray mini-van through its darkened windows.

Below, Decker sat at a small desk in the master bedroom, thinking about the Matisse in the FBI's possession. Brunner was right: without it, he'd never locate the Reserve. It still angered him that Brunner had brought up his father and his exploits in Hungary, implying his father would have found a way to retrieve the missing painting. And he was sure that it was Brunner who turned him in to the New York police. Even if he had left evidence behind at Geist's office, the cops would have needed his name to identify it. He was going to have to do something about the German.

Against the opposite wall sat the last three paintings he had retrieved. The newest addition was the Van Gogh they had gotten from Conrad Linge. It was probably worth even more than the Renoir. Again, he questioned his ability to find a buyer for them. Then he got an idea that would solve all his problems.

He picked up the phone and called directory assistance in New York. "The International Foundation for Art Research, please." The operator gave him the number and he dialed it. When a woman answered, he said, "I'm trying to get ahold of Sivia Roth."

"I'm sorry, she's not here."

"Yes, I know she's in Chicago. I was wondering if you could get her to call me."

"What is it regarding?"

"Just tell her I know where Josef Rathkolb's other paintings are. That's R-A-T-H-K-O-L-B."

"And your number?"

Decker pulled the phone away from his ear and looked at the backstrap of the receiver. Across it was a black embossed plastic strip from a label maker giving the telephone's number. He smiled. The area code was 305—Miami, apparently the owner's billing location. The call would be untraceable. Decker gave the woman the number and then said, "Oh, yeah—tell her I'm interested in the reward."

40

SIVIA'S SUITE NOW HAD A COLD, BLACK-AND-WHITE emptiness. Fallon had been gone less than ten minutes, but already she understood she was on her own. Without him and the FBI's resources, the recovery of the Reserve seemed hopeless. Suddenly the search seemed so overwhelming that she found it easier to wonder if the cache really did exist. Like a mirage on the horizon, it always appeared to be at the limit of her vision, never solidifying, never growing nearer.

But then she thought about everything she had seen: the dead Nazis, the Goering messages, the Matisse, but most of all the undiluted hate in Rochlitz's eyes when he ordered her and Fallon from his house before his wife surrendered the painting. The Reserve was real and she knew to think otherwise was simply trying to escape the difficulties ahead. She needed to talk to someone so she dialed David Citron. His wife answered, and, in a very guarded and practiced monotone, would say only that he was out of the country.

That left only Alan Singer to call, not just to seek direction, but she wanted to find out what legal problems were in store for their associate who had been arrested in Cleveland. For security reasons, it was Singer's practice to never answer the phone. Hoping he was in the office, she left a vague message that he should call her as soon as possible.

A half hour later her phone rang. "Alan?"

"Sivia, this is Rachel." It was one of the volunteers at IFAR.

"Sorry, I was expecting someone else."

"Oh, that's okay. I didn't know whether to bother you with this, but we got a call about the paintings you're looking for. He said something about a reward and I told him he'd have to talk to you."

"What exactly did he say?"

"That he knew where Josef Rathkolb's paintings were."

Sivia felt a small rush of adrenaline. "Did he leave his name?"

"Just his phone number." She read it to Sivia.

"Thanks, Rachel." After calling directory assistance and finding out that the area code left by the caller was for Miami, she dialed the number. "Hello."

"This is Sivia Roth, I was given this number to call."

"Yes, Sivia, do you know who this is?" There was something familiar about the voice, something unpleasant. "We met briefly outside Martin Bach's house."

Her breath caught in her throat; she was talking to Kurt Decker. "Why would I want to talk to you?"

"Because I can give you all of the paintings."

"And why would you do that?"

"I'm sure you're aware that I'm missing a part of the puzzle. A part which you have and I will never be able to get. Without it, I am unable to find the exact location." When she didn't say anything, he said, "I assume you have it."

From the wiretap, she knew that the second coordinate was 19. And even though Fallon had told her about the number on the back of the Matisse frame, he had never said what it was. As she wondered if he had intentionally kept it from her, she absentmindedly answered, "The FBI does, but I was never told."

"I know the feeling, which leaves me with only one option—the reward—if it's enough. Exactly how much is it?"

Sivia had no idea. "That depends on a number of factors—how many paintings there are. How much they're worth. And, I guess, how easy you make it for me."

"Well, it's more than ten masterpieces, much more, and I'm going to give you the exact location minus the one clue the FBI is holding. How much is that worth?"

"Again, I can't—"

"I didn't call you to hear 'I can't.' If I turn this over to you, I'm losing roughly a million dollars. Can you guarantee me that much?"

The reward had been the FBI's idea, and that option was now gone. "If everything is as you say, yes, I can guarantee it. Yes."

"Good. Give me some time to figure out the exchange—to make sure that you're not going to set me up with your FBI boyfriend, and then I'll call your office. It should be no more than a couple of hours. Can you wait there for my call?"

"Do I have any choice?"

In Cleveland, Darla Kincade's phone rang. "Hello."

"It's me," Decker said. "Go to Karen's now."

When she answered five minutes later, he said, "Do you know where I keep my phony passport?"

"At that other guy's house?"

"Right. Is yours still valid?"

"I think so, but I'll have to check. Are we going somewhere?"

"Most definitely, but first I need you to do me one more favor."

Fallon walked into his supervisor's office. "I thought you might like to be the one to lead me to the slaughter."

"That's not funny." Blaney picked up the phone and called the SAC's secretary. "Fallon's here, can he see us now . . . we're on our way." He got up and put his suit jacket on. "I don't want to know if you were in on this illegal wire, so please don't say anything that I would have to put my right hand into the air about. And if I were you, I wouldn't admit anything to Stamen, or anybody else."

On the drive back to the office, Fallon had considered the one question that the SAC would undoubtedly ask him: Did he have knowledge of the wiretap in Cleveland? Although he had never confessed to a felony before, he normally found owning up to a misdeed strangely exhilarating. For him it was sort of a test, a check of who he was. In fact, he wondered if he didn't sometimes wander across the blurred lines of Bureau procedure intentionally, just to feel the honorable sting of having to admit guilt and then accept the consequences. He thought about Sivia's insights into his relationship with his father and supposed this was another confused inheritance from the man who had left him little else.

But if he did confess his part in the wiretap, at some point his admission would be used against Sivia, and, although he still felt a resentment for what she had done, he couldn't bring himself to do that to her.

Fallon and his supervisor entered the dark office. Stamen was pacing behind his desk, just beyond the edge of the light coming from his desk. Once they sat down, a shaft of smoke came streaming toward them. "I hope what I am about to ask you will prove to be a waste of all our time," Stamen said. He sat down and the available light shadowed his face. He glared at Fallon. "I'm sure your supervisor has told you about the wire being found in Cleveland. Did you know anything about it?"

"This isn't a breech of Bureau etiquette you're talking about, it's a felony," Fallon said. "You know you have to give me my rights."

"An innocent person would find that insulting. I was hoping you'd simply tell me that you didn't know anything, and there would be no need for lawyers."

"You'd better read me my rights."

With more premeditation than usual, Stamen stabbed his cigarette into the ashtray until it was completely out and he had snapped it in half. "You're painting us all into a corner. The Bureau is hot on this. They're waiting for a call back with the results of this interview. They've already declared that if you admit being involved, you're to be suspended immediately."

Blaney said, "But he hasn't admitted doing anything."

Stamen gave him an unpleasant glance to let him know that legal hairsplitting was a defense that would have no audience at FBI headquarters. He turned back to Fallon. "The problem is this individual in New York, this Alan Singer, he's suspected of having ties to Israeli Intelligence."

"At headquarters, anyone who's Jewish is suspected of having ties with Israeli Intelligence. No matter what these people call themselves or think about doing, this case is about murders and looted paintings. No one's threatening national security."

"A *felony* was committed."

"They put a recorder on a telephone line to stop a murderer."

Stamen lit another cigarette. "It sounds like you know a lot about this."

"And you could probably have used it against me if you had taken my suggestion and advised me of my rights."

The SAC took a deep drag, tilted his head back, and blew it straight up. Then he leaned forward into the glare of the lamp. "Oh, you're going to be given your rights. But not by me. For right now, stay in the office until I can get a decision from headquarters."

The first thing Fallon thought of when he got back to his desk was Jack Debbin. If the Office of Professional Responsibility was coming to Chicago to conduct an investigation, they would eventually have to go to Cleveland. He didn't want Debbin to get caught in the crossfire. He picked up the phone and dialed his number.

"Debbin."

"Jack, it's Taz."

"I got a feeling this *ain't* a good news call."

"Then you've heard about the illegal wire?"

"*Heard* about it? The Cleveland PD just left. They handed the whole thing over to us, all the evidence, *and* all the headaches. In fact it's this squad's violation. Thank God, they didn't assign it to me."

"Just so you know, they're tagging me with it here. The SAC is talking to the Bureau right now, telling them where to send my last check."

"Is there anything I can do?"

"Before all this started I mentioned to the SAC I had a contact in Cleveland who was getting me toll information on Decker. Fortunately I didn't tell him who it was. I don't know if he'll implicate himself by bringing up his own knowledge of it, but I wanted to give you the heads up so you could *tidy up* before OPR heads your way."

"Funny you should mention that, I was just doing a little spring cleaning," Debbin said. "But before I dump everything, do you want the last of these tolls?"

With everything that was happening to Fallon, the last thing he thought he would have been interested in was another chance to find Decker and the Reserve. But Debbin's question made him realize that he was. "What's another count or two on the indictment." Fallon took out a sheet of paper. "How many are there?"

"Suddenly she's making a ton of calls all over the country."

"When did they start?"

"Let's see . . . the first one was early yesterday afternoon."

"After the PD hit her apartment?"

"Yeah, I guess it would be."

"Any calls to the Chicago area?"

"Nothing to Illinois, period."

"She's just sending up smoke," Fallon said.

"Yeah, that makes sense."

"Keep your head down, Jack." He hung up and looked over at Zjorn's desk. His jacket was draped across the back of his chair. Fallon called the major-case room but the phone was busy. He headed for the elevator.

When Fallon entered the room, Zjorn was just finishing a call. "Where are you heading next . . . okay, let me know." As soon as he hung up, the phone rang again.

Fallon said, "Let it ring."

Zjorn looked at him closely. "What's the matter?"

Fallon led him across the hall into an interview room. In the small nondescript cubicle there was a table and two chairs, and a window that looked down on the south end of the Loop. "The thing I didn't tell you about—what I was being so evasive about—Sivia had a wire put on the phone in Cleveland."

Zjorn looked stunned. "How?"

Fallon then told him about her involvement in *Brichah* and the subsequent discovery of everything by the Bureau. "That's how we found out about Rochlitz and were able to beat Decker's crew to the Matisse. I knew about the wire but not until after it was installed. She came to me and asked if I'd use the information. But I didn't know about *Brichah*."

"Does the front office know about your involvement?"

"They've pretty much figured it out, and that's going to be enough for me to have to take the weight on this. Because you were assigned to help me with the case, you may be interviewed by OPR. If you are, you don't know anything about the wire and you don't know who I was getting toll information from in Cleveland. And make sure you don't bring up the Reserve. If they find out about it from you, they'll find a way to connect you to everything."

"You're not going to get fired?"

"That's not important right now. But, whatever they decide, I won't be handling this case anymore. Most likely, it'll be reassigned to you. And just as important as finding Decker is recovering the Reserve."

"How am I going to do that?" Zjorn asked.

"You're the one who told me we'd have to find Decker. If he gets the last painting, which I suspect he's in the process of doing right now, he'll have all the coordinates except the one on the back of the Matisse."

"If I can't tell anyone about the Reserve, that's a lot for me to handle alone."

"After the OPR inquiry blows over, you can *discover* that there is a Reserve, and then you'll get all the help you need."

"And before this great epiphany occurs, if I need to, can I call you?"

"Of course."

The office paging system clicked on. "Will Taz Fallon report to the SAC's office immediately." Usually, the subject of the announcement was asked to dial a certain extension and then directed to a location. The SAC's secretary, normally a most discreet person, had evidently made the ominous call at her boss' direction.

Fallon smiled at him. "I wonder what that could be about." As he headed out the door, he said, "Just remember, Doc, your first priority in this is to protect yourself."

Blaney was waiting for Fallon outside the SAC's office. "He told me to make sure you have your creds and gun."

"That certainly takes the suspense out of what the Bureau's decided." Blaney shook his head, and Fallon could see that he was upset. "Pete, this too shall pass."

The lights were on in the office. It seemed almost surreal to Fallon, even more so because of what he knew he was about to hear. He and his supervisor sat down. "You are suspended pending the OPR investigation," Stamen said without ceremony.

Blaney said, "What did they give as an official reason?"

"It doesn't matter what the official reason is, because the real reason is the Bureau doesn't want one of its agents acting as a tool of Jewish militants." He held out his hand. Fallon pushed his credentials and Sig Sauer across the desk. "Two headquarters agents will be here tomorrow. You are to be available at ten A.M. for an interview. They also instructed me to have Sivia Roth brought in and interviewed tonight. Some agents are being sent to her hotel right now."

Fallon smiled. He could see her in the room with the agents interrogating her and wondered how long it would be before they, too, were compromised.

Sivia was going through her address book, trying to find someone who could help her raise the reward money. She was so preoccupied that when a knock came at the door, she opened it without looking through the peephole first. Decker and his two men pushed their way in and grabbed her.

Decker said, "Let me offer you some advice from someone who's been there—if you want to keep your whereabouts unknown, never phone anyone with caller ID."

41

FALLON'S APARTMENT WAS THE FOURTH FLOOR OF a three-story brownstone in the Lincoln Park area of Chicago's Near North Side. The onetime attic had not simply been remodeled, but rather, as evidenced by the dominance of light and angular space, architecturally restructured. The upper portion of the walls, which peaked to a fifteen-foot ceiling, were defined and softened by a network of hand-hewn pine beams. Their dark, weathered color contrasted sharply against the quiet earth tones of the walls. Four deep windows, two on either side, slanted upward toward the sun. The apartment was a single, long room. At the far end, through the kitchen and living area, was the bedroom. It was not separated by walls or a door but rather by shape and elevation. The floor, a step higher than the rest of the apartment, was partially surrounded by the circular, interior walls of the large turret that dominated the exterior of the building's north end. The ceiling rose even higher to a single coned point. A foot below the roofline, the entire perimeter was ringed with a series of small, rectangular, leaded-glass windows.

When Fallon walked in, he flipped a light switch near the door. An old wooden and brass camera tripod that had been turned into a floor lamp went on and illuminated an antique oak carpenter's bench that he used as a desk. It was worn by a hundred years of cabinetmaking and still had a large wooden vise appended to one end. Scattered across it were half a dozen books, some photographs of Mayan artifacts, and several maps of Central America. At one end, Fallon's answering machine blinked.

Unexpectedly, he found himself hoping it was Sivia. He became angry with himself for his lack of resolve. Before playing the message, he reminded himself of what she had done and to be cautious of any defense she might offer.

But instead of the soft rhythm of Sivia's peacemaking, he heard the amused voice of Kurt Decker. "Fallon, I've got something that belongs to you, and you have something that belongs to me. If you're interested in an exchange, beep me at this number." Fallon started to write it down, the first three digits were 212—New York. He knew the rest of it; it was Sivia's pager.

He dialed and after the beep, punched in his number. A few seconds later his telephone rang. "Hello," Fallon said.

"First of all, if you're trying to trace this, don't bother. I'm using your girlfriend's cellular."

"I'm not in a position to trace anything."

"Yeah, she's been telling us you were in trouble with your boss and wouldn't be able to help us. Is that true?"

Fallon knew Decker had to be convinced that he and his crew were not taking on the entire FBI. "They more or less fired me today, but I can still get what you want."

"Just as well for the girl. The agents I've seen get real clumsy around the drop site. Especially the way I set them up."

Fallon knew, Decker's arrogance aside, that he was right. During the investigation, he had shown an uncanny ability to anticipate the Bureau's attempts to capture him. "I assume we're talking about the Matisse."

"And you know what I have."

Fallon wanted to hear her voice. "The only thing I know you have for sure is her pager, and I think trading a Matisse for a small chunk of electronics would be a little foolish."

"That's why I'm not going to miss this country, there's no trust anymore."

The next thing Fallon heard was Sivia. "Taz, don't do this. He can't find the Reserve without—" Her words ended abruptly.

Decker came on the line. "Man, I know she's good-looking, but I like my women with a whole lot less attitude." Fallon heard him take a deep breath. "But that's your problem. Now that I've showed you mine, I assume you're ready to deal."

"Just tell me where and when?"

"Where's the painting now?"

"Locked up at the office."

"And you won't have any problem getting it?"

"It'll be a problem, but give me a couple of hours to make sure anyone who might be an obstacle is gone."

"Okay. Tonight—or more accurately—tomorrow morning at two A.M., come to the Burnham Harbor. As soon as you pull in, you'll see the harbor master's building. About a hundred yards south of it, there'll be a small blue dingy tied up at the wall. Row out dead east. You'll see a white buoy with the number thirty-two on it. Tie up there. Under the rear seat you'll find a brown paper bag. Inside will be your girlfriend's phone. Wait for my call," Decker said. "And Fallon, if I see anyone but you, she's going for a swim."

"Don't worry, the FBI won't be there."

Then Decker gave a short condescending laugh. "You haven't warned me yet. This is the part where you're supposed to tell me that if anything happens to her, you'll kill me."

"That's because something *has* already happened to her." Fallon hung up.

He checked his watch. It was almost five. He dialed the office. "Zjorn."

"Doc, I need a big favor. Call up to the SAC's secretary and tell her you've got something you need to lock in the vault tonight after she's gone, so she'll leave it half-unlocked."

"I didn't think suspended agents are supposed to go shopping in the SAC's safe after hours."

"You don't want to know."

"In other words, you want me to do the dirty work and not have any of the fun."

"This is not going to be fun. Besides, you could wind up losing your job, too."

"Aside from my Ph.D., I have some other degrees, one in computer science. Do you know how much more money I could be making right now? Tell me what's going on, because, whatever it is, I'm in."

"Decker's got Sivia."

"What!"

"He wants to trade her for the Matisse."

"Taz, you got to let somebody here know. You can't stop him by yourself."

"I don't want to risk trying to stop him. Every time we set a trap for him, he's been ahead of us. And now that he has the home field advantage, trying to beat him would be suicide. Besides, Stamen would never agree to turn over the painting. He thinks that good naturally triumphs over evil. There's no choice but to give them the Matisse."

"When's the drop?" Zjorn asked. Fallon repeated the details of Decker's instructions. "Okay, I'll get the painting and meet you in an hour at North Avenue Beach."

After Fallon hung up, he began to feel something he hadn't since his mother died—panic. Even during the Citron kidnapping he hadn't given in to it. So why was he now? He knew his feelings for Sivia were part of it, but there was something else, some emotional wall she had lowered when she got him to open up about his father. She had showed him that he didn't need to be ashamed of his relationship with his father, nor would he be judged harshly because of it. That's probably why their intimacy had been so intense the night before—he trusted her with his fears, and she proved to him they were unnecessary. As enraged as he felt now, he knew emotion could cloud his judgment, and maybe even cost Sivia her life.

He took in a deep breath and held it for a few seconds before exhaling. He went over to his CD player, chose an old Duke Ellington album that featured the warm, soft trumpet of Harry "Sweets" Edison, and carefully adjusted the volume. On top of the maps on his desk was an antique brass geologist's compass. He picked it up and felt a reassurance in its heavy, time-smoothed craftsmanship. The device performed a half dozen functions, one of which was a level made up of a small air bubble in a contained tube. He sat down in a thickset brown leather chair and swung his feet up on its ottoman. Balancing the hundred-year-old compass in his open palm, he made himself wait until the pre-

carious bubble became perfectly still. He stared at its motionlessness
for a while, then shut the lid. For the next hundred heartbeats or so, he
let his mind dissolve into the dark, smoky complaints of Edison's trumpet. Slowly, he let his thoughts return to Sivia and Decker.

If he was to row east, away from shore, that meant Decker was
going to pick up the painting by boat. He had probably chosen Burnham Harbor because it was large enough for him to hide among its
hundreds of boats while he made sure Fallon was alone. And if he
could conceal himself that easily, Fallon thought, so could Doc.

He tracked down the assistant harbor master on the phone and introduced himself as Agent Fallon. "We've got an undercover operation late tonight and we need to borrow a boat. Do you have
something we can use?"

"I don't know, what're you looking for?"

"Something with a low profile, but quick."

"Give me a minute while I see what we're holding keys for." After
a couple of minutes, he came back on the line. "We've got a cigarette
boat that's just been delivered and its owner isn't due for another
three days."

"That sounds perfect. My partner will pick it up in a couple of
hours."

As soon as Fallon pulled into the lot at North Avenue Beach, he spotted Zjorn. He parked next to him and got into his car. "Any trouble
getting it?"

"No, it's in the trunk. After I talked to you, I got a call from the
Deer Park PD. They had a homicide, victim's name is," he took out a
faxed report, "Conrad Linge. He's a seventy-seven-year-old German
immigrant. His daughter, who doesn't live with him, found the body
hidden in a utility shed behind the house." He handed the document
to Fallon.

He scanned it briefly and put it in his briefcase. "I guess Decker
has the sixth painting."

"All of them but the Matisse, which brings us back to tonight. He's
got to have a boat."

"That's my guess," Fallon said. "But he'll keep it hidden until he's
sure I'm alone."

"You're going to be awfully vulnerable out there. This would be a great opportunity for him to get you off his back—forever."

"Let's hope he's too busy concentrating on the Reserve to think about that. The key is finding out whether Sivia's on the boat or not. Since kidnappers don't usually bring their victims to the drop, if she is on board, it's a good bet that Decker isn't going to try anything and will make the exchange. If she isn't, I'm going to have to make sure he doesn't try to take the painting and run without releasing her."

"How're we going to find out if she's there?"

"It's not going to be easy. He won't want us to know she's there, because I'll be a lot less likely to try anything if I don't know where she is," Fallon said.

"I assume this is where I come in."

"You'll be out in the harbor in another boat, hopefully in a position to see her."

"Where do we get this other boat?" Fallon told him about his call to the harbor master's office. "What did he say about the buoy?"

"It's about a hundred yards offshore with quite a few boats tied up close by, so you shouldn't have any trouble getting lost among them, especially at two A.M."

"Where exactly do you want me?"

"They'll probably come from the open-water side, from the east. You should position yourself directly on my flank to either the north or south. You'll have to see which is best when you get out there. And you should be twenty-five to fifty yards farther out than I am because I don't think, at least initially, he'll come any closer than that."

"If I spot her, how do I let you know?"

"You're going to have to go back to the office and pick up a night scope, a body transmitter, and one of the new walkie-talkies with the wireless ear pieces. But first, go see about the boat. I'll meet you in front of the planetarium at midnight. We can work out the rest of it then."

Zjorn started the engine. "You're sure this is the best way?"

Fallon got out and when he turned back to answer him, Zjorn could see the fear in his eyes. "I've never been so *un*sure of anything in my life."

42

CARRYING A BLACK GARBAGE BAG, FALLON STEPPED down into the unsteady dingy. He reached under the backseat and found the cellular phone that had been left, as promised, in a paper bag. After putting his back to the rest of the harbor to block detection, he took a small walkie-talkie out of his inside jacket pocket, turned it on, and set it between his feet. Then, in a quiet voice, he spoke into the flat microphone taped to his chest. "Doc, have you got me?"

"Five-by, Taz. When you get tied up on the buoy, I'll be to your south."

Fallon dipped his hand into the black water and felt its icy sting. He took a moment to scan the boats, hoping to catch a glimpse of Zjorn's position. He hadn't realized just how big the harbor was. The only shapes he could distinguish in the damp darkness were the endless silhouettes of tangled masts. "Here we go," he said and placed the oar pins into the locks and started rowing.

When he got within twenty yards of the buoy, Doc said, "Okay, Taz, I've got you on the night scope."

When they had met at the planetarium, it was decided that Fallon would keep his speaking to a minimum because if Decker or his crew had any night vision capabilities, they would be able to see Fallon's lips moving, and that could only mean one thing—he wasn't alone. Without answering, Fallon coasted to the buoy and carefully made his way to the front of the rocking dingy. As he tied the bowline through the float's metal loop, he listened carefully for any unusual noises, but the only sound across the harbor's calm water was the clinking of the sailboats' halyards gently reporting their movement from side to side.

Parked close to where Fallon had found the dingy was the rented mini-van. Inside sat Rölf Brunner with two of his assistants, Claas Steinhaus and Eduard Wald. Steinhaus was six feet tall and thickly built. He had white-blond hair that hung in limp, pasty bangs across his flat forehead. Wald was considerably shorter and thin. He had a lazy right eye that was made even more noticeable because the left one never stopped moving, continually scanning the 180 degrees in front of him. Although neither of their names appeared on any records, both were employees of the German Democratic Alliance party. They worked directly for, and were paid by, Rölf Brunner. "When did you get the explosives aboard?" Brunner asked.

"When they went to get the woman Jew," Wald said. Carefully, Brunner picked up the remote detonation device and examined it. "When will you kill them?"

"As soon as we know the location of the Reserve. The nice thing about dealing with Americans is you can always rely on their impatience. So I don't think it will take Decker long to find out."

The phone in front of Fallon rang. He checked his watch—it was five minutes before two. He and Zjorn had decided to be in place ahead of schedule in the hope of drawing an early call from the kidnappers. If it came, it would indicate that Decker was already there watching the buoy. And if he was, Zjorn could start looking for any boat with a vantage point to observe Fallon's movements. Hopefully then, from his concealed position, Zjorn would be able to spot Sivia, which would give them the advantage of knowing exactly where she was.

Fallon let it ring twice more before answering. "Hello."

Decker did not like the delay. "I hope you're not going to start playing games with me."

"I'm sitting out in a dingy at two in the morning, and you're accusing me of playing games?"

*   *   *

Brunner and the other two men stared intently at the cellular scanner that was intercepting the call between Fallon and Decker. Brunner said, "How did you get Decker's frequency?"

"While Claas was placing the explosives, I ran some tests on the boat's phone."

"Very good, having access to their conversation will make this much easier."

Decker said to Fallon, "A point well taken. Did you bring it?"

"Did you bring *her*?"

"So you *are* going to play games."

"Just protecting my interests."

"Then stop stalling."

"It's right here." Assuming Decker was watching, Fallon stood the garbage bag up on end and tapped the top.

Zjorn scanned the harbor, trying to determine which boats had a direct line of sight to Fallon's position. He spotted the *Lost Weekend* as it moved ahead slowly, trying to get a better vantage point. "Taz, I think I got them," he whispered into the radio. "They're at your two o'clock, and I'm pretty close to them. Looks like they're turning to get a better angle on you. I can see a dim light in the window of their cabin below deck. If you can see it, clear your throat."

Unable to detect the boat as he slowly searched the water to his right front, Fallon didn't give the signal.

Decker said, "Hold it up so I can see it." Intentionally, Fallon held the painting up, still shrouded in the bag, to find out exactly what Decker could see. "You're getting cute again, take it out of the bag."

"They're still turning," Zjorn said. "A couple of more seconds and I should be able to see in the cabin."

Fallon said, "I want to talk to Sivia before I do anything else."

"What makes you think she's here?"

"If this is going to be a trade, she'd better be."

"You've been doing this long enough to know that it's not wise to bring your bargaining chip to where it can be taken away," Decker said.

"Call me insecure, but I'm out here without much of a fall-back position. I need reassuring."

"Well, I guess somebody has to show some good faith."

Zjorn whispered, "I can see two people in the cabin now, one male looking through some sort of scope toward you, and it looks like Sivia is in a chair behind him. I can see her hands tied to the arms of the chair."

Fallon held up the bag in front of his face as if preparing to expose the painting. He then dropped the phone, and at the exact moment it clanged against the bottom of the dingy, he said into the transmitter, "Wearing?"

"Wearing?" Zjorn asked, not understanding the question for a moment. "Oh, what's she wearing? It's kind of a beige or off-white dress and there's a row of black buttons on the cuff." Fallon remembered the expensive dress she had been wearing the last time he saw her.

As he picked up the phone, Decker asked, "What was that?"

"I dropped the phone. Okay, I'm going to trust you on this." He slid the painting out of the plastic bag and held it up.

As he did, the *Lost Weekend* picked up a little speed and came toward him. When it got within fifty feet, a spotlight from its bridge blinded Fallon. Decker said, "Well, it looks good, but I suppose the FBI could come up with a copy if they had to. What's on the back of the frame?"

Brunner sat upright and grabbed the radio-signal detonator. Wald asked, "You are going to do this now? What about the paintings?"

"So we lose those four. The important thing is to get the coordinate."

"We still will not have the sixth coordinate."

"It is the least important. The first five will bring us within a half mile of the location. I think we are resourceful enough to find it from there. Anyway, as soon as I push this button, everyone who knows about the Reserve will be dead, and we will be able to take our time locating it. And the explosion will undoubtedly be blamed on Herr Decker and his criminal activities."

Fallon said, "I've shown my good faith, now I think it's your turn. I want to talk to her."

"I told you she's not aboard."

Fallon reached into the garbage bag and took out two house bricks, holding them up in the light so Decker could see what they were. Then he placed them carefully in the bottom of the bag next to the Matisse. He twisted shut the neck of the bag. Lowering it over the side of the dingy, he let the painting sink until three quarters of the bag was submerged.

Decker's voice cut through the darkness, "Alright, alright!"

As Fallon waited, Zjorn said, "The guy with the scope is walking over to her."

The next thing Fallon heard was Sivia. "Taz, don't go for it—"

Her voice was interrupted and Decker came back on the line. "Okay, Fallon, now you know she's here. It's your turn to prove that what you have is the real item. What's the number on the back of the frame."

Fallon realized that he had gained as much advantage as he was going to. Now he had no choice but to try and make the exchange. "It's eight-eight."

"Eighty-eight," Decker said. "That sounds like the right number. Now we can—"

There was a brief, shrill tone on both cell phones just before the *Lost Weekend* exploded.

43

THE EXPLOSION CONED UPWARD, AND THE BLAST'S concussion slammed into Fallon and threw him out of the tiny boat as it overturned. He lost consciousness for the few seconds it took his body to react to the water's cold warning.

Disoriented, he slowly rose to the surface. He found himself wondering why he had chosen to go swimming with his clothes on. The next thing he noticed was a huge fireball burning fifty yards in front of him. It lighted the water's surface, and he watched the small iridescent oil patches around him change shape and color like a blue-green kaleidoscope. A boat came toward him. The driver had a faceless familiarity, possibly a character from another dream. He was calling a name: "Taz!" His name was Taz. Taz . . . something.

Zjorn reached over the gunwale and grabbed Fallon's arm, pulling him over the side. There was a long, deep cut under Fallon's left eye. "Taz, you alright?" Fallon stared back blankly for a moment and then returned his attention to the fire.

It wasn't until a couple of hours later, when Fallon found himself on an emergency room gurney, that he was able to interpret complete sentences. His cheek hurt, and when he reached up to find the source of the pain, he was surprised to find a thick cotton dressing taped across it. He shot up to a sitting position. "Sivia!"

Zjorn gently pushed him back down. "You've got to take it easy, Taz."

"Where is she?"

"There's nothing you can do. Every available agent is at the harbor."

"Where is she!"

"How much do you remember?"

Fallon thought for a second. "Everything until the explosion."

Solemnly, Zjorn said, "There weren't any survivors."

Fallon pushed away Zjorn's attempt to have him lie down. He stood up and took a moment for the waves sloshing through his equilibrium to subside. "Where're my clothes?"

In as calm a voice as possible, Zjorn said, "There's nothing you can do. They've sent for a plastic surgeon to sew you up, so just hold on. You can't go around with your face torn open."

Another wave of lightheadedness hit Fallon, and he leaned back against the gurney. "Do they know what caused the explosion?"

"I'm no expert, but that had to be a bomb."

"I remember talking to Decker on the phone, but I can't remember what was being said."

"Decker must have asked you what the number on the back of the frame was, because the last thing I heard you say was eighty-eight. Then a second later—boom."

"That's right, it was the one piece of the puzzle he didn't have."

"Well, don't worry, he won't be using it."

"No, but the person who set off that bomb will."

"Who's that?"

"There's only one person it could be—the German who hired Decker."

"How do you know someone hired him?"

"The wire."

"Did it tell you where to find him?"

"No, but I know where he's headed—to the Reserve."

"But you don't know where that is," said Zjorn.

"I've got a friend who's a Ph.D. We'll figure it out."

The white curtain that surrounded Fallon was pulled back and a slender, well-groomed man in an expensive suit, accompanied by a nurse, came in. "Going somewhere, Agent Fallon?" The nurse guided Fallon back into a prone position. "I'm Dr. Price, and I'm here to make you beautiful."

While the doctor snipped the ragged edges of Fallon's wound and stitched them together, Fallon thought about Sivia. At first, when his emotions raced forward into anger and hate, he distracted himself by concentrating on the vague pressures of the doctor's work as he pushed and pulled against the medicated numbness that had flooded across the left half of his face. But then he started to feel the strength of a childhood ally—rage. He let it heighten his concentration. He had to figure out where the Reserve was because Sivia's killer would be headed there.

But he had only two of the six coordinates. Something vague and fleeting started evading capture by his consciousness. Was it an answer or just the effects of the concussion the doctor told him he had suffered? The more he concentrated, the more elusive it became.

Finally, the doctor finished. "Because the laceration was a jagged tear, I had to cut away a considerable amount of tissue. I'm afraid you're going to have a fairly noticeable scar." He took out a pad and wrote a prescription. "In an hour or so, you will experience a substantial increase in pain. This should help. I recommend you get it filled as soon as possible." Fallon thanked him, got dressed, and followed the signs to the emergency room parking lot.

Zjorn was on the radio. "That's ten-four. I'll let him know."

Fallon got in and said, "Is that me you're going to let know?"

Reluctantly, Zjorn looked at him. "Yeah, that was Pete Blaney."

"And?"

"When I first got you here, and you were still out of it, I called to let him know what had happened."

"You didn't give yourself up on the Matisse?"

"To make him understand what happened, I had to."

"I should never have gotten you involved."

"He's at the harbor with the divers. He knows you've been released and that I'm taking you home. He said you should come in tomorrow and bring him up to speed."

Fallon had not heard anything after the word *divers*. "What did the divers find?"

"That's what he wanted me to tell you. The only thing they've found so far is a half dozen body parts. Mostly male, but a few female. I'm sorry, Taz."

*   *   *

Fallon stood in his shower being careful not to get the dressing covering his cheekbone wet. Again, the rage started to grow in him. He had to find the Reserve, and before the German.

A dull awareness started nagging at him again. He was overlooking something. What was it? He turned the water to cold and, like the pain in his face, let its shock help him focus. He started at the beginning, the night he met Sivia. Bach's house and the confrontation outside. Then to the police department, and back to Bach's. In the basement, he found that one unused frame that had led them to Marvin Risch. The thought of Marvin Risch stirred something in him. The last time Fallon and Sivia were there, what was it he said? He wondered why Rathkolb had ordered that all the frames be painted a different color. He felt some recognition in those facts, as though they were trying to push whatever he was looking for to the surface.

He started over, meeting Sivia at the restaurant with David Citron, to Bach's, to the police department, back to Bach's and finding the frame. The frame, that was it, the frame was somehow important.

As he dressed, his memory involuntarily walked him back through Bach's basement. He could see how neat it was, all the old hand woodworking tools arranged neatly on top of the workbench. He opened the bench's single drawer; surrounded by a few scattered wood screws and finishing nails were the metal dies used to stamp numbers and letters into wood. Then his mind flashed to the back of the Matisse frame, the four perfect circles that made up the 88. "That's it!" he yelled out to Zjorn.

He came into the living room where the Ph.D. was pouring a cup of the coffee. "That's what?"

Fallon opened his briefcase to verify its contents, closed it, and said, "Let's go."

"Where?"

"To commit a B and E."

44

"I TOLD YOU BEFORE, I DON'T COMMIT FELONIES without malice of forethought," Zjorn said as he pulled away from the curb. "What are we doing?"

"Do you remember who Martin Bach is."

"Sure, true name Josef Rathkolb, the keeper—and hider—of the Reserve."

"That first night, after Sivia and I finished giving our statements to the Des Plaines PD, we went back to look around Bach's house. In the basement, I found an unused picture frame that led us to Marvin Risch. Risch told us that for some unknown reason, Rathkolb had ordered him to paint all the frames a different color. You saw the numbers on the Matisse frame, what do you think was used to make them?"

"Well, they were too perfect to be freehand, so I suppose some sort of numbering tool."

"Guess what I saw in Bach's basement—dies."

"Okay, so those are what he used on the frames, how's that help us?"

"Each frame is painted with a different color. There are ten individual number dies, zero through nine. If we examine each one microscopically, we'll be able to tell by the residue paint fragments which numbers were used on which frames."

Zjorn didn't answer right away. Fallon knew his mind was processing every step of the idea, right up to the final twelve digits of the Reserve's longitude and latitude. "Pretty impressive. Even if those dies were cleaned, an electronic microscope will be able to pick up the faintest molecules of the different colors. But there are some problems. Say we find red paint on the number one die and the number three, is the coordinate thirty-one or thirteen? And even if we can figure which it is, how do we know where those two digits fit in the sequence of six?"

"Let's worry about one thing at a time. We don't even know if the dies are still there," Fallon said. "Besides, it's my job to come up with the absurd, it's yours to make it work."

Zjorn pushed the speedometer up another fifteen miles an hour.

The anesthetic had begun to wear off and the pain in Fallon's cheek was getting worse. He could feel each heartbeat as it zigzagged through the wound. It made him forget his fatigue, but more importantly, each throb renewed his anger. He took out the prescription and tore it into small pieces.

As they parked in the driveway, Bach's house looked the same. Fallon found it hard to believe he had been there only eight days ago. The same padlocked hasp secured the front door. "You got anything to get past that lock?"

"I've got a tire iron in the back."

Zjorn opened his trunk as Fallon scanned the area for witnesses. After Zjorn jammed the flat point under the hasp and wrenched it open, Fallon went in first. "Go in the kitchen and see what's available to pack the individual dies in. They're four or five inches long."

Fallon headed downstairs and was relieved to find the workbench exactly as he remembered it. He opened the drawer and like ingots of precious metal, the dies caught the light from the single bulb overhead. Zjorn came down with a handful of clear plastic sandwich bags. Fallon placed one die in each bag to prevent them from contaminating one another. When they had finished, Zjorn began inspecting the remaining letter dies that were left in the drawer. "These look like they've never been used, so the number dies were probably only used to mark the frames. There should be no previous-use contamination."

Fallon said, "That's good. You're going to have to hand carry these back to the lab if we want this done right away."

"Why me?"

"I'm under suspension, remember?"

Zjorn thought for a second. "I've got a better idea. This is not a complicated examination, we just need to know which colors are on which dies. A friend of mine, Joel Mangren, is working on his Ph.D. in analytical chemistry at the University of Chicago. He does a lot of work with an electron microscope. Let's go see him."

As Zjorn drove south on the Dan Ryan Expressway, Fallon asked, "Think this'll work, Doc?"

"If those dies were used to cut the numbers in the frames, we'll know which ones. You could almost do it with a standard microscope. With the electronic, it's almost overkill. That's the easy part. What I'm worried about is unscrambling the numbers."

After carefully scraping as much residue as possible off each of the cast aluminum dies and onto slides, Joel Mangren methodically placed them one at a time under the electronic microscope. As he watched the fluorescent screen in front of him, he made notes on a pad of paper. Fallon sat on one of the classroom chairs off to the side and watched him and Zjorn, who busied himself writing on a blackboard. He drew six dashes and then wrote one number in the fourth slot:

$$\underline{\quad}\ \underline{\quad}\ \underline{\quad}\ \underline{88}\ \underline{\quad}\ \underline{\quad}$$

Fallon said, "The third number is twenty-six."

"Off the wire?" Zjorn asked. Fallon nodded. "When were you going to tell me that?"

"I wasn't. Less for you to put in your confession. But now that you're going to be charged with multiple felonies, it probably won't make any difference at sentencing," said Fallon.

"That's very reassuring." He wrote in the number:

$$\underline{\quad}\ \underline{\quad}\ \underline{26}\ \underline{88}\ \underline{\quad}\ \underline{\quad}$$

Zjorn said, "This is what we know so far. The twenty-six from—ah, Cleveland sources—and eighty-eight from the painting you recovered. Now, if we're lucky enough to find only one set of numbers

with a four in it, that would probably fill in the first blank space because, assuming what we're looking for is in the Chicago area, the location should be in either the forty-first or forty-second parallel. If
that happens, there'll only be three coordinates that we will have to
position. As a visual aid, let's say it's forty-one." He wrote the number
in the first position:

41 __ 26 88 __ __

"Then we're halfway there," Zjorn said and sat down at a desk
next to Fallon.

For the next half hour, Mangren examined all ten dies, methodi-
cally recording the results. Finally he sat upright and arched his back.
With his notes in hand, he went up to the blackboard. Next to
Zjorn's numbers, he wrote:

#0—
#1 white, blue
#2 green, red, gold
#3—
#4 green
#5—
#6 red
#7 white
#8 black
#9 gold, blue

"There's how they break down," Mangren said.

Zjorn walked back to the blackboard. "Okay, one matches up with
seven because they're both white that gives us either seventeen or
seventy-one. The next is nineteen or ninety-one, both blue. Then
green gives us twenty-four or forty-two, red—twenty-six or sixty-
two, and gold is twenty-nine or ninety-two. And that leaves the eight
without a match because it was used twice for the eighty-eight. And
since there is only one number with a four in it, our first coordinate is
not forty-one, but forty-two. Now let's see what we have." He picked
up the chalk, erased the 41, and wrote in the new numbers:

<u>42</u> __ <u>26</u> <u>88</u> __ __

(17 or 71) (19 or 91) (29 or 92)

"But all the unknown numbers are either minutes or seconds, which means they cannot exceed sixty, so the first one has to be seventeen, the second nineteen, and the third twenty-nine."

Zjorn erased and rewrote the second row:

<u>42</u> __ <u>26</u> <u>88</u> __ __

(17)(19)(29)

"Now if you remember your high school math, specifically permutations and combinations, we can figure out how many combinations there are by trying those three numbers in the blank spaces. Because there are a total of three items, you multiply three times two times one, which equals six. So we have six possible locations to check. Not bad, huh?"

"That's great, Doc," Fallon said. "But how do we find those locations on the ground from longitude and latitude? It's not like they're street addresses."

"We need a GPS receiver."

Fallon asked, "That's the thing that works off the satellites?"

"Right, Global Positioning System. It's a handheld computer that'll give you your longitude and latitude, even your elevation if you need it." Zjorn looked at the board for a moment and said, "But there is a small problem with it, the readout is in degrees only. The frame coordinates are probably in degrees, minutes, and seconds. But making the conversion isn't difficult, finding their actual location is going to be the problem."

Mangren interrupted. "Mat, have you seen those CD-ROM digital maps?"

Zjorn said, "I think I read something about them."

"Once you bring them up on a computer screen, you can go from an overview of an area, like northern Illinois, and zoom in until you're close enough to see buildings. But the best part is as you move the cursor across the map, there are three windows at the top giving you a constant readout. One for elevation, and the other two are longitude and latitude, in degrees, minutes, and seconds. I've got a laptop I can lend you."

"Believe it or not, they issue them in training school now with your gun and badge."

"Does it have a CD-ROM capability?"

"We're the government, nothing is too expensive for us."

"Then you could load up the software and get a fix on all six locations in a matter of minutes. If one of them is in, say, Lake Michigan, you could eliminate it without having to physically go to that point. It'd save you a lot of time."

Zjorn said, "I'm sold; where's the closest outdoor outfitter?"

45

FALLON DROVE AS ZJORN BROUGHT UP THE MAP OF the Chicago area on his computer's screen. He moved the mouse around until the two small windows at the top read 42°0'0"N and 88°0'0"W. "Since we know it's going to be forty-two north and eighty-eight west, let's see where that is and use it as a starting point." He studied the map for a moment. "It's close to Schaumburg, why don't we head up there. All six of the possible locations will be north and west of that point." Zjorn made more calculations. "The distance between the two possibilities that are farthest from each other is twelve miles, so we're looking at a box twelve miles by twelve miles that all six of our coordinates fit into. How do you want to start eliminating them?"

"See which ones you can zoom in on. Like Joel said, if one's in the middle of a lake, we can eliminate it. We have to be looking for some kind of building."

Zjorn moved the mouse carefully until the windows reported the first coordinate on his pad. "The first one is in the Moraine Hills state park."

"I think we can bypass that."

"The second is in Richmond, Illinois, which is about one mile south of the Wisconsin border."

"That's a possibility. Remember, the first painting was up in the Milwaukee area."

"The next one is two miles west of there. Neither location shows any buildings at those exact coordinates, but there are some structures within a mile or so."

"Let's not eliminate them because of a lack of buildings. They're built and torn down everyday, and who knows how old that map is."

"Then the next two are within two miles of each other around the town of Woodstock. Again, there are buildings within a mile. No, wait a minute, the one farther south is in the middle of a cemetery."

"Let's skip that one, too."

"The last one is just outside of McHenry with a structure within half a mile."

"That's four possibles. Which one you want to go to first?" Fallon asked.

"I like the Wisconsin connection. Why don't we start up at Richmond, work our way south to McHenry, and then the one farther west in Woodstock. That way if they're all negative, we'll be right there to check out the cemetery, just in case."

"Do you know how to work that GPS?"

"By the time you get us to Richmond, I will." Zjorn got out the owner's manual and began reading.

An hour later they were standing in a cornfield. Zjorn double-checked the numbers on the GPS screen against his notes. "This is it. We're dead on it." Both men looked around; the only building they could see was a house almost a mile away.

"Well, let's go make a nuisance of ourselves," Fallon said.

"What are you going to do, ask if they have any looted paintings?"

"Not a bad idea."

When they got to the door, Fallon knocked. A woman in her late twenties answered, and when Zjorn held up his credentials, she said, "FBI?"

"Yes, ma'am," Fallon said. "We're out here on a wild-goose chase, looking for some stolen paintings, and your address came up." He watched her reaction carefully.

She gave a short, casual laugh. "Stolen paintings? Boy, are you in the wrong place."

"Mind if we come in and take a look around? That way we can take you off our list."

"Are unmade beds against the law?"

"If they were, I'd be in the electric chair," said Fallon.

She laughed and held the screen door open. "Make yourselves at home."

A half hour later they were back in the car headed for the next location. Zjorn said, "I think we can draw a line through that one." Fallon didn't answer. "Taz."

"Sorry, what?"

"We can eliminate that one?"

"That's what I was wondering about. Is the Reserve going to be somewhere by itself or will someone be standing guard?"

"Well, he had people holding the other six paintings, wouldn't it be logical that he would do the same with the whole load?"

"I'm not sure he would trust any one person with the entire Reserve. But I guess we won't know until we find it. What's next?"

"Just stay on this road for about eight miles."

Ten minutes later, Zjorn checked the digital map again. "I'm not sure exactly where we are. Pull up after this intersection so I can get a fix on our position." He got out and turned on the GPS receiver. After a minute, he said, "It's back this way." He pointed across the intersection they had just come through. "I don't want to lose reception; I'll walk."

By the time Fallon turned the car around and pulled into a gas station, Zjorn had made his way around to the back of the building. He was looking out into a wooded area about a hundred yards away. "This one is somewhere between here and those woods. If it's here, it's got to be in the gas station." They turned around and examined the tiny building.

"Two down, two to go," Zjorn said.

Fallon drove up to the third location, which was just outside McHenry, Illinois. Fifty feet off the road, in a stand of trees, the remnants of a house's stone foundation was just visible in the overgrown weeds. Zjorn got out again to take a reading and, walking farther away from the road, he watched the GPS's screen intently. When he finally looked up, he saw a barn that, because of the winding road back through the trees, had not been visible when they parked. Around the side of it sat a dark gray mini-van. He hurried back to the car. "Taz, there's a barn in the back with a mini-van parked around the side."

Fallon felt the blood pump faster through his wound. "Did you get the tag?"

"Yeah."

Fallon gave him the keys. "You drive." Zjorn could see that Fallon had sensed something. Both of them got in the car and drove a quarter mile and pulled onto an old, unused road that was not visible from the barn they had just left. Zjorn called in the license plate, and it came back to a rental agency at O'Hare airport. "What do you think, Taz? Makes sense this guy would have a rental." Fallon reached over the seat and got his briefcase. He opened it and took out his personal nine-millimeter automatic and two loaded magazines. "I guess you think it's them."

"I want you to drop me there and take off."

"Take off? Are you nuts?"

"There's a good chance whoever killed Sivia is inside. If he is, not everyone will be coming out."

"And what if it's you that doesn't come out, how am I supposed to carry that around?"

Fallon stared at him for a while before saying, "Okay, but I want fifteen minutes inside first."

"I don't—"

"The negotiations are over. Drop me out in front, then bring the car back here and hide it. By the time you get there, I should have my fifteen minutes."

Zjorn was stunned by the tone of Fallon's voice. Never had he heard anything so calm and yet so full of hatred. He put the car into reverse and pulled back onto the paved road.

46

AS FALLON NEARED THE BARN, HE COULD SEE THAT two strips of steel plate, each at least eight feet long, had been drilled and bolted to the adjoining edges of the ten-foot-high double doors at the front of the structure. They were welded together to prevent anyone from entering. Wanting to keep the element of surprise, he worked his way around the opposite side of the barn from where the van was parked. There were only a few windows, and they were all fifteen feet off the ground. Each was fitted with fiberboard inserts that had been nailed tightly into place.

At the end of the back wall nearest the van, some of the weathered gray siding had been broken away, and the pieces lay scattered nearby on the ground. The opening was just large enough for a person to fit through.

Fallon listened for voices, but heard only the persistent hissing of gas escaping. It was accompanied by the smell of burnt garlic. Thumbing the safety off his automatic, he stepped inside.

The afternoon sun, through razor-thin cracks in the west wall, marked the barn's interior with a dozen paper-thin sheets of light, each scoring the floor like bright yellow knife cuts.

At the far end, illuminated only by the blue-white glow of an acetylene torch, was the hulk of an ancient armored car. Time had oxidized its paint to a dusty pink. Its wheels had been cut off the axles, so it sat low in the straw that covered the floor. Someone had used a welding torch to seal the doors and attach sheets of steel plate over the windows, turning the old truck into a vault.

There were two men standing next to the vehicle. One was a powerful-looking man using a cutting torch to burn through one of the side windows. The other, apparently supervising, wore an expensive suit and Fallon could see thick scars on his left cheek, which glowed with a blue iridescence in the burning light.

The one in charge said something in German, and Fallon thought he recognized the voice from the Cleveland tapes, but the rage was hammering away at his cheekbone, and he realized he couldn't rely on his objectivity. The floor around the truck was littered with a number of brand-new tools; everything from a sledge hammer, to wrecking bars of various lengths, to steel chisels, to flashlights, and even a kerosene lamp.

They were just starting to burn through the thick metal covering one of the truck's windows. The man with the scars spoke again and although Fallon couldn't make out the words, the gestures seemed increasingly impatient.

Cautiously, Fallon moved directly behind them to limit their ability to retreat to cover. Then he yelled above the torch's noise, "Everybody freeze!"

Startled, both men spun around. It took them a moment to find Fallon in the darkness. A smirk settled across Brunner's face as he recognized him. "You are the policeman from the harbor."

"And you're the German with the bomb."

The accusation dropped Brunner's jaw. "I am here as a tourist."

"Okay, you're the tourist with the bomb."

"I am here on holiday."

"I'm curious, did the travel brochures recommend you bring your own cutting torch or buy one here?"

He looked at the bandage under Fallon's eye. "I have nothing further to say."

"You don't want to talk? You're making all my dreams come true." He waved his gun in the direction of the acetylene tank. "You and Egor, straddle the tank."

Brunner whispered something in German to Steinhaus, and he started to move away from his boss, the burning torch held at his side like a weapon at the ready. Then Brunner said, "Do you know that one of your country's great weaknesses is all the restrictions on its policemen?"

"That's so true." said Fallon as he raised his gun, aimed carefully, and fired. The bullet nicked the outer edge of Steinhaus's ear, freezing him. "Fortunately, I'm no longer a policeman."

"Then what are you doing here?" Brunner asked. "The Reserve?"

"I'm not much of an art lover, but when it comes to revenge, I'm a real pig." Steinhaus started moving away from Brunner again. Fallon swung his gun around, pointing it at the center of Brunner's face. "If he takes one more step, I'm going to shoot you through both ears—and with only one bullet." Steinhaus stopped and waited for orders. None came.

Fallon said, "Turn off the torch."

Brunner nodded at Steinhaus and he closed the valve. Fallon then backed both men up by motioning with his gun until they were straddling the acetylene tank attached to the torch. "Since you two seem to enjoy explosions, I thought maybe you'd prefer this form of interrogation." He aimed at the tank, "Tell me about putting the bomb on the boat."

Brunner said something in German, and Fallon assumed that he was telling Steinhaus not to say anything. He fired a shot that struck the floor about two inches from the tank. Neither of the two men showed any reaction. Brunner said, "An explosion would kill you also."

Fallon raised his gun slightly. "Why didn't I think of that." He snapped off another shot that hit the floor, this time an inch away. Fallon pointed his automatic at Brunner's face again. The German stared back defiantly. But then, he glimpsed past Fallon. An ugly smirk crawled across the German's mouth, "So what if we did, we killed only criminals and a Jew."

Sensing someone was behind him, Fallon pivoted, lowering himself into a crouch, hoping to find a target in time. Eduard Wald stood with a gun aimed at him. Before either man could fire, a shot came from the shadows near the opening in the back wall. Wald fell slowly forward, each of his eyes uselessly searching in a different direction. For an instant, Fallon assumed Zjorn had fired the shot, but then he realized that the sound was the quieted hiss of a silencer. From the darkened corner came a familiar voice. "Drop the gun." Fallon knew if he tried to turn and fire, he would be as dead as the man who lay in front of him. He let go of his automatic and let it drop onto the wooden floor.

He watched in disbelief as Kurt Decker stepped forward. Somehow he had survived the blast. If it wasn't for his left hand being heavily bandaged, he would have seemed immortal.

He nodded for Fallon to move by the others, and said, "Rölf, you look a little surprised to see me." Brunner gave an order to Steinhaus in guttural German, but before he could move, Decker shot him in the chest and he fell back. Although badly wounded, he attempted to stand. Taking a quick step forward, Decker rested his automatic on the bandaged left hand to steady his aim and fired again. The shot caught Steinhaus just above the left eyebrow. His powerful body resisted for a moment but then flattened out. "That's a pretty extravagant way to remind you that I understand even the most idiomatic German."

Stoically, Brunner said, "Two million dollars."

"Inside that truck are *hundreds* of millions of dollars."

"You'll never be able to sell them."

"You have only yourself to blame for this. You're the one who kept throwing up my father's ability to accomplish the impossible. Well, congratulations, you've convinced me. If I can find the Reserve, I can find a way to sell it."

"A certain sophistication is needed in dealing with the caliber of people who have the breeding and money to buy paintings of this quality. Although you are a person of infinite resources, I think you are honest enough to admit that you are not so equipped."

"You're absolutely right, but I've got something better than culture, or loyalty, or that honor you're always talking about; I've got the gun."

"This is the future of Germany you're attempting to steal. Others will come after you."

Decker laughed. "Why would they come after me, I died last night in an explosion."

"Three million."

"Is that your best offer?"

Thinking he had finally found Decker's price, he said, "Yes."

Decker raised his gun and fired twice into Brunner's chest, killing him. "I'm sorry, that's just not enough. And you, Fallon," Decker continued, "you have been quite the competitor. I don't know how you found this place, but I'm impressed."

"On the contrary, that you survived that explosion is what's impressive." Fallon tried to glance at his watch.

Decker held up his bandaged hand to display it was his only injury. "I must be lucky like my old man." Then motioning toward Fallon's watch, he said, "Expecting someone? I hope it's not your partner—he won't be coming."

Instead of the rage Fallon expected, a strange, almost euphoric evenness came over him. Although he had come to kill whoever was responsible for Sivia's death, the idea of taking a life had frightened him. But Doc being gunned down left no doubt in his mind that Decker needed killing. And Fallon suspected that his illogical restraint was his subconscious warning him to be patient. "Why am I still alive?"

Decker held up his bandaged hand again. "Simple, I'm going to need your help getting inside the truck. I've been here since early this morning, trying to figure out how to get into it when Brunner and his two stooges showed up. So I figured I'd let them do the work, even load the paintings into their van. When they left to get the equipment, I went outside and hid in the woods. They were doing just fine until you showed up."

"Then maybe you shouldn't have killed them."

"It looked to me like you were going to do that anyway. Besides, with all of you alive, things were getting just too complicated. I'm sorry if I deprived you of the pleasure of shooting them."

"Don't worry about me, I'm already making alternate plans."

Decker laughed. "Well, while you're plotting your revenge, pick up the torch and get to work on opening up that truck."

Fallon lit the torch and adjusted the gas flow until it was a seeringly sharp tongue of flame. He examined the cut that Steinhaus had started. He hesitated and then turned off the tank. Decker said, "This isn't the part where you tell me you'd rather die than help scum like me, is it?"

"Do you know how hot this burns?"

"I've torched my way into a few safes—I'd guess a few thousand degrees."

"What do you think that will do to the paintings inside?"

Decker didn't answer right away. "How else can you get in there?"

"Did you notice anything about the steel plate they were trying to cut through?"

"No."

"All the plate that's been welded on is one-inch. This window is half-inch. That's why they wanted to go in there. You've been trying to get into Rathkolb's head for a while now, what does this tell you?"

Decker thought for a second. "He wants us to go through that window . . . it's boobytrapped?"

"If I wasn't the one with the torch in my hands, I'd let you find out for yourself."

Decker took a couple of steps back and examined the vehicle as it sat flat on its axles. It appeared crouched, like a great wounded beast that is even more dangerous because it has been forced into a defensive posture. He noticed that the straw was scattered, but around the armored car it was so thick the floor couldn't be seen. Keeping the automatic trained on Fallon, he squatted down and ran the fingertips of his bandaged hand under it. Around the periphery of the vehicle he could feel the edge of more steel plate. He traced its edge for a short distance in both directions. Then he stood up and, keeping Fallon in front of him, walked around the vehicle cautiously, performing the same inspection with his foot as he went along. "The entire thing is sitting on steel plate. Why would anybody do that?"

Once Decker discovered the protective plating under the armored car, Fallon knew not only why it had been boobytrapped, but where the Reserve was. His only answer to Decker was an unemotional stare.

"I guess you're not going to be much help. Which means I should kill you, too, but I am in sudden need of a mine detector." He stared back at Fallon but the agent's mind was elsewhere. "Maybe Rathkolb thought a Nazi would be smart enough, or suspicious enough, to keep from setting it off." He glanced at the dead bodies. "Well, so much for the smart Nazis theory." He became silent again, and after a few seconds, said, "All the paintings, all the clues lead to this place, the Reserve has to be here. Why put the steel plate under the truck? It would deflect the blast upward." Decker glanced up into the rafters. "Why?" Then he said, "Of course, it's not to damage anything above but rather to protect what's below. There has to be a space under the floor."

When Fallon had come around the barn, he saw that over the years the grading had worn away, exposing the foundation. The thick slabs of limestone were set too deep to just be supporting the structure. There had to be a lower level.

"But how do we get down there?" Decker asked.

"I'm afraid I can't help you."

"I would think you'd be glad to."

"Why?"

"To stay alive a little longer, to hold onto some hope that you might somehow get out of this. And admit it, Fallon, you want to see those paintings as badly as I do. But if you're not going to help me, I'll just stack you on the pile of Germans."

"You're right, I do want to stay alive a little longer." He turned so Decker could see his eyes. "There's something I've got to take care of before I go."

47

ALTHOUGH DECKER HAD LAUGHED AT FALLON'S threat, he held his gun with a little more readiness as they walked around the barn, looking for access to the space below. Fallon had one of the German's flashlights in his hand and Decker carried the kerosene lamp he found next to the truck.

Decker said, "Any secret door or panel would have to be hidden in one of the corners, because they're the least trafficked areas and there's less chance of accidental discovery." The two men went past the first corner. It was piled high with scrap lumber. Decker moved on. Once he saw the second one, he said, "This looks good. The floor's completely covered with hay here, just like under the car." He dragged his feet under the straw, exploring the floor's surface. His foot caught on something—a wooden cleat. A foot later he found another. He followed the pattern for ten feet, with another cleat nailed down every twelve inches.

At the end, he bounced around on his toes, testing the floor. When he felt it give slightly under one foot, he found a crack that ran along the floorboards. He cleared the area around it until he discovered another crack running at a right angle, along the row of cleats. Together they formed a three-foot-by-ten-foot rectangle. "This is it. This section tips down and becomes a ramp. That's what the cleats are for, so you won't slip as you go down. Now I just have to figure out how to lower it. The latch has to be at the end that tips down."

While he continued to point his weapon at Fallon, Decker went back to the end that had given slightly under the pressure of his foot and examined the wall alongside of it. When he didn't find anything, he thoroughly cleaned out the crack at the end and followed it away from the wall. Three feet away was a wooden beam that supported the roof. Hidden at the base of it was a thick metal rod, the end of which was bent at ninety degrees and sticking up out of the floor about three inches. Farther away from the wall was a groove in the floor that the rod could travel across. He pulled it along the groove. The floor did not sink until Decker touched it with his foot. It gave way to the pressure and then came back up when he took his weight off of it. "It's being held up by a counterweight." He ordered Fallon to the end nearest the corner and told him to step down. As he did, the far end of the section slowly lowered into the void below.

"After you," Decker said. By the time Fallon stepped on the third cleat, the end of the wooden incline had touched down on the floor below. He continued his descent into the subterranean chamber's cool dampness.

Decker turned up the flame on the kerosene lamp and followed. As soon as he got off the ramp, it slowly swung back up into place. There was a knotted rope hanging from it. Decker grabbed it, and as he pulled, the ramp started to come down again. "Must have been an old bootlegger's warehouse or something."

Fallon flashed his light up and inspected the system that converted the floor into an entrance for the lower level. A large cube of limestone that weighed at least two hundred pounds sat suspended on a wooden tray. It was held in the air by thick rope that ran through two large wooden pulleys. All the parts appeared to be as old as the barn except the ropes; they had been recently replaced. "This wasn't used by bootleggers," Fallon said. "The ramp is too steep to get anything as heavy as a barrel back up. And the shallow grooves in the side of the counterweight were cut by hand. They stopped doing that long before Prohibition."

Fallon was surprised at how large the hidden level was. As best he could tell, it was about half the size of the barn above. As he walked to the far end, he saw the remnants of what looked like six cots, consisting of wooden frames interlaced with loosely woven strips of canvas, now mostly rotted. Above them, on a large limestone slab, printed in faded black paint was a Bible verse:

> And the chief answered,
> With a great sum obtained I this freedom.
> And Paul said,
> But I was free born.
>
> *Acts 22:28*

It suddenly occurred to Fallon that this had been a safe house for the Underground Railroad, part of the route used by runaway slaves on their way to the legal freedom of Canada before the Civil War. Chicago was a well-documented "station," and some of its Quaker residents were known for their unshakable abolitionist beliefs and activities.

"What are you looking at?" Decker asked. Fallon didn't say anything as he turned his flashlight into the darkness ahead.

At the end of the huge room, a corner had been chambered off by two additional stone walls. In the middle of one of them was a thick wooden door with a heavy steel-rod dead bolt on the outside. Fallon thought the room had probably been the last century's edition of an ice box, used to store perishable foods. It being on the hidden level would also have allowed the runaways to feed themselves without any help from above. On the door was a hand-painted swastika:

卍

Like the Bible verse, it was also black. How ironic, Fallon thought.

"Look at that swastika!" Decker said. "This is it!"

Fallon's eyes lingered on the Nazi symbol. There was something about it that didn't seem right. Every swastika he'd ever seen had the ends of its arms bent at right angles in a clockwise direction, but these were counterclockwise.

He thought of the truck above him—was this a warning, a warning that only a Nazi would detect?

"Open it," Decker ordered. Fallon slid the rod back, unlocking the door. He walked backward, pulling on the handle, purposely keeping the thick bulkhead between himself and the interior of the room. When nothing happened, at Decker's insistence, he stepped inside.

Decker came in right behind him. His lamp lit up the entire room.

Neatly stacked on specially constructed shelves was the Führer's Reserve. Close to a hundred paintings, all of them shrink-wrapped in thick, translucent plastic, row after row, shelf after shelf. Although the masterpieces were barely distinguishable through the milky plastic coverings, their collective presence commanded a certain reverence. Here in this small, abandoned cellar, hundreds of years of the world's best art sat with a martyred patience, as if knowing that its beauty and genius would always outlast the petty agendas of those who had stolen it.

Greed widened Decker's eyes as he pointed his gun at Fallon and told him to sit on the ground next to the wall. "I did it. I found the Führer's Reserve. I'm missing only the Sisley and the Matisse. But ninety-eight isn't bad." Then he noticed that the first painting in front of him was not encased in plastic. What he didn't notice was that it was the only one with a frame around it.

From his angle on the floor, Fallon could see that the frame was thicker behind the canvas than in front of it. "I wonder why this one wasn't wrapped?" Decker asked as he reached for it. When he pulled it off the shelf, there was an almost imperceptible mechanical click.

As he brought the painting closer so he could see it in the lantern's light, the canvas exploded, covering his face with a fine gray powder. For a moment, he seemed confused by the pranklike attack, but then his hands shot to his eyes. At the same time, the shelf, relieved of the weight of the framed painting, tipped back slowly. Then something at the back end of it fell to the floor, and glass broke. Immediately Fallon could smell gasoline. Decker had started to grunt painfully while he tried to rake the burning dust out of his eyes with his fingertips. Fallon saw what looked like wisps of gaseous fumes coming off Decker's face. Then the FBI agent smelled something he remembered from the University of Chicago's chemistry lab earlier that day—acid. The moisture from Decker's eyes was apparently converting the powdered chemical to a concentrated liquid. Then there were two thuds as something dense hit the floor. Fallon scrambled to his feet as two *pops* went off in rapid succession, the kind he had heard in training dozens of times. They were either smoke grenades or incendiary devices. He thought he knew which.

Decker was now hacking and spitting violently, trying to clear his throat and mouth. Fallon dove through the doorway just as the first grenade ignited. A small explosion followed and flames streamed out the door for a moment before returning to feast on the unburned gasoline inside. Decker's voice now became louder, not a scream, but a roar, a bellowing, like a great wounded animal. The second device exploded and the fire seemed to double in strength. Almost simultaneously, a third explosion went off. It sounded as though it were up on the barn's main floor. With the flashlight still in his hand, Fallon ran to the ramp and pulled it down.

Once he was up in the barn, he headed for the opening through the rear wall. But the room where the Reserve had been stored was directly under the opening. The fire, fed by the gasoline, was spreading through the barn's century-old timber at an incredible rate. Then he realized that the third explosion had been caused by a device set in the floor near the opening. The flames were already six feet high on the upper level. The exit was completely blocked. The entire barn had become another of Rathkolb's traps.

Fallon would have to make his own opening. Next to the armored car, he found a large crowbar. He went to the nearest wall and for the first time saw that dense panels of fiberboard had been bolted into the studs. He took the crowbar and, with a two-handed baseball swing, chopped at the panels, but after a half dozen attempts he had hardly dented it. Smoke was starting to fill the barn.

He ran back to the armored car, picked up his gun, and disconnected the torch hose on the acetylene tank. The gage showed that it was three quarters full. He brought it back to the wall and placed its valve against one of the eight-by-eight wooden beams that supported the roof. The bottom of the tank was aimed toward the wall ten feet away. Then he hurried to the pile of scrap lumber he had seen when they were looking for the entrance to the lower level. He found two six-foot sections of eight-by-eights. They were heavy enough that he had to make separate trips to carry them over to the cylinder. He laid them tightly along the sides of the tank to ensure its direction of flight.

The smoke was thickening quickly and he started coughing. It was becoming more difficult to see, so he took his flashlight and set it down close to the tank to illuminate the valve. Backing up thirty feet, he laid down on the barn's floor and sighted his nine millimeter at the juncture of the tank and valve. In theory, with the valve resting against the thick structural beam and the eight-by-eights as guides, the tank would be propelled in the direction of the wall with enough force to go through it easily. That was if he could make the shot. It had to be very accurate because if too much of the tank was hit, it could explode and spray shrapnel everywhere. If he got too much valve, it could misdirect the missile's path and send it anywhere in the barn. There was also a possibility that it could hit the armored car and set off whatever was inside of it.

He flattened himself against the floor and lined up the sights on his weapon. He fired, but a moment too quickly, jerking his head down behind his hands in anticipation of an explosion. As soon as the gun discharged, he realized his mistake. He decided that he had to chance leaving his head a little higher for that split second to ensure the shot. But if the tank was hit, that split second was enough to send its fragments at him. The smoke was now so thick it was starting to settle along the floor. He watched it swirl into the flashlight beam thirty feet away. It was now or never. Then he heard something behind him.

Standing at the top of the ramp was Kurt Decker. From his chest down, his clothes were almost completely burned away. The little that was left were still smoldering. All his exposed skin was charred. His face glistened with horrible, open wounds. One eye seemed to be cauterized shut, while the other blinked at an incredible rate. Hanging from his blackened right hand was his automatic. He spotted Fallon through the smoke and fired once.

Fallon rolled over on his back, shot three times without taking aim, and missed. Decker fired again and missed. Fallon took a short breath, held it, and squeezed the trigger. This time he hit Decker in the stomach. He staggered but didn't go down. He started toward Fallon.

Taking aim again, Fallon fired at Decker's hip. The bullet's impact ripped his torso sideways and his leg buckled, sending him to the floor. He tried to get up using his unbandaged hand, but he couldn't get his disobedient legs under him. He lost the grip on his gun and it skidded away. Cautiously, Fallon went over to him and kicked his gun farther into the smoky darkness. Decker looked up with what vision he had left and gave a short, choking laugh. "I guess we're about to find out exactly how much heart you do have."

Fallon couldn't understand how a man could endure so much pain and felt an unwanted admiration for him. He turned to go back to take up a firing position for the acetylene tank and Decker yelled, "I'm already dead, Fallon, just don't leave me like this!"

Fallon ignored him and sighted his nine millimeter on the tank's valve. He fired and the tank exploded. When he raised his head, he saw a hole in the wall slightly larger than the size of the tank. The surrounding fiberboard had now been loosened from the studs, so he picked up the crowbar that had been useless just minutes before and pried away a large piece of the material. The barn siding beyond it was splintered but the hole wasn't large enough for Fallon to escape. He went back to his two-handed swing. Between kicking, prying, and swinging, the hole was soon large enough for him to fit through.

From behind Fallon, a one-word scream ripped through the smoke and fire. "*Please!*" It was almost as if the single syllable were a foreign language that Decker had never spoken before and, even though agonizingly desperate, was having difficulty pronouncing now. As primal as it was, there was a certain dignity to it. Fallon turned toward him, raised his gun, and fired a single round through Kurt Decker's head.

Fallon pushed himself through the opening in the outer wall and into the clear air beyond. His first thought was of Zjorn. He ran to the back of the barn and found him next to the original opening they had used to gain entry. Smoke was streaming out of the hole. Zjorn lay facedown. Fallon rolled him over carefully. The pool of blood next to him was fairly large, but to Fallon's eye, not life-threatening. His breathing was shallow and rapid. Fallon pushed his second and third fingers against Zjorn's carotid artery. His pulse was weak and twice as fast as normal.

As heat and smoke seeped out of the barn through the cracks between the siding, the fire's roar began to crescendo. Fallon pulled

Zjorn up over his shoulder and hurried to the German's van. They had left the keys in the ignition. Fallon slid open the cargo door and placed the unconscious agent on the floor. He drove up to the road and for the first time noticed the sound of sirens. "That couldn't be the fire department already," he said out loud.

A pained voice from behind him said, "It's Blaney."

Fallon turned around to see Zjorn conscious and trying to pull himself up into a sitting position. Fallon put the van in park, climbed in back, and said, "Fortunately, one of us had some sense." He took off Zjorn's bloody suit coat and tore away his shirt.

"How bad is it?" Zjorn asked.

There was a single entry wound in his upper left back and an exit wound in the upper left chest. There was not much blood flow from either. "It looks like you got a major problem here. You're only going to be able to use one hand to stuff dollars bills into those G-strings for a while."

Zjorn smiled painfully. "That's okay, because then it'll take me twice as long. And with my arm in a sling, I'll probably be allowed an occasional sympathy grope," Zjorn said. "Who shot me?"

"Believe it or not, Decker."

"Decker!"

"Don't ask me, you're the one with the analytical skills."

Two Bureau cars slid to a halt on the road next to the van. Fallon opened the window. "Call for an ambulance, Doc's been hit. And you'd better follow me up the road. I think that barn is about to blow."

As Fallon turned onto the road, Zjorn asked, "Taz, what happened inside?"

"Decker and three Germans, they're all dead. Just lay back and relax. I'll give you all the details later."

"How about the paintings?"

"You know how badly Decker wanted them?"

"Yeah."

"He decided to stay with them."

48

FALLON PULLED ONTO THE DIRT ROAD WHERE ZJORN
had left his car. The other Bureau cars parked behind him. The first
one out was Pete Blaney. "Taz, where's Doc?"

"He's in the back with a through-and-through chest wound.
Decker shot him."

Blaney opened the sliding door and rolled Zjorn half-over so he
could see the wound. "How you feeling?"

"Like I've been shot."

"Hang on, an ambulance is on the way." Another agent appeared
with the first aid kit from his car and started tying compression ban-
dages around Zjorn's back and chest.

Blaney led Fallon away from the van. "What happened in there?"
Fallon explained about the Germans, and how Decker had somehow
survived the boat explosion only to hit a boobytrap in the barn.
"What were they after?"

"There were some more paintings."

"How many?"

Fallon decided not to tell him about the extent of the Reserve; he
had enough problems. "I don't know, a few I guess."

"Why were they boobytrapped?"

"Like everything else in this case, to keep them out of the wrong
hands."

"Well, it looks like that part worked. How'd you wind up here?"

"There were codes on the back of the paintings. Doc helped me figure it out."

With a look of mild disbelief, Blaney stared at Fallon for a few seconds. "You know, Taz, there are a lot of holes in this story. If I was any farther from retirement, I might want to try and fill them in. But Decker and his crew are dead and everybody will be too busy taking bows to care. And I'm certainly not looking to complicate my life. As far as I'm concerned, this case, except for a little reverse English with the media, is closed."

Before Fallon could say anything, the barn exploded. "It is now."

"You'd better come in tomorrow and get all this down on paper. I'll talk to Stamen. With the girl dead, that wiretap can't be linked to you. Unless you decide to confess, I should be able to get you reinstated."

Fallon didn't answer, and Blaney could see the mention of Sivia's death had hit a nerve. "Taz, I'm sorry."

"Yeah," Fallon said, his voice drained.

Trying to change the subject, Blaney said, "Other than putting out the fire, is there anything else that needs to be done here?"

Fallon was still thinking about Sivia. He wished he could have recovered the Reserve for her, but it was gone now. Then something occurred to him: Where were the paintings Decker had gotten from his victims? On the Cleveland tape, it sounded as though he had turned one or two over to the German. If that was so, as mobile as the Germans had been the last twenty-four hours, there was a chance they were somewhere in the van. And if Decker had gotten the last painting from Linge, that meant he had at least three of them himself. Where was his car? It had to be close by. "I think this van should be taken to the office and searched. If you can have someone take Doc's car back, I'll drive the van."

An ambulance pulled up. Blaney said, "Okay, I'll brief the police when they get here and they can secure the scene. We'll have to send an evidence team back in the morning when everything has cooled off. Don't leave just yet."

While Fallon waited, he watched the fire department battle the blaze. Two uniformed police officers directed traffic around the bottleneck, and Zjorn was taken away in the ambulance. The other agents had driven back down the road and were standing around with Blaney talking to the police. Fallon went to the rear of the van and opened the door. There were several suitcases. He hefted them, trying to judge by their weight if they could contain only the paintings. They all had the normal weight of clothing except for a large, wide briefcase that was much heavier. Inside he found an electronic scanner, the kind used for intercepting phone calls.

Under the bags was a storage compartment. Fallon pushed everything forward and opened the hatch. Cushioned by a couple of hotel towels were two paintings—according to their signatures, by Cranach and Degas—each wrapped in heavy brown paper. Fallon covered them up, closed the hatch, and pulled the suitcases back over them. So now he had two of the paintings, but what was he going to do with them?

And where were the other paintings Decker had obtained? If the Germans had the paintings in their vehicle—probably because they expected to leave as soon as the Reserve was found—then maybe Decker had done the same thing. But where was his car? Unlike the Germans, he had been smart enough not to park close to the barn, but logically it had to be hidden within walking distance. Fallon went out onto the road and looked around. The surrounding terrain was flat and open. There were only two stands of trees: the one that surrounded the barn, and the other was where Zjorn had parked the Bureau car.

At Blaney's direction, an agent had already taken Zjorn's car and followed the ambulance to the hospital. Fallon walked to where it had been parked and examined the overgrown road. Farther in, about seventy-five yards off of the main road, was a second thicket. He made sure no one was paying attention to him and then headed toward it. The ground was dry and it was difficult to detect any signs that a vehicle had recently been through there. Fallon followed a right angle turn and then he saw it—a black Chevy Blazer.

On the front seat was a GPS receiver, similar to the one Zjorn had used. A road map of the area lay on the passenger side floor. Inside a large canvas bag on the backseat were the tools of Decker's trade: a sawed-off shotgun, a similar length carbine, an old army .45 automatic, ammunition, handcuffs, a set of binoculars, and various burglary tools including a couple of ski masks. The cargo hatch was empty.

He checked above the visor and inside the glove compartment. He searched under the front and rear seats but found nothing. He sat down in the passenger seat and picked up the unfolded map. The approximate location of the barn was circled with some longitude and latitude notes scribbled in the margins. On the floor were the box for the GPS receiver and its instruction booklet.

For the next ten minutes, he thumbed through the manual, trying to acquaint himself with its basic operation. Zjorn had explained to him that a position reading was difficult to obtain while in a car, so he got out and turned the receiver on. He watched as it slowly locked onto four satellites. Then he hit the menu button. One of the lines read *landmarks*. The booklet said that the landmark function was to record locations where the operator had been so he could find the way back. Fallon scrolled down and hit the enter button. One landmark was saved: 41°91.29N, 87°53.31W.

With Zjorn's car gone, Fallon didn't have access to the digital map that would tell him exactly where those coordinates were. And he had no intention of going back to the office because someone might insist that he leave the German's van and its hidden cargo. But the manual said that a pointer screen would direct the operator, regardless of location, to the landmark. He referred to the instructions again; he had to push the up arrow twice. The display shifted and read: TO LMK 1. It gave a bearing in degrees, and distance to the location: BRG138°, DST46.06MI. Also a half circle had formed on the screen, the top of which was marked with an S to give a general direction to the landmark. A computerized arrow indicating that 138 degrees was southeast of his present location and forty-six-plus miles away. Since the paintings weren't in the car, the landmark Decker had recorded seemed like the most logical place to look. But why would he have to mark it—he certainly would know where he had hidden them. Whether it made sense or not, it was the only lead Fallon had.

He walked back to the minivan just as Blaney was driving up. "Taz, we're all through here until morning. Why don't you come in about noon; that'll give me a chance to talk to the SAC."

"Think you can get Doc off the hook for the Matisse? If he hadn't taken it, I would have."

"The headlines are going to read, 'Agent Zjorn Wounded in Shoot-out; Bad Guys Dead.' Pretty hard to make him a villain underneath that. And don't forget *the balance*: Stamen will get more good press than bad out of this, so the scales will be tipping in Doc's favor. He's going to be in good shape. Wouldn't be surprised if he doesn't wind up with a commendation."

"I appreciate it."

"Just go home and get some rest. You look awful."

"I will," Fallon said.

After Blaney left, Fallon took out a map of Illinois from the mini-van's glove compartment. Decker's landmark appeared to be some-where along the lakefront, north of downtown.

He followed the tollway to the Kennedy Expressway. Because he had met Zjorn there the night before, he got off at North Avenue and took it to the beach. He parked in the lot, got out, and took a GPS reading. As soon as the satellites locked in, he pulled up the landmark screen and then the pointing display. It indicated that Decker's land-mark was now on a bearing of 81 degrees, which was a little north of due east and at a distance of 2.8 miles. How could that be, almost three miles—straight out into the lake?

Diversey Harbor was the closest. Down on one of the docks, Fal-lon found a man in his late fifties who was hosing off his boat. In his free hand was a can of beer. "Excuse me, do you know where I can charter a boat?"

"It's too early in the season for that. Where you going?" Fallon no longer had his credentials, but he did have his business cards. He took out one and handed it to the man. "I won't be exactly sure until I get out there."

The man studied the card. Fallon could see the beer in his hand wasn't his first of the day. "FBI, huh? Don't you have a badge or something?"

"Did you hear about the explosion down at Burnham Harbor last night?"

"Sure."

"I was a little too close to it and lost my ID and a fairly nice sport coat." Fallon pointed to the bandage under his eye. "This is all I have left."

The man judiciously rattled his can of beer to see if it was empty. "How long is this going to take?"

"However long it takes to go three miles out and three miles back."

The boater thought about it for a moment. "Well, it's not like I got a board meeting to get to. Besides, I never met an FBI man before. Let's go."

As they cleared the mouth of the harbor, Fallon turned on the GPS. It now showed a bearing of 103 degrees at the same distance, 2.8 miles. Fallon gave the man the heading and when they got a mile from shore, he could see something on the horizon. It looked like some sort of structure, but he told himself it couldn't be, not in the middle of Lake Michigan. As the engines churned forward, it became larger—it was a building. Fallon asked, "What's that?"

"An old water-pumping station. There's three of them out here. They've been abandoned for years. Is that where we're going?"

Fallon checked the GPS. They were on the same bearing and less than a mile from where the computer said the landmark was. "Evidently." Now he understood why Decker had recorded the location. At night or in a fog, the GPS would have guided him there without a problem.

The old building was large, about the size and shape of a squat lighthouse. All the windows had been boarded up and the plywood was gray and warped. On the southwest side, a steel staircase came down to the water. It wrapped around the structure for about twenty feet where it finally lead up to a door. "I've got to go in there for a minute," Fallon said.

"Hey, you're the FBI. Let me get you alongside."

With surprising skill, he brought the boat to within inches of the metal staircase. Fallon hopped onto the landing. A cold draft of apprehension swept down his spine. For the first time, he found himself wondering if all of Decker's men were accounted for. He unsnapped his holster. The man said, "You'd better take this," and threw him a flashlight.

As quietly as possible, Fallon climbed the stairs. When he reached the door, which had been boarded over, he could see that the nailed plywood had been pried away except for one of the sides. He pulled it back and saw that the door had also been jimmied. He slowly pushed it open and drew his gun. It was completely dark inside. As soon as he turned the flashlight on, he heard something scramble against the floor to his left. He swung into a low stance to defend himself against an attack from that direction. Holding the flashlight as far away from his body as he could, he aimed its beam at the noise.

Curled up protectively, handcuffed to a pipe that ran from the floor to the ceiling, was Sivia Roth.

49

"SIVIA!"

"Taz!" She squinted into the brightness. "I can't believe you found me."

"How?" was the only word Fallon could get out as he fumbled for his handcuff key. Once he got the cuff off, he pulled her into his arms.

"This means you got Decker," she said.

"That boat was completely destroyed, how could you survive?" Abruptly, he held her out to arm's length. "Are you alright?"

"Where's Decker?"

"Dead. I thought *you* were dead."

She smiled. "I'm fine." Fallon looked at her clothes. She was wearing a faded, shapeless black sweatsuit. "Other than my wardrobe."

"I still don't understand."

"Decker was afraid that you would bring the FBI with you, so he set up all the smoke and mirrors. The first thing he did was find the right location, that's why he picked buoy thirty-two. He deliberately gave you enough time so you could get someone in place to help you. When Doc came early and hid his boat among the others, we were already there. Then Decker figured exactly where to put the *Lost Weekend* so Doc would think he was seeing everything. The whole point of his plan was to make you believe that we were on that boat, but Decker and I never were."

"But I talked to you on the phone."

"Remember the conference calls between Decker, the German, and Darla? What you heard in the harbor was a three-way hookup between Decker's men on the big boat, Decker and me on a smaller boat, and you. His men just listened so they would know which moves to make for Doc to see."

"But Doc saw you."

"Did he see my face?"

Fallon thought for a second. "He never said anything about your face. But he saw your dress."

"That was Darla. That's why I'm in this sweatsuit. Decker flew her in just to play me. Decker and I were far enough away not to be spotted, but he had binoculars on you, so when you did things like hold up the bricks before putting them in the bag with the painting, he could say the appropriate thing. He had them all rehearse it so they would be able to fool Doc and you with their movements. Like when you demanded to talk to me, he knew you would do that because you had done the same thing earlier in the day. Besides, it was a natural precaution on your part. His men knew to take the phone over to Darla when you wanted to talk to me, but I was on a smaller boat with Decker. Remember I tried to warn you not to fall for it. He even wanted you to think that he was trying to convince you I was *not* aboard, so when Doc spotted Darla in my dress, you'd think you were one up on him."

"Why did he go through all that?"

"He was afraid the FBI was going to try and grab him, so he set it up that if they stormed the *Lost Weekend*, they wouldn't get him or me. It was really quite ingenious." She reached up and gently pulled away the edge of his bandage and inspected the stitches. Then she gently pressed it back into place. "From the harbor?" He nodded. "It's not too bad."

"Did he know that the German was going to blow up the boat?"

"No, in fact, when it went up, as cold as he was, he was in shock. He had me lying on the deck but he was watching you in the spotlight through the binoculars. That's how he got hit in the hand. Once he realized what happened, he quietly motored out of the harbor. Then he figured out it couldn't have been more perfect. Everyone thought he was dead, and all roads to the Reserve were destroyed. No one but him had all six coordinates, so he was the only one who could find it. That's when he brought me here. *Did* he find the Reserve?"

"He found it, but it was boobytrapped. There's nothing left of either of them."

She was quiet for a moment, her disappointment obvious. "I guess evil will eventually destroy itself."

"Before he died, he shot Doc, but he's going to be okay."

"What about the German?"

"German*s*. There were three of them," Fallon said. "And like everyone else he ran into in this case, Decker killed all of them. But what about you? Since you would have been the only one to know he was alive and in possession of the Reserve, he must have had something else in mind for you."

"I think I was his backup plan. If he was caught, he could use me to deal his way out. Producing me would have been pretty dramatic, almost like bringing me back from the dead. But a funny thing happened when we got here last night, he wanted to discuss the three paintings he had. He was remarkably civil. Some of his insights into the works were impressive. But then he started asking me about how I would go about selling them. And how much I thought they would be worth. He was under the impression that, because I have dealt with a lot of stolen art, I had access to a lot of people who would purchase works with questionable provenance. He was right, I do. But if he thought I was going to help him, no matter what he did to me, he was making a big mistake."

"Are the paintings still here?"

"In that storage closet." She pointed to a door across the room.

Fallon found them on the floor, wrapped in newspaper.

She asked, "How did you find Decker?"

"I wasn't looking for him. I tracked down the Reserve because I knew the German would be there. It was him I really wanted."

She moved close to him and looked into his eyes. "Why?"

"Because I thought he had killed you."

"So does this mean we're going to be alright?"

After a pause, he said, "I don't know."

Her eyes moistened briefly, and then she forced a smile. "I think you're the first man who ever found me more desirable dead than alive." Realizing how inappropriate her comment was, she gave a strained laugh. When Fallon didn't say anything, she said, "How did you find the Reserve?"

"Let's get out of here. I'll tell you on the way back to your hotel."

After getting a key from the desk clerk, Sivia and Fallon took the elevator up to her floor. As she put the key in the lock, she said, "Funny, the last time I opened this door, Decker was on the other side."

"I'm pretty sure he won't be this time."

"I don't know if I can stay here."

"If you like, you can stay with me until you're ready to leave."

"I would appreciate it."

"When are you going back to New York?"

"That depends."

"On?"

"Who's going to take possession of those paintings."

"The agreement was that you'd take them."

"I thought maybe . . . things had changed."

"I guess some things have," he said, "but that's not one of them."

"And I guess some things just weren't meant to be. Give me a couple of minutes to collect my things, and we can get out of here."

Fallon swung the door to his apartment open and followed Sivia in, carrying the five wrapped paintings. After climbing up four flights of stairs, she seemed surprised at the apartment's uniqueness. "This is nice . . . very nice." She walked through to the bedroom and came back. "This is you." She stopped in front of his desk and scanned the items strewn across the top. She picked up the photograph of an artifact. "What is this—Mayan?"

"That's the best guess. It's a crystal skull. Supposed to be ten thousand years old."

"I would have never guessed that archaeology is a hobby of yours."

"I have a childhood friend who lives in Miami now. Every couple of years we accumulate enough vacation time and money to go treasure hunting off the coast of Honduras on an island called Roatán for three weeks. Ever heard of it?"

"No."

"It's one of the best diving spots in the world. Huge coral reefs and a long time ago, a favorite spot for pirates. The locals like you to believe there is still a lot of treasure buried there."

She laughed politely. "Somehow I can't see you rich."

"I don't think I have to worry about that. Even if we found anything, the government wouldn't let us take it out of there. Mostly we drink rum and try to stay out of jail."

"Then why all this?" She waved her hand over the items on the desk.

"It just makes it more fun. You know, something to fantasize about."

"Men do seem to live by their fantasies."

He smiled. "That can be a dangerous piece of intelligence in the wrong woman's hands."

She laughed again. "I know an exit line when I hear one. Besides, it's always been my custom to take a shower after spending two days in handcuffs. If you'll point the way."

Fallon showed her where the bathroom was. "I'll go down and get your bags."

When he returned, she was already out of the shower and sitting on the bed with a towel around her, using another one to dry her hair. "You don't have a hair dryer?"

"Sorry." He put her bags on the bed.

"I notice you don't have a television set, either."

"I had enough of it when I was a kid."

"Another legacy from your father?" When Fallon didn't answer she said, "And this apartment, is it also a protest?"

"This apartment?" He laughed sarcastically.

"You grew up in a basement flat, now you live *above* the top floor of a building. You don't think that has anything to do with your father?"

"Maybe it does." His voice was becoming angry. "And maybe it always will."

After a pause she said, "You might be selling yourself short. Don't forget you had a loving mother for eleven years. Maybe that's who you really are. Why else, even after I betrayed you, did you come and find me?"

Sivia watched his face while he thought about what she had said.

She could see the anger dissolve, and a sad reluctance take over. "I wish I could say I came for you, but to tell you the truth, I was looking for the paintings," he said. "And that sounds a lot more like my father than my mother." He turned around and disappeared into the bathroom.

Fifteen minutes later, after showering, he reappeared. There was freshly brewed coffee on the stove. He started to say something but saw the confused look on Sivia's face. She was dressed and sitting on the floor. In a semicircle were the five paintings, all facedown. "What is it?" he asked.

"The paintings . . ." she said, her voice in a stupor.

"What?"

"They're all forgeries."

50

"FORGERIES? ARE YOU SURE?"

"Positive," Sivia said. "I probably wouldn't have noticed, but I was examining the Nazi markings on the back, seeing if I could figure out which family the paintings were taken from. I didn't notice anything out of the ordinary until I turned the Cranach over. He is the oldest of these five artists. He died around the middle of the sixteenth century. Look at the nails that hold his canvas to the stretcher." Fallon inspected them. "Now look at the nails in the others."

When he finished, Fallon said, "They all look the same to me."

"That's the problem, they're *exactly* the same. All those nails are made from wire, a process that was not invented until long after Cranach was dead."

"Maybe just the Cranach is a phony."

"Look closely at the nails on each of the paintings, they're all exactly the same, as if they came out of the same box. They're hammered in at the same angle and even the same distance apart."

"You're right."

"And that's not all." She turned over all the paintings. "See how the canvases are all aged about the same. Forgers use all kinds of gimmicks to age paintings—gums, varnishes, ovens, whatever. These are all identically aged."

"Does that mean the rest of the Reserve were forgeries?"

"I don't know, you're the one who saw them."

"I didn't really get much of a look at them, they were all sealed in thick plastic. I couldn't really make out any details." Fallon stopped abruptly and then said, "Of course, they had to be fakes, too. They were wrapped like that so you couldn't see what they were. Every one of them could have been just an old worthless painting. That's why there was more than one boobytrap. He wanted to make sure that everything was destroyed, and with a little bit of luck, everyone who was involved."

"Who is *he?*"

"There's only one person it could be—Rathkolb," Fallon said.

"Rathkolb? But why?"

"That's a good question. And to answer it, we have to figure out what happened to the real Reserve."

"Maybe he did sell it off without anybody knowing," she offered. "But then why put us through all this deception—the forgeries, the codes, the murders—if he was going to commit suicide?"

"That's exactly right, he wouldn't."

"What do you mean?" Sivia asked.

"If Rathkolb was going to kill himself, there is no reasonable explanation for forging the paintings, and then carrying out this elaborate deception. So . . ."

"He didn't commit suicide."

"It answers all the questions. There are a couple of things that have been bothering me. One is Martin Bach's goatee. Remember how white his hair was, but his beard was bright red?"

"What does that have to do with this?"

"When we got the Matisse from Rochlitz, do you recall what his wife said about Bach?"

"The odd color of his beard."

"That's right. It was so ridiculous that everybody had to notice it. As a result, having seen his body, we knew that the man who distributed the paintings to the six old Nazis was Martin Bach. And because Martin Bach was passing out paintings, he had to be the man known to possess the Reserve, Josef Rathkolb. Then there was the suicide note and the letters to Rathkolb from Goering we found in the dagger case next to Bach's body."

"So you're saying that Martin Bach was not Josef Rathkolb."

"That's the only logical explanation," he said.

"Then where did Bach get the paintings?"

"Rathkolb. And he's probably the one who had Bach dye his beard so the connection would automatically be made. You saw the letter from Goering ordering everyone to follow Rathkolb's orders."

Sivia said, "Goering's paranoia was well-known. He and Rathkolb could have worked out the plan before the paintings left Germany."

"If so, the entire South American connection was probably devised by the two of them so if the wrong person came looking for the paintings, he would be set on a false trail that ended with the destruction of the faked Reserve."

"It's hard to believe that a mind could be that devious," Sivia said.

"Don't forget we're talking about the men who designed and carried out the Holocaust. This was probably no more than a game to them."

"Then my being able to trace the Sisley back to Bach was also part of his plan."

"Probably. You told me that you found out about the auction from an anonymous phone call to the foundation."

"It had to be Rathkolb," she said.

"Seems logical now, doesn't it?"

"Do you think he's keeping the Reserve for himself, or is he looking to finance some new fascist group like Goering wanted?"

"Before he was killed at the barn, the German said that Decker would be stealing Germany's future. I have to assume that he belonged to the kind of group the Reserve was originally intended for. If Rathkolb wasn't willing to turn it over to him, it can only mean that after all this time he wants it for some other reason."

After a pause, Sivia said, "He was even smart enough to send us the real Sisley, figuring it would be authenticated before the auction."

"And by doing that, he gave the rest of the forgeries credibility. He sacrificed one to keep ninety-nine."

"More than likely he shopped around to find a lawyer like Pearsay for the auction. Someone who was self-protective enough to find out Bach's whereabouts just in case some legal problem arose. Then Pearsay would have a get-out-of-jail-free card. It's not hard to find an attorney with that kind of reputation hovering around the New York art scene."

"And if you hadn't been able to get Pearsay to give him up, there probably would have been another anonymous call," Fallon said.

"So you think he was putting out enough information to keep us and Decker at each other's throats."

"In the heat of battle, attention to detail becomes very unimportant. I—"

"What is it, Taz?"

"The other thing that has been bothering me is the sixth victim." He opened his briefcase and took out the Deer Park PD report that Zjorn had given him. "His name was Conrad Linge." Fallon's voice trailed off as he reread the report. "Here it is. His daughter, after not being able to get him on the telephone, went to the house and found his body hidden in a shed at the rear of the property. When asked if her father had any enemies, she said there was no one specific, but because of the recent killings of German immigrants, he had become extremely cautious, changing all his locks and even his telephone number."

Sivia thought about it for a moment. "If he had his number changed, Decker couldn't have used the telephone pretext to find his address."

"That's right."

"Then how did they find him?" Sivia asked.

"Just like you with the Sisley, Rathkolb probably tipped them. Again, to keep everybody at each other's throats."

"But how would he know where to call Decker?"

"There was only one way to get information to Decker, and that was through Darla," Fallon said.

"When was Linge killed?"

Fallon scanned the report. "Based on the ME's opinion and the daughter's last contact with him, early Thursday morning."

"When was my contact in Cleveland arrested?" she asked.

"Around noon the same day."

"So if Rathkolb did call Darla with Linge's location, it would be on that last tape."

Fallon was at the phone dialing Cleveland. Jack Debbin answered on the first ring. "Agent Fallon. You're the reason I'm still here this late. I'm trying to finish up all this paperwork on the Decker case. Thank you very much."

"I'm sorry, but if you're still looking for him, I know exactly where he is."

"Your supervisor called and said he was ten-seven. I guess I do have something to thank you for."

"I need a big favor."

"Excuse me, aren't you under suspension?"

"A mere technicality."

"Couldn't you just lie to me for once?" Debbin said.

"Oh, haven't you heard, I've been reinstated."

"You are a master of deception. What is it that you need?"

"The guy they caught coming out of Darla Kincade's building with the tape recorder, if you have the tape, I'd like to hear it."

"Okay, but whatever your involvement was, I don't want to know about it," Debbin said. "Hold on for a minute while I rummage through the guy's desk who has the case, I'll see if I can find it." Fallon motioned to Sivia to pick up the extension next to the bed. Debbin came back on the line a few minutes later. "Okay, Taz, hari-kari rules apply."

Debbin was invoking an unbreakable death-before-implication pact between them. "Hari-kari," Fallon agreed.

Debbin turned on the recorder and laid the phone's mouthpiece on the speaker. Fallon and Sivia listened as Decker and Brunner spoke in German. That was followed by a brief lull and then another phone call started with Darla answering in a sleepy voice. A man who seemingly had a difficult time speaking English asked, "Ist he dort?"

At first they couldn't quite recognize the voice, but once they realized it was being disguised, they started noticing some familiar inflections and idiosyncrasies. They now knew who Josef Rathkolb was.

51

"MARVIN, IT'S SIVIA."

"Sivia!" Risch said. "The news, they said you were dead, in a boat explosion. This is a miracle. But how?"

"I'm fine. Another woman was killed; they thought it was me. But everything is okay now. In fact, we have rescued five of the paintings. That's why I'm calling. I need someplace discreet to keep them until I can make arrangements to ship them—you know—*east*. Do you have someplace there you keep your valuable pieces?"

"Of course, it is one of the reasons I bought this old bank building. There is a walk-in vault in the basement. You are welcome to use it for as long as necessary."

"Is now a good time?"

"I am an old man, where would I have to go?"

"See you soon."

A cold, steady rain was falling as Fallon and Sivia hurried to the front door of the Rhine Antique Gallery. They carried five large black garbage bags, each taped shut to protect the paintings from the weather. Through the window they watched as Risch quickly appeared and then shuffled with some urgency to the door. He unlocked it. "Come in, come in."

"Thank you, Marvin," Sivia said. "This is very kind of you."

Risch noticed the bandage under Fallon's eye. "What happened?"

"I lost an argument with a boat."

"Ah, the incident at the harbor." Risch nodded at the garbage bags. "But it seems your pain is not without reward."

"Yes, we were very fortunate," Sivia said.

"Well, come with me, we'll put them where they'll be safe." He led them to the back of the store and into his workshop. Sivia noticed a half-constructed wooden crate. Inside, rows of plywood strips had been screwed to the walls to form a dozen slots. The carpentry was fairly elaborate by current standards for packing and shipping. Sivia had seen a smaller, but almost identical version of the crate at Sam Weisel's gallery that had contained Sisley's *Watering Place at Marly*. Sivia wanted to try and signal Fallon, but Risch was walking too close to her.

At the back of the workshop, a stairway led to the basement. Risch went first. Once downstairs, they walked through a small area whose only furnishings were an outdated blond oak table and chair. They entered a room that revealed a heavy, steel vault door. "Please give me a moment to open it." He took out a small piece of paper and read it laboriously while he turned the dial back and forth. Once he had completed the combination, he rotated the large black handle clockwise and Fallon helped him pull the door open.

The vault was large. Along the walls were several small, featureless square tables. On top of them were expensive-looking objects: a flawless Tiffany lamp, delicately crafted vases and urns, a porcelain clock, and a dozen hand-carved jade and soapstone figurines. A glass case held at least twenty ornate pocket watches; most of them appeared to be gold. Another, music boxes. Centered in the back wall was another door. Fallon said, "You have some nice things here."

"Yes, a lifetime of collecting. If I ever decide to retire, I'll have to sell them. I don't know if I could give them up."

"Where should we put these?" Sivia asked, holding up one of the paintings.

"Well, I don't think we need to leave them in the bags. Let me get something so they won't be on the floor. I'll have to go upstairs, excuse me."

As soon as Fallon heard Risch's ponderous footsteps ascending the stairs, he went to the door at the rear of the chamber and opened it. There was a light switch on the wall just inside. He flipped it on.

The second vault was even larger. A baby spotlight hanging from the ceiling threw a narrow, bright swatch of light across an easel. Sitting on it was a pastel of a naked woman. Scribbled in the lower left-hand corner was the artist's name—Picasso. A chair and side table were positioned immediately in front of it, apparently for Risch's viewing comfort. Subdued, indirect lighting placed around the periphery of the ceiling lit the rest of the room. Set in shelf racks similar to the ones in the barn's cellar sat the Führer's Reserve—dozens and dozens of paintings in ornate gilded frames.

"My God," Sivia said, "this is it."

"That's right," a voice came from behind them. They turned around to see Risch aiming a Mauser machine pistol at them. "The real Führer's Reserve. Now, please come out of there before we have any accidents."

Risch backed up with the agility of a man twenty years younger. Fallon and Sivia, their hands in the air, followed him. Once they were in the outer room, he had Fallon take off his jacket and turn around. He pulled the nine millimeter from the agent's waistband. Then he patted the pockets in Sivia's coat.

Fallon said, "Josef Rathkolb, I presume."

"When you called, I thought you might be on to me. It did not seem logical that someone with your resources would need my humble facilities. That's why I brought you down here and pretended to leave—to see if you would look in the back vault. You both are very clever. I am curious, how did you figure it out?"

"Actually it was Sivia," Fallon said. "She discovered that the paintings we have are forgeries. And that led us to the tape of your call to Cleveland with Linge's name and address. Once we recognized your voice, everything made sense."

"It displeases me that my little deception was unmasked by a Jew, but I will soon rectify that mistake. As far as the call, I knew it was risky, but there was no other way to get Decker to that barn. Besides, I thought if the tape came into your possession, you would not listen to it but simply bring it to me for translation the way you had the others. I tried to disguise my voice, but I guess I was unsuccessful."

"The tattoo was a nice touch," Fallon said. "It had me fooled."

"It was Goering's idea. He thought if I came to the United States as a Jew, my immigration would be much easier. He was certainly right. And who would think to look for a former Nazi with a concentration camp tattoo."

Fallon asked, "Why did you start this whole Reserve hoax now? Why start it at all?"

"The discovery at Berchtesgaden."

"What's Berchtesgaden?" Fallon asked.

Sivia said, "Goering's last residence. A document bunker was recently found there."

"He left detailed records concerning the Reserve," Rathkolb said. "I knew it was just a matter of time until the specifics came to light. So I took the initiative to stage the collection's *destruction*. It had to be big and noisy so the world would be satisfied that it no longer existed."

"So that's why you wanted as many of us fighting over it as possible?"

"It wasn't easy trying to figure out who to give help to next. I not only told Decker where to find the sixth painting, but I called that television reporter and let him know that it was a Matisse you had recovered. And I certainly left you enough clues: the documents in the dagger box, the metal dies, and then reminding you about how the frames were different colors. For a while, I didn't think you were going to put it all together."

"And if I hadn't, you would have just asked me if examining the dies was possible."

"Exactly. But you did, in fact, you performed exactly as I had hoped with one exception—you were a little too independent. You were supposed to go to that barn with enough of your fellow agents that some would survive to tell of the destruction of the Reserve. If you had all died in the barn, no one would have ever known of its *destruction*. Fortunately you were resourceful enough to escape," Rathkolb said. "But of all the clues I left you, the picture frame turned out to be the most fortuitous. It was planted so you would come to me for assistance. Little did I know that it would bring you back to me whenever you needed the tapes translated."

"And that's where you got the Cleveland phone number from."

"It was on the beginning of each tape."

Sivia asked, "Who painted the forgeries?"

"They *are* exceptional, aren't they? It was my wife, Hilda; before she died, she had completed fourteen of them. Since you have brought only five bags, I assume one of them was destroyed either in the harbor or at the barn. And I had to boobytrap one with aluminum trichloride at the barn. In case you didn't get to see it happen, with any moisture at all, that powder turns into concentrated hydrochloric acid," Rathkolb said. "That leaves only twelve of the copies. But they are so convincing. She was quite an artist, don't you think?"

Fallon left the question unanswered. "Who was Martin Bach?"

"He was my cousin. We came to this country together. He was a little slow but could be quite vicious when called upon. During the war he became very dependent upon my connections to keep him out of the army, so when we immigrated, he did whatever I told him, including delivering the paintings to the Guardians, and even taking the cyanide." Rathkolb smiled again. "He thought it was a new type of liquid vitamin."

"And you had him dye his beard?"

"So people would remember him. As you call it, a nice touch, no?"

"Killing a member of your family always is."

"Was Marvin Risch a real person?" Sivia asked.

"Oh, yes. In fact, this is his number on my arm, in case camp records were ever checked. And he *was* a goldsmith, just eighteen years old and he already knew how to bribe the guards. His dealings came to light during one of my many trips to the camps. We *interrogated* him for three days to get the most intimate details of his life." He turned to Sivia, viciously aiming his words at her. "The *Reichsmarschall* would send me to the camps . . . to get written transfers of ownership for your people's works of art. It was very stimulating. In exchange for their cooperation, I would issue them vouchers for safe passage for themselves and their families out of the country. The men were always so noble, always insisting we couldn't have anything unless all their relatives were included. So I would feign reluctance at giving in so it would appear that we were sincere in our promises. We even went to the trouble of having trucks take them from the camps . . . to ensure the success of any future negotiations with those who were watching. We had them driven far enough away so the shots couldn't be heard. They always believed us."

"I thought the Reserve was supposed to finance a new Reich," Fallon said. "The brief acquaintance I had with that German, he seemed like your kind of sociopath."

Rathkolb tightened his grip on the pistol. "The men of today's Germany will never have the courage to undertake what we did. They are more concerned with themselves than the future of their country. Our kind of patriotism no longer exists in the world. Besides, I gave everyone a chance to find the Reserve. They all failed. It was the final test. I had decided that if they couldn't find it, they would never be able to use its power."

"So you're going to show them by—what—selling or keeping all those paintings for yourself?"

Rathkolb laughed. "Do you think I need money? When the paintings left Germany, Goering sent a half-million dollars in gold with them. It was mine so I would never be tempted to violate the Reserve. I have more money than I ever could spend."

"Then you and the paintings are going to sit down in this basement until you die?"

"I would probably have done that without another thought, but going through the considerable trouble of this deception made me ask the question, what am I saving the Reserve for? There will be no new Nazi order, so before I die, I must utilize it. But how? Then it came to me: one more magnificent act, so incredible that I, like the Führer, would never be forgotten and, most importantly, not have to die a death as embarrassingly unheroic as Goering's."

"If that's all you need, I can help you out right here," Fallon said.

Rathkolb raised the pistol to eye level and pointed it at Fallon's face. "Get down on your knees." Fallon thought about rushing him, but Rathkolb stood far enough away to easily get off an accurate shot before Fallon would reach him. He lowered himself to his knees. "Nothing is to be taken seriously with you Americans." Rathkolb laughed. "You want amusing? I'll give you something to laugh about. Do you know what methyl isocynate is?"

"Isn't it that new drug they're using to treat raving lunatics?"

"Raving lunatic—I'm sure that's what they'll call me when they judge what we're about to do to your Zionist friends." Rathkolb smiled with a renewed viciousness. "The people of Bhopal, India, know what it is."

Sivia said, "Union Carbide—the gas leak."

"Very good, *Sivia*." He growled her name mockingly, making it sound like profanity. "Of the eight hundred thousand people who were living there, two thousand died immediately. Another eight thousand have died since. Two thirds of the population were afflicted with everything from spontaneous abortions to stillbirths to offspring with genetic defects. Twenty thousand are now blind or have cancer. It can be an extremely effective tool. But where best to use it? And then it struck me." She refused to look at him so he put his free hand under her chin and pulled it up until he could see her eyes. "Care to venture a guess?"

That he was asking her, and not Fallon, told Sivia that his target was Jewish. Her eyes turned stony. "No."

"The greatest concentration of Jews in the world—Israel."

"I've been to Israel, you'll never get an ounce of that stuff through their security, even *with* your tattoo."

"We don't have to get it into the country. Just to its shores."

Fallon said, "That's twice you've said *we*. Who is we?"

"I assume you have heard of the Middle East terrorist group *Al Sunnah*."

Fallon gave a short, sarcastic laugh. "Somehow I can't see you making friends with anyone who doesn't have blond hair and blue eyes."

"Under normal circumstances, you would be absolutely right, but nothing will unite strangers quicker than a shared hatred. And I have the FBI to thank for allowing me access to them. When your agency arrested some of their members for those Wall Street bombings a year ago, their lawyers were prominently mentioned in the news. I sent the late Martin Bach to them with a large envelope. Inside was a sealed letter addressed to the group, along with fifty thousand dollars in cash. The letter stated that I wished to make an extremely large contribution to their defense fund, if they would assist me with a project of mutual interest. Martin told the lawyer that the enclosed money was a trifling sum compared to what would be donated. For a while it was comical. They thought I was an FBI—how do you call it—sting. It took months of testing me and my following their false instructions before we actually met. When we did, I told them what I had in mind. They said if they agreed to it, something of that magnitude would be extremely costly. I handed them Polaroid photographs of ten of the best paintings in the Reserve. Then I gave them an estimate of its total worth."

Defiantly, Sivia said, "They wouldn't be able to sell them."

"That was one of my concerns, but in less than a month they contacted me again. They said we had a deal and explained that they had access to several oil sheiks who were interested and, because of their historic disregard for world opinion, wouldn't care if someone questioned the provenance of the works. In fact, for them it added a certain amount of respectable contempt within the Arab community that they had been taken from Jews. So it was agreed that I would make a down payment of ten masterpieces. That crate upstairs in my workshop—the one you were so interested in—is to transport them. They will be sold and the proceeds will fund this final, glorious act."

Sivia said, "Your *glorious* plan can't possibly succeed. The Israelis are not fools." Rage hardened Rathkolb's eyes. "You said you have been to Israel—Tel Aviv?"

"Of course."

"To Haifa?"

"Yes, once for a day."

"Then you know they are two of the three largest cities in the country. Tel Aviv has a population of over a million people in and around the city, and Haifa in excess of a quarter of a million. A total of just under half of the country's population. But more importantly, they are both located on the Mediterranean Sea. Late this summer, each port will receive a cargo ship. Guess what will be in their hold."

Fallon said, "They can't contain as much of that chemical as a manufacturing plant."

Rathkolb laughed. "I thought you to be better informed. You obviously don't have any idea how little of that liquid insecticide caused those deaths in India—forty cubic meters, that's all—about half the size of a railroad car. The ships that we are purchasing have a capacity of over four thousand metric tons apiece. That's roughly enough space for three hundred half-railroad cars each."

"Even if you could get that stuff into the harbors, vaporizing is a whole different problem."

"Again, you are wrong. It is a very unstable compound and has a boiling point of just forty degrees centigrade. Do you know what started the leak in Bhopal? A small amount of water. It simply seeped into the storage tank and caused a violent chemical reaction, resulting in a vapor cloud. And the whole accident was over in an hour. And all it took was a little water."

"Who's going to stay aboard those ships and risk that kind of death?"

"One night when the wind is favorable, they will unseal the containers and quietly scuttle the ships while the country is asleep. By the time the gas is released, they will be out to sea. Sixty minutes later, it will be over. Even if something goes wrong, these people are suicide bombers," he said. "And like everything else in this world, with enough money, the seemingly impossible becomes a historical fact."

Rathkolb turned to Sivia and she could see it was his intention to torture her as much as possible before killing her. "Why aren't you laughing at my *lunacy* now?" She stared back, trying not to let her emotions show. "Don't you get it? It's the ultimate irony. We're using the Jews' own paintings to finance their destruction. And when *Al Sunnah* has completed this act, I will give them the rest of the Reserve. It will continue to be used for that purpose long after we're all dead. It's wonderful, half a century later, it's being used to carry out Hitler's directive. It truly is the Führer's Reserve."

Fallon said, "You are nuts."

"You still don't see the irony. The gas the insecticide gives off is cyanide . . . the same that we used in the camps. We're doing it all over again, and paying for it with the Jews' own money."

Tears started running down Sivia's cheeks. The color had drained from her face; she suddenly seemed frail. "How do you know they're not lying to you about everything, just trying to get the paintings?"

"Don't think that hasn't occurred to me. But just as you have through this entire ordeal, you brought me the answer with these forgeries. You were considerate enough to return these five to me. The ten photos I showed them were of forgeries. But because I had passed them out as part of the false trail, I had only seven left and was going to have to include three real paintings in the down payment. But now, I won't have to risk anything. I don't know how to thank you."

Fallon smiled. "After we figured out you were Rathkolb, do you think we would actually bring *all* the forgeries here? Did it ever occur to you that we might have told someone about you and left a couple of the paintings with them to prove what we said?"

Rathkolb didn't know whether Fallon was bluffing or not. If someone else did know that the real Reserve still existed, that probably meant that they knew about him, too. But if all the forgeries were there, Fallon had to be bluffing. "Well, we will just have to take a look at them and find out."

Fallon reached for the closest one and Rathkolb raised his gun menacingly. "Not you. She can do it."

There were two bags close to Sivia. She pulled the tape open and took the paintings out one at a time. Rathkolb looked at Fallon again; the FBI agent still had the same smile. "Now the rest of them. Quickly," he told Sivia, using his gun to wave her over to the bags closest to Fallon. She picked one up, and after opening it fumbled with it, as if the painting was stuck to the bag. "It's snagged on something," she said, reaching into the bag. Rathkolb was watching Fallon carefully and failed to see the fear in Sivia's eyes as she hesitated for a moment before bringing the bag up to chest level.

It exploded with three deafening gunshots that echoed metallically through the unvented vault. Rathkolb stumbled back two steps and then fell against the door with an awkwardness attainable only in death.

52

SIVIA'S FACE WENT WHITE AND HER KNEES STARTED to buckle. Fallon grabbed her and put his arm around her waist. "It's okay, there was nothing else you could have done. He was within seconds of killing both of us."

"Thank God you hid that gun," she said.

"When I saw that look in your eyes, I wasn't sure you were going to be able to do it."

She took a deep breath and said, "I'm okay now . . . I want to see it again." She went into the back room and sat down in the chair. For the next few minutes, she just stared at the Picasso.

When she got up, Fallon said, "You were definitely right about his less-than-honorable plans for the Reserve. But when you came up with the idea of coming here and getting it out of him, I have to admit, I pictured that hidden gun winding up in *my* hand."

She got up and looked at the shelved paintings in silence. Finally, she turned around. "Well, what do you want to do? This is a sure-fire way to get your badge back."

"Just go call whoever you have to."

She came over and kissed him lightly. "Thank you."

"I'd better get out of here before I become a witness to anything else. Will you be alright here by yourself?"

"I should be."

"Why don't you come wait upstairs so you don't have to be alone with him," Fallon said.

When they got to the front door of the shop, she said, "We'll look for the ledger that Schwend's sister told us about and the gold Rathkolb said he—"

Fallon held up his hands. "I already know a lot more than I want to."

She kissed him again, this time slowly on the lips. He showed no emotion. "I'm sorry you demand such perfect loyalty, but we live in a world where the more you want out of life, the less perfect it becomes. Maybe you just don't want enough out of your life."

He started to say something, but instead turned around and walked out into the early morning rain.

It was a few minutes past noon when Fallon arrived at the office. He was halfway through the reception room before he spotted her. Sivia sat dressed in an pearl gray silk suit. Next to her was a large package wrapped in brown shipping paper. The heavy twine on the outside hooked into a temporary carrying handle at the top. She smiled and stood up. "Hi."

"What are you doing here?"

"Your boss is waiting for us."

"Us?"

She smiled and pointed at the package. "Could you carry this for me?"

Fallon picked it up, and they were buzzed through the security door.

When they walked into Ralph Stamen's office, Fallon was surprised to find David Citron sitting there. The curtains were thrown back and the midday sun streamed through the windows. Citron stood up and offered his hand to Fallon. "Taz."

Stamen asked Fallon, "How're you feeling?"

"I'm fine."

The SAC leaned over his intercom. "Sue, have Pete Blaney come in here, please." He turned back to Fallon. "You've had a busy forty-eight hours."

Fallon glanced at Citron. He didn't know how much Stamen had been told and was hoping Citron would give him some indication so he wouldn't divulge anything he shouldn't. Instead Citron just smiled, almost as if enjoying Fallon's dilemma. "I guess so."

Stamen spoke directly to Citron, "Well, it looks like we're in agreement then. The inquiry concerning the Cleveland wiretap will be closed, and there will not be any further investigation of Miss Roth or Agent Fallon. In return, the FBI will take custody of the five masterpieces, and they will be processed through the proper Department of Justice channels. When the legal owners can be identified, the paintings will be turned over to them or their heirs."

The door opened and Blaney came in. Citron said, "Ralph, I'm going to have to ask for one minor concession. After you announce this sizable recovery to the media, to save face, one of our organizations will issue a statement praising the FBI's good work in finding these works, but the request will be made that the Department of Justice complete their investigation and return the property as expeditiously as possible."

"I have no problem with that," Stamen said. "Pete, how about unwrapping the paintings and setting them up in a display."

Blaney took the package from Fallon and placed it on a large table. It was directly under a large red, white, and blue plastic FBI seal. As the paintings were unwrapped, Stamen started lining them up next to one another. Fallon could see that the SAC was arranging a television camera shot.

Still unsure of exactly what was going on, Fallon picked up the Cranach. As soon as Stamen was distracted, he turned the painting over and glimpsed at the stretcher nails—it was the forgery.

Stamen took the painting from Fallon, put it with the others, and went around to the other side of his desk. He checked the alignment and then said into his intercom, "Sue, get ahold of Kathryn and have her set up a news conference for four o'clock."

Citron stood up. "Ralph, it looks like we're all set here. Thank you for your help."

"Thank *you*. And Sivia, I'm so glad you're alright." She extended her hand gracefully and he held it for a moment. "Have a nice trip back to New York."

Fallon started to leave with the others when Stamen said, "Taz, I need to see you for a minute."

Sivia said, "I'll wait for you out in the reception area."

Blaney sat down next to Fallon. The SAC took Fallon's credentials and gun out of his drawer and pushed them across the desk. "I don't know whether to scream at you or shake your hand. I couldn't even begin to figure out how many rules and laws you've violated." He smiled. "Or how you accomplished some of the things you have. But the tiebreaker for me was when Citron walked in here and said he was willing to be your source. The Bureau will be very happy about the paintings, but that you've brought David Citron aboard is an im- measurable accomplishment for us. From the way you originally talked about how he was resisting recruitment, you must have been surprised when he agreed to do it."

Fallon picked up his credentials and weapon and smiled. "I'm still not sure I believe it."

Once they were outside the door, Fallon said to Blaney, "Pete, thanks for hanging in there with me."

"Like I told you, it's all in the balance. On one side is a major news conference plus the recruitment of a top source, on the other is the burial of an embarrassing Bureau problem. For Stamen, it wasn't even a close call."

Fallon stood with Sivia while she waited for an elevator. "I appreciate everything you and David did, but it's only a matter of time before they find out they're forgeries."

"I wouldn't be so sure, they're awfully good. Even if they do figure it out, by that time, your boss will be retired or transferred. And what will the FBI do then, have a news conference and tell the world, 'Hey, you know all those millions of dollars worth of stolen paintings we recovered? Well, we were duped.' I don't think so. Anyway, our pur- pose was to get your job back, and no matter what else happens, that's not going to change."

"What are you going to do now?"

"The foundation's sending me to Amsterdam on a late flight. There's a sculpture there they want me to try and trace. What about you?"

Fallon looked away and shrugged his shoulders halfheartedly. She could see it was an unintentional protest against ending their rela- tionship in such an insignificant way, as though they had met briefly on a trip and were about to exchange addresses for future letters they both knew would never be written. "Taz, I don't want to leave it like this, either, but for you there's far more safety in distrust. And as long as you're dependent on that, there'll be these good-byes," she said. "If you're going to insist on continually proving yourself to someone who is dead, I suggest it be Jack Rymill instead of your father."

He knew she was right. When he thought that she had betrayed him, his reasoning had been distorted by a fear of disloyalty, of another abandonment. But her only crime was that she failed to tell him about *Brichah*. And now it was apparent that had been only to protect him, as she had today when she and Citron, at some personal risk, came to save his job.

Blaney stuck his head out the door. "Good, you're still here. We've got a robbery. The manager and a teller have been shot. I need everybody available to respond." He disappeared back inside.

When the elevator doors opened, Sivia kissed him and got in. "Well, it looks like it's time for you to go save the world again."

"Somebody once told me that if I kept trying to do that, I'd never be happy. I think maybe it's time I try for something a little smaller."

"Like?"

"I'm not sure . . ." He stepped onto the elevator and, as the doors started to close, put his arms around her. "How big is Amsterdam?"

About the Author

Paul Lindsay was born in Chicago, Illinois. He graduated from Mac-Murray College in 1968, and, after a failed attempt to outwit the draft board, wound up serving a tour of duty in Vietnam as a Marine Corps infantry officer. His luck held when he joined the FBI and was assigned to Detroit, Michigan, for the next twenty years. Although he is the author of *Witness to the Truth*, *Codename: Gentkill*, and *Freedom to Kill*, this book is the only thing that presently stands between him and a career as a bank guard.